"Not at this speed." There [...]

"Get on his starboard wing [...] and keep with him . . ."

"That's a Roger, HomeBase. [...] [...]ng more, and we're with him. Six hundred feet, and closing to five hundred. Straight and level."

Back in the TFCC, Murdock followed the exchange closely. If anything went wrong there would be no need for the third platoon of SEAL TEAM SEVEN. He could see the radar tracks as the four planes angled southeast toward the target island.

"I'll be damned, Captain," Red Tomboy said. "The near MiG is moving in closer to me. The fucker is fifty feet away. I can see the bastard through the canopy."

"Stay steady, Red Tomboy, we don't want to play wing tickle with him at your speed."

"I'll Roger that."

The air went dead for a few seconds.

"Shit, Captain, he's motioning me . . ."

"Pull back, Red Tomboy. Pull back . . ."

SEAL TEAM SEVEN
Pacific Siege

**Don't miss these other explosive
SEAL TEAM SEVEN missions:**

By Keith Douglass

THE CARRIER SERIES:

CARRIER
VIPER STRIKE
ARMAGEDDON MODE
FLAME-OUT
MAELSTROM
COUNTDOWN
AFTERBURN
ALPHA STRIKE
ARCTIC FIRE
ARSENAL
NUKE ZONE
CHAIN OF COMMAND

THE SEAL TEAM SEVEN SERIES:

SEAL TEAM SEVEN
SPECTER
NUCFLASH
DIRECT ACTION
FIRESTORM
BATTLEGROUND
DEATHRACE
PACIFIC SIEGE

SEAL TEAM SEVEN
PACIFIC SIEGE

KEITH DOUGLASS

BERKLEY BOOKS, NEW YORK

Special thanks and acknowledgment to Chet Cunningham for his contribution to this book.

SEAL TEAM SEVEN: PACIFIC SIEGE

A Berkley Book / published by arrangement with the author

PRINTING HISTORY
Berkley edition / June 1999

The Penguin Putnam Inc. World Wide Web site address is
http://www.penguinputnam.com

ISBN: 0-425-16941-3

BERKLEY®
Berkley Books are published by The Berkley Publishing Group,
a division of Penguin Putnam Inc.,
375 Hudson Street, New York, New York 10014.
BERKLEY and the "B" design are trademarks
belonging to Penguin Putnam Inc.

PRINTED IN THE UNITED STATES OF AMERICA

10 9 8 7 6 5 4 3 2 1

SEAL TEAM SEVEN

THIRD PLATOON*
CORONADO, CALIFORNIA

Lieutenant Commander Blake Murdock. Platoon Leader. 32, 6'2", 210 pounds. Annapolis graduate. Six years in SEALs. Father important Congressman from Virginia. Murdock recently promoted. Apartment in Coronado. Has a motorcycle, loves to fish.
WEAPON: H&K MP-5SD submachine gun.

FIRST SQUAD

David "Jaybird" Sterling. Machinist Mate Second Class. Platoon Chief. 24, 5'10", 170 pounds. Quick mind, fine tactician. Good with men in platoon. Single. Drinks too much sometimes. Crack shot with all arms.
WEAPON: H&K MP-5SD submachine gun. Administrator for the platoon.

Ron Holt. Radioman First Class. 22, 6'1", 170 pounds. Plays guitar, had a small band. Likes redheaded girls. Rabid baseball fan. Loves deep-sea fishing, is good at it. Platoon radio operator.
WEAPON: H&K MP-5SD submachine gun.

Bill Bradford. Quartermaster First Class. 24, 6'2", 215 pounds. An artist in spare time. Paints oils. He sells his marine paintings. Single. Quiet. Reads a lot. Has two years of college. Squad sniper.
WEAPON: H&K PSG1 7.62 NATO sniper rifle or McMillan M-87R .50-caliber sniper rifle.

Joe "Ricochet" Lampedusa. Operations Specialist Third Class. 21, 5'11", 175 pounds. Good tracker, quick thinker. Had a year of college. Loves motorcycles. Wants a Hog. Pot smoker on the sly. Picks up plain girls. Platoon scout.
WEAPON: Colt M-4A1 with grenade launcher.

*(Third Platoon assigned exclusively to the Central Intelligence Agency to perform any needed tasks on a covert basis anywhere in the world. All are Top Secret assignments.)

Kenneth Ching. Quartermaster's Mate First Class. Full-blooded Chinese. 25, 6'0", 180 pounds. Platoon translator. Speaks Chinese, Japanese, Russian, Spanish. Bicycling nut. Paid $1,200 for off-road bike. Is trying for Officer Candidate School.
WEAPON: Colt M-4A1 rifle with grenade launcher.

Harry "Horse" Ronson. Electrician's Mate Second Class. 24, 6'4", 240 pounds. Played football two years at college. Wants a ranch where he can raise horses. Good man in a brawl. Has broken his nose twice. Squad machine gunner.
WEAPON: H&K 21-E 7.62 NATO round machine gun.

James "Doc" Ellsworth. Hospital Corpsman First Class. 25, 5'10", 160 pounds. One year pre-med, then he ran out of money. Prefers small dark-eyed girls. Single. Competition shooter with pistol. Platoon corpsman.
WEAPON: H&K MP-5SD/no-stock, 5-round Mossburg pump shotgun.

SECOND SQUAD

Lieutenant (j.g.) Ed DeWitt. Leader Second Squad. Second in Command of the platoon. From Seattle. 30, 6'1", 175 pounds. Wiry. Has serious live-in woman. Annapolis grad. A career man. Plays a good game of chess on traveling board.
WEAPON: The new H&K G-11 submachine gun.

Al Adams. Gunner's Mate Third Class. 20, 5'11", 180 pounds. Surfer and triathlete. Finished twice. A golfing nut. Binge drinker or teetotaler. Loves the ladies if they play golf. Runs local marathons for training.
WEAPON: Colt M-4A1 with grenade launcher.

Miguel Fernandez. Gunner's Mate First Class. 26, 6'1", 180 pounds. Has a child with a woman in Coronado. Spends his off time with them. Highly family-oriented. He has family in San Diego. Speaks Spanish, Portuguese. Squad sniper.
WEAPON: H&K PSG1 7.62 NATO sniper rifle.

Colt "Guns" Franklin. Yeoman Second Class. 24, 5'10", 175 pounds. A former gymnast. Powerful arms and shoulders. Expert mountain climber. Has a motorcycle, and does hang gliding. Speaks Farsi and Arabic.
WEAPON: Colt M-4A1 with grenade launcher.

Les Quinley. Torpedoman Third Class. 22, 5'9", 160 pounds. A computer and Internet fan. Has his own Web page. Always reading computer magazines. Explosives specialist with extra training.
WEAPON: H&K G-11 with caseless rounds, 4.7mm submachine gun with 50-round magazine.

Rodolfo "RG" Gonzalez. Damage Controlman First Class. 26, 5'10", 180 pounds. Loves to surf, prays for a storm for better waves. Is Second Squad's tracker. Speaks Spanish, Italian, and Russian.
WEAPON: Colt M-4AI with grenade launcher.

Jack Mahanani. Hospital Corpsman First Class. 25, 6'4", 240 pounds. Tahitian/Hawaiian. Expert swimmer. Bench-press 400 pounds. Once married, divorced. Top surfer. Wants the .50 sniper rifle.
WEAPON: Colt M-4AI with grenade launcher. Replacement for Gonzalez after he's shot up in Iraq on the first phase of this mission.

Joe Douglas. Quartermaster First Class. 24, 6'1", 185 pounds. Expert hand-to-hand and unarmed combat. He's an auto nut. Rebuilds classic cars. Working on a 1931 Model A Ford Roadster. Platoon's top driver, mechanic.
WEAPON: H&K 21E 7.62 NATO round machine gun. Second radio operator.

Fred Washington. Engineman Second Class. A black man. 24, 6'0", 180 pounds. Is driven to succeed. Taking computer college courses. Doesn't carouse much. Is writing a novel about the SEALs.
WEAPON: H&K MP-5SD submachine gun.

1

Tuesday, 9 January

33,000 Feet Altitude
Near Kuwait Border

Newly promoted Lieutenant Commander Blake Murdock watched his fifteen men in the murky gloom of the interior of the special C-130 Hercules. They were flying at night near the northern Kuwaiti border next to Iraq, too high for anyone on the ground to see or hear the plane. This area was outside the Iraq radar envelope.

The Hercules was the one they had used before, painted totally black with no insignia, armed and equipped specifically for covert night flights over hostile territory.

Murdock patted the side of the big plane. He knew it was the most versatile and widely used military transport in the post–World War II era. The four big turboprop engines growled away outside. He'd heard that a C-130 had even been flown off a Navy carrier without the use of a catapult or arresting wires. The plane had a 133-foot wingspan, which made Murdock wonder how they did it. Right now they were flying at the plane's ceiling of 33,000 feet.

The big plane lumbered through the thin air at 350 mph as the sixteen SEALs rattled around in the big cargo compartment. The Third Platoon of SEAL Team Seven, based in

Coronado, California, under command of NAVSPECWAR-COM, Naval Special Warfare Command, was now assigned to and under the direct orders of the CIA. Murdock began inspecting each of his first squad's seven men. They had checked the rigging, gear, weapons, and combat vests of each other. Now Murdock went over it all again, then had two men look over his latch-up. When he was satisfied, he saw that Lieutenant (j.g.) Ed DeWitt had given his seven-man Second Squad a similar routine.

"When the fuck we going to get there?" Engineman Second Class Fred Washington asked. He was the only black man in the group, and confessed he sometimes felt like the platoon's "Nominal Nigger." "Hell, I can say that, but you shitheads better not," he had said during late-night drinking binges.

"We get there when we get there, Slowfoot," Lee Quinley cracked. He was a Torpedoman Third Class, from Maine, and the platoon's computer expert.

Even though they had made jumps like this dozens of times, each one was new and different, and presented the ever-present dangers of any jump.

Murdock looked at his watch, and punched the light button. In the glow he saw that they had fourteen minutes to their drop point. They had been sucking oxygen from masks provided in the plane ever since they passed fifteen thousand feet. He motioned the men around him, talking loudly so they could hear.

"Nothing new from the top. We go in as we planned. Let's stay within fifty feet of each other on the drop, and pull up when we get down there for an easy landing. We don't want any broken legs or sprains on this jump. Any questions?"

Bill Bradford, Quartermaster First Class, waved. He was a hulking six-two, and did marine oil paintings in his off time. "When do we start to use our portable oxygen?" He was the new man in the platoon, taking over Magic Brown's spot after the machine gunner had been knocked out of action in the *Deathrace* operation in Iran.

"We'll turn on our personal oxygen system in about three minutes, as soon as the red jump light goes on," Murdock said. "That will put us ten minutes from our jump point. We have two hours of oxygen in each bottle, which should be plenty."

"How long to touchdown?" Ron Holt, Radioman First Class, asked. Holt was a rabid Dodgers fan. When baseball wasn't on, he'd rather go deep-sea fishing than eat.

"We jump on this HAHO at about thirty-two thousand. We'll be on static lines to open our chutes automatically to keep us bunched as close as possible. Then we should have seventy-two to seventy-five minutes gliding down.

"By then we should be about fifteen miles inside Iraq, and near the small town of Osadi. That's the objective. This High Altitude High Opening routine should put us down within half a mile of the target. We'll use the Motorolas, and if we see we're overshooting, we'll circle so we can come down close to the target."

The red jump light came on.

"Let's turn on your portable oxygen and have a radio check. Second Squad first."

Murdock listened to the earpiece as the Second Squad chimed in to DeWitt.

"First Squad report," Murdock said into the lip mike. It was connected to a wire that went under his shirt collar, and down inside his cammie shirt to a waist transceiver unit clipped on his belt. Another wire led to an ear speaker. The seven men responded with their last names, and the Platoon Leader nodded.

Murdock watched his men. He'd been with some of them for two years now as Platoon Leader. They were his guys. They had bonded together in live-or-die combat situations more than a dozen times and were closer than blood brothers. They would die for each other. He remembered three of his men who had done just that. He shook his head, not wanting to think about those three.

The loadmaster came out of the cabin into the big hold, and motioned to Murdock.

"Sir, about six minutes from the drop. You better get the men hooked up and ready."

Two minutes later the squads lined up, one on each side of

the big cargo hatch at the back of the plane. Thirty seconds later they felt the whoosh of air as the nine-foot-long ramp lowered from the top of the plane. The jump light still showed red.

Murdock watched the loadmaster, boss of this phase of the operation.

Three minutes later, the light turned from red to green.

Murdock nodded. "Go, go, go," he barked into the lip mike. The sixteen SEALs ran forward in two closely spaced lines, out of the big hold, and off the end of the ramp into the blackness of the Iraqi night. The time was a little after 2100.

Murdock sensed the jolt of apprehension as he always did on a jump. Then he took the last running step off the ramp, and surged into the darkness. The freezing cold hit him like icewater in the face, jolting past the ski mask protection, icing his nose in an instant even under the oxygen device.

The moment he was free of the craft he went into an arch move, his arms and legs spread out like a bird so he wouldn't tumble. After only six seconds he felt the drag chute pull from his main chute, then the gradual slowing as the rectangular, steerable chute deployed.

The air was so thin at 32,000 feet that the chute came out gradually and took some seconds to fill with the thin air. The steerable chutes lowered a man's free-fall speed much more gently than a big round chute would do.

There was no disemboweling jerk on the parachute straps as a falling body slowed suddenly from free fall to fully supported. Murdock had experienced that quick stop on other jumps halfway upside down. The straps around his legs and shoulders would slam him upwards, bringing a groan; then the chute over him would take up the load, and the pain would ease into a slow throbbing. He always worried that he had crushed his balls in those regular jumps.

He grabbed the straps and looked around. He saw the bobbing glow lights. Each man had one and held it so it could be seen by the others. This was one way to help them stay somewhere near each other. Murdock swallowed and tried the lip mike. He hoped it hadn't frozen up.

"Platoon, use your compasses. We're on a bearing of

three-forty degrees. Let's hit it dead in the chops. Radio net report First Squad." Murdock listened as seven men responded. He heard DeWitt check in his men. Sixteen SEALs primed and ready to go. His fingers screeched in pain even through the special gloves as the cold bit into them. At thirty thousand feet it must be well below zero. More than an hour more of gliding, but it would get warmer.

The Platoon Leader looked at his altimeter, and punched up the small light. It showed 30,100 feet. He wasn't sure what the ground-level height was here, but it couldn't be more than five or six hundred feet. A long ride down.

He looked around, and spotted six of the glow lights. Ingenious little devices. A plastic tube with two compartments each containing a separate chemical or element. Bend them and break the seal inside, and the two substances combined to give off a healthy glow. Most of the six-inch-long tubes were good for six to eight hours.

As they glided toward the Iraqi village, Murdock went over the briefing. Their objective was a modest house in the small village of Osadi. It was controlled by a local war chieftain who was a renegade from the Iraqi Army. He was known as El Raza. Saddam Hussein hadn't tried to catch him, probably deciding it was too much trouble. El Raza ruled like a bandit lord over the locals. His house was heavily defended, according to the latest reports. He had troops, machine guns, maybe even land mines. The house would be a fort.

Two days ago, El Raza had slipped into Kuwait at night with a dozen men, and captured a well-known Kuwait leader in a small town only five miles from the Iraqi border. The kidnapped man was highly placed in the Kuwait government. He had come to his relative's home at this border town for a holiday.

Kuwait was powerless to get him back. They couldn't afford to invade Iraq. They had no special forces who could rush in and break him free. El Raza had demanded two million American dollars as a ransom for the man, Fayd Salwa. He said if the ransom wasn't paid within forty-eight hours, Salwa would be sent home a body part at a time in a basket.

Don Stroh, the SEALs contact with the CIA and main order-giver, had been clear.

"You go in HAHO as silent as a SEAL. You take down this El Raza and rescue Salwa and we'll pick you up outside the town with a chopper. Maybe a six-hour mission from drop to pickup. All done at night and the Iraqis won't know who hit them, especially El Raza."

When the SEALs received the orders, they had hung up their close-quarters shoot-out weapons, and left from North Island Naval Air Station four hours later.

A gust of wind rocked Murdock's steerable chute, and he felt the drift, but quickly pulled the glide chute back on course. He saw the glow lights of the other men making the same correction.

"Halfway down," he heard DeWitt say in the Motorola earpiece.

"Yeah and warmer," David "Jaybird" Sterling, Machinist Mate Second Class, said. Jaybird was the platoon noncom administrator and boss. "Why the fuck does it stay so cold out here?"

It was clear and cool. Murdock was always surprised how cold it could get in a desert: 110 during the day and down into the forties at night.

Far ahead, he saw a faint glow. It had to be the town of Osadi. According to their best maps, this was the only town in the whole territory for fifty miles around. It was why El Raza had chosen it as a haven from the Iraqi Army. He felt isolated and safe. When he'd deserted, he'd taken a company of his men, and all the arms they could pile on armored personnel carriers.

Twenty minutes later, the soft glow ahead had turned into fuzzy lights. They were low enough that Murdock could see some of the terrain below. Desert, a few ravines, a scattering of low brush and weeds, lots of sand and rocks. Good old desert.

"Looks like we're dead-on on the old cracker barrel on this one, people," Murdock said. "My skyhook shows that we're at just under five thousand feet. We could come in a tad short, so don't waste any altitude maneuvering. Ed, can you see all of your men?"

"All but one. I think his glowworm died. He was close in last I saw him."

"Yeah, Commander. Franklin here. My light died like a stiff prick at a church service. I got glowworms on both sides of me."

"Roger that, Franklin," Murdock said.

They came to ground a half mile short of the village. Everyone made it down without any injuries. They had practiced this landing enough that they should know how by now.

They didn't bother to bury the chutes.

"They'll know we've been here tomorrow, so why bother?" Murdock said. They checked equipment and got their issue weapons in their hands, and Murdock moved them out.

The scout, Joe "Ricochet" Lampedusa, Operations Specialist Third Class, led the troops, with Murdock right behind him and Ron Holt, with his SATCOM, right behind Murdock in case he was needed in a rush. First Squad scattered out behind at ten-yard intervals. The ten yards was standard for most combat situations. One lucky explosive round or one hand grenade wouldn't put down more than one man at a time.

Second Squad, with (j.g.) DeWitt in the lead, followed the First Squad. They both were in a modified diamond formation, and hiked along at a pace of fifteen minutes to the mile.

A half-moon cast a suggestion of light over the desert. Here there were occasional tufts of grass, a few cacti, and now and then a low growth that must hug runoff gullies formed when sudden downpours bathed the desert.

Still a quarter of a mile from the first lights, Lampedusa went down, and the rest of the SEALs dropped into the dirt as well.

Murdock met the motorcycle enthusiast halfway.

"Some kind of a truck, no lights," Lam said. "Parked out there about a hundred yards from that last building."

"A roving mounted patrol?" Murdock asked.

"Doubt it. The rig hasn't moved for five minutes. I've been watching it."

"Let's pay your truck a visit." Murdock turned, and motioned for the rest of the men to stay where they were. In the darkness, the signal went from one man back to the next, until it worked all the way through Second Squad.

Murdock and Lam bent over, and ran silently toward the truck. Murdock saw that it was some type of Russian personnel carrier. It had a machine gun mounted facing forward. The rig was parked so it nosed away from the settlement.

Without warning, the truck's headlights blazed a path through the desert night. Murdock and Lam were well out of the beam, but they went to ground and didn't move. Murdock figured it was two minutes later before the lights snapped off. He had kept his eyes tightly closed during the light show. When he opened his eyes, he found his night vision not affected. He snapped up the NVGs, Night Vision Goggles, and checked the truck.

He could see a man at the steering wheel, but he wasn't sure if there was another man in the cab. Murdock motioned, and he and Lam moved to the left to come up more on the side of the rig. Murdock carried his standard-issue weapon, an H&K MP-5SD submachine gun with the stock extension closed. It had been customized for the SEALs with a special stock, handgrip, and safety. It had tritium dots on the sights for night shooting. It could spit out one 9mm round at a time, bursts of three, or full-auto fire.

The scout carried his usual Colt M-4A1, a .223-caliber that fired single shots or full automatic at seven hundred rounds per minute. Like all SEAL M-4A1's, his also had an M203 40mm grenade launcher under the barrel.

They moved forward in a crouch until they were forty yards from the rig, then went down to a crawl. Cradling weapons across their arms, they went by elbows and knees another fifteen yards. Both weapons carried sound suppressors. Murdock used the NVGs again, nodded, and brought up his H&K. He sighted in and put a three-round burst through the open side window.

After the silenced burst, the two SEALs came to their feet and charged the small truck. They found two uniformed men in the front seat, both dead. There were no troops in the back.

Murdock stood and waved the SEALs forward. He had silhouetted himself against the town's lights. The men came up in formation, and the platoon moved forward.

Lampedusa knew where the fortified house should be. He checked the buildings, then swung around to the right.

Murdock figured there couldn't be more than two hundred inhabitants in the place. The house they wanted was in the second row from the outside. They weren't blocks exactly, more like cow paths or maybe goat trails.

Lam went down again to the dirt fifty yards off the first row of buildings, and Murdock crawled up to him.

"Figure it should be right in there, between these closest two buildings. Looks the same as the satellite pictures we got."

Murdock put his NVGs on the slice of territory they could see between buildings. As he watched, he saw an armed guard walking across the area.

"Must be it, they have sentries out." He touched his lip mike. "DeWitt, up here." They hadn't worked out the final assault on the place because there wasn't enough intel. Now they would parcel out the assignments.

Murdock and DeWitt talked for three minutes; then Murdock moved ahead with the First Squad. There were no people on the streets. There were streetlights only every two hundred yards. None shone on this area.

First Squad slid between the buildings, which looked like commercial enterprises, and spread out along a narrow street that fronted the target house. It sat twenty yards in back of the avenue, and had a stone wall around it that was only three feet high. The house itself had two stories, was made of stone and mortar, and looked sturdy.

Ed DeWitt brought his men up, and sent half of them to each side of the house between buildings, and wherever they could find an open field of fire against the house.

The guard Murdock had seen before came again, evidently walking a circuit around the house. He carried a rifle over his shoulder, and walked at a leisurely pace as if thinking about what he would do when he got off duty.

They waited. Another guard came out of the shadows, and

talked with the rover, then went back where he had been. Now, with the NVGs, Murdock could see him. Murdock searched other shaded areas, and found another front guard.

"DeWitt. Check for fixed guards on the sides. We've found two out here."

"Roger that."

Murdock pointed to Bill Bradford, the new sniper for the First Squad with his H&K PSG1. It fired a 7.62 NATO round from the high-precision sniping rifle. He had a 20-round magazine, a long, heavy barrel, and a pistol grip at the trigger. It had a fully adjustable stock, a 6 x 24 telescope, and a sound suppressor.

Bradford lifted the rifle, and looked through the scope. The light-gathering properties brought the target into clear focus. He checked the first hidden sentry, then zeroed in on him and fired. He shot just once, then moved to the other sentry and cut him down with one round.

"Take em down if you got 'em, Ed," Murdock whispered into his mike. He heard two muffled rounds from the side, then silence.

"Ready to go," Ed said on the Motorola.

Before Murdock could move, three floodlights snapped on, bathing the whole front of the house and the yard with light.

"Do them," Murdock said. Ten silenced shots whispered into the night. All the floodlights died from hot lead.

"Move it, First Squad," Murdock said into his mike, and the eight men lifted up and stormed the front of the house. They took gunfire from firing ports and out the windows.

Seven of the SEALs blasted through the twenty yards, and slammed against the house. One man was down. Murdock ran back and grabbed him, and then ran forward, half dragging Ron Holt to the wall.

"Caught one in the left arm, Commander. Sorry."

As they talked, Kenneth Ching, Quartermaster's Mate First Class, had pasted two globs of TNAZ plastic explosive on the house's front-door hinges. He set timers and looked at Murdock, who gave him a thumbs-up. Ching pulled out the activating switches. Then he ducked under a window, and rushed away fifteen yards along the house.

The twin explosions came almost on top of each other. Doc Ellsworth, Hospital Corpsman First Class, got to the blown-in door first, and tossed in a flashbang grenade. He dodged to the wall beside the door, shielded his eyes, and held his hands over his ears. The series of sharp, powerful, but non-lethal explosions erupted inside the room coupled with six brilliant strobe lights. Both light and sound blasted out the open doorway.

When the last strobe faded, Murdock and Doc Ellsworth pulled down their NVGs and jolted through the door. Murdock took the right side, and Doc the left part of the room.

Doc blasted his MP-5 twice. The two bursts of three rounds cut down two Iraqis on his side of the room. Murdock had no targets.

"Clear one," Murdock said as he and Doc charged to a door at the other side of the room. They hit the wall next to the door, and Murdock threw a flashbang grenade inside. The screeching, pulsating sound roared through the room as the series of brilliant strobe lights flashed through the doorway. The two SEALs waited flat against the wall on both sides of the open door.

As soon as the last strobe faded, the two charged into the room. No one was inside. The third room was to the left. They hit it with one more flashbang grenade, then jolted through the door, their MP-5's ready. Murdock cut one kidnapper in half with a fully automatic burst from his weapon. The man's face showed surprise as he dropped the knife he was about to throw, and he crumpled to the floor dead.

Doc put a burst of three 9mm rounds into the second Iraqi, who still held his hands over his ears. The kidnapper took the rounds in his chest, slammed backwards against the wall, and slid down slowly, leaving a wide red smear.

There were no more Iraqis in the room. There also was no hostage.

"Where the hell is he?" Murdock asked. Doc shook his head. They had cleared all the rooms in the house. There was no kidnap victim.

"Pull back, Second Squad, pull back to the desert. We need some recon. We're right behind you."

2

Tuesday, 9 January

El Raza's House
Osadi, Iraq

Murdock motioned to Doc, and they eased out of the house. The explosions that had ripped open the door evidently had attracted no attention. They saw no one, no lights or vehicles.

As silent as sixteen wisps of smoke, the SEALs exfiltrated from the area back into the desert, and hit the dirt facing the small town.

"He wasn't there," Murdock told DeWitt. "No fucking hostage, just some Arabs who looked surprised as hell that they were dying. Jaybird, get up here."

Jaybird slid in beside the two officers.

"Any other intel on this town?"

"Not much. The house was our target. They said something about a military HQ El Raza uses. It's at the other end of the town, maybe six hundred yards north."

"Best bet we have," DeWitt said. "Hope to hell we don't have to search every building in this little place."

"The HQ sounds good," Murdock said. "Let's get on our horses and move up there. We know nothing about the building?"

"Afraid so, Commander. Be a good time for a guided tour."

"This is turning out tougher than they told us," Murdock said. "So what's new. Jaybird. Find Douglas, and tell him to take Gonzales with him and go back and see if that truck we passed will run. If it will, have them drive it into the desert and come up beside us here about a quarter of a mile out. We might need it fast. Have them keep pace with us as we move. Go.

"Ed, let's go up the hill here and find that HQ. It should be the biggest building in the town. At least we hope it is. You keep your squad outside ours as we go north. When we get there we'll recon the building, and see what we need to do. If that kidnapped guy isn't there, I don't know what the hell comes next."

"Guns Franklin," DeWitt said. "He speaks Arabic and Farsi. We grab ourselves a prisoner and let him talk to live."

"Good. Let's move."

First Squad walked silently north along the outskirts of the small town. The road in back of the houses outlined the community and kept everyone inside. They walked a half mile, then hit the dirt and checked the area. Murdock and Lampedusa went past the buildings inside the town to see if they could find a large building.

They moved silently from shadow to shadow. Past the first row of houses, the area changed. Here there was a central open area, as if it could have been a market at one time. At the far end stood a building larger than the others, but of the same stone and mortar construction.

Murdock and Lampedusa studied the area for five minutes. They saw no one move. There were no guards around the building. They could see none on the roof or in what looked like a small guardhouse near what appeared to be the front double doors.

"A church, a mosque?" Lampedusa asked.

Murdock shook his head. "No minaret, no tower with small balconies, which is always attached to a mosque."

"So, maybe it's the HQ."

"Let's go and see."

They darted from one bit of cover to the next, keeping near the smaller buildings to the side of the open area. When they came to the front of the large building, they found a Russian-built weapons carrier parked and facing outward. A heavy machine gun, maybe a .50-caliber, perched on a mount.

The two SEALs nodded, faded to the side, and went around the place. Two windows near the back showed lights. At the back of the building they found six armored personnel carriers that had to be Russian-made. They also spotted a fuel dump of 55-gallon barrels, and a concrete-block building that could hold ammunition and weapons.

"Make a nice bonfire," Lampedusa said.

"If it comes to that. Easy in, easy out. But that doesn't look like it's going to happen. Let's bring up the platoon and take a look inside. Might be troops in there, and officers and maybe a kidnapped hostage."

Five minutes later, they found the platoon lurking fifty yards outside the perimeter road. The truck they had liberated growled along in the desert beyond them.

Murdock told the men the situation.

"We know about three doors. Front, back, and side. There may be another door on the far side. We'll go in the back door, since the lights are in that area. I'll go in with two men from Second Squad. First Squad and the rest of Second will back us up covering the side doors and the front.

"We'll use silencers and knives whenever possible. We don't want to roust out El Raza's whole army. Our only objective is to find this hostage and get him out of here. Bring in Franklin and his helper from the truck. We need all the guns we have. Let's move."

Murdock chose Quinley and Washington for his assault team, and moved up on the rear door, past the silent weapons and personnel carriers and the fuel dump. Murdock held up for five minutes watching for a guard, but none showed. He and Fred Washington darted to the rear door and tried it. Unlocked. He turned the knob, and opened the panel an inch. No lights showed inside.

Murdock, and two men, slid into the room. It was a storage area, holding various goods. He had on his NVGs, and found a door across the ten-foot-wide room. Unlocked.

He opened it two inches. Faint light showed beyond.

Murdock switched his MP-5 to three-round burst, and stepped inside. It was a supply room loaded with uniforms, rations, ammunition, and other goods. A single work light burned overhead.

The men found two doors. Lights showed under both of them. Murdock opened one and stepped inside. Three uniformed men worked over a radio panel. Murdock's three-round burst put down two of them. Another three rounds from Lee Quinley's silenced H&K G-11 nailed the other one.

Another door showed ahead. Murdock moved to it. Washington opened it, and they both looked in. It was a barracks, with twenty men sleeping on double-decker bunks. The silenced shots had not awakened them. Washington eased the door closed, and they moved to the next one.

Beyond this door, opened a long hallway. There were six doors leading off it. At the far end, sat a sentry at a desk. He was either sleeping or reading. Murdock switched his subgun to single-shot, and fired twice. The guard jolted back against the wall, and then slumped off the chair to the floor.

Murdock and Quinley ran to the guard as Washington covered their backs. The guard was dead. They checked the first door. An office. The second showed a storeroom. The third door opened onto a pair of cells. Two men were in one, three in the other.

"Any of you speak English?" Murdock asked. One man looked up quickly.

"I do. Who are you?"

"Are you Fayd Salwa?" Murdock asked.

"Yes. Are you Americans?"

"Right, we're taking you home," Quinley said. He looked at the lock on the door. A small key chain hung on a nail near the door. He grabbed it, tried two keys. The third one unlocked the cell. He opened the other cell as well, and ushered all the prisoners out. They saw the open door and ran.

Tears brimmed Salwa's eyes as he grabbed Murdock in a bear hug. "I have prayed to Allah to rescue me, but I never thought it would happen."

Murdock touched his lip mike. "I have the package. We're coming out." Just as he said it they heard automatic-rifle fire in the hallway. Murdock peered around the door frame from floor level, and saw three men in military uniforms moving down the hall, checking rooms as they came.

He pushed his MP-5 around the door frame, jolted out so he could see, and sprayed the advancing guards with three triple-round bursts. All the soldiers went down. One crawled toward his dropped rifle. A burst of rounds from Quinley's G-11 put him down and dead.

"Which way out?" Murdock asked Salwa.

"I don't know. They only brought me here tonight. I'd like to have a weapon. I was in the army, I can use one."

Murdock gave him the Mark 23 O pistol off his belt. Salwa chambered a round and pushed on the safety.

"Let's try to the left, past where the guard used to be," Quinley said.

Murdock agreed. "Those sleeping men back the other way must be awake now after that rifle fire."

Murdock talked to his Motorola again. "Ed, we've got some bad guys shooting in here. Create a diversion outside, the side entrance, and the back. Keep them busy. We'll try to get out."

"Roger that. How about a nice gasoline fire back here?"

Murdock took the lead. Salwa was in the middle with Washington, and Quinley bringing up the rear. They ran past the three bodies, and to the end of the hall where the guard lay dead.

A connecting hall went both ways. Murdock chose the right-hand one, and had gone only a dozen steps when two soldiers came around a bend in the hall. Murdock brought up his MP-5 and got off three rounds. Salwa right behind him fired four times, and the two soldiers went down.

The three SEALs and Salwa ran toward them. One of the soldiers lifted up with his AK-47. Before he could fire, Salwa put a .45 round in his head. The man slammed backwards as brains and blood splattered against the wall.

Murdock waved his thanks at Salwa, and they ran on. The corridor dead-ended at a double door. Salwa shrugged. Murdock tried the door. Locked.

Someone behind in the hall fired at them. Quinley turned,

and chattered off six rounds down the hall at two uniformed men. They ducked out of danger. Murdock looked at the door. It was their only way out. He stepped back, waved Salwa and the two SEALs back, and put a three-round burst of the 9mm slugs into the area of the door lock. The panel shook on impact, then swung open a foot.

They darted through the opening, just as the men behind them fired again.

The room was a total surprise. Two naked men with military blouses draped over chairs were in two beds, each of them with two naked women. Murdock and Salwa grabbed the men's clothes, and backed toward a far door. Quinley and Washington kept their weapons aimed at naked bodies. The far door was unlocked.

Salwa peered through the open door with Murdock. Murdock nodded, and the four men hurried through into the next room, a small kitchen. Beyond that they found another corridor with a door at the far end. This door opened to the outside. Murdock had no idea which side of the building they were on. He checked outside.

No troops were visible. He looked both ways again through the darkness, and to the right saw a growing light. He frowned, then realized it came from the flickering of flames. The men darted out the door, and ran twenty yards to a parking lot where a number of civilian cars and three military rigs stood.

Murdock hit the Motorola. "Ed, where the hell are you?"

"We're near the back door where you entered. The fire's burning nicely, and we have about twenty troops who don't like us too well. They keep shooting at us."

Then Murdock could hear the rifle fire.

"Use the rest of the Second Squad back there to cover you, then start leapfrogging back into the desert. We still have the package. We'll try to meet you at that truck we borrowed."

As Murdock said it, someone from the door they had just left opened up with automatic-rifle fire. Quinley went down beside the front of a car, and peppered the door with his 4.7mm caseless rounds.

"Salwa, can you get one of these personnel carriers started?"

"Give it a try. You have a knife?"

Murdock gave him his K-bar, and the Arab man vanished into the nearest half-track. More fire came from the side door, and now a new threat showed at the front of the building.

"The damn rig with the Big Fifty has swung around on us," Washington whispered. A dozen rounds slammed overhead.

"Don't think they want to shoot up their half-tracks," Murdock said.

A moment later a line of men from the front of the building came running at them with assault fire. The nearest civilian car was riddled. The three SEALs returned fire, and half the shooters went down. Fewer rounds came then, and Quinley put in a new 50-round magazine and fired again.

Another line of gunmen ran forward from behind the first.

Murdock heard the rumble of an engine start.

"Ready," Salwa shouted. Quinley, Washington, and Murdock jumped in the half-track, and it rolled away from the front of the building, then did a ninety-degree turn, and headed straight for the desert. Two hundred yards into the sand and rocks, the rig slowed, and pivoted around so its .50-caliber machine gun on the front could work the rear of the building.

For the first time, Murdock looked at the fire. It seemed that half the gasoline drums had blown up, splattering burning gasoline over the rest of the stored goods.

Murdock got to the Fifty, loaded in a belt of ammo from a box, and charged in a round. He leveled the weapon at the rear of the complex, and jolted off five rounds.

He was surprised at the force the rounds going off made on the gun itself and the mount.

Murdock touched his mike. "Ed, that's me on the Fifty. Get your men the hell out of there."

"Pleased to oblige there, good buddy. We're on our way. Leapfrog it is."

"We're moving out too. We'll keep their heads down for a while."

As he spoke, they took machine-gun fire from near the

front of the building. The other rig with the .50-caliber whammer had changed targets. Murdock swung his weapon around, and sent two bursts of six rounds at the flashes he could see. The other gun didn't return fire. He put six more rounds into the same area, then hit the back of the building again.

"Murdock," DeWitt said. "I sent Douglas out to get the truck and bring it in to meet us. We should have a hookup in about five."

"We'll move north to find you. If you see a half-track coming, it's probably us. Don't fire."

"That's a Roger. We've got one wounded, not serious, but will take some looking at."

"First we've got to figure out how the hell to get away from here without a bunch of El Raza's men tailing us. Our chopper guys don't like to get shot at. This bunch could even have some Stinger ground-to-air missiles."

"Those shoulder-fired kind?" Ed asked.

"Yeah, the kind the terrs use sometimes. We're coming to find you."

3

Tuesday, 9 January

Desert near Osadi, Iraq

Murdock settled back in the half-track and watched behind him. Within three minutes he saw lights coming toward him. They must be some of the other half-tracks of El Raza. He had a choice: try to outshoot them, and give away his position, or continue to roll along without lights, and stay lost in the desert.

"Ed, no lights on your rig. I've got lights behind me, but no return fire so they don't know where we are."

"That's a Roger. We've met the truck. I've got six men inside, and eight hanging on the outside. Where to?"

"We've been heading east—that should put us far enough away from the town so now we can cut due south. The border is closest to the south."

"Will the chopper care?"

"Less Iraq airspace they have to cover, the better they'll like it. Can't tell what good old Saddam might have sitting around here with wings on it, and air-to-ground missiles on the wings."

"Due south it is. How do we join up?"

"I'll stop our rig and listen," Murdock said. "Should be able to hear that grinder of yours out here."

"That's a Roger. We're turning south."

In the half-track, Salwa had heard the transmission from Murdock. He looked at the American. "Shut it down now?"

Murdock nodded. The rig stopped and Murdock stepped away as the engine died. He turned slowly trying to pick up some sound. Quinley was beside him.

He touched Murdock's shoulder and pointed. Murdock turned that way.

"Three or four half-tracks chasing us," Quinley said. "Sounds like more than one engine."

Murdock thought he heard it, but it faded. It was to the left. Salwa started the engine, and they moved over the dark desert at ten miles an hour.

"Sometimes there are little wadis out here fifteen feet deep from the runoff," Salwa said. Murdock nodded. They drove south for ten minutes; then Murdock had the engine turned off and they listened again.

Nothing.

Far off they saw headlights.

"Looks like they're still going east," Murdock said. "Let's hope we lost them."

Then he saw more lights, two pair that were heading in much the same direction as he was. He hit the mike.

"Ed, you have two rigs chasing you? Headlights to the rear?"

"Yeah. Figured something was back there—they just turned on their lights."

"Keep on the same bearing. We'll see if we can come up to the side of those two half-tracks and give them a good SEAL hot-lead welcome."

They drove faster then. A half-moon gave some help. Salwa had grown up in the desert, and knew even with the lights off how to tell a shadow from a gully, at least now that it was vital. The rigs with lights on were going faster, but Murdock had the angle on them. He figured in another two miles he'd have them at a two-hundred-yard range. All he had to do was blow their tracks off or kill the engine with the half-track's mounted Fifty.

Ten minutes later, Murdock could see the lights, and the

faint shadows of the rigs themselves. He was at four hundred yards. He closed to two hundred, and used the rig's mounted machine gun to shoot at the first half-track.

The fifty-caliber spoke loudly in the desert silence. He missed with the first rounds, corrected, and slammed six, then twelve rounds into the side and front of the moving rig. It sputtered and died. The headlights went out.

He saw the second rig stop and turn to bring its gun to bear on Murdock's muzzle flashes. Murdock got off a ten-round burst, then two more five-round bursts before the other gunner could get in action. He saw the front of the rig dissolve in steam; then the fuel tank blew in a gushing explosion fed by the diesel fuel, and the fight was over.

"Oh, yeah, beautiful," Ed DeWitt said on the Motorola. "I'd say the two are about a half mile behind us, and they were gaining on us like crazy. Can we use lights now?"

"Hell, no. There are still three or four half-tracks out here hunting us. We join up, get another five miles south, then call for our chopper pickup, and in an hour or two a big dinner. What time is it?"

"Just past twenty-three hundred," DeWitt said. "Come and find us. I can loan you about six men."

"Turn off your engine. Let us know when you can hear us, then guide us in. We can't be more than a mile or two apart."

Murdock found the rest of his platoon ten minutes later. They overshot them, and had to come back.

"Got you," DeWitt said on the radio.

Then Murdock saw the truck with men hanging all over it. Salwa pulled the half-track up beside it, and they redistributed the men for better mobility.

"Let's have a casualty report," Murdock said to the men.

Holt came up and showed Murdock his arm. "The slug went on through, no big deal. Doc put some gunk on it and wrapped it up proper-like. I'm fit for duty."

"But no hundred-foot rope climbs, right?"

"Yeah, that would be tough."

The second squad wound was only a bullet graze. Doc wrapped it and they moved.

"Let's keep it quiet now, and listen for engines. Somebody

get on top of the truck and look for headlights. Be nice if we had a thousand-foot hill to use for a lookout."

They watched and listened for ten minutes. Murdock was satisfied they didn't have any of the hunter half-tracks close to them.

"We'll motor another twenty minutes due south, then put in our call for the chopper. Everyone watch for headlights out here."

Twenty minutes later, they had covered several miles to the south, and hadn't run into any sign of the Iraqi hunters. Murdock called a halt, and they listened again. Then he waved at Ron Holt.

"Fire up the SATCOM. Let's get out of here."

Holt took the fifteen-pound radio off his back, and opened the flap with the antenna. He set up the small dish, and aimed it somewhere near where the Milstar satellite should be in a synchronous orbit 23,300 miles over the equator. The radio gave instant communications by the satellite with anyone, anywhere in the world. They could call the President, or their families back in Coronado.

It was fifteen inches high, three inches square, and had power from ten watts all the way down to one tenth of a watt for short-distance clandestine operations. It had the capability of voice, data, or video transmission and receiving, and encrypted each message automatically. It could send out a lengthy message in a burst of energy less than a tenth of a second long to make it almost impossible for an enemy to find the transmitter.

Murdock took the pad, and typed in his message: "Have package, waiting pickup. Murdock." He used the MUGR, the Miniature Underwater Geographic locator. It usually worked underwater with an antenna that drifted to the surface, where it contacted the three closest positioning satellites for triangulation to pin down the location anywhere on the globe to within ten feet. He took the reading off the dry-land model, and entered the coordinates in his message.

Murdock reviewed the words, then punched the button to encrypt it, and it was sent a moment later in a quick burst of power.

"Now we sit down and wait for our bird to come," Murdock said.

Fayd Salwa had been following the procedure with interest.

"This is fascinating to me," he said. "When I was in the army we had nothing like this. We had a weapon, and sometimes bullets, and if extremely lucky a truck so we didn't have to march so far. It wasn't a good army."

"These gadgets are fine as long as they work," Murdock said. "Once we had a SATCOM that took a pair of slugs right in the middle, and it was just fifteen pounds of worthless junk."

A moment later, a message came back on the SATCOM.

"Help on the way. ETA ten minutes."

Murdock nodded, and told the troops. How long did it take a chopper to fly ten miles? Only he didn't know where it was coming from. The border with Kuwait might be more than ten miles away to the southeast, he knew.

Murdock checked each man. Nobody else had been wounded, no other physical problems. They had been lucky to get in and out with so little damage. It was always a deadly chance going into these blind situations. Sometimes they simply didn't have enough intel.

Five minutes later, they heard a noise to the southeast. They let the sound grow until they knew it was a chopper. Murdock let it fly directly over them at a hundred feet until he was sure it was a U.S. machine. Then he popped a red flare, and the bird circled around and landed a hundred yards from them.

"Let's get the hell out of Dodge," Murdock said. The men had been standing waiting; now they started to run across the sand to their air bus out of Iraq.

They were still fifty yards away, when Murdock heard the whooshing sound he had nightmares about, an incoming Rocket Propelled Grenade. These lethal rockets were deadly, easy to use, and to conceal.

Before he could yell at his men to take cover, one rocket hit the chopper, and then another, and a third. The bird, with its big rotor chugging around, burst into flames; then the fuel

exploded, and there was nothing left but fiercely burning bits
and pieces of machine and the dead crewmen.

"Hold!" Murdock shouted. "We can't help the poor bastards! Let's find the shooters!"

They all hit the sand, and listened. Over the roaring fire of
the chopper they managed to hear some high-pitched chatter
and a fired round or two. Murdock pointed to the left, where
there was a small gully.

Murdock whispered into his mike. "Ed. Take your squad
fifty yards south. We'll move north, then we move up on that
gully. A surprise party."

It took them only a few minutes to get in position, and then
move forward. At the edge of the small arroyo, they stopped
and peered over the side. It was an armored personnel carrier
with a dozen men around it. They were celebrating the
destroyed chopper.

Murdock gave his men time to set up; then he aimed his
subgun at the closest troops below and kicked off a twelve-
round burst. At his signal, the rest of the weapons opened up.

There was no immediate response, as the men below dove
for any cover they could find, mostly behind the armored rig.
Then gunfire answered the SEALs.

Murdock ducked back a minute, and rolled to the left to
establish a new firing position. Half of the men along the lip
of the gully did the same thing.

Bill Bradford settled in behind the big M-87R .50-caliber
rifle, and zeroed in on the vehicle. The big McMillan
bolt-action rifle had a ten-round magazine hanging out the
bottom of it. Bradford put his eye to the Leopold Ultra MK4
16-power scope, and triggered off the first round.

The AP, armor-piercing, round splattered through the hood
and exploded deep inside the diesel engine, killing any more
movement by the rig. He then concentrated on the cab and
blasted three rounds in there. He had loaded the magazine
with alternate AP and HE, and the effect riddled the personnel
carrier, turning it into an elongated bit of flotsam on a sea of
sand.

Murdock rattled off three-round bursts at the dimly lit
targets. The SEALs continued to take return fire, but the men

below must have figured they were outgunned. No RPG rounds came their way. The Iraqi troops, or the men from El Raza, must not have been able to tie down a good target.

After four minutes, the firing from below tapered off, then stopped. The survivors evidently knew when to quit, and had faded into the desert night, moving away from Murdock and his team.

"That's a wrap," Murdock said on the Motorola.

It was too late to check for survivors in the chopper. The three RPG rounds had brought a nearly immediate fuel explosion, and there was no chance anyone could have lived through the blasts.

"Move out, double-time back to our transport," Murdock said into his mike. "We need to get away from this fucking grave site. Somebody in that personnel carrier might have radioed in the shoot on the enemy bird, and that will bring all sorts of visitors to this place."

Holt jogged up beside his commander. "Should we give a report on the chopper, sir? Somebody back there will be wondering."

"Right, but in a half hour. By then we should be well away from this death scene. The time won't matter to that chopper crew."

Fayd Salwa came up on the other side of Murdock. "Could I offer a suggestion? Distance from that scene is the key, but they will expect us to run directly for the Kuwait border. If they search for us it will be there. My suggestion is that we turn and go southwest, which will put us into Saudi Arabia in about fifteen miles. I know this area."

Murdock considered it. He nodded. He touched the lip mike. "Men, we're changing direction a little, southwest instead of southeast. We're heading away from where the bad guys will be looking for us. This direction will put us in Saudi Arabia, a friendly nation."

Back at the motorized rigs, they loaded up and moved out southwest. If they were only fifteen miles from the border, there was a chance they could get there quickly.

Murdock could imagine the worry about the chopper back at its base. He pulled up the rigs a mile from the crash site and

sent a cryptic note on the SATCOM about the chopper, asking
for another pickup. A message came back quickly.

"Positive there are no survivors? No chance for another
pickup. Our radar shows numerous Iraqi aircraft moving into
your area. Try to make a run for the border."

Murdock sent back a message that there was no chance for
survivors. Then they moved with lights off.

They had gone no more than a mile when Murdock halted
the rigs and turned off the engines. The sound he had thought
he heard came again; then a jet fighter roared over their heads
at two hundred feet.

"He couldn't see us and he doesn't have good enough radar
to spot us on the ground. We'd be so much screen clutter. He's
fishing, but we've got to be careful. We'll keep the trucks a
hundred yards apart, and move slowly toward the border.
Maybe eight miles from here now."

The men heard a swooshing sound, and all of them dove
out of the rigs and hit the ground.

Another Rocket Propelled Grenade. It slammed into the
ground ten yards from the truck, but shrapnel sprayed
forward, smashing the windshield, puncturing the gas tank,
and chewing up the fuel line on the engine.

"Where did it come from?" Murdock asked his mike.

"From the north," Ed DeWitt said. "I've got three men
moving that way. There's a little gully over there. They could
be on the lip of it. Anybody hit by that hot steel? Casualty
report."

"Yeah, L-T. Adams. I picked up a scratch on my leg. Tore
my cammies. Not bleeding much."

"L-T. Douglas. Caught some of that steel on my right arm.
Dug in deep. Doc better take a look."

"I'll find you, Douglas," Doc said.

A moment later, they heard gunfire, then more gunfire.

"Nailed two of them, L-T," Gonzalez said on the Motorola.
"They have some kind of a jeep rig and bugged out before we
could get anybody else. Don't think we hurt their transport
much."

At the truck, Joe Douglas had been checking it out. He

ground the starter six times. Nothing. With a small flashlight, he looked the engine over.

"No way, L-T," he told DeWitt. "The engine is a mess, fuel line is in ten pieces, a bunch of wiring is chopped up. Take me a week to make it run. Besides, all the gas leaked out. Lucky it didn't blow up on us."

"Let's get to the half-track," Murdock said on the radio. "We'll load as many on it as we can; the rest of us will jog along beside it. We'll change off every two miles. We've got a border to find."

Ten minutes later, they heard a chopper coming. The men scattered away from the half-track. Murdock manned the fifty-caliber MG. He knew the chopper gunners could see the half-track in the pale moonlight. It wasn't supposed to be here. That would be enough for a shoot.

He got off six five-round bursts with the big weapon, but wasn't sure if he scored any hits. Then the bird was coming in on a missile run, and Murdock jumped off the half-track and sprinted away thirty yards before the missile hit the vehicle. The first explosion was enough to destroy it; then a secondary explosion ripped through it, and the half-track became various refrigerator-sized pieces of junk scattered around the desert.

As the chopper came over the rig on its firing run, the SEAL platoon returned fire. Bill Bradford had his Big Fifty out, and got off six rounds as the chopper came over. The last two jolted into the chopper and it began trailing smoke. It tipped left and nearly hit the ground, then righted itself, before it lost power and dropped straight down three hundred feet and burst into flames.

"Take that, Turkey," Bradford called, and the rest of the SEALs cheered.

Murdock hit his mike. "Listen up. We're on foot, and still seven or eight miles from the border. Mr. Salwa knows the territory, so he'll be our guide. We'll form up in a column of ducks ten yards apart and move out of here at double time. That chopper radioed in our position for damn sure. Let's motor."

They kept moving, with Murdock setting the pace at a

brisk six miles an hour. He kept a lead scout out a hundred yards and a rear guard as far back as he could see the main body. As far as they knew, no one followed them though the half-moon Iraqi night.

They hiked hard for an hour, then took a break. Lam roamed the area around them, and came back reporting that he saw nothing except two night birds, and heard only a few small scurrying night animals.

Murdock had Holt fire up the SATCOM again, and he reported shooting down the Iraqi chopper. He told them they were aiming southwest for the nearest point of the border with Saudi Arabia. He asked for any orders.

The reply came back quickly. "Kuwait border area alive and active with Iraqi troops and choppers. Do not try to approach. We can send no airlift support. Keep us informed. Good idea on the Saudi border. Good luck."

The SEALs sat in the sand and rocks of the Iraqi border area resting. The kidnap victim had stayed close to Murdock. He thanked Murdock again for his rescue.

"Our army simply doesn't have any commandos like you folks. We don't have the skills. Now it is my hope that we can get to one of the borders safely. It would not go well for me if either El Raza or Saddam Hussein's men caught me."

When Holt had the SATCOM packed up, they moved again. They had heard more jet aircraft, but they were miles away evidently searching a different area. There was a lot of desert out there to cover, Murdock decided.

They had hiked for fifteen minutes on their southwest course when Murdock heard the unmistakable sound of helicopters heading toward them.

"Two choppers, maybe three coming in from the north," DeWitt said. "I can see searchlights."

"Spread out and get into the dirt," Murdock said. The SEALs scattered twenty yards apart, lay down in the sand and rocks of the desert, and spread handfuls of the sand over their cammies to make them even harder to see. Weapons were hidden under their bodies.

The choppers made a pass two hundred yards to the north

of them, then circled back, and came within a hundred yards of their position.

"Nobody move, don't even breathe," Murdock said softly into his lip mike.

Murdock watched with surprise as the two choppers settled down to a landing four hundred yards away. The birds landed about fifty yards apart, and were larger than he had first thought.

Each chopper had on landing lights, and he could see twenty combat troops jump down from each one. The troops formed up, and then spread out in a skirmish search pattern and began walking directly toward where the SEALs lay.

4

Tuesday, 9 January

**Southeastern Desert
Iraq**

Ed DeWitt and Jaybird moved up beside Murdock.

"Range to the choppers?" Murdock asked.

"Four hundred yards," Jaybird said. "We can't outrun them. We'll have to stand and fight sometime."

"Let's hit them with the Fifty, kill the choppers, then we can take on the troops," DeWitt said.

Murdock watched the enemy troops move forward cautiously. The SEALs had another ten minutes before the Iraqi soldiers overran them.

"Get Bradford working with the fifty," Murdock said. "With his first shot we use the MGs on the choppers, and the rest of us with long guns get down on the troops. Go."

Ed left to pass the word to his men. The sixteen SEALs moved up into a line of skirmishers facing the enemy troops. Two minutes after the decision, everyone was in place, and Bradford fired his first round. It hit the lead chopper in the engine compartment. Its rotor died where it had been idling.

The other SEALs with long guns opened up on the troops advancing on them. Four or five went down before the Iraqis hit the dirt. The two machine guns chattered at the choppers. One burst into flames. The second one had died in place.

Then Joe Douglas and Horse Ronson turned their machine-gun sights on the advancing troops. When the MGs took over, the Iraqi troops were pinned down. They couldn't advance into the deadly machine-gun and rifle fire, and they couldn't stand up to retreat.

Miguel Fernandez with his sniper rifle picked off a soldier whenever he found one moving or showing above the desert terrain.

The firefight was too far away for those men with the MP-5's. Murdock used his radio, and told all the MP-5 shooters to crawl to the rear. Thirty yards away was a small wadi that had been dug out by the occasional cloudbursts. He got them into it, then pulled back everyone but the machine gunners. He stayed with the MG men until the rest of the platoon was in the gully.

He signaled for Ronson to cease fire and get to the rear and the safety of the wadi. He used Douglas to keep up firing across the spread of the enemy troops.

They were taking only an occasional round from the Iraqi troops, who had just lost their transport. They could be thinking about the long walk back to their base.

"Let's go," Murdock told Douglas. He folded the bipod, and they ran the first twenty yards before the Iraqis realized they weren't taking fire anymore. A few rounds came, then more. Murdock and Douglas hit the dirt, and crawled. At the same time, the SEAL long guns from the top of the wadi spoke, and silenced the Iraqi weapons.

Mudock and Douglas rolled over the lip of the ravine, and tumbled to the bottom six feet down.

"Let's move," Murdock said. "Form up, and double-time out of here, down the gully, and when we get some distance, we'll bug out southwest. Move, move, move."

They ran down the ravine. It gradually got deeper but headed to the south, so they kept in it.

By the time they had been running for five minutes, Murdock called a halt on his radio. "Lam, take a look over the rim, and see if you can spot anybody trailing us."

Lam crawled up the ten-foot-high bank, and stared back the way they had come. He used his NVGs, and checked out every area he could see. When he dropped down from the bank, he shook his head.

"Can't see a rat's ass of them out there, Commander. Not a farting one."

"They're probably trying to figure out if they have any radio to contact their base," DeWitt said. "If no radio, they'll have one fucking long hike."

Murdock turned to Salwa. "Any of this area look familiar to you?"

The Kuwaiti official shook his head. "Not right here. There are wadies like this all over this end of the desert. The rain comes down in bucketfuls, and runs off just as fast."

"So, it's southwest again. Let's get up the bank, and on the move. The time is now oh-oh-forty-five. We have maybe six hours to sunrise, if we're lucky."

Four men went up and over the bank. Before anyone else could climb the bank, they all heard rifle fire from somewhere in front. The four men dropped back down again.

"Whole shitpot full of them not a hundred yards out there," Lampedusa said. "Looks like they came down another arroyo somewhere and found us."

Murdock motioned the long guns to the top of the bank. He sent three men with MP-5's down each way along the gully for thirty yards.

"Look over the top of the bank, and shoot if you've got a target," Murdock told the men with long guns. "We don't want them any closer. Let's use some forty-mike grenades if it looks good. Now."

He moved up, and watched over the lip of the ravine. He could barely make out a line of Iraqi troops in front. They would go to ground with the first shot. His MP-5 wouldn't get that far.

"Fire when ready," he said to his lip mike. The two machine guns and the two sniper rifles blazed and chattered. Murdock thought he saw three men hit in the firing; then the troops ahead dropped into the dirt making poor targets. His men ducked below the ridge as they took return fire.

Lampedusa was back at the top of the bank with his NVG,

and his Colt 4-Al. He picked out a target through the Night Vision Goggles and fired.

"Yes," he said, and dropped down.

Murdock handed his NVGs to Horse Ronson, who popped up with his machine gun and soon fired three five-round bursts, then came back down to his protection.

"Them assholes don't have no cover out there," Ronson said. A flurry of rounds slammed over the top of the ravine; then all four long guns went back up, and Lam made it five. The long guns took turns firing to keep the Iraqi troops pinned down, as Lam loaded a 40mm grenade and fired. He was long. He fired a second round, a WP, and saw the flash as the furiously burning white phosphorus rained down on half a dozen of the Iraqi shooters out front.

Down to the left, Murdock heard some firing. He ran that way to find his three men with MP-5's crouched along the side of the ravine, firing straight ahead.

Murdock felt some rounds slam past him, and he pasted himself against the side of the ditch, then hurried on to his three men.

"Skipper, we caught four of them trying to outflank us along here. We dropped three of them, but missed the fourth. Figure he's long gone now heading for the rest of the troops."

"Let's look at the bodies," Murdock said. They were only fifty feet up the gully. Two of them had AK-47's, and the third some foreign make of submachine gun.

All were dead.

"Bring the two AK-47's," Murdock said. "We might need them. And get all the ammo you can find." Murdock looked at the submachine gun, and dropped it. He preferred his MP-5.

"Stay here and watch for any more of them," Murdock said. "I'll bring you back in as soon as I think it's safe."

He ran back to the main body. Jaybird saw him coming in the darkness, and intercepted him.

"That first man over the side got hit, Commander. It's Gonzalez. Doc says the round went into his upper chest. Not sure if it missed his lung or not. So far no trouble breathing. He can walk, but he won't be doing much with his weapon."

Murdock found Gonzalez. Doc was still with him.

"Hang in there, Gonzalez. Doc is fixing you up. We're almost to the border. A piece of cake from here. Do what Doc tells you, and take it easy."

Doc went with Murdock off a dozen yards. "Not good, Commander. Bullet's up high, might have missed a lung, but it might have punctured it and it could collapse."

"How far can he walk?"

"Don't know. I just hope he isn't bleeding inside. I'll stay with him."

Murdock nodded, and checked with Jaybird on the top of the bank.

"They tried one rush, but went down when we opened up again with the MGs. My guess is they are down to maybe twenty who can fight. The odds are getting better."

"Let's get all of the Colts up here, and throw out about twenty forty-mike-mike. That's the best way to rout them. If we can make them run, then we can choggie down our ravine. Don't know where the hell it's going, but it's away from here."

Jaybird called up the men with the Colt carbines that could fire the grenades. He had five Colts.

"Five rounds each," Jaybird said. "Alternate HE and WP if you've got them. Let's get this fracas settled."

Murdock told the MG guys to do twenty rounds each just before the grenades went out. They did.

The grenades fell just after the machine guns tapered off. Murdock watched from the top edge of the bank. He saw one Iraqi leap up, and run to the rear. Good. Five grenades had dropped in, and he could hear some screams. Then the second volley. Just as it ended, two more men raced away to the rear into the darkness.

Murdock used his mike. "You six flankers, come in. We're going to be shagging ass here in about three."

Murdock watched the last three volleys of grenades explode on the Iraqi troops. Some were long, two were short, but enough hit the flattened troops to rout them. When the last of the small bombs went off, Murdock used his NVGs and saw six men limping to the rear. Six more leaped up and ran hard back the way they had come.

Murdock used the mike again. "Doc, you and Gonzales head down the gully. We'll follow it another mile if we can. At least it gives us some protection. We'll catch up. Don't push him too hard."

Gonzalez heard the message in his radio. He snorted. "What the hell he mean, not push me too hard. I'm a hairy-assed, nookie-fucking SEAL, goddamnit. I can keep up with this shitty outfit any day."

Doc Ellsworth agreed with him. Doc took Gonzalez's weapon over his shoulder and helped him stand.

"Okay, now nice and easy, RG. We ain't in no damned race here. We just move, right?"

Doc was surprised how slow Gonzalez walked. The bullet had done more than drill one small hole. It hadn't come out his back, so it was inside somewhere causing all sorts of hell. Doc hoped that Gonzalez could last for a mile.

Murdock and the rest of the platoon moved out a few minutes later, and caught the slow-moving Gonzalez quickly. Murdock slowed the pace, put Lam out in front, and told him to check the sides of the ravine every few minutes. He had Jaybird riding Tail End Charlie as rear guard.

Murdock figured the pace was about three miles an hour. If Gonzalez could maintain it for two hours, they should be right next door to the Saudi border. A damn big if, he knew.

He called Ed up and laid it out. "War games, Ed. We're in this situation, and you're El Raza. You know about where we are. What are you going to do after the choppers didn't nail us?"

Ed took a deep breath. Murdock had caught him doing that several times when he wanted a minute to think. He shifted his weapon to the other shoulder, and motioned with his right hand.

"First, I'd get some troops out in front of where it looks like we're headed. I'd cover both of the borders. Say about three miles away from the line. Put a blocking force of all the men I could spare. We know El Raza had two hundred men at one time. We lowered his force by at least a dozen, maybe fifteen or twenty.

"He has some choppers. Just how many we don't know. So I'd use choppers or half-tracks and move eighty men into blocking positions along the Saudi border and along the Kuwait boundary. Then I'd sit and wait for us to fall into the trap, or for daylight when my jets could do the job."

"El Raza doesn't have any jets."

"Then whose were those we saw?"

"Probably Uncle Saddam. He may be in the equation now. If so, he's got all the firepower, and men, he wants. But would he pull El Raza's chestnuts out of the pot? Why would he?"

"To give Uncle Sam a bloody nose. He's already shot down one U.S. chopper and should be able to prove it. If he could capture or kill sixteen U.S. military men on Iraq soil, he could shout invasion and all sorts of wild things in the world court of public opinion. And he'd win the round."

"Good. About what I had decided on, the blocking move. If he has eighty men for each spot, how long a line could he use to be sure to block us?"

"Eighty men at twenty yards apart at night would be the best he could do. That's sixteen hundred yards. Damn near a mile. Seventeen hundred and sixty yards in a mile. Two eight-eighties that I used to run for the Academy track team."

"If we hit the screen, we'd have to take out three of the sentries to give ourselves a safe passage between them of eighty yards. Almost a football field. Which I didn't play on for the Academy." They both chuckled.

"So, if Lam can spot them in time, and if we manage to hit the wrong spot where they are, we need to take out three sentries in a row," DeWitt said. "Wish we had bows and arrows. Even our silenced sniper rifles are going to make too much noise."

"Knife work," Murdock said. "You, me, and Jaybird."

Lampedusa came back every ten minutes. He was surprised how slowly they were moving, then remembered Gonzalez.

"I can't see shit up there," Lam told Murdock. "Don't look

like there's anybody ahead or behind us. Think we shot the fuck out of that chopper bunch."

Murdock told him about what he and DeWitt had been talking about.

"Makes sense. Only how do you know they'll put them twenty yards apart?"

"We don't. It's what I'd do in his situation," Murdock said.

"What if he figures by our hits on his people that we're heading for Saudi, not the other one, and he puts all one-eighty along that border?"

"Then we'll have a better chance of hitting his nearly two-mile picket fence, but still just as good a chance of getting through," DeWitt said.

"Yeah. Okay. I want to be one of the guys with the knife."

"A volunteer," DeWitt said.

"We'll worry about that when you spot those pickets. Remember, this is Iraq. They'll probably be talking and most surely smoking. Should be fish in a fucking teacup."

The pace had slowed. Murdock wondered about carrying Gonzalez. He was 180 pounds. Ronson could pack him for half a mile. Then what? No, they were stuck with the best pace that their wounded man could do.

Murdock went up to see them. Gonzales looked worse. Doc gave him another shot of morphine from the small one-time-use ampoules, and he perked up a little.

"You tell me where you hurt, Gonzalez. None of this hero shit, you understand?"

"Yeah, Doc. Too damn tired to argue."

"How tired? Like you aren't getting enough blood to carry oxygen to your muscles?"

"No, just tired. My arms feel like they're about to fall off, but they ain't."

Gonzalez wasn't wearing his combat vest with his ammo and other items. It usually weighed about twenty pounds. Doc had given the Colt carbine to someone else as well.

"So, buddy, just keep moving them big feet one ahead of the other, and we'll get out of this chickenshit country."

"Amen to that. How far?"

"Not a clue, nobody will tell me. We'll take it one step at a time."

Later, Murdock thought he heard an aircraft, but he couldn't be sure. Nobody else heard it. He was fantasizing. He checked his watch. It was 0130. They had five hours to daylight. Salwa had put on Gonzalez's combat vest, and had his Colt. He gave Murdock the .45 H&K pistol.

"I'm more used to a long gun," Salwa said.

The ravine kept getting smaller and shallower. They were moving upstream. A half mile more and they were back on the desert floor. They shifted their heading back to the southwest.

Salwa came up to Murdock. "Hey, now I know where I am. We're near some caves—I don't remember what they called them. Back in my student days we came here on a field trip. Relations between the countries were better then."

Murdock gave the Kuwaiti a drink from his canteen.

"I'm remembering a little more about this area," Salwa said. "There were several of the large caves. Ancient ones with hints of a previous civilization."

Murdock put his canteen back on his belt. "How big were the caves?"

"Huge. But it was a long time ago."

"Might be a good defensive position if we get tracked down," Murdock said. He took off the NVGs and handed them to the Kuwaiti. "Take a look around, you might see something familiar."

Salwa took the goggles, and stared around the landscape for a minute. Then he caught up, and walked again beside Murdock.

"Yes, I did see something. The start of a wadi. It's nearly on our course. I think if it's the right wadi, that I can find the caves."

Murdock talked with Ed DeWitt and Jaybird. They agreed.

Ten minutes later they moved in a slightly more southern direction, and soon found a wadi, or gully, that was small, but grew deeper as they walked along it.

"Yes," Salwa said. "This is the one. The caves should be less than a half mile ahead."

Murdock went to the front of the line and checked in with Gonzalez. He looked decidedly worse than he had a half hour before. As he walked beside Murdock, Gonzalez stumbled, and Doc had to catch him. Murdock talked to his mike.

"Ronson, come up to the front."

A minute later Ronson came striding up. He took one look at Gonzalez, picked him up like a baby, and carried him forward. He had given his machine gun to Murdock.

"Half a mile, and we take a break," Murdock said. Gonzalez had closed his eyes. Murdock knew how proud he was to be a SEAL. He didn't want anyone helping him. Only now it was absolutely necessary.

Murdock went back to the middle of the line, and told DeWitt about the assist. The big problem now would be daylight. Before then they had to have somewhere to hide or be across the border into Saudi Arabia. The caves might be the answer. That is, if they didn't run into the blocking force before it got anywhere near light. Murdock wanted to be well into Saudi Arabia by the time the desert sun came up.

The caves would give them good protection for a rest. If the Kuwaiti was right, and if he could find them in the dark.

5

Wednesday, 10 January

Near Wadi al-Batin Caves
Southeastern Iraq

The Third Platoon hiked along the wadi for half an hour. Murdock heard something and hit the dirt, and the rest of the platoon went down as well. He turned. The sound had come from close by.

Fayd Salwa chuckled. "Commander, I'm afraid it's the alarm on my watch. It's new, and I've never figured out how to turn it off, so I set it at two-fifteen A.M., and two-fifteen P.M. Sorry."

"False alarm," Murdock said into his lip mike. "Let's move."

He grinned at Salwa. "Hey, don't worry about it. Just glad we weren't sneaking up on somebody. At least now I know what time it is. We have, what, maybe four hours to daylight?"

"Sunup about six-thirty, or oh-six-thirty." Salwa looked ahead again through the NVG. "Yes, yes. This is the way. The caves are no more than a hundred yards ahead. We'll go down a steep place in the wadi here."

Five minutes later, they had dropped in the gully to twenty feet below the level of the desert. The first cave was nothing but a black hole in a rock wall.

"First one isn't much," Salwa said. "Let's go to the middle one. It's huge."

Fifty feet down the wadi, they came to the second cave. The wadi was open on the top, and the cave showed black and dank on the right-hand side. Murdock took a pencil flash from his vest, and aimed it into the cave. The thin light went only a few feet.

"It's more than a hundred feet deep, and thirty feet wide," Salwa said. "The ceiling is up about twenty feet. Lots of room."

Murdock stared at it. "How far are we from the border, and can we make it there before daylight?"

"From here, four miles. I know. We hiked in when I was in school. Four miles, four hours, usually no problem."

Murdock rubbed his jaw. Gonzalez would be a problem. "Take a break," he said into the Motorola. "Fifteen minutes." He turned back to the Kuwaiti. "Do any of these caves have water in them, drinkable water?"

"This one does. Far back."

Three of them carried all the canteens, and found a small spring that came out of seemingly solid rock, gurgled down twenty feet, and vanished underground again. They filled the canteens, and using both Murdock and DeWitt's flashlights, worked their way back to the front of the cave.

Murdock told Holt to make another SATCOM contact giving their MUGR coordinates. The reply came back quickly.

"You now have a better location. Kuwait border still too hot to cross. Might have a chance since you're near the Saudi border. Give us an hour to do some consulting with our allies."

"Not much of an answer, Commander," Holt said.

"No answer at all."

Just before the end of the break, Joe Lampedusa, the platoon scout, hit his mike.

"L-T, we've got company. Commander, that is. A small vehicle of some kind with bright lights just slid down the steep grade, and is about fifty feet up the wadi. Maybe a dozen men with it."

Murdock ran for the entrance. The two machine gunners, Joe Douglas and Horse Ronson, beat him to it. They went prone, and set up their machine guns, then charged in the first round as silently as possible.

The Iraqi men in the rig left it, and investigated the first cave. Six of them were visible in front of the headlights.

"They can't miss us," Murdock said. "Get two grenade throwers up here," he told his lip mike.

Kenneth Ching and Guns Franklin slid to the ground and dug out hand grenades.

Murdock waited a minute; then more men came in front of the small rig, and the motor started. Murdock jolted off six rounds from his MP-5SD, and the machine guns chimed in with a series of five-round bursts.

Four men in the headlights went down. The truck's windshield shattered. A hand grenade burst at the side of the rig showering instant death. The second grenade that exploded was WP, white phosphorus, and it sent unquenchable blobs of the fast-burning phosphorus spraying into the cave, and across four more men, who went down screaming. The sticky substance burned through uniforms, then into flesh, and through it and bones as the soldiers bellowed in agony.

There was no return fire. The men were so caught by surprise, and the fire coming at them was so intense, that all died in their tracks, or ran out of the wadi hoping to escape the sudden death.

Murdock took the men with him from the cave mouth, and charged the jeep with assault fire. There was no opposition. They checked the bodies in the pale moonlight. Only one was alive. He was dispatched with a round to the head. SEALs take no prisoners, leave no wounded.

Five minutes later, the platoon had saddled up, and moved out of the wadi heading due southwest for the Saudi border.

"Only four miles," Murdock said. "A little over four miles to the border. We can do that standing on our pricks and waving our arms. Any questions?"

"Yeah," somebody said on the radio. "Who the fuck were those guys?"

"Don't know, don't care," Murdock said. "Either Saddam's

troops or El Raza's kin. They're dead, and we're going home."

Gonzalez was doing better. The fifteen-minute break had rejuvenated him. He wanted to walk. Doc told Murdock Gonzalez couldn't walk far. Murdock had Bill Bradford, the next-largest man in the platoon, walk beside Gonzalez for when he was needed.

They hiked across the barren desertlike landscape for a half hour, and were about to head down a gentle slope when Murdock saw Lam go down ten yards ahead. Murdock and the rest of them hit the desert sand and rocks.

Just ahead in the moonlight, they could see a small campfire. They heard the sound of music, some stringed instrument with lots of weird sounds and the plucking of the strings.

Murdock, Ed DeWitt, and Jaybird crawled up to the scout, and watched the scene below.

"How many men?" Murdock asked.

"Twenty to twenty-five," Jaybird said.

"More like thirty to thirty-five," DeWitt countered.

"Yeah, Commander, at least thirty," Lam said.

"Too damn many of the fuckers to go through them. We take a small detour and quietly move around the sleeping dogs and let them make their music." Murdock looked at the shadowed faces of the others. "Any other suggestions?"

"Go around," Jaybird said, and the other two SEALs nodded. They backtracked a half mile, then did a wide roundabout of the camp. They never came within a half mile of it, and when they were safely around, they moved back on the compass course that Salwa gave them.

Before they finished their backtracking, Gonzales fell to his knees. Bill Bradford put him on his back piggyback-style, and told him to hold on. Bradford carried him as if he was a feather pillow.

Twenty minutes later a chopper came out of the dark sky with a searchlight probing the sandy ground. It moved over the land slowly, searching with its long beam.

"Almost a mile away," Lam said.

"Yeah, but coming this way," Murdock said. "They must

have had a radio contact with that last bunch we took out in the wadi."

"So we keep going?" Jaybird said.

"Absolutely," the Platoon Leader said. "Let's pick it up a little and tell Ronson to break out that Fifty he got from Bradford. We might need it if that chopper pilot spots us."

"We gonna play Chiricahua if they get close?" Lam asked.

"Fucking right. Best way to become invisible. In the meantime, we move faster."

They stretched out their stride, and rolled across the desert-like landscape at nearly six miles to the hour. Then the chopper changed directions, and came directly at them. When it was a quarter of a mile away, Murdock hit his lip mike.

"Indian it, you guys. Down and sandy. Cover up everything but your eyes. Move. Now."

Salwa caught on quickly, and scooped the sand and rocks over his dark clothes while lying prone with his head down. Murdock added some rocks and sand to the civilian, then covered himself. He had taken a good look at his men. They were dispersed at least ten yards apart. Most looked like lumps of sand and rock. He saw no telltale sign of uniforms, boots, or weapons.

"Ronson, keep that Fifty loaded and handy. Don't fire unless the chopper spots us and opens up. Then take him out."

"Roger that, Commander."

They waited.

Murdock lifted his head two inches, and took a look. The chopper was doing S turns in a good search pattern, but still heading dead for their position. There was a chance they would be in the gully between the S turns, but there was just as good a chance they would be directly under the moving beam. Whoever was on the light did a good job of covering the spots between the turns where the chopper wasn't directly overhead.

It came closer. Murdock had kept his lip mike free. Now he spoke softly into it. "This is it. He's about a hundred yards out. It's down and dirty for us. Ronson, keep it ready but out of sight. Right?"

"Aye, aye, Commander."

The chopper was at three hundred feet, Murdock figured. An ideal height. It gave enough spread for the light, and kept the chopper low enough so the observers could pick out things on the ground. He hoped they weren't good at their jobs.

The bird came closer, swung away from them in the S turn, then came back almost directly overhead. Even at three hundred feet the downdraft blew around some sand. Just enough to make it harder to see what the searchlight picked up.

Then Murdock pushed his face into the sand, and held his breath. The chopper swung back, and angled directly over the length of the platoon.

Murdock could feel the brilliant light moving toward him; then it came directly over him, and he held his breath again. The beam hovered over him a moment, then moved on. At any time Murdock expected to hear a door gunner's machine gun chattering away, spraying the SEALs' backs with deadly slugs, but no sound of shooting came.

The *whup, whup, whup* of a big chopper filled the air, and Murdock let out his breath as the sound faded a little as it edged away. Then it came louder as the Iraqi chopper did another S turn, then started to fade as it kept moving away from them. When the bird was half a mile away, Murdock called the men out of the sand.

"Fucking ants they got here are as big as fucking rabbits," Joe Douglas said. It broke the tension, and the men brushed off the sand and got back in their double diamond formations. They moved out to the southwest with Lam on point.

Ed DeWitt jogged up, and fell into step beside Murdock.

"That might have been one of Saddam's choppers," Ed said. "If El Raza had a few, we must have shot them down by now. But would El Raza call in Saddam's birds? I don't know."

"Could be. I still like the idea that he'll put out a blocking force. He could do it with the trucks and half-tracks he has left. How is Gonzalez holding up?"

"He's weaker. Ronson and Bradford are taking turns

carrying him. Slowing us some, but not much. When we gonna get out of this chickenshit sandbox?"

"Soon, we hope. Soon."

"Eat dirt," Lam said on the Motorola, and the Third Platoon went into the Iraqi topsoil.

"Commander, you best look at this," Lampedusa, on the point fifty yards in front of them, said.

Murdock and DeWitt double-timed up to Lam, and went into the dirt beside him. Ahead they could look down a gentle slope. It had probably been made by runoff water over centuries of cloudbursts. In the middle of it, three hundred yards away, they saw three vehicles in the faint moonlight. There were troops around them, evidently eating a meal.

"Oh-three-hundred chow-down," Lam said.

The officers had their NVGs up and working.

"One weapons or personnel carrier, two smaller rigs," DeWitt said. "I'd say maybe twenty-five men."

"Good uniforms, good equipment," Murdock said. "That would make them Iraqi Army. Some of Saddam's outlying troops. They must be looking for us, or may be just in a blocking position."

Jaybird had come up and checked through Murdock's NVGs. "Oh, yeah. Good gear. Definitely not El Raza baby. I move to take out their transport with the Fifty, then get on our horses and run like homeboy bastards for Saudi."

Murdock took the NVG and checked again. "We put the twenty-one-Es thirty yards apart for convergence. Then we bring Bradford and the Fifty in here. We put twenty forty-mike-mike on them as well, with half HE and half WP. Should do it. Call up the men, Jaybird."

Five minutes later, the SEALs were in position. Murdock pointed at Lampedusa, who angled his Colt M-4A1 with the grenade launcher on it, and the scout fired the first 40mm grenade. At once the Big Fifty and the machine guns and the other grenade launchers fired.

Bradford's first .50-caliber round hit the larger weapons/personnel carrier in the engine and blew it apart, which started a small fire. The men below bellowed in panic, throwing away their meals and dodging for cover. The machine guns riddled them, putting a dozen down and dead before they could find any cover.

"Die, you sonsofbitches," Horse Ronson bellowed over the nine-round bursts of the 7.62 NATO slugs that slammed out of his H&K chattergun. He aimed and fired again, chopping down a pair of men charging away from the trucks.

Miguel Fernandez zeroed in on a man trying to get out the door of the burning rig. His H&K PSGl sniper rifle fired, and the Iraqi slammed against the truck door and sagged down dead in an instant.

Al Adams judged the distance with his 40mm grenade launcher and fired. The first round was long. He adjusted. and dropped the next two right in the churning mass of frightened men below near the trucks. The mortarlike grenades kept dropping in on the Iraqis even when they found something to hide behind. The WP showered like white waterfalls, and the Big Fifty knocked out the other two vehicles before anyone had a chance to start the engines. There were only a dozen shots fired from below at the SEALs.

Within forty-five seconds it was over. Two of the rigs below burned brightly in the Iraqi night. Bodies sprawled around the vehicles. Murdock guessed eight to ten had escaped into the desert wondering what hit them and how an 0300 supper had turned into a death knell for so many of them.

Murdock checked the scene of the slaughter below again with the NVGs. He nodded.

"Let's saddle up and get out of here," he said. "We definitely can't use their transport."

Fayd Salwa kept shaking his head. "I don't see how you did it. So quick, so deadly. These weapons you have are truly remarkable. All I ever had was a rifle that worked sometimes. Truly amazing." He smiled. "I'm grateful that we are on the same side in this difficult situation."

"Good," Murdock said. "How far are we from the border?"

Salwa thought for a moment, looked around at the moonscape, and nodded. "Yes, I recognize that small wadi back there. I'd say two of your miles."

"Two miles and it's oh-four-twelve. Two hours to sunup. We better hustle."

They marched again. Murdock knew there was no chance to fly in a chopper for a pickup. Not with Iraqis angry and working the border with Kuwait. They would probably be over here along this end of the Saudi line as well.

The SEALs kept hiking. The coolness of the desert night crept into their cammies, and neutralized the sweat. At 0440, Murdock called a halt and looked at Salwa.

"Where's the damned border?"

"It should be close by," the Kuwaiti said. "I've been here a dozen times. Unless . . ."

"In two hours it'll be light," Murdock said. "They'll have every plane in this sector up searching for our asses."

"My mistake somehow," Salwa said. "I'm sorry. I thought we would be in Saudi Arabia by now. We must be in a slightly different sector."

"Just slightly," Murdock said.

They marched across the desert again in the morning darkness.

Ten minutes later, Lam hit the mike. "Better get up here, Commander. I think we found the fucking picket line."

Both officers and Jaybird went up to where Lam lay in the dirt on a slight rise. Ahead, across a quarter mile of desert, they could see winking lights, and hear some metal-on-metal sounds.

"Could be the damn cooks getting breakfast ready," Jaybird said.

The NVGs showed a different picture. Even at that distance, Murdock could pick out individuals. The men were in a defensive picket line stretched across in front of the SEALs. It looked like they were spaced about thirty yards apart. He saw no telephones or wire. Some of them could have radios. The SEALs would have to chance that.

Jaybird saw the same thing. Then Ed DeWitt nodded. "Sure as hell it's their picket line," he said. "Where do we go through?"

Murdock looked over the line again. Slightly to the left, he saw a concentration of men and a half-track. That would be the center of the line.

"Their center looks to be to the left. We'll angle five hundred yards to the right, and try for our penetration. Jaybird, Lam, and I will go in with our K-bars. Ed, you'll have the con if we don't come back. Try an end run. They'll be looking for you. Let's move the troops."

They hiked parallel with the line for ten minutes. Then Murdock stopped them, and told everyone what they would do.

"When you hear 'Clear left, right, and center,' you come for the center of the slot. We'll keep our radio transmissions to a minimum. They might have some kind of receiver that would show up our signals. Any questions?"

"Wouldn't silenced rounds do the job?" Fernandez asked.

"Too risky," DeWitt said. "It's the noise factor. We can't take that chance. We'll work the program. As soon as we get the all-clear, we'll go through the fence in single file, five yards apart on the double. Don't let any equipment jangle or make any noise. You know the silent routine."

Murdock pointed Jaybird at the middle target. He took the one on the right, and Lam had the left one. They moved out like shadows on the desert floor. They were fifty yards from the targets, and crawled the last twenty. Murdock saw that his sentry was smoking. Good, it would hamper his night vision. Murdock drew his K-bar fighting knife and crawled forward.

The sentry moved, flicked his cigarette away, and took six steps toward Murdock. He gave a long sigh, and urinated. He was totally relaxed.

Murdock came out of his crouched position, and surged forward ten feet, his boots pounding the ground. The sentry heard his steps, and half turned. Murdock's K-bar drove into his side, through his shirt and upward, slicing through part of the intestine and lung, then into his heart.

The Iraqi's eyes went wide. He started to say something; then his mouth opened in a scream that never made it out of his throat. His knees buckled, and he fell toward Murdock, who caught him and eased him to the ground.

Murdock touched his lip mike. "Clear right."

Jaybird had the center. He crawled the last thirty yards, slow and sure. Twice he saw his man look out front, scanning the area. Then he seemed to relax, and concentrated on cleaning his fingernails with a small knife.

The soldier's rifle had been slung over his shoulder with the muzzle pointing down. It would take precious seconds to get the weapon up and ready to fire. Deadly seconds.

Jaybird held two K-bars. One he had balanced for throwing. He held it in his right hand. He moved forward again on his elbows and knees. Twice he had to stop when the man looked across his position.

Closer. He was within twenty feet of the man now. Too far for a throw. He edged closer, six inches at a time. The sentry coughed, and looked to his right. He whispered something that Jaybird couldn't hear. Evidently the one he tried to call to didn't hear him either.

The sentry sighed, reached his right hand into his pocket, and pulled out a pack of cigarettes. Jaybird worked closer. When the Iraqi soldier's match flared, totally destroying the man's night vision, Jaybird lifted up from ten feet and threw the K-bar with one swift motion.

Hours of practice had made Jaybird an excellent knife thrower. The long blade and handle turned over once, and the point of the K-bar drove into the sentry's chest just to the left of his heart. With the throw, Jaybird had charged forward.

When the knife pierced his chest, the sentry let out a groan of surprise, caught the blade with one hand, and fell to his left. Jaybird was on top of him in seconds, his other K-bar slashing deeply across the soldier's throat, severing his left carotid artery and jugular vein. The man gasped once and died as blood drained from his brain.

Jaybird quickly searched the body, found nothing of value, and hit his mike. "Clear center."

Lam had a tougher target on the left. The man looked hyperactive. As Lam crawled up to twenty yards, the sentry kept pacing back and forth. He checked the area directly in front of his post, and the landscape on each side as well.

Lam stopped within twenty feet of the sentry. If the Iraqi took a good look directly in front of him, he would be able to make out Lam flat on his belly. Lam brought up a borrowed, silenced MP-5 on single-shot. Just in case. He held the K-bar knife in his right hand. The sentry made his ten-yard hike on either side, and came back.

Lam knew he couldn't risk going any closer. He felt around on the ground, and found a fist-sized rock. He'd revert to his old kid games of war in the Oregon mountain brush. He hefted the rock, then threw it at some dead shrub directly behind the sentry. The bush was no more than a foot high, and half of it had died from lack of rain.

The rock hit the dead branches and snapped them, making a surprisingly loud sound in the desert silence. The sentry spun around, his weapon up and ready.

Lam came out of his crouch, took a dozen silent steps toward the man, then surged forward sprinting the last six steps, his arm held in front of him like a lance with the K-bar a straight extension of his arm.

The sentry must have heard him at the last moment. He spun around just in time for the blade to drive deeply into his chest. It missed his heart, but slashed through his lung, and chopped in half a major artery supplying the lungs.

The Iraqi sentry sagged, then slammed backward from the force of the knife thrust. Lam let go of the knife. The soldier tried to scream, but had no voice left. His eyes closed, then opened. His hands reached for weapons that were no longer there.

Lam bent over him, pulled out his knife, and stabbed the wounded man once more, driving his K-bar into the soldier's heart. He waited a moment, and saw the life fade from the sentry's eyes. Then he touched his mike.

"Clear left," he said. Lam crouched over, and ran silently to the right. He spotted Jaybird a moment later, and dropped beside him. Murdock was on the other side. They each pointed outward in defensive postures. No words were spoken.

Lieutenant (j.g.) DeWitt heard the third "Clear," and waved his men forward. All had weapons at the ready, with rounds chambered and safeties pushed off. They walked quickly single file, following DeWitt toward the center position, where Jaybird had vanished. They were five yards apart.

The silent file came out ten yards to the side of the three SEALs covering for them, continued on through, then spread out to ten yards between men. The three sentry-busters moved in at the end of the line, and walked backwards for a hundred yards watching the rear.

They were two hundred yards past the line when a single rifle shot sounded behind and to the right where the center of the picket line had been.

"Double time, let's get out of Dodge," Murdock said into his mike.

They ran forward. Murdock heard movement to his right. He stared into the darkness, then used the NVGs.

"Hold it in place and in the dirt," he said into his mike. A second later a flurry of rifle and submachine gun fire erupted to the left.

"I spotted about twenty troops over there just before they opened up. Some flankers. They know where we are. Fire at those muzzle flashes now!"

The stretch of desert erupted with the SEALs' firepower. The snipers with NVGs picked off targets that showed themselves. Most of the Iraqis were flat on the ground firing at where the SEALs had been standing.

Murdock figured the range: two hundred yards. Maybe less. "How is our supply of forties?" he asked on the mike.

Radio reports came in that they had twenty-four rounds.

"Let's each man shoot half his rounds. Make them on target, no more than two hundred yards. Fire now."

The MP-5 weapons were of no use. Silenced, they were effective at no more than fifty yards.

Murdock wished now that he had a long gun. All he could do was watch. He concentrated on using the NVGs.

"Five of them moving up on the left flank," he said into the mike. At least three guns shifted fire there, and the flankers fell back dragging two wounded.

The 40mm grenades began dropping on the enemy troops. They took several direct hits along the line of shooters. After taking ten rounds of the grenades, the Iraqi troops surged ahead fifty yards to get out of the barrage, and went on firing.

The two SEAL machine guns worked overtime as the Iraqis moved up, cutting down five of them.

"How many out there?" a voice on the Motorola asked.

"I've got about twenty left," Murdock replied. "Get those forties back on target."

Another half dozen of the grenades dropped in on the Iraqi troops. The firing died off for a moment, then picked up as some of the troops ahead of them made a fast retreat to the rear and vanished—probably into a wadi, Murdock decided.

Then the retreated troops covered for the rest of the soldiers as they raced to the gully and out of sight.

"Hold your fire," Murdock said into the mike. "Looks like the bad guys have had enough for now. Anybody pick up a wound?"

The net went silent for a moment; then a voice came on, and Murdock was sure who it was.

"Yeah, got a scratch, upper right leg. Hurts like hell."

"Ching, that you?" Doc Ellsworth asked.

"Yeah, not sure how fast I can walk."

"Where are you, middle of the line?"

"Front, near the front."

Murdock ran that way, and saw Doc ahead of him. Doc got there first. Kenneth Ching was down, and holding his right leg.

"Ed, get the rest of the platoon out of here, and take Salwa with you," Murdock said into the mike. "Due southwest. Move them. We'll catch up. Watch out for Gonzalez. Trade off on the men carrying him. Move."

Doc examined the leg with the help of a shaded mini-flash hung around his neck. "Bullet went through. Looks like it missed the bone. Hurts like hell." He bandaged it and got Ching on his feet.

"Limp a little and see if you can walk," Doc said.

Ching tried. Limped and walked. He made it ten yards with Doc and Murdock beside him. Murdock had Ching's Colt carbine.

"Yeah, I can make it. Got one of them shots, Doc?"

Ellsworth used a one-time shot of morphine, and Ching perked up.

"Yeah, let's go," Ching said.

They caught the rest of the SEALs three hundred yards ahead. The main body had slowed. Doc left Ching, and went to check on Gonzalez.

They had stopped, and Fred Washington and Fernandez were taking turns carrying the hurt man.

Gonzalez couldn't hold on anymore. His eyes were going glassy and he mumbled.

"Fireman's carry," Doc said. "It'll keep his head down and he won't fall off that way. We better move again."

Murdock came to the front of the column with Salwa. They kept hiking across the desert at a slower pace. The coolness of the desert night crept into their cammies and neutralized the sweat.

Another half mile, and Murdock called a halt. It was almost 0500. "Salwa, where's the damned border? Is it marked here?"

"It should be close. I've been here a dozen times, unless . . ."

"In an hour it's going to be light," Murdock said. "They'll have every plane in this sector up searching for us to burn our asses."

"Sorry. My mistake. I thought we would be in Saudia Arabia by now. We must be in a slightly different area."

"Just slightly," Murdock said, his anger edging through.

Murdock checked on Ching. He was limping worse, but he waved away any help. "Hell, I'm a fucking SEAL," he said.

They walked for another half hour at three miles an hour on the same compass bearing. The darkness began to evaporate around them. It would be dawn in half an hour.

Murdock stopped the men and dispersed them. He turned to Salwa.

"Now what? Just where the fuck are we?"

Salwa studied the landscape ahead of him. It looked much the same all the way around to Murdock. Salwa turned to Murdock, smiling. "Yes, yes, now I see. We hit the notch. A small area of Iraq that bulges into Saudi Arabia. It's not more than three miles deep. We hit it almost in the center."

"Three more miles, you're sure?"

"No, we're two thirds of the way there. A mile more. Yes, absolutely. Guaranteed."

Murdock had just about given the order to move out when he heard the jets.

"Figures," Murdock said. "They can't miss us out here." He hit the lip mike. "Company. Probably MiGs. Not sure what number, but doesn't matter much with targets like us. If they spot us, and they almost certainly will, we disperse at least twenty-five yards apart. Got that? At least twenty-five. We want to be as lousy a target as possible. Let's stretch out our diamonds now and move. Salwa says we have another mile to the Saudi border. Let's move out."

It took the MiGs ten minutes to find them. They had been on a grid search, and when they turned and came over the SEALs at sagebrush level, Murdock knew their ID had been confirmed.

"Ground fire when they come back," Murdock radioed. "You know the drill, fire in front of the bastards, long lead. Ground fire can be damned effective. Give it a try."

The two MiGs came one at a time, and the machine gunners and the long gun men had time to fire at both in succession. The jet fighters used their cannon, spraying the area with 20mm explosive rounds.

The trouble with jet aircraft strafing a ground target at five hundred miles an hour is that the rounds land from forty to sixty feet apart, depending on the angle of the aircraft. It makes for a lousy hit ratio on as small a target as the dispersed SEALs were.

After the first pass, Murdock hit the mike. "Casualty report, anybody hit?"

The air was silent a moment. Then Doc Ellsworth came on.

"Looks like Gonzales got hit by some shrapnel on his right leg. Not too bad. But doesn't help his general condition. I've got it under control. We'll still have to carry him to the border."

There were no more casualty reports.

"We hit the sonofabitch?" Ron Holt asked.

"Don't think we had any hits, Holt. Anybody else pick up

lead?" Silence. "Okay, Doc. Stay with Gonzalez from here on in. Let's try to get invisible with sand before the birds fly back." The men spread out farther in the dirt and covered themselves with splotches of sand and rocks, weapons hidden under their bodies.

The jets came again, in the same formation. This time the machine gunners and Bradford with the Fifty had a better idea how to aim. The three men popped up when they saw the planes coming. Bradford picked up the strafers as early as he could, and fired for a nearly head-on shot. He had time for just one shot, and triggered it off imagining that he could see the flight of the big .50-caliber round of explosive, armor-piercing destruction.

Joe Douglas had his H&K machine gun angled upward to meet the jets as well. Once they got overhead, it was too late. He fired a twelve-round burst as one of the MiGs was a hundred yards away. The twelve slugs and the plane met at tremendous speed, and Douglas prayed that he had made some hits.

When the long gun men were sure they hadn't fooled the pilots, every long gun fired, as the jets screamed overhead at less than fifty feet, then pulled up sharply and started their three-mile-wide circle to come back on target. The second MiG went around normally; then a thin trail of smoke came out of the craft. The smoke increased as the big plane wobbled slightly, then slewed to the left, and began to lose altitude.

The SEALs stood and cheered as the MiG dropped lower and lower until it tried a wheels up landing in the desert at more than 150 miles an hour. It hit, bounced, flipped over twice, and burst into flames.

The SEALs quieted and looked at Murdock.

"Okay, we got a lucky hit. The other MiG turned north, and must have hit his afterburner. We better hit ours too. Form up, and let's move out."

Doc Ellsworth fell into step beside Murdock.

"Gonzalez is in damn serious condition. I don't know what that slug hit inside him, but it ain't good. He could use a doctor about now. We're carrying him and trading off every quarter mile. Four different guys. We can make five miles an hour."

Murdock nodded, and Doc went back to Gonzales. Murdock waved Salwa up. "What happens when we get to the border? Are there guards all along it? Wire, trenches, or just a single strand of wire identifying the border?"

"Usually nothing to mark the border. A survey post every six or eight miles. The jets would attract attention from the Saudis. My guess is there will be some kind of mobile force along the border here wondering what's going on."

"What part of the Saudi border is this?"

"The Irwado sector," Salwa said. "That I'm sure of."

Murdock used his Mike and told Ron Holt to come up. They called a halt, and Holt set up the antenna and aimed it. Then Murdock typed out a message.

"Advise Saudis in the Irwado sector that friendlies are about to cross their border area inbound from Iraq. Make sure they know we are seventeen friendlies coming in."

He got a quick response, and hoped that the message would be passed down from hand to hand until it got to the commander of whatever force maintained this sector of the Saudi Arabia border.

They marched.

There was no sign of any more Iraqi troops or planes.

A mile farther on, they came to a small rise, and Murdock called a halt and went up with Lam and Salwa to check it over. Ahead they saw what looked like a small military vehicle. Murdock figured it was a quarter of a mile ahead. He let Salwa look through his binoculars, and the Kuwaiti agreed.

"Yes, a utility rig the Saudis use along the border. Usually only three or four men and an officer."

Just as he stopped talking, they heard the chatter of a machine gun and rounds sang over their heads. The men pulled back under cover of the rise.

"Who has a green flare?" Murdock said into the Motorola.

"Yo," Colt Franklin said.

"Fire one high toward the border," Murdock said.

The green flare sailed high, burst, and floated down on its small parachute. At once another burst of machine-gun fire came over the top of the rise.

Murdock checked the landscape. A small ravine led to the left toward the border. It was ten feet deep. He kept his men under cover of the rise, and moved them into the gully. It had some bends and twists, and should get them within fifty yards of the Saudi patrol.

When the gully began to play out, Murdock lifted up to the top, and checked the Saudi troops. It looked more like they were thirty-five yards away. Salwa was at his elbow.

"Can you yell at them from here and make them understand who we are?"

Salwa bobbed his head. "Yes, I can try. We all speak Arabic. If this doesn't work, I suggest a white flag."

Salwa moved up another twenty feet, found a place he could stand, and edged his head over the top of the wadi.

He shouted something in Arabic. Waited, then said what Murdock figured was the same thing again. They waited. In a period of silence, Murdock heard shouting from the other side. Salwa shouted something back to them, then said it a second time. After that he slowly lifted over the top of the gully and put both hands in the air.

He shouted again, and motioned below him.

Again a short silence, then chatter, and yelling from the other side.

Slowly, Salwa put his hands down, and turned to look at Murdock. "Yes, it's all arranged. They know who we are but are still suspicious. Hold your weapons pointing at the ground, and come up one at a time. I'll go first. Then another one. Only one man in sight at any one time. I told them you're Americans, and they are impressed. They saw the jet crash. When I get to them, I'll explain about our wounded man. Have the big man carry him out last when you tell him to on your radio."

Salwa moved out of sight, then walked toward the Saudis. When he was gone, Murdock lifted over the edge, then told the men to come one at a time and slowly, with their weapons down.

Ten minutes later the Americans were across the border into Saudi Arabia. The officer there had radioed for more transport. They had made it. Murdock made a mental note to have a serious talk with Don Stroh about the quality of the CIA's extraction operations. This one was a flat-out failure.

6

Saturday, 13 January

Naval Special Warfare Section
Coronado, California

Third Platoon of Seal Team Seven had been home almost twenty-four hours. Murdock's five casualties had been treated in an Air Force hospital near Riyadh, Saudia Arabia. All except Gonzalez had been cleared for transfer to the Balboa Naval Hospital in San Diego.

Gonzalez was flown to Germany to one of the best military hospitals. He would get specialized treatment. The doctors had no idea how long he would be hospitalized or when he would be cleared to go to Balboa. They had dug the slug out of his upper chest, but were still evaluating the internal damage the steel-jacketed slug had done.

Ron Holt's slug through his left arm had not been a problem. The doctors said he could return to full duty in three weeks. The same prognosis had been given to Ken Ching, who had a bullet through his right leg.

Al Adams and Joe Douglas both had shrapnel wounds from the RPG, but they were not deep or serious and were already starting to heal. The two SEALs didn't require any more hospitalization. The four injured men who came home were all released from Balboa and told to return in two weeks for a final checkup.

Murdock sent a hot dispatch to Don Stroh. Never before
had he been hung out to dry for so long, taking so many
needless casualties. He knew Don would have an answer for
it all. He also put the same comments in his after-action
report that went through Master Chief MacKenzie and thence
to Commander Masciarelli, the skipper of the Seal Team
Seven and Murdock's immediate boss.

With that out of his way, Murdock settled down to putting
the pieces of his platoon back together. Balboa had certified
the four injured SEALs fit for light duty.

"Shit, there ain't no such thing as light duty in the SEALs,"
Ron Holt said. "Be fucking lucky if they don't pile it on us
double because we was dumb enough to get hit."

All of the men had liberty, including Ed DeWitt, and now
Murdock sat in the strangely empty and quiet office of the
Third Platoon checking his roster. He recognized the sound of
the footsteps in the hall outside long before the body came
through his door.

Without looking up he said: "Good morning, Master Chief
MacKenzie."

The master chief, who ran the eight platoons in SEAL
Team Seven, had previously been Platoon Chief of the Third
Platoon, and still had a special feeling for the group, even
though many men had come and gone since his term there.

"Didn't catch you when you stepped over the quarterdeck
this morning, Commander. Were you avoiding me?"

"Hard thing to do, Master Chief." Murdock grinned and
put his polished black shoes on the edge of his desk. "Hell,
George, you know I couldn't do that if I wanted to. Even
polished my belt buckle this morning for your inspection."

"How are Gonzalez and your lucky four wounded?"

"You know Gonzalez is in the hospital in Germany. Hard to
tell when they will transfer him to Balboa. The other four are
SEALs and labeled fit for light duty. You know what that
means around here."

"Figured. You going to want a replacement for Gonzalez?"

"Be a good idea. Run someone in as a temporary replacement. If Gonzalez doesn't get cleared in three weeks, he
won't be ready for any action we might have within two

months, so we'll make the temp permanent. You've done it before."

"You want to pick from my roster?"

"This afternoon. If it's all right with the master chief and if you can squeeze me into your loaded appointment calendar."

"Might be a problem. Later on that. I read your after-action report before I passed it on to the skipper. The old man is going to be pleased."

"Well, hot damn, George. You came all the way over here to tell me I did a good fucking job for a change?"

"That and to remind you that you owe me a steak dinner."

"What the hell for, George?"

"Because I'm the master chief and I keep your ass out of the fire, and save your neck from getting chewed every week by Commander Masciarelli. Why else?"

They stared at each other for a minute, then both chuckled. They had been working together for more than four years now. First when Murdock had been an instructor for the tadpoles coming through the BUDS/S training. Then for over two years since Murdock had taken command of Third Platoon.

"You don't think you were too rough on the CIA for not getting you out of Iraq?" MacKenzie asked.

"Not half tough enough. They hung us out to dry again. Hell, they didn't even try with a second chopper. They let us sit in there and fight our way out."

"Which you did destroying a shitpot full of Iraqi equipment including shooting down two choppers and one MiG jet fighter."

"Yeah, we got in a couple of lucky rounds. I've still got a huge bone to pick with Don Stroh. Figure he won't be around for a while."

"Not for a while, Murdock. Not until ten-hundred today."

Murdock scowled. "Don't shit me about this, George. I'm still not cooled down about how they fucked us in Iraq."

"Get over it, Commander. That's the way the CIA plays the game. Once the mission is completed, the personnel are secondary."

"But we hadn't extracted the civilian yet. The mission wasn't over."

Master Chief MacKenzie dropped into the chair beside Murdock's desk.

"What's bugging you, George?"

"Nothing, nothing at all."

"That's why you're sweating? Why have you cleared your throat six times since you came through the door? It's your psychosomatic throat problem, remember? You always get it when you're nervous as hell."

"So?"

"So what's bugging you?"

"The other platoon chiefs are giving me static about your platoon's facial hair and haircuts. I know, I know, you have special permission from the old man, but it bugs the other SEALs. You know how close I watch every man who steps across the quarterdeck. No beards, no goatees, no long side-burns. Face hair can interfere with the proper use of under-water gear."

Murdock sat there grinning, enjoying this as much as anything in the past few months.

"True, Master Chief. All true. Tell them when they work for the CIA they can wear face hair too. End of argument."

"Why?"

"You know damn well why, Master Chief. Sometimes we go in undercover, no uniforms, no weapons, getting the lay of the land. Three or four of us show up clean-shaven with white-side haircuts a half-inch long, lean and mean, we're gonna scream to everyone who sees us that we're military. We need to be low-key sometimes. It's got our dicks out of trouble several times in the past year, and now I won't let the guys all go clean-shaven and short-haired. That's why, George."

"Yeah, I guess I have to live with it. If Commander Masciarelli kissed the CIA ring, not a fucking thing I can do about it."

"Anything about the commander getting transferred out?"

The master chief perked up and looked at Murdock critically. "You just trying to lift my spirits or what? No word anywhere about any command changes around here. Not that I wouldn't welcome it. Our leader is bent all out of shape because he lost command of Third Platoon. He says all he is to your platoon now is an impotent pussy of a figurehead. He hates Don Stroh and the CIA with a white-hot passion. That's why I want to steer Stroh away from here as soon as he arrives."

The command master chief rubbed his face for a minute. "Oh, business. You're not going to need any replacements for your four other wounded men, I'd guess, since you haven't asked for any."

"True. We have a month to six weeks and we'll be ready to dance again, if you get us a top-notch replacement for Gonzalez. Don't want to mess up the platoon. We've had too many changes lately. Interferes with our teamwork."

MacKenzie checked his watch.

Murdock frowned. "Master Chief, that's the third time you've checked your timepiece in the past five minutes. You late for a hot date somewhere?"

MacKenzie stood, and walked around the chair grinning. "Indeed I am, young man. A hot date straight from Washington, D.C. Like I told you, your buddy Don Stroh is due at ten-hundred. He's late. Want to come out to the quarterdeck with me and greet him?"

"Not especially."

"Might be interesting. You can read him off about hanging you out on a tough titty in Iraq."

"Now that you mention it."

A knock sounded on the doorjamb, and a seaman came around the corner. "Sir, a visitor." He backed away, and Don Stroh, wearing a red hibiscus, Hawaiian shirt, and walking shorts, stepped into the room.

"Commander, what a beautiful job in Iraq. Haven't had time to tell you what an outstanding job you and your men did over there. Your transport got deep-sixed, and you made adjustments and brought out the hostage, and all of your men with only one major wound. Remarkable. The President sends his congratulations."

"You and your Company almost got us all killed, you

fucking well know that. What the hell is the matter
with . . ." Murdock stopped. "Shit, I can chew you out later
when Master Chief MacKenzie can't appreciate it. Instead
we'll take a cash bonus of five thousand for each of my men."
He paused. "That was a joke, Stroh." Murdock took the CIA
contact man's hand. Master Chief MacKenzie jumped out of
his chair, and waved Stroh toward it.

"Nope, no time to sit down, we can talk later," Stroh said.
"I'm here on vacation. I want to go albacore fishing.
Understand that's the best of the tuna family, and I want to
catch about a dozen."

Master Chief MacKenzie looked at Murdock.

"Albacore, you sure?" Murdock said. "Problem is the
albacore fishing was spotty this year. It started in June and
finished in August. All the surface fishing is over now."

"So why are the half-day boats going out of Seaforth? I just
called them and made three reservations for the 12:30 boat.
Said they had good catches this morning."

Murdock chuckled. "Yeah. Those landing guys lie a lot.
What they're catching now are rock cod, some mackerel, and
maybe a calico bass or two."

"Hey, a fish is a fish. Come on, our poles, licenses, and
tickets are all paid for and waiting for us." Stroh laughed
when Murdock started to protest. "Hey, I won't let you say
no. I'm your boss, remember? Anyway, this will give you a
chance to chew me out for letting you find your own way out
of Iraq. Things just fouled up, and I'm sorry. Now, get your
tail in motion. We have to drive all the way down to Mission
Bay to the landing."

"I'd like to go, but the master chief here gets seasick."

"You lie, Commander. The car is ready. Where's your hat?"

They pushed off from the Seaforth dock at 1235, and
stopped at the bait barge to pick up anchovies; then they
headed out the channel to the Pacific Ocean, and turned north
toward the La Jolla kelp beds that spread out for a half mile
seaward. It would take them almost an hour to get to the first
fishing stop. They signed in, and got their numbers for their
burlap sacks to hold their catch. Murdock saw that there were
thirty-two fisher-persons on the boat.

Murdock bought three beers at the small galley, and they settled down at the tables.

"Now, Stroh. Tell me what kind of foul-ups on your end almost got me and my men killed by Saddam Hussein."

When they docked a little before 1800, they all had fish in their numbered gunnysacks. In the parking lot, Murdock went through the sacks, picked out the mackerel, and gave them to a Vietnamese family who waited nearby.

"Fish fry at my condo tonight," Murdock said. "Master Chief, see how many of my guys you can round up."

The evening was a raucous success. Three of the other condo owners complained. Six of the SEALs had shown up, including Lieutenant (j.g.) Ed DeWitt and his lady, Milly.

A little after midnight, Don Stroh got around to telling Murdock why he really came to town.

"Frankly, the NSC is worried about North Korea. State has no idea what's going on over there. The situation is volatile and we want your Third Platoon on a carrier in the area where you can be on instant call. You'll fly over when we think it's about ready to blow. No timetable yet. That should give your four men time to heal up enough to be operational. You're getting a replacement for Gonzales, I'd imagine."

"Tomorrow or the next day, yes. My other men will need at least a month to get healed, and then another month to get back in condition. I can't have them running twenty miles with bullet holes still healing in their legs."

"This isn't next week, Murdock. Just a little advance warning. Hell, Berlin or Mexico or Antarctica might blow up before then, and you'll be off somewhere else. This is just the hottest thing on our agenda right now, for your future calendar."

"The National Security Council is uptight again, huh? So we go over there and sit on the fucking carrier and wait for something to happen?"

"About the size of it. Look at it this way. You won't have to do all that tough desert training out at Niland."

"How long do we wait on board the toy boat?"

"Not sure. A month at least, maybe two months. You can

do physical training on the deck, dodge Tomcats landing. You can take target practice off the flight deck, work night problems when there's no flying. Be a change of scene."

"But we still just sit and wait."

"About the size of it."

"We'll get some tough training in before we go. Don't tell the men about this yet. We'll surprise them a week before we leave."

The next morning the men were still on leave, and Murdock spent half the morning with the master chief sorting through prospects for a replacement for his team. There were eight men fresh out of BUD/S training who had not been assigned a SEAL Team yet. Murdock figured he needed more larger men in the platoon.

He liked two of them. One was a tough Chicano from Los Angeles. He admitted that he'd been in a gang there, but had bailed out and moved away from town. He was clean, no police record, no behavior problems, and had an outstanding record in BUD/S. He was six-two and weighed 210 pounds.

The second man was half Hawaiian and half Tahitian. He'd been in the Navy for four years, was a first class corpsman, but said he wasn't looking for the doc job in a platoon. He'd grown up on surf and sand in San Diego. Could bench-press four hundred pounds, had been married for a while and had a three-year-old daughter in Los Angeles, and had the all-time SEAL record for the three-mile ocean swim without fins. His papers said he was six-four and weighed 220 pounds.

Murdock decided he had to see the men. Master Chief MacKenzie had them both at Murdock's office at 1300. He took the Latino, Manuel Guzman, first. Murdock liked the kid on first sight. He was twenty-four, had been in the Navy for four years, and had a brush cut that hadn't grown out much from the BUD/S training period.

Guzman stood at attention until Murdock told him to sit down. He did so stiffly, looking nervous.

"Guzman, why do you want to be in Platoon Three?"

"You're the action around here, Commander. You get more assignments than all of the other platoons combined. I like action. I used to work the flight deck. I didn't want to get sucked into the intake of a jet."

Murdock nodded. He'd seen it happen once on a carrier. He didn't want to watch it again.

"You have a family?"

"Parents in LA. Two sisters. A batch of uncles and cousins I don't really know. I got out of town when I quit one of the clubs they have up there."

"You seem a little tense, Guzman."

"Yes, sir. Officers make me that way."

"Not a good quality for a SEAL. You know that I went through BUD/S training the same as you did. Only I had to score ten percent better on everything than the enlisted. The instructors love to pour it on the officer tadpoles. Didn't you have any officers in your class?"

"Yes, sir. Two. Both rang the bell."

"They don't do that anymore."

"We still call it that. Put your hat down by the bell and bug out. We say they rang the damned bell."

"You're Second Class."

"Yes, sir. Striking for first on my next chance."

"You know it's hard to keep up with your specialty and do the job as a SEAL."

"Yes, sir. I want the next grade."

Murdock stood. Guzman stood at once, and came to attention.

"Thanks, Guzman, Master Chief MacKenzie will be talking with you."

Guzman started to salute, then dropped his hand, did a snappy about-face, and walked out of the room.

Murdock went to his door, and motioned to the next man, Jack Mahanani. The man rose out of the chair across the squad room, and filled the door frame when he walked in. He stood at ease, and grinned at Murdock. Murdock told him to sit down. He did with a smooth, controlled movement that many big men lack.

"Damn, sir. Been hoping like crazy to get a shot at the Third Platoon of Seven."

"Why's that, Jack?"

"Hell, you guys get all the best assignments. Seems like you're in the field damn near half the time. Hear you almost lost a man on your last run. Bitchin'. But then that means I got a shot at filling in his place."

"How much do you weigh, Jack?"

"Two-forty. I keep it right there. I know the SEAL limit is two-forty-two, so I don't get in no trouble."

"Hear you like to swim."

"True. My mom says I'm half dorado. I'd rather be half white shark, but you take what you can get."

"You did the rough-water three-mile without fins?"

"Oh, that. Yeah, kind of embarrassing. I beat all the instructors who challenged me. They roasted me for a week."

"All-time record, I hear."

"Yeah. My Tahitian mom is to blame. She made me swim every day off Mission Beach in San Diego. Said every Tahitian should be a swimmer."

"You're a Hospital Corpsman First Class, but don't want the corpsman job in the platoon. Is that right?"

"I could do it if your regular man goes down. Rather use one of them big fifty-caliber McMillan eighty-sevens."

"You should be able to handle it. Jack, how do I pronounce your last name?"

"It's Hawaiian, my dad's moniker. Mahanani, just the way it looks. Pronounce every letter."

"Thanks. Now, why do you want to be in Third Platoon of the Seventh?"

"Like I said. You guys get all the action. Training is fine, but I hear some of these platoons here have never fired a damn shot in anger on a mission. I don't want to play at war that way. I want some real action."

Murdock grinned. He liked this kid. "Jack Mahanani, I think we can guarantee you some real action. If you come with us, we'll get you blooded in a big rush."

Murdock stood up. Jack stood.

"Jack, you'll be hearing from Master Chief MacKenzie. You're supposed to report back to him now."

As soon as he left, Murdock got on the phone to Mac-Kenzie.

"Yes, George. I want Jack Mahanani. Write out the orders for him. He's to report here at zero-eight-hundred Monday morning."

"The swimmer. He's quite a specimen. You can use him. I'll get the paperwork done. He's all yours. I'd guess you'll go on a training sked."

"You guess right, Master Chief."

"Whatever you need, have Jaybird give me a call."

"Will do. Thanks."

They hung up, and Murdock looked at his master training chart. What could he pull out to help integrate Mahanani into the platoon?

Holt, with the slug through his left arm, could do all of the training exercises except the O-course. Adams and Douglas, with their minor shrapnel wounds, could take the pace on any of the training. Ken Ching, with the slug through his thigh, would have to go light on marching and swimming for a week, maybe two. He'd be left behind on the first week's workouts. Murdock decided to assign Ching to a series of upper body workouts that wouldn't bother his leg and would keep him busy.

Mahanani could fit into Gonzalez's old slot in the Second Squad, but that would be up to DeWitt. He might want to adjust his squad somehow. The big Hawaiian would be the man if they put a McMillan Fifty with the squad. Murdock had often thought of having two of the long-range weapons in the platoon. This might be the time to try it. He'd talk to DeWitt Monday.

Murdock took Sunday off. He stayed at his condo, slept until noon, then called Ardith and ran up his phone bill.

"I'm recuperating from a nasty cold, I'm tired, crotchety, and I wish I was there so you could pamper me a little," she said. "I can use a lot of pampering right now."

"Hey, wish I was there too. Maybe in March."

"But this is only January. March is not acceptable." There was a pause, and she gave a long sigh. "Damn, Murdock, why can't we at least work on the same side of the country?"

They went on talking for a half hour.

"I hear things are heating up over in North Korea," Ardith said.

"Wouldn't know, I'm not at the seat of government. I'm just a lowly cog in the military machine. Nobody tells me anything."

"I bet. Hey, fair warning. If I hear about you getting ready to shoot off somewhere on a mission, I'm going to have an urgent need to do some government work in San Diego. Fair warning."

"Heard and understood. No complaints from this side of the country. I better let you go. Pamper yourself. A bubble bath, and then a long nap, some coffee, and maybe some white wine while you watch the flames in your fireplace."

"Oh, yes. I'll remember doing that when you were here."

"Good night, beautiful lady."

"Thank you, and good night to you."

Murdock hung up. Why couldn't life be simpler? Why couldn't Ardith have a nothing job, and jump at the chance to live in San Diego, and be with him all the time? He snorted. Hell, then she wouldn't be Ardith, and he probably wouldn't look at her twice.

He went for a two-mile walk, then watched an old movie on TV, and got to bed early.

Monday morning, Murdock put Third Platoon into a light training schedule. They were near Niland in the California desert at the Naval Chocolate Mountain Gunnery Range for two days. They had some new weapons Murdock wanted to test. The men who had not fired the now-standard H&K G-11 caseless-round automatic rifle got all the firing time they wanted with it.

"Every man here has to be proficient with every weapon we carry. Who hasn't been checked out on the fifty-caliber sniper rifle yet?"

There were three men, including Mahanani. Murdock told Bradford to give Mahanani lots of work on the big weapon. Bradford took them to the "B" range, and they each took twenty-five shots. Then Bradford gave them all a quick course in breaking down and cleaning the heavy-firing long gun.

Murdock and DeWitt had talked about Mahanani before they left.

"Yeah, let's put him in Gonzalez's spot in the formation," DeWitt had said. "I like the idea of having a Fifty in my squad. It'll give us a little more firepower when we need it. He's big enough to do the job. What does he weigh?"

Murdock had told him 240.

"I just hope I don't have to carry him out of some firefight like we did Gonzalez."

Murdock showed the rest of the men a weapon that looked strange. It had a bipod, shot a NATO 7.62 round, and could be used to fire around the corner of a building or a wall. The weapon was placed around the corner, then the gunner sat in the protected spot, looked through a right-angled flexible telescope, and fired the weapon with an electronic trigger.

Murdock got off two three-round bursts, and turned it over to Jaybird.

"Too much trouble to set up," Jaybird said. "Yeah, I'm crazy, but I want reliability and mobility. Anyway, I don't shoot around too many corners these days."

Most of the other SEALs who tested the new around-the-corner weapon agreed.

Murdock gave Jaybird a move-out signal, and the Platoon Chief rousted the men out into their combat positions in a pair of diamond formations.

Murdock came in front of the formation, and looked over the men. "Ching, fall out and stand guard over our goods here and our favorite bus. We're going on a hike, and the doctors don't want you working that leg as much as we're going to. You get to do any series of upper-body exercises you want to. We have some free weights in the bus, and there are always push-ups and chin-ups. Give yourself a good hour's workout. Then take it easy, and heal up. We want you back going flat out in a week."

Ching fell out, and Murdock saw a flicker of emotion on the man's face. He figured it was relief at not having to go on the march.

Murdock led them out on a ten-mile march with full
operational loads, including combat vests with standard-issue
ammo for the various weapons. Every man also carried two
filled canteens, his weapon, a smoke grenade, four hand
grenades, a first-aid kit, a plasma kit, twenty-five feet of
quarter-inch nylon rope, a weapon field-cleaning kit, a K-bar
fighting knife, a large plastic garbage bag, sunscreen, cam-
ouflage makeup, sunglasses, water purification tablets, waterproof matches, and four chemical twist-to-start light sticks.

The men wore their desert cammies, with an assortment of
headgear ranging from balaclavas to floppy field hats to
bandannas.

They headed out for Hill 431, and Murdock led the pace.
Halfway there they moved into their combat field diamond
formations, with Second Squad leading and Scout Lampedusa a hundred yards out in front.

At the top of the small peak, Murdock spoke into his
Motorola, and the men moved into a long line of skirmishers
five yards apart along the rim of the hill.

"See that old snag down there that we've shot at before?"
Murdock said into his lip mike. "That's the target for today.
Machine gunners, give it six bursts of five rounds. Bradford,
be ready. You're next with three rounds. Let's blow that snag
away this time. Douglas and Ronson, you may fire when
ready."

When Bradford had fired, Murdock came back on the net.
"What's the range to the snag?" He got several ideas.

"The right answer is two hundred yards. Let's see who can
lay a forty-mike-mike right on the target. Each of you give it
four tries." The five SEALs equipped with the Colt M-4A1
with the M-203 grenade launcher under the barrel started
firing.

After a dozen rounds went out, Murdock came back on the
radio. "Remember, this is like horseshoes and fraggers. Close
counts. Nudge them in there."

When the firing stopped, the desert was so quiet they could
hear a hawk call a half mile off.

Murdock lifted his subgun and chattered off six rounds.

"That's enemy fire from our rear. What's your first reaction?"

"Get our asses over the ridge and protection on the downslope," Jaybird called.

"Do it," Murdock bellowed. The fifteen men jolted over the ridgeline, and six feet down the reverse slope. They crawled back up until they could just see over the ridge, and readied their weapons.

"How about some return fire on those attackers below?" Murdock whispered into his lip mike.

Fifteen weapons sprayed hot lead down the slope ahead of them until Murdock gave them a cease-fire. Murdock pulled the men around him.

"Anybody remember where the hog's back is?"

"To hell and gone north," Quinley said.

"Another dog-fucking ten miles," Ron Holt added.

"True, I have to keep you puppies in shape. You could be coming into some light duty, who knows?"

Jaybird laughed. "Bet you do, Commander. Don Stroh didn't come out here just to go fishing and have a fish fry."

"You know anything more, you tell us, Jaybird," Murdock said.

"Just guessing," the Platoon Chief said.

"We've got company at three o'clock," Lampedusa said.

Murdock looked out from their ridgeline, and saw a trail of dust spiraling up in the quiet desert air.

"He's moving too fast for the terrain," Lam said.

"Got to be a Humvee," Joe Douglas threw in.

The Humvee is the U.S. military light-utility truck that replaced the time-honored Jeep. It's a multipurpose 4x4 wheeled vehicle with automatic transmission, power steering, and a Detroit Diesel 150-hp diesel V-8, air-cooled engine. Top speed is 65 mph with a range of 300 miles.

"What the hell is a Humvee doing out here?" Ed DeWitt asked.

As they watched the dust trail come closer to them, they saw a green flare, pop in the sky over the dust trail. The rig was still two miles away, and the flare faded quickly.

"Trying to get our attention," Murdock said. "Jaybird, fire

a green flare and let's get moving down this asshole of a mountain. Maybe we've got an assignment."

"Could have talked to us on the SATCOM," Holt said. "Oh, yeah, we haven't had it turned on this morning."

"Do it," Murdock said.

They stopped, and Holt broke out the SATCOM and aimed the fold-out dish antenna. As soon as he had it aligned, and the set turned on, it gushed with voice transmission.

"Commander Murdock, respond ASAP. This is Commander Masciarelli. This message will repeat every five minutes."

Holt switched the set to transmit in the clear, and Murdock took the mike.

"Commander Masciarelli, this is Murdock. Message received, standing by."

Less than a minute later, the speaker came on.

"Murdock, you'll be having company there today. Special Agent Olivia Poindexter. She works with the Company, and has a group of special items to show you. You may want to extend your stay in the field for testing. In case you decide to, I've sent rations for your platoon for four more days. Advise the master chief of your schedule. Questions?"

"No, sir. The Humvee is in sight now, and we're moving toward it. Murdock out." Murdock looked at his platoon.

"You heard the man. We've got a date below with the people in that Humvee. Let's not keep them waiting too long at the boulder field down there."

Ed DeWitt walked beside Murdock.

"One of Don Stroh's guys is bringing us some new weapons to test?"

"That's what it sounds like. The Agency has some great little items, but usually they don't share much. I'm interested in what they're going to show us."

Twenty minutes later, they hiked over the last of the boulder field that had stopped the Humvee. A civilian sat in the front seat. The driver was a seaman.

Murdock put his men at ease fifty yards from the Humvee, and walked up with Ed DeWitt to the vehicle. They were thirty yards away when the civilian stepped out. She was slender, a brunette, and wore khaki pants and shirt. Sunglasses protected her eyes, and her hair had been cut short and stylish. She turned toward them, and waited.

"Be damned," Ed DeWitt said.

"Probably," Murdock said, and grinned. They stopped a respectable six feet from the woman, and both men came to attention and saluted.

"Good morning. I'm Lieutenant Commander Murdock. This is Lieutenant (j.g.) DeWitt. I understand you want to see us."

Up close, he could see that she was tan, more sturdy than he had first thought, and smiling as she took off her sunglasses. The two SEALs took off their shades as well. Her smile was delightful.

"Gentlemen, I'm Olivia Poindexter. I often work with Don Stroh, who you know. He asked me to show you some of our newest, and best, defensive and offensive weapons and gadgets. I hope this isn't too much of a problem for you?"

"Not at all, Miss Poindexter. We're always glad to see anything that Don thinks might help us in our missions."

"I'm aware of what you've done in the past, Commander. I respect your work, and your skills. I'll try not to show you anything that might not be appropriate."

"We want to see everything you've brought, Miss Poindexter," Ed DeWitt said. "We're always watching for new ways to do our job."

"Your material is back at the bus?" Murdock said.

"No, it's with us, but we can off-load there."

"We're about six miles from the bus," Murdock said. "We'll see you there in an hour or a little less."

She lifted her brows. "Six miles an hour, Commander. That seems a little fast for men with full field gear."

Murdock grinned. "Watch us."

The SEALs didn't even grumble when they went into double time over the desert terrain. They had done it before, many times. Now they had a good purpose to get back to their Navy bus, which served as their headquarters there in the Navy bombing range. It was near noon and that would mean chow. Even MREs sounded good right then.

Murdock's watch showed exactly fifty-two minutes had elapsed when he brought the men to a stop in front of the bus.

"Let's eat," Murdock said, and the men dropped their gear and grabbed MREs from the bus. They sprawled around it in what shade it could provide. The California desert sun beamed down at them in its winter warmth. The high desert should be showing about sixty-five degrees during the day, down to forty-five at night.

Murdock handed the CIA agent an MRE.

"Ever had the pleasure of dining on one of these, Miss Poindexter?" he asked.

"Please call me Livy. It's short for Olivia. My mother started it a long time ago. No, I can't say I've ever been in a four-star hotel that offered these. Are they good?"

"Relative term. They aren't bad, and they keep the troops alive, which is the important element. Sometimes they're better than my own cooking."

"I've heard that bachelors either learn how to cook rather well, or spend a lot of time eating out, true?"

"Absolutely. I'm huge when it comes to beef Stroganoff, and my enchiladas aren't bad either."

She tore open the brown plastic wrap on the MRE. Murdock watched her.

"Look, I'm eating French," she said. "I have chicken à la king."

"One of our chef's best," Murdock said.

She delved into the contents of the dark brown envelope.

"There's peanut butter—yummy—and crackers, a spoon, cocoa beverage powder, a beverage base powder, and this inch-and-a-half-tall tiny little bottle of tabasco sauce. How delightful."

"You missed one whole envelope," Murdock said.

"There's more?" She laughed as she said it, and he was pleased she was taking it so well. She could have insisted on driving back to the tiny wide space in the road called Niland for a civilized meal.

"Oh, I see what you mean. Instant coffee, cream substitute, sugar, salt, chewing gum, matches, toilet tissue, and hand cleaner. Really, you shouldn't have been so extravagant. I'm not as high-level as Don Stroh."

They both laughed.

"When we have time, and firewood, we make real hot coffee, and hot chocolate even," Murdock said.

"All the comforts . . ."

The sailor who drove her out unfolded two tables and set them up beyond the Humvee. He carried a half-dozen boxes from the vehicle, and then waited nearby. He had finished his MRE in record time.

"Things still tense in Korea?" Murdock asked her. "Don told me we might be moving out to a carrier off the peninsula sometime soon."

"Tense is a good word. The North seems to think they can push and push, and nobody will shove them back. The time might be near when South Korea will shove back without our permission. Then there will be real trouble over there. The big problem is, it looks like the North is massing troops along some of the border, which could be really, really bad news."

The men finished the MREs. Murdock noticed that she didn't eat all of the chicken à la king, but did better on the crackers and peanut butter. He had mixed up the drink solution for her with a canteen of water, and she liked that.

"Time to get to work, Commander," she said.

"Please, call me Murdock. Everyone else does."

"Good, informal is better. What I have is a series of gadgets and weapons—some you may know about, some you might have heard about. Some are off the shelf, and others are experimental, and many are one of a kind. Yes, some of it is spy stuff that you can't use, but Don wanted you to check it out. Maybe your undercover operations could utilize some of our standard equipment. I've brought some of that too."

Murdock called to Jaybird, and he rounded up the men and sat them in the dirt, sand, and rocks in front of the table. Livy went up to the table, and leaned against the edge of it. She smiled.

"Good afternoon, gentlemen. I hope you had a good lunch. Now it's time to go to work. What I'm showing you is a combination of currently available tools that many of our agents use, and quite a few far-out and still-in-development weapons that you might be interested in.

"I know firepower is your trademark. The ability to put massive amounts of lead into a given target or area in the least possible time. Good. Nothing beats it. We have some items that just might help you in that task, and some that might work better even than massive firepower.

"The first item isn't in that category. It's a tool you can use in your training that can be just as effective in a pair of rooms in your headquarters as a full-scale operation in your Kill House."

She held up a Glock 17 automatic in one hand and a tube that looked like a ballpoint pen in the other.

"This is Range 2000, developed by IES, an Israeli company. It consists of a sophisticated digital video-projection system controlled by an IBM-compatible computer with a 133-megahertz Pentium chip. This machine can 'branch.' That means the sequence of events that unfolds on the screen in front of you is determined by your reaction to individual segments as they come on the screen.

"This tool is aimed at police, and gives them the options of using the right body language and talking so they might not have to use force. If force is required, they must choose what level of force, such as pepper spray, a baton, or their pistol.

"The laser insert works in almost any pistol with the addition of various sleeves, and is powered by a hearing-aid battery good for twenty-five hundred laser shots.

"The video tapes you confront can be made in various local locations, and then edited for the use you need. You play out the scene, 'shoot' with the laser in your own pistol, and get a score on your action, timing, and hits.

"The cost of this system is about thirty-five thousand dollars."

"Lots of luck," somebody in the platoon called out, and everyone laughed.

"Yes, it costs a little, but if such training could save just one of your lives, it would be well worth it. At least to the guy who would have died."

The sailor next handed her a sawed-off shotgun. She loaded one round into the chamber and closed it.

"This is a weapon you know something about. It's a little

hard to show you here in daylight, but I just put in the chamber a Starflash round. When fired into a room, the round erupts in a shower of sparking fireballs that ricochet wildly throughout the room. They are intended to be distracting and confusing, and by the time the persons in the room realize what's happening, you are in there doing what you do so well."

She looked around. "Questions."

"Are those rounds available?" Doc Ellsworth asked. "I carry a Mossburg pump, and they would surely come in handy."

"Yes, available to police and to the military. I'll see that your master chief gets the address." She paused.

"Now, since you mentioned shotguns, here's a new thought. The finest shotgun in the world, and the one used most by SWAT police across the country, is the Italian made Benelli 12-gauge 12l-M-1 recoil-operated semiautomatic shotgun. The Benelli has been called the masterpiece of ballistic handiwork. I have one here, and you can test it out. The semiautomatic feature may be the most important element in the kind of fast-fire situation you guys specialize in. Oh, the Benelli also has an optional mini-flashlight fitted on the barrel."

"We do a lot of work in the dark," Jaybird said. "Does the mounted flashlight have a handy switch for on and off?"

"To simplify matters, it's on the back of the flashlight. It could be rigged with a solenoid down by the trigger housing. Any questions?"

There were none, so she went on. She picked a yellow tennis ball from a box. "Any of you play tennis? If you use one of these, it's a love game every time."

She stepped forward, and threw the tennis ball as far as she could away from the men. It arced out forty feet, and when it hit, went off with a sharp cracking explosion.

There were some murmurs from the men.

"That's a camouflaged impact grenade. As long as it hits something fairly solid, it will explode. It's about the same power as your usual M-67 fragmentation grenade. Now, tennis, anyone?"

"Probably not, Livy," Murdock said. "We don't do that much undercover work."

"Fair enough. Here's an item you should be aware of. We don't know all about them yet, but they are on the market, and we expect that they have been sold in some quantity to terrorists."

She held up a weapon with an inch-thick solid barrel and a folding stock.

"This is the Russian-built VAL Silent Sniper. As you can see, it's sound-suppressed, and has a twenty-round magazine for the nine-millimeter rounds. It fires the heavy bullet at subsonic velocity due to the silencer. The nine-by-thirty-nine round is said to penetrate all levels of body armor out to four hundred meters.

"Now, the folding stock makes it easy to transport and conceal. That's why we are certain that this weapon will be showing up more and more around the world in the hands of criminals and terrorists.

"We haven't completed our testing of it, and only recently obtained two of them, so we should know more in the future."

"How much does it weigh with that heavy barrel?" Colt Franklin asked.

"Good question. Actually, it weighs two and a half kilos, almost exactly the same as your Colt M-4A1 carbine, and your H&K MP-5 when they are without the suppressor."

She watched the SEALs for a moment. "Any questions about this weapon? You may never see one; then again, the next batch of terrs you hit may have a potful of them."

She looked at Murdock, then went on. "I understand that you use the Heckler and Koch G-11 as a standard weapon. Good. I like it. It works well in the field. And from a security standpoint, it leaves no brass to be identified later by some irate nation.

"We understand that Germany is now in the process of bringing out an advanced version of this weapon, which was created in 1990, but we don't have any of the new models yet. We'll keep you informed if and when we get one and what the availability is."

"What about some real spy stuff?" Al Adams asked.

Livy smiled. "You mean like an umbrella with a poison dart in the end, a BMW with a rocket engine and machine guns under the headlights, and a pen that explodes when it's turned the wrong way?"

"Yeah, like them."

"Sorry, most of those extreme measure items went out with the Cold War. There really are few enemies now that our field agents are asked to kill. From what I hear, this platoon's body count is probably higher than that for all the Company personnel in a year."

She looked around. "Commander Murdock. That about takes care of my indoctrination for you. Don Stroh says he'll have some items to talk to you about from time to time. Just to keep you informed."

"Thank you, Miss Poindexter. Tell Don we'll be waiting for his call. Now, it's time the foot soldiers out here got back to basics. Today is the land phase of our training. I understand you have brought us some more rations."

"Yes, they were unloaded into your bus when we arrived." She looked around. "Thanks, guys. Have fun in the sun, and don't get those nice clean uniforms all dusty."

The seaman quickly had the displays boxed up and put back in the Humvee. He started the engine, and the Humvee moved back down the lane toward the gate, and then back toward San Diego.

Murdock stretched and looked up at the sun. "Okay, SEALs. You have five minutes for a piss call. Then it's back to work."

They hiked away from the bus with full vests and weapons, combat ready, in their sweat-stained cammies.

A half mile out, they halted, and Murdock gave them hand signals. He wanted Ed's squad to take the lead in a diamond formation. His squad would follow in another diamond. The signals told them to stay ten yards apart.

"Anytime you see a red flare, that will be the signal that we're taking fire from that flank. You will form into a line of skirmishers to that side, take cover wherever you can find it, and return fire on my first burst of three rounds. Move out."

7

Monday, 12 February

Chocolate Mountain Gunnery Range
Niland, California

The Third Platoon of SEAL Team Seven had been moving across the barren landscape of Southern California for two hours. It had been almost a month since the four men in his platoon had been wounded in Iraq.

The two men with shrapnel gouges had healed completely. Ron Holt, with the bullet through his arm, was back to ninety percent and had been taking training with them after only a few days' rest. Kenneth Ching, with the slug through his thigh, had been the slowest to heal.

After a month, though, he was back to full training. This was his second hike in the desert. He was holding up well, Murdock decided. Every day when Murdock came over the quarterdeck and waved at Master Chief MacKenzie, he expected to find orders from Don Stroh. There were even news accounts now of the North Korean saber rattling along the border. Commentators said it was intended to distract the population from being so short of food and other necessities. The idea was to hate the Americans instead.

Murdock was pleased the way his men had recovered and moved back into the training-and-conditioning mode. Condi-

tioning was the most important aspect now. Mahanani had
blended in well with the rest of the platoon. He was easy-
going, never got angry, could lift his weight in elephants, and
was the first to be there when another man needed help.

At the moment they were about halfway through a twenty-
mile hike. It wasn't colorful or dramatic or even interesting.
It was step after step, sweat it out, swear it up, but by damn
get there.

Ken Ching slogged along just in front of Harry "Horse"
Ronson. Now and then Ching lagged a little behind Ron Holt,
who was ten yards ahead of him.

"Come on, Chinko, let's keep up with the rest of them,"
Ronson called from his spot just behind Ching.

Ching looked back, and gave Ronson the middle-finger
salute.

Ronson bristled. He hated that sign, had been in more than
one bloody brawl because of it. He tried to put a cap on his
anger, but couldn't.

"What's the matter, Chinko, can't take a little ribbing?"

"I can take any shit you can shit out, bastard horseface,"
Ching said, his anger coming through instead of good-natured
jawing.

Ronson charged him. Murdock, working as Tail End
Charlie in the formation, saw the move, and sprinted up to the
pair just as they came together. Ronson landed a pounding
right fist against Ching's jaw, and the shorter man sagged
backward, but at the same time launched a roundhouse kick
that caught Ronson in the belly and drove him down to his
knees.

"Hold it," Murdock barked as he stepped between them.
"What the fuck is this all about?"

"The old Chinaman there can't take a little teasing,"
Ronson said.

"This big horse's ass wouldn't know a little of anything if
it hit him in his fucking face," Ching said.

Ed DeWitt heard the ruckus and stopped his squad, which
was in the lead. Jaybird halted the other squad. Everyone had
heard at least some of the exchange.

Murdock sat Ronson and Ching in the dirt and made them

look at each other. "Hey, you two assholes. So you're both pissed off about being on another conditioning hike. So what the hell do you think you're drawing the big paychecks for? You earn your pay with your training sweat. When we get into action, that's the payoff of all of our work. You two know all this. We're a team, remember? We work, we function, we kill working together as a fucking team."

"Oh, shit," Ronson said.

"Yeah, Ronson, you'll be shitting blood if you don't get with the program here," Murdock said. "Teamwork means each of us relies on the man next to him to protect his ass. He doesn't, and you're in graves registration before you can piss purple. You read me, you two?"

He watched them. Ching had taken two or three long breaths; at last he nodded. Ronson looked away, spat on the ground, and slammed his palm onto his thigh. He stared up at Murdock, and the edge of a grin showed. "Shit, yeah, Skipper. I'm with you."

"Okay, get on your feet, shake hands like a pair of SEALs, and let's get back to work. Ching, you move to rear guard where your regular spot is. A little separation right now won't hurt.

"Ronson, you try to keep your yap shut for a while, you read me, sailor?"

"Yes, sir."

"Same formation. Ed, let's move them out."

Five minutes later a red flare burst to the left of the platoon. Silently the men shifted to a line of skirmishers along a low ridge, and when Murdock chattered off three rounds from his MP-5, the rest fired down the slope into a dry wash three hundred yards below.

All of the men wore their Motorola radios with lip mike and earphones. Murdock let the firing continue for a minute, then spoke into his mike.

"Cease fire. Remain in place."

Murdock lifted out of the sand and rocks, and moved along the men, checking their positions, seeing who had found any cover at all. He glanced up just as Ching lifted up, swung his

Colt Carbine around, and ran toward where Harry Ronson lay looking the other way.

Before Murdock could yell, Ching fired off three rounds, and then three more. Ronson jumped up, his face wavering between surprise and abject fear.

Murdock charged over, and saw Ronson staring at a spot two feet from where he had been. There a four-foot-long rattlesnake writhed in a death struggle. The head of the snake had been chopped off by the six .223 slugs.

Ronson shook his head, kicked the still-spasming snake, then ran to Ching and grabbed him in a bear hug. Tears brimmed his eyes, but never made it to his cheeks.

"Ching, you beautiful motherfucker, don't you never die," Ronson said. It was the highest praise one SEAL could bestow on another. "We need you in this fucked-up outfit."

Murdock looked at the snake, then at Ching. "Nice shooting, man. You even got an angle so you wouldn't spray Horse. Let's all take ten and settle down." The men gathered around, and stared at the snake.

Joe Douglas looked at it, and then up at Ching. "Your prize, man, you killed it. You want the skin? I'll skin it out for you. Make a bitchin' headband."

Ching nodded.

They watched Douglas take out his knife and slit the snake from tail to what was left of the head, then strip the skin off it. He looked up.

"Hey, anyone for rattlesnake steak? It ain't bad, honest. We used to have it when I went hunting over in Arizona."

"You eat it," Washington said.

"Have to cook it first. We probably don't have the time."

He was right. Five minutes later, Murdock called them together. "See that ridge up there with the notch? How far from us is it?"

The guesses ranged from one mile to ten.

"It's about four miles. We're looking across a small valley, and that always messes up your distance perspective. Usually the point is farther away than it looks when viewed across a low area. We have a company of regulars tracking us. They're fresh, and moving fast. We need to get to that ridge, and then

PACIFIC SIEGE   91

surprise them when they start up it. We'll double-time for fifteen minutes, then walk for fifteen, and alternate that way until we're there.

"Jaybird, keep time on that stopwatch of yours. First Squad takes the lead. Lampedusa, a hundred yards in front. Let's move out."

The men were dragging by the time they hit the top of the ridge. Murdock spread them out in a line of skirmishers on the reverse slope so they could just see over the top. Then he fired a red flare into the small barren valley they had just crossed. He kicked out three rounds from his MP-5, and the rest of the platoon opened fire.

"Cease fire," he called after about thirty rounds per man.

"Bradford, break out the Fifty. Pick a target, and get off five rounds at your pace. Machine gunners, set up and support his fire when he finds a target. Go, go, go."

Bradford picked out a rock about four hundred yards away, and hit it with three of the five shots. The machine gunners chimed in, and when Bradford landed his fifth round, they all ceased fire, and the California desert returned to its quiet mode.

Far down the ravine they saw two black hawks circling on a rising air current. Halfway down the slope a desert jackrabbit left his nest under a thin sage and scurried across to another spot of concealment.

Murdock let them rest a minute. It was nearly 1700. They were about ten miles from the bus. He positioned the squads side by side across fifty yards of desert ridge.

"We're going down the far side here, men. I want you to work as a squad. Four men move out twenty yards, hit the dirt, and fire to the front to cover the other four men moving up. Then the ones who just came up move out twenty, hit the dirt, and cover the first four, who leapfrog. Work that way down the rest of the way to the bottom of the slope. Be careful of your fields of fire. Stay even with the other squad, and don't shoot anybody. Clear?"

They worked the basic fire-and-move drill until they all were at the bottom. By that time it was almost 1800.

"Find a spot and enjoy your MREs. You all were told to pick one up before we left."

Murdock let them rest for a half hour. It was well dark by then in the California desert. He talked with Ed DeWitt.

"Think any of the men know where we are from the bus?"

"Jaybird. Probably Lampedusa. The rest of them could be out here all night."

"About time we had a night drill on using the compass, finding your way back to the bivouac."

Ed grinned in the darkness. "Gonna be half of them sleeping out here tonight without a blanket."

"Be good for them. We'll drop them off at two-hundred-yard intervals by pairs. Then let them find their way back."

"We keep Jaybird and Joe with us?" Ed asked.

"Right. Otherwise they would team up, and get everyone back."

Ed chuckled. "Yeah, we've been too damn soft on these guys lately. Be good for them."

"By the way, Ed. Which way would *you* strike out to find the bus?"

Ed laughed. "I know the exact direction. You couldn't get me lost in a jungle."

"Good, you get the con as we head back. First we need a little bit of night-firing practice. What haven't we done lately?"

"We could do an LZ defense."

"Yes, get them into it."

DeWitt called the men around him, and explained the exercise. "We have wounded, we're in enemy territory. We've called for a helicopter lift-out. The choppers are on their way, five minutes out. They request a red marker flare. We shoot out a flare at a good LZ, and then form a perimeter around it. We defend it against attacks from all sides. Who has a red flare?"

"I do," Jack Mahanani said.

"Fire it out about a hundred yards line of sight. As soon as it hits, we converge on it and deploy around it thirty yards away in a circle. Go, Mahanani."

He fired the red flare. It arced out, hit the ground, and kept burning.

"First squad to the right, second squad to the left. Let's defend our LZ or we'll never get out of here. Go, go, go."

They ran for the flare, and went down in prone positions facing outward thirty yards from the red light. Ed's three-round burst from his MP-5 started the firing. They kept up the firing for a full minute; then Ed used the Motorola.

"Sustain fire, but on five-second intervals. Conserve rounds. We don't hear the chopper yet."

The firing tapered off, then came on with single-shot rounds at intervals. After two more minutes, Ed called a cease-fire.

"Come on in around me for an evaluation," Ed said in his mike.

The men assembled.

"Jaybird, what happened?"

"Went fine. We fired too fast at first, but we didn't have any targets so we overshot. With something to fire at, we'd be more conservative. I'm almost dry on ammo."

"Douglas," Ed said.

"I ran out of ammo. It's been a long drill. Like Jaybird said, with real targets I'd be more conservative. Knowing we were waiting for the chopper, we'd all save more ammo for the landing and to protect our men as we loaded."

"That's about it, men. Let's form into a column of ducks, First Squad on the right side, Second Squad on the left, and get ready to move out."

"Where to, LT?" Doc Ellsworth asked.

"Anyone have an issue compass?" Ed asked.

Two of the older hands groaned.

"You wouldn't, LT," a plaintive voice called out.

"Would, and will," Ed said. "This one is called getting home alive."

"Oh, damn, I think I'm coming down with appendicitis," Ron Holt called. Half the men laughed. The other half didn't know what was coming.

"Move out to the north," Ed said. He put Joe Lampedusa leading one file and Jaybird the other.

"No talking, this is a quiet maneuver." Ed led the group generally north. Murdock brought up the rear. Every two hundred yards he tapped two of the men on the shoulder, and told them to hold their position for ten minutes, then regroup.

He had dropped off four pairs before one of them said something.

"Commander, this is a find-your-way-home drill, right? We ain't gonna regroup." It was Horse Ronson. He was with Fred Washington.

"Well, now, Horse, you figure it out. Just hope to hell you have your compass."

As they walked away, Murdock could hear Horse swearing up a storm.

In twenty minutes, they had dropped off all the pairs of men except the leads. Jaybird had watched behind him. He had it figured out.

"Hell, Commander, I know how to get back," Jaybird said. "No compass, but I got me the stars. I'd be the first swabby back at the bus."

"Maybe not, Jaybird. You see, you're with us. We four, no more. Lieutenant DeWitt here is going to be our guide and scout to get us back to the bus. Before dawn, we hope."

Ed muttered something they couldn't hear, and took his compass out of his combat vest. He stared at the stars in the clear sky overhead, and then pointed. "We go south and west. We've been working generally north and east. Should work."

"I figure we're about twelve to thirteen miles from the bus," Murdock said. "What do you think, Joe?"

"Closer to fifteen, Skipper. It's now about twenty-hundred. If the LT can do the job, we should be in our blankets by midnight."

It was almost 0100 before the foursome arrived at the bus. Two teams had beaten them back: Ronson and Washington, and Doc Ellsworth and Joe Douglas.

Another team came in about 0200, but the last six men didn't make it back until an hour after daylight at 0630.

Murdock and the others had fires going for coffee and hot MRE main dishes. The last men in ignored the food, and fell on their blankets for a quick rest.

"Sack out," Murdock said. "We don't have our first call here for another hour and a half."

Al Adams groaned, and pulled his blanket up over his head. "I may never walk another step in my lifetime," he growled.

Murdock let them sleep in until 0800, then rousted everyone out.

"Today we get to wash the dirt off our cammies in the good old canal. It should be a fun morning."

Before they left the bus, Murdock checked in on the SATCOM with Master Chief George MacKenzie.

"Checking in about my laundry list. Anything new there at the zoo?"

"Not so you could notice, except it's much quieter than usual with the Third Platoon out gallivanting around the countryside."

"Anything from our friend and fisherman Don Stroh?"

"Not nary a word, sir. You did have a personal call from Washington, D.C. The nice-sounding lady did not leave her name or number."

"Thank you, Master Chief. She never leaves a name. She figures I must know who's calling."

"And do you, lad?"

"Aye, that and I do," Murdock said with a brogue to match the Scotsman.

They both laughed.

"Master Chief, I'm figuring at least another day here. I'll check in tomorrow morning and see what's happening."

"Aye, do that."

"We're done here. Out."

At 0900 the SEALs marched away from their "home" at the Chocolate Mountain Gunnery Range toward the Coachilla Canal. Technically it was outside of the gunnery range boundary, but the SEALs didn't let that stop them from utilizing the wetness for training purposes. The authorities that ran the canal that fed water to the water-starved Imperial County from the Colorado River aqueduct had never complained about a little bit of wetness training in their water.

The SEALs were ready for combat. They had restocked their combat vests with their regular supply of ammunition,

grenades, and other operational gear, and stuffed in one MRE
each. Just one today, not two, which should mean a shorter
training day. Everyone had his issue weapon.

"Let's move out," Murdock called. "Diamond formation
with Lam out front a hundred. Let's go."

It was less than half a mile to the canal. Murdock watched
the water, tossed in a piece of dry cactus wood, and saw it
swept downstream.

"Looks like about five knots today," Murdock said. "Motorolas in the waterproof. No rebreathers and no fins. Just a
nice little swim. Let's go downstream for a quarter of a mile;
then we'll come back up against the current."

They waded in and swam by twos with their buddy lines
attached. Murdock took the point, and when he stopped, he
stepped out on the bank and waved the others to turn around.

"Okay, upstream now. Swim for it. Doc, Quinley is
wounded. Has a bad arm and can't swim. How are you going
to get him upstream?"

Quinley had been pulled out of the water as the others
began to move upstream.

"Ronson, Fernandez," Doc called. "Get back here, and help
me with a casualty."

The two came back and waited. Doc took out of his kit an
inflatable collar that looked like half a life vest, attached it
around Quinley's neck, then pushed a pin and it inflated.

"Left arm or right," he asked Quinley.

"Left."

Doc strapped Quinley's left arm to his side, and his wrist
and forearm across his chest. He tied two buddy lines
together, and looped them around Quinley under his armpits.

"On your back in the water," Doc told the casualty. He
gave the buddy lines with loops tied in each end to the two
SEALs. "You're towing him, and I'm keeping his head out of
the water," Doc said. "Let's move, we're too far behind the
rest of the platoon."

Murdock swam behind Doc and his patient.

The system worked. The two strong swimmers in front had
tied the buddy lines around their chests so they could do a
powerful crawl stroke. They moved upstream against the

current, but had no chance to overtake the other swimmers now well ahead of them.

Murdock had told Ed DeWitt to stop them about where they'd entered the water a quarter of a mile ahead.

The SEALs had strapped their weapons across their backs, and swam hard. It was work against the current. Murdock had told Bradford to leave the big fifty-caliber rifle on the bus. No way he could carry it and his MG and swim upstream.

Halfway there, Ronson and Fernandez swam to the near edge of the canal and rested.

"Can you make it?" Doc asked them. Both nodded, but didn't waste any breath answering.

Ten minutes later, the last five men came to the point of departure, and crawled out of the canal.

"Hey, don't know what you guys are panting about," Quinley said. "I'm fresh as a four-dollar whore and ready to do the swim again."

Both Ronson and Fernandez slugged Quinley in the shoulder.

"Maybe I should really break your fucking arm," Ronson bellowed, then collapsed on the side of the canal, still breathing hard.

"Teamwork. Teamwork. It's all got to be teamwork," Murdock said, pacing among his men. His cammies still dripped from the canal water. "What happened back there that shouldn't have? Anybody?"

There was no reply.

"Two men were called back for special duty, to tow a casualty. Two of you should have at least taken their weapons, made their work a tad bit easier. Teamwork. We work together to stay alive. If this had been a real mission, we might have lost either of the two men towing the casualty, or the wounded man himself, or all three. Think, men. Think about the good of the group. We all depend on each other. Just like carrying the logs down at BUD/S. We think teamwork here, it'll save our butts on a mission.

"The facts are, we have a mission in the oven. It's not quite ready yet, but in the near future we'll be flying out of here and going to the Far East, where we'll be berthed on an aircraft carrier while the brass monitors a situation about ready to blow. If and when it erupts, we'll be nearby ready for action."

He looked around at the tired men. They seemed to perk up a little.

"You get ten minutes to rest. Then we'll double-time out to the old gunnery range and practice throwing grenades. That means we swing past the bus to take on a couple of cartons of the little hand bombs."

A half hour later at the grenade range, they took turns throwing the smooth and round M-67 grenades at truck tires positioned at twenty, thirty, and forty yards away. Each man threw until he dropped a grenade in the twenty-yard tire, then had two shots at each of the longer throws.

It took Ron Holt eight throws to get the first grenade inside the twenty-yard tire. They threw from behind a log-and-sandbag barricade. Murdock used his field glasses from forty yards away to spot the targets.

Doc Ellsworth had the best arm in the platoon. He laid his second fragger in the twenty-yard tire, hit the thirty-yard circle on his second throw, and nailed the forty-yard tire on his first.

"Come on, you dirtbags," Doc crowed. "Let's see a little competition around here. Do I have to show you how every fucking time?"

Nobody beat the medic that day at throwing hand grenades.

They closed out the morning with a five-mile forced march, and wound up back at the bus. Everyone slumped in the shade of the bus or sat inside, and broke out his MRE.

"Holt, fire up the SATCOM. Somebody is trying to reach us."

"Your radar ears again, Commander?"

"Damn right."

"They should have like E-mail on this thing so it could pick up a message and record it so we could get it anytime."

"Hard to do without turning it on, Holt. Go."

The minute Holt had the antenna positioned and snapped on the set, they had a call come in. It was encrypted, but came through the machine in clear voice.

"Murdock, this is Stroh. Give me a call when you can. Things are moving."

"Not yet," Murdock growled. "It's too damn quick. We need more time to get the men ready."

He nodded at Holt to set for voice transmission encrypted, and picked up the mike.

"Murdock here, looking for Don Stroh. My ears are on."

There was a pause while the machine encrypted and sent the message. Another came back a minute later.

"Murdock. Stroh. Things moving faster than we thought. We need you to be out there a week from today."

Murdock scowled at the set. He was far enough away so the men couldn't hear.

"Can't do it, Stroh. I have that new man. We need more time to integrate him into the team. You know how we work closely together. Can't you push it another week?"

"I can, but the President can't. He cut the orders to my boss, and I'm just the messenger. A week tomorrow from North Island, three o'clock P.M. You'll be going to the USS *Monroe*. You've been on her before."

"Aye, aye. Can't argue with the Commander in Chief. We'll be ready, but we may need a week to recuperate on that Navy pleasure-cruise ship."

"That sounds better, fishing buddy. I'll meet you on the carrier. I'm out of here."

Murdock signaled to Holt to turn off the set. "Not a word of this to the men. I'll tell them tonight. Go eat your chow." Murdock found Ed DeWitt in the back of the bus, and told him what he'd just found out.

"We're pushing it to get ready," Ed said. "Remember, we've got a new man in my squad."

Murdock worried it. "Yeah, that's what's been bugging me. He has good individual skills. It's the teamwork I'm thinking about. We'll do some basic teamwork back at the Grinder. Get a little down and dirty. We'll make sure that Jack Mahanani will be totally integrated into the team."

"A pair of men roping down a thousand-foot cliff is a good way to imprint cooperation."

"Yeah, Ed, and a good way to lose a man if something goes wrong. Let's use a little more subtle method."

Ed finished his peanut butter and crackers. "What's for this afternoon?"

"Not sure. We need the rest of the day here, then five days of intensive water training, then we should be ready."

"How about the injured-buddy drill?" Ed asked.

"Each one carry one?"

"Sounds good."

"How are Ronson and Ching getting along?"

Murdock grinned. "Hell, like twins. Ching blasting that rattlesnake about ready to plant his fangs in Ronson's ankle turned Ronson into Ching's buddy for life."

"Damned good thing. Ronson was hot. We use a diamond formation?"

"Right. We go out four miles, then get hit by a whole division so we pull back with our wounded."

"Who carries who?"

"Next man in line in the diamond. Or if it's a mismatch, switch it around so it works. You designate your wounded and who carries who. We'll move back halfway, then switch, and the one carried then totes his buddy."

"Sounds good to me. Hope you don't have to pack out Ronson and his two hundred and fifty pounds."

Murdock grinned. "Easy, who's going to get Mahanani and his two-forty? Better make it Ronson. They deserve each other. Let's get these noodle-knockers into the field."

8

Tuesday, 13 February

Chocolate Mountain Gunnery Range
Niland, California

Third Platoon worked its way into the desert four miles from the bus, and Murdock called a halt.

"This is as far as we're going right now," Murdock said. "We're under a simulated attack. Eight of you have been wounded, and can't walk. Right now I want every man over two hundred pounds up here. Move."

Ronson, Bill Bradford, and Jack Mahanani came forward.

"Now I want you to pair up. Ronson and Mahanani are a match, Bradford, I'll take you up as my partner. You one-eighties match up with each other, and then those a hundred and seventy, and the hundred-and-sixty-pounders. Come on, we don't have all fucking day."

Four men were in the two hundred class. Five men were in the 180 class, five at 170, and two at 160. Murdock moved one of the lightest 180 men down to the 170 class, and the two 160's matched up.

"Pair up in weight class and let's get moving."

"How can I carry this big lug?" Mahanani asked, looking at Horse Ronson.

"Doesn't matter how, just do it," Murdock warned. "Remember, two miles back toward the bus, we switch the injured for the carry guy, so be gentle. It could be payback time."

Murdock took 215-pound Bill Bradford in a fireman's carry, and began walking back toward the bus. The others yelped and bellowed, but at last everyone got moving. Ed DeWitt, in the 170-pound class, carried his man first.

The over-the-shoulder fireman's carry was the favorite, but some did it piggyback. Doc Ellsworth tried dragging 160-pound Les Quinley by the shoulders, letting his heels dig furrows in the desert. He soon gave up, and did the fireman's carry.

Murdock stopped at two hundred yards and rested, waiting for the others to catch up.

"Don't look so pissed off, you SEALs," Murdock said when everyone had made the first stop. "You know that the only easy day was yesterday. Let's move out."

Lugging a combat-ready SEAL with weapon and ammo across the California desert is tougher than it looks, Murdock decided. When he got to the one-mile point, he put Bradford down and rested.

The others straggled up. Jack Mahanani was the last man in, with Horse Ronson bending him nearly double. He dropped into the sand and gasped for five minutes.

"Don't you ever get wounded so bad we got to carry you, Ronson," Mahanani said when he could talk.

"We'll take a breather here," Murdock said, "Then we switch horses for another mile, and call it good. You riders shouldn't be tired at all."

Horse Ronson stood and stretched. "Damn, I'm ready to go now, okay, Commander?"

Murdock nodded.

Ronson picked up the 240-pound Mahanani in a fireman's carry, adjusted him a moment, then ran for twenty steps and burst out in a roaring laugh. He settled down to a walk, and moved away from the others quickly.

"Hell, might as well get everybody moving," Murdock said. "Don't anybody try to catch Horse. Just be sure to get your buddy out of the line of fire. That's a mile ahead."

The mile of travel took them forty-five minutes. Horse and Mahanani were sleeping when the rest of them arrived.

Two of the men who had been carrying were so tired they could barely stand. Murdock gave them all a half hour to get their muscles back in order; then they walked the two miles back to the bus.

"Let's load up and get out of here," Murdock said. He had their attention. "Our orders came down. We fly out of North Island in a week. That means some tough training between now and then. We'll be ready. We're going to sit down on that carrier somewhere in the Far East and wait for developments in Korea. The top is about to blow over there, some of our experts say. Now, let's get out of here."

They arrived back at the SEALs quarterdeck at 1700, and Murdock gave the men the night off.

"Be back here at 0730 tomorrow ready to kick butt. We've got a lot to do in the next few days. A good night's sleep will help. Now get out of here."

He finished some paperwork, talked with Master Chief MacKenzie at the quarterdeck for a minute, then nosed his Ford Bronco out of the parking lot onto Silver Strand Boulevard and headed north into Coronado.

At his condo, Murdock parked in his slot and went up the steps two at a time. He started to put his key in the door, then paused. It was open a half inch. Instinctively he reached for his .45, but it wasn't there. Murdock listened. He could hear music. What burglar was going to turn on the stereo while he looted the place? Murdock nudged the door inward an inch, and looked through the slot.

Nothing.

He pushed it in farther, and smelled something cooking. In one swift move, he jolted into the condo and glanced into the kitchen.

Ardith Manchester had just taken a taste of something cooking on the stove. She looked over, grinned, and put down the spoon.

"Heard you were back from Master Chief MacKenzie. I

like him. Dinner isn't quite ready. Lots of time for you to take a shower." She paused. "Or for us to take a shower."

They met halfway across the kitchen, and he kissed her long and deep. She gave a little sigh, and melted firmly against him.

"You'll get filthy from the desert," he said.

"Good, as long as it's with you."

They kissed again, gently, softly, and she spun away from him.

"Dinner is almost burning." She waved at him, shooing him out. "You get wet, and I'll finish dinner."

Murdock never knew what they had for the meal. He watched Ardith, and couldn't stop grinning.

"How?" he asked her.

"The CIA has absolutely no secrets from my daddy. He's been on top of the Korean thing for two months. When the President gave the CIA the word, Daddy knew about it twenty minutes later, and then I did, and I tried to call, but couldn't get you, so I packed my small bag, grabbed a plane out of Washington National as soon as I could. I picked up three hours coming this way. Fantastic."

"That's a good how. You know about our assignment?"

"Not the hour you leave, but I know the day. Next Tuesday."

They put the dishes in the under-counter washer, and dropped on the sofa. Murdock sat there watching her. He'd seldom seen a prettier woman. Long blonde hair that cascaded around her shoulders, five-nine but seemed taller, slender, sexy, with the softest blue eyes he'd ever seen. High cheekbones so she looked like a model. White teeth almost perfect, but with one small notch to give her a real look. Then there was her smile.

She turned it on now. Glorious. He couldn't get enough of it.

"What?" she asked.

"Just want to sit here and watch you for a minute. You have the time?"

"I have a week's worth. I told my boss he could take his job and vote on it."

They laughed. She could get away from her father's Senatorial office anytime she wanted to.

"Still turning down those job offers from the agencies that have been trying to hire you?" he asked.

"Only two of them. Nothing really interesting so far. I'd get buried in the mass of people. I like it where I am."

She stared at him; then a small frown grew on her pretty face.

"What?" he asked.

"You look tired. Are you pushing your men too hard, and yourself right along with them?"

"Probably. The more we sweat in training, the less we bleed in combat."

Ardith winced.

"Sorry, no more SEAL talk," he said. "What about you? Did you get that new car?"

"No. I'm saving my money."

He frowned. She was usually never short on cash. "Why?"

"Girl stuff. What about that new camera you were going to buy?"

"Haven't yet. Waiting for the new technology."

Ardith laughed, and he loved the sound of it. "Like me waiting for the new technology on computers, right? It changes every month, so I'm still waiting for the ideal setup."

"You have a computer at home."

"Yes, it's two years old and already a dinosaur. I can't even read the JPG files."

"Way ahead of me. I don't know what a JPG file is."

"With pictures and graphics and things."

He slid over beside her.

"No more talk," she said.

He nodded and kissed her. His hand found her breast and she sighed, and pushed back against his hand.

She came away from his kiss. "Right here on the couch?" she asked.

"It would save time."

"It would be a first."

It was.

Later, they sat in front of the fireplace on the floor, and watched the wood burn.

"Real wood, logs and sticks," Ardith said. "I like that. You haven't been to our cabin up near Rhododendron, have you?"

"That's some kind of a flowering shrub. It's a town too?"

"Yes, just a little place up on Mt. Hood. Beautiful in summer, fantastic in the winter when the heavy snows come. We'll have to spend some time up there."

"Yeah, I'd like to. Only not for a while."

Ardith watched him, her face still flushed, her eyes pleading. "You really have to go?"

"Yes. But we have nearly a week. During that time I have to finish training. A new guy in the platoon is always a worry. Men who have been in combat form a bond, a loyalty that imprints us so hard that it makes for lifelong friendships. When we can stay alive together, with teamwork and support, it makes the relationships so tremendously powerful. The new guy hasn't had any of that. He knows the routines, where to go, what to do, but he doesn't have the emotional bonding yet."

She snuggled against him. "I can't feel the power, the bonding, but I can understand it. No more whining from me. Just hold me tight, and I'll pretend that you'll never let me go."

"I won't let go of you. I'll have to be gone sometimes, but I'll never let go of you. Hey, this is the Navy. A good Navy woman knows about separation. Most of the men have a six-or-nine-month blue-water deployment, bobbing around on an ocean somewhere."

"No more whining," Ardith said. "Korea. I don't think the North is going to invade the South. Their economy is nearly bankrupt. They have thousands of people starving. How can they launch a military offensive?"

"War takes the people's minds off their problems and the shortage of food. Gives them somebody to hate out of country. Great strategy for a failing government."

"Will it work?"

"Usually it doesn't. The army runs out of food or guns, and

the enemy overwhelms the military, then takes over the country, and almost always it's worse off than before."

"Except World War Two and the Marshall Plan."

"True."

They were both quiet then, watching the fire. He stood, and put more wood on the blaze, then settled back beside her.

"Oh, yes, I like this," Murdock said. "So much better than sand fleas in your ears and sand crabs crawling up your leg."

"Is it true you turned down a chance to be an aide to the CNO?" Ardith asked.

"True. I don't polish boots well."

"You know the Chief of Naval Operations. It would be a plush, prestigious assignment for you."

"I'm not on the admiral track. If I'm lucky I might make captain before my twenty are up. If I don't, it won't matter that much."

"But you can't be a SEAL for ten more years, can you?"

"My knees wouldn't hold out for that long. We lose more good men with worn-out knees than any other physical problem. But I might be able to move up in the operations end."

He held her then, and she made soft noises in her throat that he knew meant she was content, happy at least for the moment. She stirred, and looked up. Then she put one of his hands over her breasts.

"I promised myself I wouldn't bug you about moving on from the SEALs to another job in the Navy. But I guess I am. I'll say it once more and then not again. I truly hope you will move on from the SEALs soon before you get yourself killed or smashed up, and find a nice safe shore job where we can be together."

She looked at him seriously, then reached out and kissed him so gently on the lips he barely felt it.

"Now, please make love to me again, and again, and again. I don't plan on getting much sleep tonight."

He opened the sides of her robe and kissed her breasts.

9

Wednesday, 14 February

Naval Special Warfare Section
Coronado, California

At slightly after 0800 the Third Platoon took to the water of the Pacific Ocean just off the BUD/S training area. They wore full black wet suits with their desert-pattern cammies over them. They had their complete combat-ready vests, weapons, Drager LAR V rebreathers, and fins.

Murdock told them before they left it would be a twelve-mile swim. No heroics, no surprise attacks from the depths by SEAL instructors, just a conditioning swim out and back. Most of it would be underwater.

Murdock put Ed DeWitt at the lead. They would follow a compass heading from the sand in front of BUD/S O-course straight across to Zuniga Point at the southernmost landfall of North Island Naval Air Station. It was exactly six miles across the inward sweep of the Pacific there. This course had been used by the SEALs many times in training.

Ed DeWitt dropped down to fifteen feet below the surface, set up his attack board on the right azimuth, and kicked out. The attack board is a molded plastic device with two handgrips and a bubble compass in the center. It also has a depth gauge and cyalume chemical lights regulated with a twist knob for the amount of light needed to read the instruments.

The SEALs were paired by their six-to-eight-foot buddy lines, and strung out in a file behind DeWitt. The usual routine was to stay close enough to the swimmers ahead to be able to see them. That kept the platoon from being spread out too far. There were no radio communications in the wet.

Murdock and Joe Lampedusa swam at the tail of the string, and became the rear guard. Murdock had told DeWitt to stop halfway through the swim and he'd take the lead. He wanted Jaybird to set the pace for training.

They were a mile into the swim when Murdock saw a shape coming up to his right. He looked closer, and saw the white flash of the belly of a large animal. He stared through the shimmering water, and the creature turned and swam directly toward him. It stopped a dozen feet away, and studied him from large curious eyes.

It was a Pacific dolphin, smaller than the ones that perform at Sea World, but just as curious. He knew these mammals traveled in pods or groups, so he stared around. He found a dozen moving up behind him, and then they flowed around him, and next to the line of SEALs. He could see them going to the surface and jumping, then returning time and again to inspect these strange-looking creatures that had invaded their territory. He figured there must be a hundred in the pod.

Then before Murdock could turn and look, something nudged him from behind. He glanced back, and found a four-foot dolphin smiling at him with big eyes.

This wasn't the TV Flipper; this was a wild sea creature. Murdock put out one gloved hand, and the dolphin backed off, then came forward. Murdock touched the side of the creature, rubbed along its back.

Then, on some unheard signal, the dolphin turned and jetted away. The rest of them must have gone with him. Murdock looked over at Lampedusa, who gave him a thumbs-up. He stared forward to see the pair of SEALs they had been following, but the pair was out of sight. Murdock checked his wrist compass, turned slightly, and gave a tug on the buddy line. He and Lampedusa swam forward twice as fast as they had been, and in thirty strokes saw the kicking feet of a pair of SEALs ahead of them.

They all surfaced at the three-mile point, and the first thing Murdock heard was about the dolphins.

"Must have been a hundred of them," DeWitt said. "They played around, jumped and dove, one hit our buddy line and almost tore it off me. Amazing."

Everyone had something to say about the dolphins. Two of the men had touched the creatures.

"Man, they are fast," Jaybird said. "I bet they can swim thirty knots."

When the talk quieted down, Murdock got things moving again. "Everyone all right? Any complaints?" None surfaced. "Okay, Jaybird and I'll take the lead, First Squad behind us. Ed, play catch-up at the tail end. Let's move, we've got a lot of swimming to do."

Murdock gave Jaybird the attack board. "You've got the con, Jaybird. Let's motor over the last three miles to the point."

Jaybird put his mouthpiece back in, and dove. Murdock caught up with him, and tied him to the buddy line. They leveled out at fifteen feet under the choppy Pacific, and Jaybird angled them along the right bearing for the point.

SEALs swim at a given pace. Every man can tell by the number of strokes he takes underwater how far he's traveled. The distance is usually off by no more than ten yards over half a mile. That's part of the reason for these continuous re-training and conditioning swims. Underwater positioning, even in murky harbor water, had been of vital importance in missions past, and would be in future assignments.

Jaybird motioned upward to Murdock, and they came to the surface. They were about thirty yards off the tip of Zuniga Point.

"Low tide, so more of it's exposed," Jaybird said.

They waited for the rest of the SEALs to surface, then treaded water for another few minutes.

"Let's go home," Murdock said. "Mahanani, you're our Second Squad tracker. I want you on the attack board and lead out. Team up with Jaybird and I'll take your buddy-line partner."

They were over halfway back to the starting point when Murdock saw in the clear water twenty feet to one side a solitary cruising shark. He checked it out, pulled the buddy cord, and pointed to it. Fred Washington nodded that he saw the shark.

Murdock watched it. He knew sharks were curious, and this was a blue, not known for having a vicious streak. The shark moved closer and closer to this strange thing in the water. In its tiny brain, the shark must have had only one purpose, to find out if this flailing, unstreamlined creature was good to eat.

It moved closer. Murdock had been up close before with sharks. On one exercise they had baited two sharks up to a boat, and gone overboard to see how the blue sharks reacted.

Now the blue came closer. Murdock figured it was no more than four feet long. Everything looks much larger underwater. The dark eyes seemed to be checking out this strange swimmer. It nosed closer until it was less than three feet from Murdock. He stopped swimming. The shark came closer.

Murdock struck out through the water as hard as he could with his fist, and slammed it into the nose of the shark just over its closed mouth. The shark jolted backward, turned, and swam away.

Washington gave a jerk on the buddy line and a thumbs-up; then they went back to swimming for home.

Twenty minutes later on the beach across from the BUD/S O-course, Washington told the others about the shark. By that time it had grown to eight feet long and its mouth was wide open ready to take off Murdock's leg.

"You actually punched a shark in the nose, Commander?" Joe Douglas asked.

"It's a common way to treat blue sharks around here. Most of them aren't vicious, but they are curious as hell. A good slap on the nose and they'll cut and swim away fast. Now that the nature hike is over, how did you like the swim?"

"Just a warm-up, Skipper," Ching said. "When are we

going on a long swim, like out to the Coronado Islands and back?"

"Ching, you're going soft," Jaybird called. "That's only fourteen miles round trip. How about we swim from here up to Oceanside and back? That would be about an eighty-miler."

The men hooted him down.

"You go, Jaybird," Doc Ellsworth said. "I'll pace you in a kayak."

Murdock got control again. "You'll get wet enough in the next four days to satisfy most of you frog-hoppers. Now, have some chow, and report back at the O-course at thirteen-thirty. Move out."

As Murdock ate his noon meal, he kept trying to figure out a way to show Ardith just how important to him the Navy and the SEALs were. He figured she knew that the SEALs were formed out of the Navy's Underwater Demolition Teams that were put together during World War II. They were assembled first as the Naval Combat Demolition Units to clear mines and underwater obstacles from harbors and beaches where military landings were planned.

They quickly became the UDTs, and worked in the Pacific clearing and charting beaches on Kwajalein, Saipan, Leyte, and Okinawa before the Marine amphibious invasions.

There was little need for UDTs in Korea, but they did work on the Inchon harbor, and did some behind-the-lines demolition work. This soon developed into a companion group called the Special Operation Teams for land or water use. From that, the SEALs were formed, the name indicating that they could function from and on the Sea, strike from the Air, or come in by Land.

President John F. Kennedy pushed for a stronger unconventional war capability in 1961. Then, on January 1, 1962, SEAL Team One and SEAL Team Two were formed. The SEALs had an expanded role after that.

They were tasked to do reconnaissance, take on covert missions against any and all enemies, to destroy bridges, harbors, ports, and other strategic targets. Their first mission was to work out tactics for these missions, develop training for completing them, and select and train with weapons to help them do the job.

From there the SEALs were ready for Vietnam; then they went in at Grenada and Panama and during Desert Storm.

Weapons, tactics, and personnel changed over the years, but the mission remained the same. To do an attack on a given enemy quickly, often silently, with sudden overwhelming firepower, and to pull out with as few casualties as possible.

Now the SEALs were a part of the Naval Special Warfare Command. Group One was located in Coronado, where SEAL Teams One, Three, Five, and Seven were headquartered. Group Two was in Little Creek, Virginia, where SEAL Teams Two, Four, and Eight were situated.

Murdock pushed the rest of his food away, and headed for the quarterdeck. Maybe he should have Master Chief MacKenzie talk to Ardith. He snorted. Oh, hell, yes, that would sink him in a rush. There had to be a way. He had five more days to find it, and to make Ardith understand.

The SEAL mystique was a hundred times more than the "brotherhood" of a college fraternity. It was much more than blood brothers who took a blood pledge. In combat most of them had bled for the others on the team, for the mission, for the cause, for the SEALs.

The officers were unlike those in any other service or component of any military unit in the world. The officers took the grunge training the same way the other SEAL recruits did. The officer might be a lieutenant (j.g.) or a full lieutenant, but he took his bars off during training, had sand kicked in his face, and was tormented physically and mentally the same as the other tadpoles.

Every officer in a SEAL unit had been through the same rigorous training as the lowest-ranked man in the team. The only difference in training was that the officers were expected to score ten percent higher than the enlisted men in every test.

This type of no-officer-country ethic formed a bond so close between officers and their men that they would kill for each other, and often had to on a combat mission.

Murdock shook his head. How did he tell all this to Ardith, and make her understand? How could he do that, and not wind up making her hate the Navy in general, and the SEALs in particular?

"Commander, the men are on the O-course and ready to go," Jaybird said to Murdock, breaking into his thoughts.

"Yes, Jaybird, good. You have the two stopwatches and the clipboard with you?"

"Right here, Commander. Are you all right? You seemed to be a thousand miles away."

"Yes, Jaybird. I'm fine. Let's go and do the damn course, and see if we can break some personal bests."

10

Wednesday, 14 February

Naval Special Warfare Section
Coronado, California

Murdock stared at the O-course at the far end of the SEALs complex built along the blue of the Pacific Ocean. He'd heard it called the toughest obstacle course in the world. He figured the description must be right.

He had Jaybird put the men in combat-formation sequence to run the course. The better each man knew where he fit into the combat formation, the better. The First Squad ran it first, then the Second Squad.

"Combat formation," Murdock called. "You know the routine. You'll leave at thirty-second intervals, and we record your time when you hit the finish line. Move them out, Jaybird."

The O-course was put together to toughen and strengthen the SEAL candidates. During the first phase of training, the BUD/S candidates must complete the O-course in fifteen minutes. By the time they are finished with their training, those who make it all the way through must complete the course in ten minutes. Most SEALs finish the training doing the course in six to eight minutes. The current record for the route was 4:25. It would be broken soon.

Murdock watched the men. The eighteen-foot-long parallel bars with rungs between them weren't hard for them anymore. Mostly a matter of technique. Then came the two stump jumps. Next the seven-foot low wall to climb, and the eleven-foot high wall with a rope to help you climb up.

Then the men worked under the barbed-wire crawl for thirty feet where the space between ground and barbed wire comes close to six inches. The cargo net climb looks easy, if you stay near the side, and make your legs do most of the work. No problem, except it's fifty feet up, and then fifty feet down the other side.

The balance logs roll when stepped on, and then comes the log stack, a pyramid of logs cabled together four feet high that you run up and down with your hands behind your head.

The rope transfer looks easy. Climb a rope up twelve feet, reach out, grab a steel ring, swing to a rope on the other side, and slide down. The trick is catching the ring. Some men have a tough time doing it.

Murdock walked into the course watching the men. He'd do the course when the last man had started. He had a personal best of 6:14 he wanted to beat.

The double hurdle is the toughest on the lot. One log hurdle is five feet off the ground. You jump up and belly flop on it, lift yourself to your feet on top, and jump to the next hurdle, ten feet high and four feet away. You have to stand on it, then drop to the ground.

The problems increase: the sixty-foot rope bridge, another log stack, a five-story slide for life down a rope, a swinging rope, then another wall, a balance beam, a five-foot inclined wall, and a twelve-foot-high climbing wall with one-inch-wide cleats to grip and stand on as you climb up one side and down the other.

When the SEALs finished the course they got their time from Jaybird, then did twenty push-ups.

Murdock slid into place at the end of the line, and took his run through the course. He passed one man, but tried not to notice. He pushed hard, and came to the last hurdle thinking he had a great time.

"Six-eighteen," Ed DeWitt said, reading the watch for

Murdock. Ed had taken over so Jaybird could get in his turn on the O-course. All times were recorded on the clipboard after the man's name.

Murdock did his twenty push-ups, all the time wondering how he was going to convince Ardith that he had to stay in the SEALs. Maybe Ed DeWitt's woman could help. She seemed content with Ed doing his job. It might be worth a try. They could set up dinner out tomorrow night. Or maybe just an informal after-dinner at his place.

Jaybird had sent the First Squad on a two-mile run through the soft sand along the Silver Strand toward Imperial Beach to the south. The Second Squad left as soon as the last man was through the O-course. Murdock led them out, and they met the first group coming back. Jaybird talked with Murdock a moment, and grinned.

By the time Murdock had his team back at the Grinder, the court between the SEAL buildings where many physical exercises and drills were conducted, Jaybird had checked out three IBSs. He had the men carrying two of them on their heads toward the surf.

Murdock and the Second Squad grabbed the third inflatable boat, and raced the First Squad to the water. At the edge they stopped.

"Launching in these four-foot swells should be good practice," Murdock said. "Have a small storm moving on-shore from the south, that's why we have the four-foot sets. Great for you surfers, if you had the time. Let's go out beyond the breakers, then make three runs in surfing the swells if we can. Just don't dump the boat. If any team dumps the boat, you get a ten-mile run. No combat gear on, no weapons, should be a piece of cake. We'll each do three in and out from the sand. Let's do it."

For this exercise there were six men in one IBS and five in each of the other two. The semi-rigid inflatable boats were much the same boats they used in combat situations, except these had no motors, just SEALs with paddles.

The three teams hit the water at the same time, using their past training to get the boats through the first breaker, and then over the next one, and into the calm of the Pacific swells.

All the men were soaking wet by the time they launched the boats, got them through the second four-foot breaker, and crawled inside. They paddled out to the swells, and on a signal from Murdock paddled for the shore, intent on surfing in on the large breakers without upsetting the boats. This could be the dangerous part.

On exercises for the BUD/S students, each man wore an orange life vest to help him stay afloat in case of a dumped IBS, and to help make finding the swimmers in the surf easier.

The first boat with DeWitt hit the breaker just right, and surfed along the top for a moment before it nosed down. The men leaned to the rear to keep the front of the boat from digging into the water and getting upended. They made it.

Murdock watched the second boat go in. Jaybird piloted it, and had it almost to the point to start down the face of the wave, when a larger-than-usual wave caught the boat and, with its tremendous power, tipped it over and sent the five men splashing into the neck-deep water.

Murdock's men paddled their boat to the area, and counted bobbing heads.

"We're missing one man," Jaybird screeched at Murdock. The IBS had ridden the foaming water well into shore upside down.

"Find him!" Murdock bellowed. He dove off his boat into the water just in back of the large breaker. The other four men in his boat did as well, and all tried to search the four-foot-deep water. Sand stirred up by the breakers cut visibility to three or four feet.

"Walk it," Murdock yelled when he surfaced. The five men who had been in his boat joined hands with the other four SEALs from the second boat, and they walked across the spot where the boat had flipped.

Nothing.

"Again, closer in," Murdock roared over the pounding noise of the crashing waves.

They walked again, hoping to find a body on the bottom or being washed out by the rip currents.

"Here!" Horse Ronson bellowed. He duck-dived, and a

moment later came up holding Les Quinley's head above water. They rushed him to shore, cleared his mouth, then did mouth-to-mouth CPR.

Doc Ellsworth took the first turn. He had worked barely two minutes when Quinley coughed and spat up water in Doc's face. Quinley gasped, shuddered, and then began breathing.

"Jaybird, run up to the quarterdeck and get an ambulance down here fast," Murdock said. "We're taking no chances."

Three minutes later, Quinley tried to sit up. They told him to stay flat on his back.

"What happened, Quinley, do you remember?" Murdock asked.

Quinley frowned, spat up some more salt water, and shook his head. "Not much. I saw us going over. Damn wave was the biggest I've ever tried to come through. Then we flipped, and something damn hard hit me on the top of my head, and that was it."

The Navy ambulance roared up to the soft sand and stopped. A doctor and a corpsman raced across the beach, and knelt beside Quinley.

"Check him out, Doc," Murdock said. "We pulled him out of four feet of water. He wasn't under more than three minutes, maybe four. CPR got him breathing again."

The Navy doctor checked his chest, then his back, then his pulse.

"How do you feel?" the doctor asked Quinley.

"Fine, sir. Just took a little underwater swim."

"A SEAL, right?"

Quinley nodded.

"Still, I better check out your gills. Can you walk to the rig?"

Quinley nodded again, and stood with some help. He wouldn't lean on anybody while walking through the sand to the ambulance.

"I'll be back for chow," Quinley said.

Jaybird had the men right the boats and collected the floating oars.

Murdock looked at the men and shook his head. "No, let's

knock it off for today. Jaybird. Get the boats checked in and dismiss the men. We're on for 0500 tomorrow morning."

The next day he talked to DeWitt about bringing Milly over for the evening about nineteen-thirty, after dinner.

"Ed, I want Ardith to see that a couple can be together even though one of them is a SEAL. Would Milly be a good example to show to Ardith and to talk about it?"

"Hell, I don't know. Sometimes Milly gets really uptight about my staying in the SEALs, especially when we ship out." He frowned, and paced the small office. "Yeah, I think it will be okay. I'll tell Milly not to scare her off." He stopped, and stared at Murdock. "I'd guess you really like this lady."

"Yeah, I'm afraid I do. Maybe I like her too much. She's hoping I'll take a job running the Navy from the Pentagon in a nice nine-to-five job so I'll be home every night."

"She's not Navy then."

"Her father is a U.S. Senator from Oregon."

"Oh, boy."

They both laughed. "Then we'll see you about nineteen-thirty," Murdock said.

That night the affair started off politely and innocuously. Then Ardith stood, put down her beer, and frowned.

"Milly, when Blake told me that you'd be coming over tonight, I figured that you'd be spoon-feeding me the Navy party line. You know, how great it is being with this swabby, and how it's for the protection of the nation, and how it's the most patriotic duty that anyone could have anywhere."

"By George, I think she's got it," Ed said.

Ardith shot him a serious look, then sat down beside Milly. Ardith was a contrast to Milly. She was tall, blond, and slender. Milly was shorter by a head, with dark hair and eyes and a nearly olive complexion. She was also a little on the chunky side.

"Now, Milly," Ardith said. "Tell me exactly what it's like living with a Navy SEAL, especially how is it when he's out there somewhere getting himself shot at by the bad guys."

Milly took a quick look at Ed, then caught a deep breath. She pointed at Murdock. "You must like this guy quite a lot to be asking about this. At least you won't be living this problem day in and day out. You're in Washington, D.C., you said." She paused.

"Well, I guess I'll have to say it's worth it, living with Ed," she went on, "despite all the drawbacks of SEAL country, and the separations. The night training, and the odd hours he sometimes has, I can put up with. Every relationship has something like that.

"It's these missions they go on that get to me. I didn't tell Ed for a long time, but I'm on hold while he's gone. I don't eat well, I don't sleep a lot, usually I lose about ten pounds, and I get these migraine headaches.

"Psychological headaches? Sure, but they still hurt just as bad. Now, that's about all I want Ed to hear. Ardith, why don't you and I go powder our noses somewhere, and have a girl-to-girl talk."

The two women went into the kitchen, then into the bedroom. Murdock looked at Ed, and shook his head. "Man, did I figure it wrong. Sounds like your bringing Milly over here provides Ardith with the final nails in my coffin."

"Never can tell. Milly sometimes talks to the jury a little."

"Milly know about our orders?"

"She knows we're going shortly. Can't just spring that on her the night before. Takes her a little getting used to each time."

"Oh, man. No wonder there are only two of the sixteen of us with live-in women. Maybe SEALs and long-term women don't mix."

"It's a damn tough mix, Murdock. To make it work there's got to be a lot of give-and-take on both sides."

Murdock looked at the bedroom, and cut off any idea of going in there. That would really do him in. He tried to figure out a defense, but gave up.

"Isn't there a Bulls game on?" Ed asked.

They watched most of the first half.

When the women came out of the bedroom, Murdock knew that Ardith had been crying. She'd repaired the damage, but not quite all of it. She waved at Murdock.

"Hey, Navy guy. I need some help in the kitchen."

When he got out there, she closed the door and kissed him soundly, holding him so tightly he wondered where one of them stopped and the other one started.

She came away from him slowly, the bright smile back on her pretty face.

"Now, I hope that made up for the long girl talk we had. We went over a lot of different things. What to expect. How it works when your man leaves. How to handle it. I learned a lot. Did you know that Milly has a master's degree in electronics, and that she's an engineer and is the top trouble-shooter at an electronics firm that makes all sorts of computer hardware?"

Murdock shook his head.

"Milly says she makes three times as much money as Ed does, but it doesn't bother him," Ardith added. "Isn't that fine?"

They cut the pie and heaped on vanilla ice cream, and Murdock carried the four pie plates on a big tray into the living room.

"Dessert is served," Ardith said. Murdock noticed she was sounding too bright and cheerful. That in itself was a bad sign.

They ate the dessert, talked a while, and found out more than they wanted to know about Milly's work at the electronics firm. Then Milly said it was time they went home.

"Five A.M. at the quarterdeck, I hear," Milly said. "You guys will need a little sleep."

When they left, Ardith took Murdock's hand and led him to the couch. She sat down as close to him as she could get. She kissed him on the cheek, and watched his expression.

"Hey, don't look so glum. I'm on your side, remember? Milly and I had a good talk. I learned a lot from that lady. I got some of my priorities straightened out. I've been thinking too much about me, me, me. I was making it ninety percent me and ten percent Navy."

"But what about—"

She cut him off with a finger over his lips.

"Hey, let me finish. I'd be thrilled pink and purple if you would come to D.C. in some Navy capacity. That just isn't going to happen, not right away at least. You turned down that aide spot to the CNO. Gutsy."

She paused and kissed him on the lips, then pulled away.

"I figure the kind of work you're doing will have an active-duty time of about four years. You've done two, that leaves two more. The CIA people say the average length of service of their field agents during the peak of the Cold War was about four years. Same here.

"Now, I think that you and I are smart enough to arrange things so we can have the best of both worlds. Between or after missions, you'll get some leave time and can come to D.C. Now and then, I can slip away for a week or two out here—say, every two months or so. That kind of an arrangement I can live with. What do you think?"

Murdock grinned, and put his arms around her. He kissed her with clear intent. She edged away.

"Really, what do you think of my suggestion?"

"I think it's a great idea. I also think that State should have you in the Middle East negotiating that Arab-Israeli thing. It would be settled in two weeks flat."

She laughed, and kissed him again.

"I think that was a yes," she said. "Now, as in any serious negotiations, we must seal the bargain. I think the bedroom is over there."

Murdock led the way. It was the best negotiations he'd been in for a long time, and the bargain-sealing lasted half the night.

The next three days flashed by so fast Murdock hardly remembered what training he and the SEALs went through. When the morning came for their departure, he had come in an hour late after a long good-bye with Ardith.

"I don't want you to go, but as a good Navy woman, I won't tell you that," she'd said. "I'll smile, and kiss you good-bye, and cry on my own damn time."

He'd kissed her again, put her in a cab for the airport, and driven his Bronco to the SEALs parking lot outside the quarterdeck. It was time.

It was a bare-bones trip. Each man took only his issue

weapon and alternates, but no ammunition. They had their combat vests and re-breathers, but no IBS—Inflatable Boat Small—or any grenades.

"I'm not sure how long it will take us to get there," Murdock said. "The Pacific is a big ocean, but there doesn't seem to be any hurry-up on this trip. We might even get fed on the way. We'll take along two MREs per man just in case. Any questions?"

"This floating bathtub will have everything we need if we get a hot call?" Jaybird asked.

"If they don't when we get there, I'll requisition it and have a COD fly it on board. The *Monroe* should have everything we need."

When they got to North Island Naval Air Station two miles through Coronado, they found a Gulfstream II jet waiting for them. The slightly modified large executive jet could take nineteen passengers.

It carried a Navy crew of three, and had a maximum ceiling of 42,000 feet and a top cruise speed of 581 miles an hour. The maximum range was 3,275 miles. Murdock figured they might make three stops: Honolulu, Wake Island, and Tokyo. He didn't even know if the U.S. had an airfield at Wake Island anymore.

Murdock looked over the craft as they waited to board. The low wing had a 25-degree leading-edge sweep, a 3-degree dihedral from the roots, and low wing fences at midspan.

The trailing edge showed one-piece, and single-slotted, Fowler flaps inboard of the inset ailerons.

The T-shaped tail had a broad, shallowly swept vertical fin with a small dorsal fillet and full-height rudder. On the top of the tail were swept, horizontal stabilizers with full-span elevators.

He knew it had dual Rolls-Royce turbofan engines with Rohr thrust reversers mounted on short stubs located high on the rear fuselage. It used wing tanks for fuel storage. The entry door was on the forward left side between the flight deck and the passengers' cabin. There were five oval porthole windows on each side of the fuselage.

He decided it would do. Better than a lumbering C-130 for the long flight. He figured the food service would be lousy.

A few minutes later, they climbed on board, stowed their vests and weapons, and settled down into real commercial-airliner-type seats for the ride. Everyone was safely on board when a crew chief checked them and nodded. A moment later a blue-clad woman came out of the flight deck and watched them for a minute.

"Oh, stewardess," a SEAL voice called.

The woman smiled, and turned so they could see the railroad tracks of a full lieutenant on her collar. She was grinning.

"An easy mistake to make, sailor, but don't do it again. I'm Lieutenant Frazier, and I'm your pilot on this milk run. We'll stop in Honolulu for you to stretch your legs and fill your stomachs. I hope you have a good flight."

11

Tuesday, 20 February

USS *Monroe*, CVN 81
Off Sendai, Japan
Murdock and his platoon settled into quarters on board the big aircraft carrier as it plowed north in moderate seas toward the Tsugaru Strait between the northern Japanese Island of Hokkaido and the big island of Honshu.

The jet had made three stops. Then, at a field near Tokyo, a COD had lifted them off the ground, and put them down on a pitching deck in choppy seas on board the carrier working north along the Japanese coast. It had been a good ride.

The carrier had been off Sendai steaming south when word came from CINCPAC to reverse directions. The quickest way to North Korea lay through the Tsugaru Strait between Honshu and Hokkaido, rather than going all the way down and around Honshu, and maybe even Kyushu, before turning north six hundred miles to come close to North Korea.

Stroh had sent them a packet of material giving background on the Korean situation, what the North had been doing, and how the U.S. and the South Koreans had responded. It didn't look good to Murdock. He had never trusted the North Koreans; now it looked like they were about to make good on an oft-threatened drive to unify the peninsula.

Once on board, Murdock and Jaybird worked with their carrier liaison, Lieutenant Commander Bolling, to draw the ammunition, additional weapons, and supplies that they wanted to have on hand for immediate selection in case they were alerted for a definite mission.

They brought in four IBSs, and left them as uninflated as they could be. Jaybird had his lists and requisition forms. He ordered wet suits for each man, extra cammies, a second SATCOM radio as a backup, and a hundred other items that the platoon might need if, or when, it went into action.

Murdock went to the wardroom, found an unused phone tap, and plugged in his laptop computer to send an E-mail to Master Chief MacKenzie back in Coronado.

"Master Chief MacKenzie. Request an E-mail report to MurdocSEAL@USSMonroe.Navy.mil. Will check my E-mail daily until we move into action. So far Mahanani is working well with the platoon." He had no unread mail, so he closed up and went back to his quarters.

The weird time change hit the platoon hard. They had crossed the International Date Line, and automatically they were about a day ahead. Not a whole day, but enough to ruin their sleep pattern for a day or two.

By the third day nothing new had come over Murdock's E-mail. They were back on schedule by then, and Murdock got the SEALs to an area they were assigned to on deck for PT and jogging. Murdock never got tired of watching the catapults throw the 74,000-pound Tomcats into the air. They went from a dead stop to something over 140 miles an hour in five seconds.

The big ship ran into some nasty weather just south of the strait, and had to lay off the tip of Honshu for a day before they entered the narrow Tsugaru Strait.

At 1043, Murdock was summoned to the Communications Center. Admiral Kenner, commander of the carrier task force, stood to one side looking worried.

"Murdock, you're on the horn to D.C." a captain said the moment the SEAL stepped into the room. "Somebody by the name of Stroh."

Murdock picked up the hand mike. "Murdock here."

"Good, they finally tracked you down. Things are blowing up over there. Not in Korea. We've got a hell of a problem up there in Japan, just north of you a ways. The *Monroe* and her carrier task force commander have new orders. Now you get yours. Your full platoon is now on standby alert.

"Briefly, some asshole general in the Japanese Ground Self Defense Force has gone ballistic and invaded the Kuril island nearest to Hokkaido. The Kuril Islands were formerly owned by Japan, but were deeded to Russia after World War II as reparations for damage done to Russia by the Japanese war machine. You're getting a fax with all the background on the area, including the anger between Japan and Russia over the islands.

"Our problem is, Japan doesn't have any kind of force to go in and take the general back home. *We* may have to. The *Monroe* has turned, and is now heading for the island of Kunashir, which this general now holds. He claims he has captured the small Russian military post on the island, and is holding the whole island for Japanese settlers to move in and reclaim ancient family property that was stolen from them by Russia. It's not a pretty picture."

"How many men does this general have on the island?" Murdock asked.

"No one is sure, but the figure of two hundred has been used, that being the number of Defense Force soldiers missing from posts in the northernmost section of Hokkaido. You've nothing to do right now but get ready. I'm told by the admiral that it will take the carrier about ten hours to get there at the best flank speed he can maintain under the current weather conditions. He will have aircraft monitoring the area soon, and reporting back. Right now we're in negotiations with Japan on exactly what they want us to do, what we want to do, and what will be the best for everyone, including keeping the Russians from doing anything stupid.

"As you might expect, the Russians are screaming at the top of their tremendously loud voices about their homeland being invaded, and they want immediate withdrawal. The only problem with that is, the Japanese military has no control over General Raiden Nishikawa, the rogue warrior now occupying the island of Kunashir."

"Japan doesn't want to go in shooting down its own troops, is that part of it?" Murdock asked.

"Precisely. It doesn't want *us* to waste the Japanese rebel troops either. It's looking for some other solution before Russia blasts the small force into DNA with rockets, missiles, and strafing attacks."

"Roger that, Stroh. We'll put together three SEAL scenarios, and have something to talk about. It's the island of Kunashir, about two hundred invaders, local Russian military captured or dead, and Russia furious. What are the Russians doing?"

"At last reports they're sending a battle group out of Vladivostock, including the nuclear-powered aircraft carrier *Ataman*, NP-400. The name *Ataman* means 'head man' in Russia, usually refers to a Cossack. Our people say its the best-equipped, most powerful carrier they have and with the latest Russian planes in their fleet."

"How far is it from the island?" Murdock asked.

"We've worked that out here, Mr. Stroh," Admiral Kenner said. "Vladivostock is roughly six hundred eighty miles from the island. If they can make twenty-three knots, that would mean about thirty hours to get there. Of course, they will have aircraft in the area long before that."

"So you'll have the high ground," Stroh said. "That's all we know here now, Murdock. We'll keep you up to date on developments. Our people are faxing you some background on this situation now. It should be there by the time your people can run down to the communications room. Good luck."

They signed off, and the six men in the room looked at each other.

"We could take out the two hundred men with rockets and missiles, and put a holding force on the island in an hour once we're there," Admiral Kenner said. "But that's not the job they want done. Damned diplomacy again. We'll never be rid of it."

"How have the Russians reacted?" Murdock asked.

The admiral frowned. "Our latest report is that they have sent out a flurry of broadcasts aimed at Kunashir Island. They have demanded that the Japanese general pull his troops off the island and give it back to the Russian military. They have warned General Nishikawa that they have a task force heading north from Vladivostock with enough firepower to pulverize every Japanese invader on the island and to thwart any reinforcements that might be on the way from Japan. They are not at all happy, and from the tone of the radio messages we've heard, sound just as trigger-happy as all hell."

"I'm not sure how the SEALs can help," Murdock said. "Usually we don't operate against friendlies. That's evidently what the Japanese government considers this general and his invaders to be. The Russians won't have any problem with blasting them straight into Hell."

A captain who Murdock didn't know spoke up. "We'll have to consider it friendly territory, and go into a defensive mode against the Russians. That's going to go over like a fragger with them. We'll have to put a defensive air cover over the place, then spread out our force off the island where the main town is and the Japanese troops are situated. Sounds damned near impossible."

Murdock stood. "Gentlemen, I better get with my men and start some advance planning, what we can do and what we can't. I'll have some suggestions in four hours."

A Captain who Murdock figured was the CAG spoke up. "Admiral, weather tells me these strong winds should moderate in an hour. It's now a little after thirteen hundred. Sunset up here is about seventeen hundred. We'll have time to get a pair of Tomcats over the site and report back."

"Do it," the admiral said.

Murdock left to talk to his men, and try to figure out what they could do to help relieve the situation that had all the elements of an international incident that could pit the U.S. nuclear carrier task force against the Russian group.

The SEALs had been given a large classroom for their operations. Murdock met them there. Jaybird handed him a big envelope with his name on it.

"Faxes, the messenger told me."

Murdock told the men the situation. "So that's the dope. We may have to go in there. If we do, how do we go in, and how do we get this rogue general out of there without shooting half of his command? Work on it. I want to check out these faxes."

He scanned the six sheets, then figured the men should know about them, and called them around.

"Listen up. This is the situation we'll be walking into. The Kuril Islands are Russian territory, a string of islands that extends seven hundred and fifty miles from the southern tip of the Kamchatka Peninsula south to the northeastern corner of Hokkaido, the northernmost of the Japanese islands. The chain separates the Pacific Ocean from the Sea of Okhotsk. There are fifty-six islands of any size that cover about six thousand square miles.

"They are part of the Rim of Fire around the Pacific Ocean, and have a hundred volcanoes on them, with thirty-eight still active. Earthquakes and tidal waves are common.

"The climate is severe, usually long, cold, and snowy winters followed by cool, foggy, and wet summers. Vegetation ranges from tundra in the north to dense forests on the large southern islands. Crab fishing is virtually the only occupation. Some vegetables can be grown on the southern islands.

"The main town is Golovnino on the southernmost island of Kunashir.

"This island chain was part of Japan for centuries. In 1945 the chain was ceded to Russia as reparations for damage done to Russia by the Japanese during World War II. All of the Japanese on the island chain were taken back to Japan, and Russians were brought in to replace them."

Murdock looked around. "Kind of like if we gave Florida to Cuba because of the Bay of Pigs invasion. The Japanese are ancestor worshipers. Family lines and family graves are of major importance. Thousands of Japanese lost their family graves when they were forced away from their long-time homes in the Kuril Islands.

"As I said, a Japanese general in the Japanese Ground Self

Defense Force invaded the closest island, and one of the largest, named Kunashir, with an estimated two hundred men, and now controls the island.

"Russia is really pissed, and is sending a big carrier force north. Our carrier battle group is steaming up that way, and should beat them to the island by something like ten hours. Aircraft from both sides soon will be buzzing over the island. Things could get nasty.

"So to repeat my question: If Japan says we need to go in and solve the problem, just what the hell do we do, and how do we do it?"

Jaybird cleared his throat. "Skipper, we've been working on it. Have to be a surprise move at night, and silent in the IBS. We go in with all weapons with silencers and try to nail down this Jap general. When we get his ass, his people will fold in a minute."

"Yeah, might work," Horse Ronson said. "But why not just drop in a few cruise missiles, blow them all to Hell, and then go in with our platoon and mop up. Fucking lot quicker and easier."

"You're forgetting what I told you earlier," Murdock said. "So far the Japanese government does not consider these men as enemies. They don't want to simply blow them away and let Russia move back in. They don't want to lose the troops, or kill off a few hundred Russian civilians who are bound to get in the way."

Doc Ellsworth groaned. "So what do we do, arm wrestle these guys while they're shooting at us? How in hell can we do that?"

"Hey, if it was easy, they'd let the Marines do it," Ed DeWitt said. That brought a round of cheers.

"Now, we get down to business," Murdock said. "We have to go in silently. The IBS sounds the best for that. We'll need to know exactly where the military HQ is on the island. They're probably using the one the Russians built. But where is it? Will the Ground Self Defense Force troops have sentries and men on guard? We've got to know a lot more before we can do much more detailed planning."

12

Tuesday, 20 February

Military Headquarters
Golovnino, Kunashir Island
Kuril Island Chain
General Raiden Nishikawa hovered over his best radio operator in the communications room of the concrete-block building that had housed the Russian military command on the island. It now served as his headquarters. He had broadcast his demands hours ago, and waited for responses.

Twice already he had seen American jet fighters sweep over the island. He had given strict instructions not to fire at any aircraft unless it fired first. The two twin-tailed planes had made three low-level runs, then climbed high, evidently on a continuing surveillance.

He had no objection to that. He had received another set of orders from his former commanding officer on Hokkaido. They were terse and angry. They told him to cease his aggression against Russia, to disarm his men, free the Russian prisoners, and return to Japanese soil within four hours.

General Nishikawa had not even acknowledged receiving the message. His proclamation of independence had gone out on the radio more than ten hours ago. He had broadcast it on military frequencies in English, Japanese, and Russian. He was sure that the whole world now knew of his victory in liberating his home island of Kunashir. Already he had found the site of the graves of his grandparents and great-grandparents. The graves themselves had been obliterated, and a school now stood over the spot. He had prayed for an hour over the hallowed ground three times already. He would go again soon.

Others in his command had found the sites of the graves of their ancestors, and had paid their respects as well. More than half of his men here had ancestors in graves on the island.

Capturing the island had been simple. General Nishikawa had planned it carefully. He'd known there would be a U.S. carrier battle group in the Honshu area. He'd also checked the Russian calendar, and had selected a two-day Russian holiday. Three quarters of the Russian military would be on leave; those on duty would be on a traditional two-day drunk. It had looked remarkably simple on paper.

He had landed his two hundred troops on the pier at the island's largest town, Golovnino. The only two military sentries on duty had been so drunk they couldn't stand. He had tied them up, and left them there. He and a hundred men had simply walked into the military command post, and found only a dozen Russian soldiers there, none of them with a weapon. The officer in command had been a new lieutenant, and half drunk. Two shots had been fired in the whole invasion. One by an invader not familiar with his weapon, and one by a Russian sentry who wasn't quite as drunk as he seemed. No one had been wounded by either round.

Now General Nishikawa ordered the commo sergeant to bring him a typed report on all radio transmissions they'd received. He marched back to his office, cold and spartan in furnishings. Not at all like his large, comfortable office on Hokkaido. He sat at his desk, looking at the results of his men's sweeps of the outlying posts. The island was more than 160 kilometers long, but never more than fifteen kilometers wide.

Most of it was heavily forested on one side, with little room for any agriculture. There were two military posts out about fifty kilometers, but both had been captured by his troops, with only two dead Russian soldiers. He was secure. Until the big powers decided what to do. He was convinced that Japan would not send any force against him. Many in the government had spoken out about Russia returning the Kuril Islands to their rightful place as part of the Japanese homeland.

What Russia, and even the United States, might do was the problem. He hoped that the U.S. would steam the battle group northward, and serve as a block against the Russian force. If it came down to an attack by any of the three powers, his small force would be smashed within minutes. He didn't think that would happen.

There would be a diplomatic settlement. Perhaps Japan would win the southern half of the island chain, perhaps even just take back Kunashir, and let Russia keep the northern, mostly unpopulated, and smaller islands. That seemed reasonable.

All he wanted was to be able to worship at the graves of his ancestors. He was here now, but wondered how long he could stay. Nishikawa was an inch under six feet tall. The Japanese on Hokkaido had been known for being the tallest Japanese since the start of the century. He knew Ainu blood flowed in his veins, but most of the Ainu characteristics had been lost through intermarriage.

The Ainu were the earliest residents of Hokkaido, the Kuril Islands, and the large Russian Sakhalin Island, and they were not related to the Mongoloid native people of the other Japanese islands. But none of that mattered now. Now his ancestors were far more important. That, and what the Russians would do when they arrived. He knew they would be coming. A knock sounded on his door, and the communications sergeant came through.

"Sir, a radio message to you from the Russians." He handed a typed sheet to the general.

"General Nishikawa. We know who you are, and why you have invaded sacred Russian soil. We know of your small force, and how you captured our island. We do not wish to start World War Three. However, you must, I repeat MUST, take your troops off our island and return to Japan.

"We will allow you seven days to do this. Our military forces are powerful. Even now they are heading for Kunashir. Our aircraft will be monitoring your movements. If you do not evacuate our island within the seven days, your force will be crushed with powerful missile and aircraft attacks, and you will be annihilated to a man. There is no room for compromise. You are occupying sacred Russian soil and if you do not leave, you must suffer the fatal consequences." The message was signed by Captain Admiral Vladimir Rostow.

"Dismissed," General Nishikawa said, and the sergeant did a smart about-face and hurried out of the room. General Nishikawa opened the desk drawer, and took out a framed photograph. He stared at it, then smiled and touched each of the faces in the picture: his wife and their three children, two boys and a girl. He looked at it again, smiled, and brushed tears from his eyes, then gently put the treasure back in the drawer.

There was still a chance. The U.S. might step in and serve as a buffer between the island and the Russians. The Japanese Diet might pass some quick legislation to make his move legal. Russia might be willing to back down on its threat.

A slim chance still existed that he might have his dream. He would send all of the Russians on Kunashir Island on to other islands in the chain, then bring in his relatives and as many of those Japanese who had ancestors resting on this hard rock of an island who wanted to come. A chance. Yes, perhaps a good chance.

He called for Major Hitachi, his second in command. He had promoted him the day they embarked for the island. Hitachi was short, a little heavy, a career soldier, and excellent with the men. He also had ancestors buried on this island. They had yet to find Hitachi's ancestors' graves, or where their graves might have been.

"Major, I'm taking the utility vehicle and going to the school. I'll be back in an hour. Keep track of anything coming in by radio. Ignore all transmissions from Defense Forces radio."

"Yes, sir," Hitachi said. "I'll keep track of it."

General Nishikawa left at once. He stepped into the

Russian-style jeep, and the driver gunned away. He knew without asking where the general wanted to go.

First they stopped at an unused crab processing plant that had been turned into a prisoner-of-war compound. Fifty-six Russian soldiers were held there, including their commander, a Russian major who had suffered a minor injury when he had fallen down in a drunken stupor while being transported from an elaborate party the night of his capture.

General Nishikawa inspected the guards, looked in the large room where the prisoners were held, and then talked to his lieutenant in charge of the captives.

"Yes, sir. All is quiet. The men seem to think that they will not be held here long. They say in this cold weather it's much better to be in here rather than standing guard in the snow and ice. They assure me that it will snow again soon, and the temperature will drop well below zero degrees."

"Keep them locked down, keep them fed and warm. We are not the enemy of these men."

They drove from there directly to the school, now empty by decree. On the far side of the playground, the earth had been leveled. General Nishikawa paced off twenty steps from the corner of the play area, and put a mark in the soil. He stepped off sixty paces from the pine tree growing at the side of the playground, and put another mark. Between the two had been a small hill that had contained the tombs of his family for over a hundred years. Now there was nothing but bare earth, and the marks of dozens of children who usually played over this area.

Tears squeezed out of his eyes as the general knelt in prayer on the sacred ground. He didn't want to admit it, but it must be that the hill, and his ancestor's remains, had been bulldozed into the small gully that had been directly in front of the hill. Now the gully was filled all the way to the school.

He wailed and cried openly for the souls of his departed ancestors, and for the evil that the heathen Russians had heaped on their souls by desecrating and destroying the graves.

For an hour he knelt on the ground praying.

By the time he returned to his military headquarters, there

were three long typed messages on his desk. Each had come over the radio, since he had cut the telephone cable from Kunashir to Hokkaido. He settled down to read the messages. He knew they would be denunciations from the Russians, from the Americans, and from the senile and impotent Japanese politicians in the Diet.

Before he could read them, a thundering roar shook the building. He rushed outside where two guards pointed away from the headquarters.

"Aircraft," one said.

Three minutes later, two jet fighters again came in low over the town. The fighters did not fire, but their afterburners shook the whole community. As they flashed directly over the military headquarters building, General Nishikawa saw the identifying red stars on the wings.

"Ah, so. The Russians have arrived," the general said. The planes made one more thundering low flyover, then headed northwest for the Soya Strait between Hokkaido and the Russian island of Sakhalin. That way they would not penetrate the Japanese airspace on the way back to their Russian aircraft carrier somewhere to the southwest.

General Nishikawa hurried back to his office to read the three dispatches. The one on top was from Tokyo. The Prime Minister himself ordered him to end his invasion of Kunashir, and return his force to Hokkaido.

"If you do not comply with this order, you will be declared a traitor to Japan, and will be dealt with according to Japanese parliamentary law. You and your men will be outlaws, branded as cowards, and rebels, and forever denied entry into Japan. For the good of Japan, cease this outrageous invasion, and return to Japan at once. I guarantee you leniency if you return within two days."

The message was signed by the Prime Minister himself.

He could not do it. Nishikawa had sworn a vow of vengeance against the government that had destroyed the graves of his ancestors. He would not give up until he had caused them as much damage as they had done to his family.

The second message was sent by the United States ambassador in Tokyo.

"General Nishikawa: We appreciate your situation, and your honorable try to recover the graves of your ancestors; however, we do not agree with the way you have gone about it. We have a battle group steaming your way. The ships, planes, and men should be off your eastern shore shortly. We will attempt to put a screen around your headquarters with an air cover, and Naval ships along both coasts near the southern end of the island.

"If requested by the Japanese government, we will take action against you to subdue your force, and remove you from the island within the seven-day limit the Russians have imposed. It will be your option whether you oppose our forces or not. If you choose to fire upon our troops and aircraft, we will respond with all of our capability.

"We hope that we do not have to engage your forces in combat; however, we are ready, and ultimately able, to do so. We look to your timely response to our message."

It was signed by the United States ambassador to Japan, Lloyd Contreras.

Nishikawa stared at the message and shook his head. "Mr. Ambassador, I'm sorry, but I'm not leaving my ancestors again. This time somebody will have to blow my dead body off this island. This is my ancestral home, and I intend to either live here or die here."

He wrote down the same words and started to take them to the sergeant in the radio room. Then he stopped. Let them wonder. Yes, let them guess at what he would do. It would last longer that way. For a moment he wondered if he only had five more days to live. It was possible. General Nishikawa shrugged.

The third message was from the Russians.

"Our planes have flown over your complex by now. We know where you are, and our computers are plotting the flight of our missiles, which will hit you with pinpoint accuracy. There is no hope that you can win. Give up now, and retain your life and the lives of your men. You have made your statement. The Russian government has always been ready and willing to discuss the future of the Kuril Islands. That offer still stands.

"You still have your transport, the small boats you nego-tiated the channel in to arrive at Kunashir. Move to them now, within the hour, and you'll be safe in Japan before sunset.

"If you do not comply within the seven-day deadline we gave you, the military headquarters there, and any of your troops we can find, will be blasted into eternity, and quicker than you ever thought you will be visiting with your ancestors."

General Nishikawa looked up as someone knocked on his door.

"Come."

The communications sergeant hurried in. He smiled.

"General, sir. We have figured out the Russian radios here. We now have a network of the handheld units in four outposts. The lookouts posted make a net call every hour on the hour, and anytime that they see anything suspicious.

"The first reports came in just now. They can see no planes or ships, and everything with the local population is calm. There are enough food stores in the kitchen area to feed our people for just over a week. Then we'll need a new food source."

"Thanks, Sergeant. There won't be any need for any more food. A week should do us fine. You've read the radio messages. We'll be lucky to still be eating anything after a week."

The sergeant saluted, did a smart about-face, and left the room.

General Nishikawa stared at the three messages spread out on his desk. He didn't trust the Japanese government.

The United States spoke softly, but carried a huge stick.

The Russians spoke bluntly, but had given him a week.

He could not figure out why, but he was the most afraid of the United States' message. The big battle force, with missiles, rockets, and eighty-five aircraft, would be offshore within a few hours. He had to decide how to deal with them. The Russians would wait. It would be the Americans who presented him with the immediate threat.

He took out the two swords of the samurai and held them, the long one and the deadly shorter blade. Yes, at least one of his ancestors had been a samurai. He had been a military retainer of a Japanese *diamyo* practicing the chivalric code of Bushido. Honor above all. He stared at the smaller blade, then gently put it in the wooden sheath, then the silk wrappings, and placed it in the bottom desk drawer. Soon he would carry it with him at all times. Soon, but not yet.

13

Tuesday, 20 February

USS *Monroe*, CVN 81
Off Hokkaido, Japan

The sixteen SEALs sat near the bow of the big aircraft carrier near the starboard side, usually reserved for parked aircraft. The area had been cleared, and the SEALs were about to have a live firing drill. Each man sat on the deck with six magazines for his particular weapon in front of him. Each magazine had only three rounds in it.

"You know the drill," Murdock told them from where he sat in the middle of the line of SEALs. "As soon as you hear me fire, you fire your weapon, empty the magazine. Then eject the magazine, and load the next one. Fire and eject, load and fire, and eject until you are finished with the six magazines.

"Machine gunners, fire out the ten rounds on the end of one belt, load and charge the second belt, and fire ten rounds in two five-round bursts. Speed in reloading is the key here. Last man done gets thrown overboard."

"You wish," somebody cracked, and they all broke up.

Murdock went on. "You guys with the H&K G-11's. Fire two three-round bursts and reload. Do that three times. Everyone up to speed?"

He looked around, lifted his H&K MP-5SD, and fired over the rail into the Pacific Ocean. At once the fifteen other weapons roared, and the stuttering of the three-round bursts caught a lot of sailors on the deck of the big ship by surprise. After a moment's hesitation, the work on the huge floating airfield went on as scheduled, with two Tomcat F-l4's launched off the deck by the catapults.

Murdock slammed the second magazine into his subgun and fired, punched out the empty, and loaded again.

Jaybird Sterling gave a rebel yell as he finished his sixth clip. He was the first one done. The machine gunners and the caseless-round G-11's finished next, and then the rest of the submachine guns, the sniper rifles, and the Colt carbines in that order.

Murdock checked his wristwatch. "Yeah, okay, nothing spectacular. Now clean up the brass and let's do some double time up and back over here out of the way."

They worked out for another hour; then Murdock sent them below for the evening meal. He found a note on his stateroom door that he was wanted in the admiral's cabin. The door was open to a small outer office where a lieutenant commander sat behind a desk.

"Commander Murdock. Right this way. The admiral is interested in what you've come up with. He also wants to ground you on some other details."

Inside the admiral's cabin, it looked more like a luxury liner suite. A couch along one wall, a large desk and a swivel chair, even a bookcase along the other bulkhead.

Murdock came to attention in front of the desk. "Lieutenant Commander Murdock reporting as ordered, sir."

"At ease, Commander." The admiral pointed to a chair. The rough command presence was gone for the moment. Small worry lines showed around the corners of the admiral's eyes, and he seemed to have aged five years since Murdock had seen him.

"Damned touchy situation we're heading into, Murdock. I want you to know that. Our battle fleet is going to be between that Japanese invader of part of Mother Russia and a Russian battle fleet. Things could get downright dicey."

When do we arrive off the island, Admiral?"

"Another three hours. Be dark by then. The seas have calmed, and we have constant surveillance over the little town, but that's all we can do right now. I'm hoping you have a quick way to go in and get the general out of there before the Russian Navy pulls up just outside of our pickets."

"Afraid not, sir. Our best scenario is to go in silently in our inflatable boats. Get ashore without being seen, then try to take down the command headquarters with stun grenades and fancy footwork. If we have to treat these invaders as friendlies, it really ties our hands. We're usually more of a shoot-and-scoot kind of operation."

"I was afraid of that, Commander. We've got one ELINT Viking up now. The Russians are less than two hundred miles away coming at flank speed. They've made four overflights of the island, just to let us know that they can do it. They're coming in from the west, which means they have to go around Cape Shiretoko, then motor about fifty kilometers down Nemuro Strait between the cape and Kunashir Island. They would still have to go around the southern tip of the island to come up on the town of Golovnino, where the Japanese invaders are.

"My guess is they will bypass the cape, stay out another twenty kilometers or so, and come in on the east coast on the Pacific side. Which means we have a little more time. We're talking about eight hours, maybe less if they push it.

"I've been warned by CINCPAC to be extremely careful about taking any action against the Russians. If they shoot first, we are authorized to return fire in kind if one of our aircraft or ships is in deadly peril."

The admiral let out a long sigh, picked up a much-chewed cigar, and clamped it in his mouth. He didn't light it.

"Shoot and scoot, yeah, I like that. Hell of a good way of doing this business. Only we can't, not on this one." He looked at Murdock, who suddenly had a whole new perspective on this level of command. "You have any more ideas on this fucking island?"

"Forget Japanese sensitivities and drop a pair of missiles on the command headquarters, then go in and mop up and airlift out any living Japanese, and leave the place to the Russians by the time they drop anchor off the town."

The admiral laughed. "Don't I wish I could. CINCPAC would have me by the balls before I could radio in an after-action report. I'd be retired in Coronado before you could flick your Bic."

A phone on the desk beeped twice. The admiral picked it up and listened. "Yes, I'm coming down. Tell those young men to keep their cool."

The admiral stood, his game face back in place. "I've got to get down to TFCC. You might want to tag along."

Murdock hurried forward to follow the admiral.

The TFCC is the Tactical Flag Command Center. It contained tactical display screens showing what ships and planes were where in his command.

A short walk later, the admiral and Murdock stepped inside the center, and both stared at the display screen.

"How close?" Admiral Kenner asked Captain Olson, the CAG.

The Carrier Air Wing Commander checked the screen. "Two bogies, sir, probably from the Russian carrier still out about eighty miles from the tip of Hokkaido. Their course seems to be set just to miss the Japanese island. Estimated speed about seven hundred knots. We have two Tomcats on an intercept course with contact somewhere past the point of Hokkaido in approximately twelve minutes."

"Get them on tactical," the admiral said.

Ten seconds later the call went out. "Red Tomboy, this is Home Base."

The response came at once.

"Home Base, yeah. We've got those two bogies on a hot meet. What the fuck are we supposed to do?"

Admiral Kenner took the hand mike. "Red Tomboy, this is Admiral Kenner. Do not initiate any action. Do not lock on with radar. Make it a flyby-and-wave. Absolutely do not engage."

"That's a Roger, Home Base. No engagement. Should we turn and bird-dog them?"

"Red Tomboy, maintain loose contact, don't attempt to escort or influence their flight direction."

"Roger, Home Base. Out."

Admiral Kenner handed the set back to Captain Olson. The admiral again studied the screen that showed his ship placement.

"All our units in their proper locations?"

"Right, sir," the watch officer said. "Everyone in the specified protection screen."

"Good. That task force could have a Russian Boomer along with it. We've got to be especially alert. What's our ETA on the island?"

"Less than three hours now, sir. We've sent out signals for the spread of our ships. We'll be four miles off shore."

"I'll wait for the intercept, Captain Olson," the admiral said.

It was a sit-down room with all the video screens at chest height, and a shelf for work areas below them. Murdock had never seen this part of a carrier in action. He watched the lines on the screen start to converge.

Suddenly he was glad he was just a lieutenant commander, without the responsibility for the carrier task force and the lives and welfare of ten thousand men and a billion dollars worth of hardware that the admiral had.

The lines on the screen almost met; then both veered slightly until they were parallel but looked almost on top of each other.

"Can't be separated by more than maybe a hundred feet, sir," the radar specialist said.

Admiral Kenner grunted.

The lines continued in a straight line.

"Heading is still directly for the northernmost point of Hokkaido," a second tech said.

The admiral turned to another console. "Let's try to bounce a signal off our ELINT and try to raise the commander of the Russian task force. It's time we had a talk. Don't we have an expert Russian translator on board?"

The watch officer frowned. "Yes, sir. I'll round him up. A

Chief Johnson, as I recall." He turned and talked to another operator, who left his station and hurried out of the TFCC.

Three minutes later, the translator was there, looking at the message the admiral had written out. He went over it four times, then nodded at the console operator.

The chief spoke in Russian: "Hailing the Russian task force now steaming up the Sea of Japan toward Hokkaido. This is Admiral Kenner of the USS *Monroe*, CVN 81. We urgently request that you respond to our call so we can have a conversation about our mutual problem."

The chief released the mike switch.

Everyone in the TFCC waited.

The dead air time stretched out.

"A minute," the chief said. He looked at the watch commander, who held up his finger in a wait sign.

"It's been two minutes," Admiral Kenner said. "Repeat the message, word for word."

"Admiral, we're on an international hailing frequency," the chief said. "I'm almost certain they monitor that frequency. We should be able to raise them on it. They may need some time to decide how to respond."

"Do it again," Kenner said.

The translator again spoke in Russian into the microphone. When he ended the message they waited.

A minute later the speaker came to life. The words were in English. "Admiral Kenner. May I offer my compliments on your seamanship. This is Admiral Vladimir Rostow, leader of Task Force Twelve now moving toward Kuril Islands. I see no need for us to talk. This is a Russian problem, not one for the United States. It is our island that has been invaded. We have given the renegades seven days to leave the island or face total annihilation. There is no room for negotiations, only the total withdrawal of the invaders by our deadline. I trust this makes our position clear."

The men in the TFCC looked at one another as if the Russian admiral's words were about what they expected.

Admiral Kenner pointed at the chief to continue. He picked up the hand microphone and went on reading in Russian from the prepared statement:

"Admiral Rostow. I appreciate your position, but now is the time for words and not bullets. We are now off the coast of Kunashir Island, and will shortly be in communication with General Nishikawa. I understand your concern. This is a minute force led by a highly emotional traditionalist Japanese. I feel there is a strong probability that we can talk him out of his position so your military men on the site can re-establish Russian control. We look forward to working with you on this delicate problem. Thank you."

There was a moment of silence; then another voice came back in English. "Admiral Rostow requests that this channel be kept open and monitored twenty-four hours a day for any emergency. Signing off."

The admiral lowered his brows and firmed his jaw. He turned, and looked at the screen showing the four aircraft.

"Sir, the aircraft are approaching the islands. They were north of Hokkaido, then swung south toward the first Kuril island."

14

Tuesday, 20 February

USS *Monroe*, CVN 81
Off Hokkaido, Japan

Murdock settled into an out-of-the-way spot in the Tactical Flag Command Center and watched developments. He checked the screen on the tactical display. Each ship and plane in the fleet was shown, and evidently all was going according to plan. The big carrier was nearing the top end of the northernmost Japanese island of Hokkaido.

Now all they had to do was slip between some Russian-held islands just beyond the point, and motor about twenty-five miles west to get to the target island. He wasn't sure how close the whole task force would come to the island.

The radio speaker came to life on the tactical frequency.

"Home Base, this is Red Tomboy." The voice was Lieutenant Harley "Red" Remington in his F14 Tomcat high overhead.

"Home Base here. Go, Tomboy." It was the CAG speaking.

"Guess you're following our pictures. Our visitors are still coming in at Mach One from the southwest. Same orders?"

"You're on a meet-up course with them in about four minutes. Same situation. Two of their planes buzzed that little target town a couple of hours ago."

"This still a meet-and-greet program?"

"Roger that, Red Tomboy. Unless you can talk Russian."

"No way, Home Base. We'll monitor. Out."

High in the daylight sky, Red Remington switched back to the intercom, and talked with his RIO in the backseat of the Tomcat.

"Pokey, we still got that pair of bandits coming in?"

"Sure as little girls have small tits. Steady and on target. They will just miss the tip of Hokkaido's Shiretoko Point, so they won't overfly Japanese territory, and then be a nickel's worth from Kunashir Island."

"Where do we meet them assholes?" Remington asked.

"In that little strait between the island and Hokkaido, maybe halfway."

"You ever seen a couple of hot-loaded MiGs up close and personal before, Pokey?"

"Shit, no. Neither have you. These guys could blast us out of the sky."

"Yeah, and we can return the favor, and they both know it. Watch for any lock-on. He locks his radar on us, we quick do the same and fire first. A fucking radar lock-on is a hostile act, and gives us weapons free. That's right out of the CAG's mouth."

The RIO snorted. "Hell, he ain't about to lock on. He's way out here away from his buddies. Two on two, but we might have eight or ten more Cats up here somewhere just waiting."

Remington checked his instruments, then the heads-up display, and looked out where the MiGs should be. Nothing.

"I've got them on my screen," the radar intercept officer said from the backseat. "Had them for a few seconds. Still straight and on course."

They were quiet for a minute. Red Remington grinned as he pushed the Tomcat through the air at slightly over Mach One. He loved this plane, wouldn't be doing anything else in the world even if he could. There was a relationship between the pilot and the aircraft that he couldn't explain. It was damned near spiritual.

"They both are making their turn, so they're just past that point, and coming around to a southeast heading," Remington heard in his headset. "You should have them visually before long."

Remington scanned the sky ahead the way he had done countless times before. Still nothing.

"Altitude? We on the right level here?"

"They could be a hundred feet above or below us," the RIO said.

"Got them visual at one o'clock," Red said. "I better check with TFCC." He switched to tactical, and at once received a call from the ship.

"Red Tomboy, you have visual?"

"Just obtained, Home Base. Does he turn or do we?"

"You ever played chicken, Red Tomboy?"

"Not at this speed." There was a pause. "Oh, yeah, he's drifting to his left, he'll overfly the island that way."

"Get on his starboard wing and stay five hundred feet off and keep with him. Be a good host, and show your visitor around. Take no hostile action unless they lock on. Confirmed?"

"That's a Roger, Home Base. He's turning more, and we're with him. Six hundred feet, and closing to five hundred. Straight and level."

Back in the TFCC, Murdock followed the exchange closely. If anything went wrong there would be no need for the third platoon of SEAL Team Seven. He could see the radar tracks as the four planes angled southeast toward the target island.

"I'll be damned, Captain," Red Tomboy said. "The near MiG is moving in closer to me. The fucker is fifty feet away. I can see the bastard through the canopy."

"Stay steady, Red Tomboy. We don't want to play wing-tickle with him at your speed."

"I'll Roger that."

The air went dead for a few seconds.

"Shit, Captain, he's motioning me. He's pointing down with his finger, then he's waving for me to follow."

"Pull back, Red Tomboy. Pull back, and let him go down, and follow him. Stay with the two of them."

"Oh yeah. We will, Home Base."

Captain Irving Olson, the CAG, watched the images on the radar screen. He was the boss of all the planes on board, a pilot himself who now had trouble getting in enough air time to stay qualified.

"Second contact," he said to the men in the room. "So far, so good. At least we aren't shooting at each other. So that's about it, Admiral. Second contact, no gunplay, follow the leader. My guess is the MiGs will buzz the military HQ down there the way the first two did to let that Jap general know they're still around."

"Let's hope that's all that it is."

"Yes, sir, I agree. How about sending a message to the Russian admiral asking him to curtail his overflights until we get this worked out a little better? In another two hours, we'll have ships around the southern tip of the island where that little town is. We don't want some trigger-happy sky jockey to start shooting up there."

"I hope the message to Admiral Rostow covered that, Captain."

"It didn't specifically mention aircraft, but I guess the same message would apply. We'll just wait and see what happens."

They watched the four blips on the screen approach, then pass over the small town on Kunashir Island, then curl around and climb away.

"Home Base, looks like the guest shot is over. The Ruskie guy came up close and waved good-bye. Then they both kicked in their afterburners, and ripped back the way they had come."

"We copy that, Red Tomboy. You need a drink?"

"Getting under half a tank. Probably should send us some juice or get us back home."

"We'll send out a tanker. Resume your station over the south end of the island."

"That's a Roger, sir."

The CAG was just ready to reach for the phone when it buzzed. He picked it up.

"Yes, sir," he listened. "Holy shit. Confirmed?"

He pushed the ship's telephone tight to his ear.

"Yes, right away." He passed the phone to Admiral Kenner, who listened, then hung up.

"Gentlemen, we're in a state of alert. We have unconfirmed but substantial reports of a Russian OSCAR, an attack sub, in the vicinity. He's been shadowing us for two days as near as the ASW people can figure. They weren't sure what it was. He's been playing up and down in the thermal layer and staying just far enough out of range, but today the layer double-crossed him and one of our 3-SBs with a MAD boom that trails fifteen feet in back of the plane got a good fix on him."

The 3-SB is a Lockheed antisubmarine-warfare plane originally built during the Cold War as a submarine hunter/killer. It was upgraded to its "B" classification early in the 1980's. In addition to its acoustic ability, it's a superb surface surveillance and command control platform.

It's armed with APS-137 ISAR radar, and Forward Looking Infrared Radar. It can carry Harpoon antiship missiles, MK-46 torpedoes, and sixty sonobuoys. The plane has a sophisticated acoustic sensor suite monitoring any sonobuoys it drops, and uses the Magnetic Anomaly Detector.

"The crew picked up more than enough signals today to generate their suspicions," the admiral said. "We're not sure where their OSCAR went or what he's up to, but that changes things drastically for us."

Murdock frowned. "How?"

"For one thing, we won't thread our way through the line of islands between us and Kunashir. We'll want to keep more maneuvering room in case we need it. That means we'll go farther north and around the fifth island and this side of the sixth. Then we'll still have maneuvering room, and our shield ships can maintain positions around the *Monroe*."

Murdock nodded. "An OSCAR—that's the Russians' biggest, deadliest sub?"

"One of them, Commander. She has nuclear-tipped torpedoes. If just one of those hits our hull at any point, it would blow us out of the water and vaporize everything for a mile around. You see why we're concerned."

The admiral was talking with men at the displays.

Later in Admiral Kenner's quarters, he and a yeoman worked over a radio message to the commander of the Russian fleet.

The admiral had written down what he wanted to convey, and the yeoman put it into as polite terms as he could muster. When he finished writing, he read it to the admiral.

"To, Admiral Vladimir Rostow of the Russian fleet on board the *Ataman*, NP-400, aircraft carrier. Dear Admiral. I am Vice Admiral Nathan Kenner of the USS *Monroe*, CVN-81. Two of your aircraft just met with two of ours, and all four did a flyby on the Russian island of Kunashir. No offensive action was taken by anyone. It is our hope that you will allow the U.S. planes to monitor the island without the presence of Russian aircraft. We also hope that there will be no possible conflict between our two forces.

"We will keep planes over the island on a twenty-four-hour basis, and inform you directly of any activity by the Japanese now occupying your Russian territory.

"We will cooperate with you in every way we can to solve this problem without the use of any hostile action against the Japanese invaders of your island. We understand you have given them a seven-day departure deadline, now two days old.

"Please respond."

Admiral Kenner listened to the words, made two small changes, and had the yeoman take it to the Communications Center, where it would be broadcast in Russian and English to be sure the Russians would hear it.

Admiral Kenner did not mention the Oscar-class submarine. He was delighted that his ASW men had spotted it, but he frowned in concern at the same time. Why was it shadowing his task force? Was it practicing to see how close it could come without detection? Or was it in the process of working out an attack plan that it would carry out in the near future, as a part of a general attack by Soviet forces in several parts of the world?

No, that was not logical. Russia did not have the capability to fight a global war. They were economically strapped. Their nuclear arsenal had been fractionated and mostly disbanded. Their Navy was in the best shape, but their Air Force was not in any condition to take on the U.S. No, the Oscar must be there for some other reason.

Admiral Kenner knew he could not take hostile action against the submarine if it were just following them. He could scare it and the crew by letting them know that the U.S. fleet knew of its presence, by dropping practice depth charges and firing dummy torpedoes at it to show that he could battle it mightily before it had a chance to attack.

Admiral Kenner peaked his fingers, and sat at his desk. He wondered how long he would have to wait before there was some response from the Russian admiral. Not long, he hoped. This was a nasty little job that had to be handled with diplomatic care. He was not a diplomat—everyone would tell you that. He wanted to get this matter closed up quickly so they could continue their journey past Hokkaido and down the Sea of Japan toward Korea and their real mission, which could involve military action. If anything happened with North Korea, he wanted to have the *Monroe* right in the middle of it.

His telephone rang.

"Yes?"

"Admiral, we have a response from the Russians."

"Read it to me."

"Yes, sir. It says: 'Admiral Kenner. I have received your message. It is totally unsatisfactory. The United States Navy has no business in this affair. This is between the Japanese general who invaded Russian soil and the Russian military forces.

"'We ask that you remove your screen of ships from around the island, and that you keep your aircraft on your deck while Russian pilots assess the situation and provide the force needed to defeat the rebel Japanese.

"'We give you one day, twenty-four hours, to remove your ships and to keep your aircraft out of Russian airspace.

"'By order of Admiral Vladimir Rostow, Commander of the Russian Task Force Twelve.'

"That's it, sir."

"Thank you. Send a copy to my cabin. Is the CAG there?"

"Yes, sir."

"Admiral, Captain Olson."

"Irving, you heard the response. Is he bluffing?"

"Yes, sir, with his afterburner on. His two MiGs were pussycats. Waved at our guys, motioned for them to follow to do a buzz over the town, then waved good-bye."

"Joys of command, Captain."

"Admiral, I suggest we keep our air CAP over the town. How long is it going to take us on this fucking detour before we get our ships around the island?"

"No more than two hours. We'll be in position by dusk. Our E-2C says the Russians are still more than six hours away."

"Think they'll come into the strait between the island and Hokkaido?" the CAG asked.

"Not a chance. Would you want your task force bottled up in there?"

"It's twenty-five miles wide."

"That's what I mean. No maneuvering room."

The line was silent for a time.

"So, Admiral, any new orders?"

"No. Keep your planes up. Dawn to dusk should do it. We don't need twenty-four-hour watch. Dawn tomorrow."

"The Oscar?"

"Maybe yes, maybe no. He might be playing tag with us. I know some of our skippers do the same thing with the Russian fleet. So far we haven't lost one, but we could. So could this Oscar take a final dive."

"Aye, sir. Steady as she goes. I've got some work to do. Anything else?"

"That's all, Irv. Get to work."

Admiral Kenner hung up the phone, and motioned to the yeoman that he should leave. He did. The admiral went to the couch in the corner of his quarters, took his shoes off, and stretched out. He wondered what had happened in North Korea. Nobody had sent him a word about it since this panic came down about the rebel Japanese general. He'd have to check on CNN. They would know what was going on as soon as the Pentagon did.

The damn OSCAR. What the hell was it doing harassing his fleet? That would be the next thing he'd ask Admiral Rostow on the Russian carrier.

15

Tuesday, 20 February

USS *Monroe*, CVN 81
Off Hokkaido, Japan

That evening, after chow, Murdock got his men together in the training room. He looked around until he spotted Jaybird.

"Sterling, did you bring that little laptop of yours along?"

"Yes, sir."

"Did I tell you not to bring it?"

"Not this time, Commander."

"Get it, let's plug it in and see what we can find on the Internet."

"We playing war games, Commander?" Jaybird asked.

"In a way. I'm smelling non-lethal here, and I know that NAVSPECWAR back in Coronado must have a half-dozen things on the shelf. Before I ask them for some of them, I need some nomenclature, some ideas, some names. Hope you have a good search engine."

"Yes, sir, Netscape. I can find anything."

Ten minutes later, they had the laptop computer plugged in to the 120, and hooked up to a phone line. Somebody said that more than sixty percent of the men and women on the ship used computers and E-mail to keep in touch with the home folks.

"Okay, do a search on non-lethal weapons. Must be a lot of stuff."

"You mean we might actually have to go into that island without our weapons?" Jaybird asked.

"If things go from bad to worse, and Russia gets frisky, and the Japanese Diet holds its position, and the Japanese give us permission to go in at all, it could be with kid gloves and no bang-bang."

"Great, just what I signed on with the SEALs for, some combat wrestling and judo practice," Jack Mahanani said.

"Got something," Jaybird said. "It's about the S.I.P.E. system tested by the Army back in ninety-two. Enhanced and secure infantry protection equipment. Here's a rifle with a sensor on it for infrared imaging, laser sight. A helmet with built-in night vision, and heads-up displays like on jets.

"One evaluator said the elements of the system would be too heavy for the average GI, would be too awkward, and hard to maintain."

"That's their idea of non-lethal?" Murdock said. "Try something else."

Jaybird clicked on another locations, typed in the key words again, and yelped.

"Yeah, here's about twenty of them. This one is interesting. It's from the Department of Peace Studies in England. Says there's a whole new generation of non-lethal weapons from battlefield lasers which blind enemy troops, to acoustic weapons designed to disorient and demoralize. They say an entire battalion can be disabled without the attackers firing a single shot."

"I've heard about some of the enhanced acoustic weapons," Murdock said." Wonder if NAVSPECWAR would have anything like that?"

"I'd ask them if I knew their E-mail address, Skipper."

"Didn't you tell me once that you had Don Stroh's E-mail address in D.C.?"

"True, in my little file."

"Dig it out and let's send him an E-mail."

"Let me get out of the Web, and to the good old Internet."

Twenty seconds later, he grinned. "Got it. DStroh@AOL. com. What do you want to ask or tell our spook buddy?"

"Subject non-lethal. Don. Does NAVSPECWAR section have any non-lethal weapons we might be able to use if we have to go into that island sans bullets? Any other non-lethal devices, ultrasound, chemical, or biological, that you know about you can airmail to us in two days? Must know soonest. Use Jaybird's E-mail address for reply. Hope you read your E-mail often. If no reply in twenty-four, I'll phone you."

Murdock used the phone in the room, called his liaison commander, and got the name and number of the top ordnance man on the ship, a Lieutenant Commander Rawlins. Murdock called him. He had a quick answer.

"Commander, I don't have any of that fancy stuff you're talking about in non-lethal. All I have are rubber bullets for NATO-sized rounds, and six stun guns the master-at-arms sometimes checks out to handle unreal wild men. You know, they're good only for three or four feet, not much more, and are attached to wires. Only other thing remotely in that field is the flashbang grenade, which I'm sure you know about."

"Yes, we use them. You don't have any of the ultrasonic guns that I've heard about?"

"I haven't even heard about them. Wish I could help you. Maybe NAVSPECWAR in Coronado could do you some good."

"Good idea, Commander, thanks."

Jaybird kept working the Web.

"Some crazy ones here, Commander," Jaybird said. "How about this one. It's a rifle that shoots a thin nylon webbing out and over a guard or sentry, tangling him up in it so the attackers can go up and cuff him.

"Or this one that shoots out a sticky substance like a flamethrower would, only this is so sticky the target can't use his weapon, or even walk out of the stuff."

"We need something off the shelf," Murdock said. "Keep looking. I'm going to see if I can get a call through to Don Stroh. We don't have the time to wait twenty-four."

Murdock called Don Stroh's office. The call went through encrypted, bounced off two satellites, and then de-encrypted before Murdock heard the response. The sound of Stroh's voice was a little strange, but it was him.

Murdock laid out the idea for non-lethal weapons.

"Yeah, we thought about that. Not much you have. You aren't even supposed to know about the ultrasonic acoustic weapons."

"Sure, sure, but can you get us some? Do we have to carry a fucking generator with us? Are they portable or worked from a chopper? Give some information here, Don. Otherwise we could be going in and arm wrestling these guys for control of the chunk of rock just about the time the Russians let loose half a dozen big rockets on it."

"Easy, down, boy. It's still in the talking stage."

"Yeah, Stroh, talking. Like ultimatums and deadlines and threats. How about NAVSPECWAR in Coronado? They have anything we can use?"

"Murdock, you're a pushy bastard."

"That's why I get along so well with an asshole like you." They both laughed.

"Okay, we have what is now called an enhanced acoustic rifle," Stroh said. "It's self-contained, has a range of five hundred yards, and can slam a sound blast into a room or against a sentry that he'll never hear, and it'll put him down and unconscious for up to six hours. After that, he returns to normal with little or no damage."

"Sounds perfect. Can you get us twenty of them in two days?"

"I can scrounge up two, if I'm lucky. We have one out at Langley for testing, and I'll get one or maybe two more. But don't tell anybody you have them, or the NAVSPECWAR guys will roast me head-first over an open campfire."

"Colorful, you're colorful. You mean they were right there in my front yard and I didn't know about them? How many shots to a weapon?"

"They work off a high-charge special battery. It takes up the whole stock. I don't even know how it works. We've used one ten times before having to plug it into one-twenty for four hours to recharge."

"Great, so we'd have twenty to thirty shots, and maybe a hundred Japs running around the island."

"Hey, be politically correct. That's Japanese Home Guards. We lost 'Japs' back in World War II. Now, one blast of the acoustic into a room will knock out everyone inside. They are especially effective in a contained space. They are ultimately directional, line of sight. They won't go through a house, but will go in a window or an open door. Some guys could bounce them off trees and walls like you do a beeper for your car lock. Anyway, you just cut off the head of that Self Defense general over there, and the rattlers won't do much harm."

"Talking in riddles now. I get it. Might be enough to get us onshore and to find the headquarters. Which comes to my next question. Do you have any satellite shots yet of this island? You've had plenty of time."

"We can't shift orbits of those babies in a few seconds, you know, laddie. Takes some time. We're working on it. As soon as we get anything on that little town on that first island— Kunashir, I think it is—we'll fax them to your little boat."

"Thanks, and the blowguns in forty-eight?"

"Faster if I can find the right aircraft connections."

"Put them in one of those business jets and scoot them across the pond. How are things in Korea?"

"Settled down a little. Your task force will still sail down that way when you clean up the Japanese problem. Anything else?"

"Just wondered when the Christmas bonus checks will arrive from our favorite uncle."

"Wrong uncle, swabby. And I still say I caught the most fish that we could eat."

"Good night, David."

"Good night, Chet. You're not old enough to have heard them, Murdock."

"I'm a student of TV history."

Murdock hung up the phone. Three acoustic rifles. Better than what they had now. He forgot to ask if anyone else would hear the sound the weapons made. If the target didn't hear anything, it was reasonable to extrapolate that no one else would hear it either.

Back in the SEALs' room, Jaybird was still on the computer. He looked up and grinned.

"All sorts of weird shit on this thing. One guy keeps yelling that the non-lethal weapons are a sham. The military wants them to knock out the defenses of an enemy, then they roll in unopposed and massacre the stunned or blind defenders. They say that the non-lethal weapons will help kill more people than ever in any war that they are used in."

"Yeah, he's probably right. Anything we can use?"

"Nope. Two more kinds of sticky-sticky-goo stuff that is dropped out of airplanes and covers a whole battalion of dug-in troops, freezing them in place so completely that they can't even move a trigger finger."

"Jaybird, take the men out of here and get some sleep. Tomorrow we see who can do a thousand push-ups. You'll all need your rest."

"A fucking thousand," Kenneth Ching asked. "You've got to be kidding."

"You'll find out tomorrow."

Ed DeWitt fell into step with Murdock as he left the room. Murdock told him about the acoustic rifles.

"Great if they work," Ed said. "If we have to go in there non-lethal, it's gonna be a hell of a mess."

"It already is, Ed. See you in the morning."

Twenty miles almost due south of the American task force, Russian Captain Barsloff Natursky brought his killer submarine down under the thermal layer, and cut her speed to five knots. The RNU *Shark*, SMN-23, had been shadowing the American task force for the past week. It was only an hour ago that his people had the first indications that the Americans had spotted him.

He had become too bold, he realized now. He had crept too close to the screening ships around the huge nuclear carrier, and one of the frigates on the perimeter had heard his nearly silent screws. Some lucky sonobuoys had taken good readings on him before he slipped away through the thermal layer where the hunters would get his signal confused with the surface noise.

Now the *Shark* was far out of their range. It was a record nonetheless. No other Russian Oscar-class boat had ever done what he had done in the masterful shadowing of an American task force.

Now the confrontation.

An hour ago he had gonel nearly to the surface, and extended his communications antenna above the water for the regular signal transmissions. To his surprise he had three messages from the carrier *Ataman* in the Sea of Japan. Now he knew of the takeover of the small Russian island north of Hokkaido, and what it meant. He had been put on a Level Three Alert—to be combat ready in fifteen minutes, and to stand by for later information. A Level Four meant impending military action was imminent. An Alert Five was the call for an all-out war.

He had fallen too far behind the American task force.

"All ahead two thirds," he ordered.

"All ahead two thirds, aye," the watch officer said.

Captain Natursky left the attack command center, and went back to his cabin. The smallness of his quarters satisfied him. He had been on submarines for thirty years. He felt at home here. These quarters were much larger than any he ever had at sea before. It was simply a larger boat, over 13,900 tons standard, and 18,300 tons submerged. He had a crew of 107 men, and could stay at sea for over a year if the food supply held out. He had so much firepower it shocked and amazed him.

But it never awed him. He had at his total and complete individual command 24 tubes to launch the largest rockets ever fired from the sea. Each with twelve independently targeted nuclear warheads. A total of 268 targets that he could aim at, hit, and totally destroy with nuclear holocausts. He could target cities anywhere in this half of the hemisphere.

Captain Natursky smiled grimly at the idea that he could totally annihilate an enemy. He, Captain Barsloff Natursky. No one else in the whole world had this much firepower. He took a deep breath, then picked up a book of Russian poetry

written in the nineteenth century, and was at once lost in the
rhyme and meter of the glorious verse.

A knock sounded on his door. He waited. The knock came
again. When it sounded the third time, he bellowed for the
person to enter.

A lieutenant walked in, and held out an envelope. It was a
sealed, yellow Top Secret envelope. The captain nodded at
the officer, who handed him the message and retreated,
probably glad not to be verbally thrashed for disturbing the
captain.

Natursky opened the envelope, and unfolded the yellow
paper, which was always used on the machine that printed out
the messages that came in encrypted.

"Captain Natursky. Continue to shadow the American task
force. The carrier is the USS *Monroe*, CVN-81. She has
eighty-five aircraft on board, including high-tech antisubmarine planes, and ASW ships. Be cautious. We are speeding to
the Russian island of Kunashir. The invasion by the Japanese
rebels still holds. We will talk them off or blast them into
eternity so they can visit with their ancestors.

"Stay on Alert Three. There may be no problem, but we
prefer to have you ready and waiting in case things get out of
hand and we need to destroy the carrier.

"Outstanding work in trailing the task force so long and
going undetected. Do they know that you're there yet? Make
any reply, comments, and suggestions during your next
regularly scheduled transmission time."

The message was signed by Admiral Vladimir Rostow.

The captain smiled. He marked his place in the book of
poetry and put it down. He was no longer in the mood for it.
He left his quarters, and moved to the combat plotting room,
where he had laid out a normal pattern of the ships that
surround an American nuclear aircraft carrier. He knew
precisely what ships were used, where they would usually be
stationed in a screening maneuver, and what weapons and
ASW devices they carried.

More importantly, he knew the total capability of the
carrier's ASW planes and ships. Understanding them, and

how the Americans worked with them, was vital to his own survival.

Now he studied the board, and moved some ship symbols. He knew what he would do in command of such a task force if attacked by a submarine. But what would the Americans do?

He laid out several scenarios, plotting exactly how he on the *Shark* would respond. He smiled again, the second time that day. Yes, he had worked out two problems, memorizing precisely what action he would take for each one.

Before he realized it, the three hours were gone and the lieutenant from communications was back asking if he had any messages to send during their short communications window. The captain said he did, and went forward to the commo center to write out his messages for the encrypting computer.

16

Tuesday, 20 February

Golovnino, Kunashir Island
Kuril Island Chain

General Raiden Nishikawa sat in his small office in the headquarters building waiting for some new reply from the messages he had sent out. He had received preliminary responses from two of the recipients. The Russians had been sharp, demanding, insulting, and militant. The Americans had made quite clear that they would do what the Japanese government wanted them to do. He had not heard anything from the Diet.

The Japanese legislature had a strong group who thought as he did. That Russia should return the Kuril Islands to Japan, to their historic home. Hundreds and perhaps thousands of Japanese had ancestors still on the Kurils. Many of the tombs had been desecrated by the Russians. There had to be an accounting.

Unfortunately, the Diet had talked and talked, and argued, and even become violent at one point, but nothing had been accomplished. He had hoped that the Diet would be a strong backer of his move to regain the ancestral home of his people.

He glanced outside. The darkness was his enemy now. He had long ago decided that if any attempt was made to retake the island, it would be done at night under the cover of darkness. Yes, it would be so.

The general couldn't rest. He walked to the door, back to the window, and at last stepped outside. He dismissed his driver, and took the Russian jeep down the poorly paved street to the schoolhouse where the playground covered the remains of his ancestors. Silently he paced to the exact spot where the tombs had been for a hundred years before the Russians bulldozed them under and leveled off the hill into the ravine.

He knelt and prayed for an hour at the spot, then rose, marched back to the jeep, and drove away. He inspected two of his sentry posts, then heard the Russian handheld radio begin to chatter.

He returned the call, and the message was clear.

"General, this is the sentry at the main pier. We see something in the bay maybe a hundred yards off shore. They look black, and humped up. We think they could be frogmen coming in, or some such invader."

"I'll be right there."

He drove fast through the streets the half mile to the pier, and ran out on the long wooden dock. His two sentries at the end were looking through binoculars.

They didn't have night-vision goggles, but the binoculars would amplify the light to a degree just as it did the distance. He took one of the binoculars, and stared at where the men pointed.

He saw them, more than a dozen ominous black humps. Some of them moved slowly. A moment later he saw a flash of white and smiled. Yes, a tusk, he was certain of it. He lowered the glasses, and gave them back to the soldier.

"Good work spotting the creatures out there. Only they aren't frogmen or invaders. They are walruses. *Odobenus rosmarus,* the common walrus that can grow to twelve feet long and weigh twenty-seven hundred pounds.

"They're resting. I've seen them do it before. The storm at sea must have pushed them in here. In the morning when it's light, they'll pick out a handy beach and take a good long nap."

The soldiers were embarrassed.

"No, you did the right thing. We have to be ready for any kind of invasion. I think if it comes, it will be in the dark. Stay vigilant."

He got in the jeep, and drove back to his headquarters. He found the bottle of sake, and filled a small glass. Right now his spirits needed a lift as much as his body.

He wondered what the Americans would do. They would know precisely what weapons he had and how many men. The Defense Force could tell them that quickly. But what would they do?

He was well aware that either Russia or the Americans could blast him and his men into small incinerated pieces at the touch of a button. The Russians had given him seven days. Two of those were almost gone. He had sensed a moderate tone in the blustering of the Russians. They had been given a serious black eye militarily, and did not enjoy that at all. But how much of a spectacle would they make of their small problem?

At least he had brought the travesty of the Kuril Islands on the world stage better than anyone had done in the past twenty years. He could remember his father shouting on street corners about the desecration of the tombs. Nothing had been done.

Now three or four billion TV watchers must have seen, and heard, about the Kuril tragedy. But the news would fade fast unless something dramatic happened.

What could be more dramatic than the Russians blasting the building he sat in into kindling wood and gravel, killing him and half of his force? That would make the world news for another few days. Maybe then the Diet would act. Perhaps they would demand from Russia that a wrong done fifty years ago be righted.

Idly, General Nishikawa wondered how he would die. He had always envisioned a pitched battle with rifle and bayonet, perhaps pistols, in the final assault. Somehow he was always the defender.

He realized that he would not like to die in the dark. No, the sunshine of a bright day would be better. That way he could chose the time and the place. If, of course, he had to die. He was not ready yet.

However, events he had set in motion, and now was living through, might very well define the conditions of his death, and he would have no say in it. He hoped that it would not be at night.

For just a moment he thought about the two samurai swords in the bottom drawer of his desk. He gently lifted out the smaller of the two blades, and slid it into the wooden scabbard. He held it a moment, then pushed it into his belt. He would carry it now, something symbolic, something to remind himself of the strict code of the samurai.

General Raiden Nishikawa looked out the dark window again, and watched a pale moon rising. This would not be the night. Nothing would happen before dawn. Dawn was a Western time to begin a great battle.

This would not be a great battle. If the dogs of war were unleashed against him, it would be a massacre, not a battle. He set his jaw, and thought of his ancestors.

This samurai would not waver in his determination.

But what would the Americans do?

Admiral Vladimir Rostow settled back in the Combat Control Center of the Russian carrier *Ataman* and listened to the MiG pilots reporting in after their latest run over the occupied island of Kunashir.

The *Ataman* was ready to fight. It was an advanced version of the Kuznetsov Orel-class carrier, type 1143.5/6 CV. It was the only carrier in the Pacific Ocean Fleet commanded by Admiral A.A. Drogin. The *Ataman* had completed sea trials and aircraft landing operations in July of 1998, and been sent immediately to the Pacific Ocean Fleet.

She carried the latest SU-33 Flankers, and the SU-25 Frogfoot fixed-wing aircraft. She'd originally had only twenty-two jet fighters and seventeen helicopters of the Ka-27 Helix models. But for an attack mission, her aircraft total had been increased, and now she had sixty operational planes on board.

She was different from the American carriers in that she

had a fourteen-degree ski jump on the main takeoff deck and a second angled deck of seven degrees.

Admiral Rostow knew he had the firepower to take care of this mission with ease. He had the SSM missiles, twelve Chelomey SS-N-19 Shipwrecks with Granit launchers. The missiles had internal guidance with command update, active radar homing up to 450 kilometers at a speed of Mach 1.6. The warheads could be 500-kiloton nuclear or 750-kg high explosive.

He was ready. Usually he could make thirty knots, but the weather and high seas had cut his speed.

The admiral had been surprised when two American fighters met his MiGs and followed them buzzing the island. The Russian pilots had acted on impulse. There was no time to ask for instructions from their commander. Yes, the pilots had made a good move. It would lull the Americans into thinking that all the Russians were soft and friendly—just before the Americans died.

Rostow had itched for some kind of confrontation such as this. He had been passed over once for the top Admiral of the Fleet rank. Someone in the chain of command had called him indecisive and softhearted on an evaluation report. If Rostow ever found out who it was, he would kill the bastard.

Nothing could stop a career in the Russian Navy cold like those two criticisms. Indecisive? He would show them. He had quickly rejected the American admiral's suggestion that he hold off his aircraft and not put an observation plane over the Russian island. The Americans had no right even to hint at such an arrangement.

His own radar observation platform plane would be in place in about an hour. It had grown dark outside, and his officers had told him they had just passed the northern tip of Kunashir Island, and would soon swing directly south along the western flank of the 115-kilometer-long island. The village of Golovnino was near the southern tip of the island. He had avoided the closer route, through the Nemuro Strait between the tip of Hokkaido and the Russian island.

There would be little maneuvering room in that narrow waterway if the American fleet chose to attack his force in the strait. This was much the better plan. The other Russian islands in the chain were eighty kilometers to the east—plenty of maneuvering room here if he needed it.

He had radioed Moscow with the situation, but there was no rational word back. The satellite communications were not the best, and he had received no firm directives about what actions to take. With no specific orders, it was up to him to facilitate the return of the island to the Russian flag the best way that he could.

His second in command had once been a political officer in the old regime, and he had expressed great concerns about how it would look on the world news reports if they simply wiped out the Japanese with bombs and missiles.

The whole world would make such an uproar that nothing would save Rostow's career. How he wished he could use all of his power, and blast the Japanese rebel's headquarters into rubble, and splatter this general all over his ancestors' ancient burial sites.

He saw the dispatch from Captain Natursky of the *Shark*. It was his ace in the hole, his counterstrike that the Americans knew little about. They only had hazy indicators that there could be a Russian sub out there watching them. Even that much would be enough to send the combat planners on board the big American carrier into spasms of activity planning for all contingencies.

He had given the Japanese general seven days to evacuate Russian soil, even before he received any instructions from Moscow. They were used to such immediate non-lethal actions by field officers, especially those in the Naval Service so far from normal communications. What was he going to do in the meantime?

He would continue his aerial surveillance. He would keep at least two fighters over the village during daylight hours. He had talked with his staff about sending in his Ka-27 Helix helicopters at night, and surprising and capturing one and then another of the small outposts, some thirty kilometers from the small town. Possible. He could do it almost surely without firing a shot.

When the Japanese Self Defense Force soldiers, who had

never fired a shot in anger and who all were unbloodied by war, heard ten large helicopters landing all around them, they would surely give up and surrender to the first Russian soldier they saw.

Admiral Rostow had five hundred seasoned Russian Marines on board his carrier. They were a new breed of fighting men, dedicated, stressed to the point of breaking, trained in the latest tactics, weapons, and equipment of a fast-deployment force. He would put them up against any combat team in the world.

But could he use them?

Better yet, how *best* could he use them?

A communications officer approached him with a yellow envelope. He took it with a nod, and ripped it open. The folded yellow paper held the message straight from the encrypting machine.

"FROM: CAPTAIN NATURSKY. CATCHING UP WITH THE AMERICAN TASK FORCE AROUND THE CARRIER *MONROE*. WILL STAY OUT OF ACOUSTIC TRACKING RANGE, BUT CLOSE BY, AND AWAIT YOUR ORDERS. MAINTAINING ALERT-3 STATUS.

"END."

A radar specialist came up to him with a sheaf of papers. The admiral nodded.

"Sir. Our reports for the past five hours show no American fighter aircraft overflights of the village. That would be since dark local time, sir. Our aircraft is still monitoring the area, and can now check our own position and that of the American fleet."

"Where is the American carrier?"

The man looked at his reports, and readouts. A moment later he glanced up.

"Sir, as of twenty minutes ago, the American task force was centered about ten kilometers off the southernmost coast of Kunashir. Our position is a little over forty kilometers north of that."

"How far are we from the island?"

"Fifteen kilometers to the east, sir. Our destination is some ten kilometers farther south, which would leave us about thirty kilometers from the Americans."

The admiral nodded, dismissing the technician. He looked at his watch officer.

"Signal all ships to slow to five knots. I want the fleet to come to dead in the water in ten kilometers. All screening ships will continue to make their rounds."

"Slow to five knots, aye, sir. Inform all captains."

The admiral listened as the order was repeated three more times by the strata of the command in the room. A moment later, he could sense the big ship bleeding off power as she slowed.

He waved at the captain who had immediate command of the flagship.

"See that I receive any communications from Moscow at once. Also, keep me apprised of any movement of the Americans, or any activity our observers notice by the Japanese. I'll be in my cabin."

The admiral had less than thirty feet to walk down a companionway to his cabin. On this ship, it was three large rooms: one for planning and tactics. A second one for meetings. The third, smallest of the group, held a full double bed, bathroom, dressing area, and a sofa at one side. A bookshelf was well stocked. There were compact discs of fifty composers. A video rack held the best Russian movies, and some Western films with Russian subtitles. A seventy-two-inch TV set had been securely bolted to the floor.

Rostow dropped on the couch, and took off his shoes. Why did his feet have to hurt? His doctor told him it was arthritis, but not the kind that could be treated with drugs. This was degenerative arthritis, where the cushioning cartilage between the bones simply wears out, and gradually disintegrates, leaving the bones to grind together, creating a wide range of pain and trouble.

It was intermittent, which angered him more than anything. He couldn't depend on his left ankle to hurt all the time. Only when he had something important to do.

He didn't look at the framed picture on the dresser. This

was not family business. After it was over he'd stare at the picture for hours, and write long letters home.

For now he had a job to do, and he'd do it. He would blast those invading Japanese off sacred Russian soil, and he would do it his way, then let the diplomats sort out the pieces. Right now he hoped that the Japanese on Kunashir ignored his seven-day warning to leave. Then they would understand the might and the power of Russia. His Russia. His battle group.

17

Wednesday, 21 February

USS *Monroe*, CVN 81
Off Kunashir Island
Kuril Chain, Russia

In the early morning sunshine, the sixteen SEALs sweated on the flight deck on the starboard side just in back of the bow, where usually fighter aircraft and helicopters were parked. All sixteen men were hard at work. Murdock had dropped the thousand-push-up order down to 150. Each man did his own count.

Speed was important here, to put as little continuous pressure as possible on the muscles. Some men did the exercise twice as fast as the others. When finished, each man simply dropped to the deck and gulped air into his lungs.

Murdock was not the fastest. He and Ed DeWitt did the workout right along with the men. Murdock finished in the middle of the crew, and waited for the slowest man.

"On your feet, and shake out your arms," he called. "We need a little double-time drill, and maybe some timed fifty-yard runs. First we'll play follow the leader, and please, don't anybody jump off the ship. They won't go back for you."

"But sir," someone said. "We're not moving."

"Shithead," Jaybird chirped. "The fucking current is moving at least five knots."

The double time ate up twenty minutes, and had the SEALs, in their cammies, sweating again and sagging to the deck.

"Any orders yet, Commander?" Jaybird asked.

"None. I checked with communications this morning. I did get an E-mail from Master Chief MacKenzie. He's jealous and wishes he was with us."

Murdock called the men around him and told them about the Enhanced Acoustic Rifles, the EARs.

"Will they work?" Lampedusa asked.

"Stroh said they will. Thanks for volunteering, Joe. We'll use you as our target when they arrive and you can tell us how effective they are."

"They work," Lam said quickly. "Commander, I know they work, no sense wasting a shot testing one." Everyone laughed.

Then came the fifty-yard wind sprints down the flight deck and back.

That afternoon, the SEALs checked their equipment in the assembly room. They they inflated the IBSs to be sure they had no leaks. Then they deflated them and put in the extra inflation canisters.

"Why we checking our weapons if we can't use them?" Jack Mahanani asked.

"If we go in with the non-lethal directive, we'll still take our weapons," Murdock told them. "It could turn into a shooting war in the flick of a trigger finger. Anytime a SEAL is fired at, he has weapons free to return fire. So get them puppies bright, shining, and well oiled. I have a feeling we'll be going in, and that it won't stay non-lethal for long."

"What's the Ruskies doing all this time?" Les Quinley asked.

"Damned if I know," Murdock said. "They send planes over to check. From what I heard in the mess, the Russian Naval force with their carrier is about twenty klicks up the coast waiting and watching. They were the ones who gave the little general seven days to get off the island. Now they're stuck with it."

"The Ruskies gonna blow hell out of that Jap general?" Al Adams asked.

"Who knows," Murdock said. "Got a feeling they won't. Be damn bad international press for them. Giant squashes small Japanese beetle with overkill. Not good press at all. They could send in a limited landing force and deal with the general's men one on one."

"If we go, it should be before the seven days are up and before the Ruskies can get a landing force on site," Jaybird said.

"That's what I'm hoping for," Murdock said. "I'm going to check with the brass upstairs. Keep things moving down here. Remember, we could be out of this five-star hotel on an hour's notice."

Upstairs in the Tactical Flag Command Center, the mood was watchful waiting. Several communications had been monitored, and translated, that went from the Russian carrier to the little general. Murdock read the transcriptions. The two seemed to be sparring, feeling each other out in the first round.

Admiral Kenner came in, and everyone snapped to attention.

"As you were." He looked at the Watch Officer. "Anything new?"

"Not much, sir. The Japanese Diet has refused to pass any kind of a motion that would show a position one way or the other on the invasion. The strength of support for return of the Kurils seems to have surprised the lawmakers. The only word we have from the Japanese government is to reiterate its position that any move by us must be non-lethal. We're right back in the hole."

"That Russian carrier, the *Ataman*, does she usually carry any Russian Marines?"

The Watch Officer held up a finger, and turned to a manual he had open on one of the shelves around the room.

"Yes, sir. The book on it says there can be up to five hundred Russian Marines on board."

·

"They wouldn't need five hundred. A hundred with auto-weapons could whack out those Japanese Self Defense Forces. None of them have ever been shot at before." The admiral rubbed his face with one hand, then frowned.

"When would the Russian Marines land?" the admiral asked. The men in the room shook their heads. The admiral looked at Murdock.

"Commander, you've done land-operation fighting. When would the Russian Marines go in?"

"Two days before the end of the cease-fire, sir. Give them an element of surprise."

"How many men would they take in?"

"Fifty at night should be enough to take down the command post. Then the rest of the job would be simply mopping up. Once the general is taken, most of the rest of the troops probably will drop their arms in a heartbeat."

The admiral nodded. "Commander, if you are to take your SEALs in there, when would you go in?"

"Tomorrow night, three days before the deadline. Surprise, beat the Russians by a day, and get it wrapped up before dawn."

Admiral Kenner smiled, rubbed his jaw, and turned back to Murdock.

"Commander, I've heard something about EAR. Can you fill me in on this? I know you're working directly with the CIA, and your clearance is undoubtedly twice as high as mine, but I'd like to know what this EAR is about?"

"Need to know, sir?"

"Absolutely. Down this way to my cabin." He turned to the rest of the room. "Carry on here."

They went along a companionway, turned left, and into the admiral's quarters. It was the largest Navy seagoing living area Murdock had ever seen. There were three rooms. The admiral popped a can of soft drink and tossed one to Murdock.

"We've got a top-secret flight coming in this afternoon. A jet rush-rush job. I don't know where they put the cargo, but a Stealth bomber flew the goods into Tokyo this morning at dawn, and a COD is bringing them up here as we speak. What's so damned important it can rate a Stealth bomber?"

"Sir, EAR stands for Enhanced Acoustic Rifle. It's a still-experimental weapon under study. It's non-lethal, which would satisfy the Japanese requirement. We might get three or twenty, I don't know which. They have an effective range of five hundred yards, and can put a victim down and out for up to six hours and not injure him in any way.

"Shoot one into a room, and the acoustic burst ricochets around the room disabling everyone inside. Line of sight and only ten shots per weapon before they need to be recharged for four hours. That's all I know."

"Interesting. Sounds like it would fill the bill for the Japanese. You still want to go in tomorrow night?"

"Yes, sir. If we can get in before the Russians, there should be fewer Japanese dead bodies."

"I'll make that recommendation to the CNO and to the ambassador to Japan. I had a signal from the Chief of Naval Operations. He says he knows you, and that I should give you every consideration. You have friends in high places."

"All in the line of duty, sir."

"Anything you need, let me know."

"One thing, sir. If these EARs come and work, and if we do go in tomorrow night, we will be taking along our regular weapons and full loads of ammunition. I won't go in naked, and have them start throwing hot lead at my men with no way to respond."

"That's no problem. Only thing is, we don't have to tell our Oriental friends that end of the equation."

"No, sir. Thank you. I better get back with my men. Will the EARs be delivered to our operations room when they arrive?"

"Within five minutes of hitting the deck, they'll be in your hands."

"Thank you, sir." Murdock snapped to attention, did a perfect about-face, and walked to the door.

"Oh, Commander."

Murdock turned.

"Remember, anything you need, let me know."

"Aye, aye, sir."

Murdock went into the companionway, and headed back to his men. Now they had something to work with, a possible time for hitting the island. "Yes!" he said, and punched the air with his fist.

Just after Murdock left the admiral, his phone rang.

"Yes?"

"Admiral Kenner, we've got some action on that Oscar again. Nothing certain. Want you to take a look."

"I'll be right down."

The call had come from Monasto, the TAO in the Combat Direction Center, CDC, six decks below the bridge. The location made the center more secure in case of an attack.

The CDC was the top nerve center of the carrier. It used to be called the Combat Information Center, but the new name showed how the operations had changed, and how the carrier battle group now controlled all the factors in a wartime situation.

A huge wall-sized blue screen in the main compartment dominated the area. It displayed every contact held by every sensor in the whole task force.

Commander Monasto sat at a desk in front of the bulkhead display. Beside him was the CDC officer. Enlisted specialists in the rest of the compartment monitored aircraft, and manned radar and data consoles.

The ASW problems were taken care of in another area directly behind the CDC. It coordinated tactics with the DESRON five decks above its location. At the end of the compartment sat two parallel rows of consoles that were used exclusively by operations specialists who correlated and deconflicted radar signals from every ship and plane in the task force.

Every man not on a console snapped to attention when the word came.

"The admiral is on deck."

"Back to work, people. What's the latest situation?"

"Sir, the frigate *Ingraham* had a series of intermittent acoustic contacts that they couldn't classify," Lieutenant

Jefferson said. He was the top ASW man in the room. "The signals were the same frequency, but kept fading and coming back. The frigate launched a chopper, and dropped twenty sonobuoys on the heading. From the last one they got a steady sounding that the sonar techs described as a Russian Oscar with the right blade count. Before the bird could drop more sonobuoys, the Boomer evidently dove, and then went silent. So we lost him."

"How far from the frigate?"

"A bracket, sir, of twelve to twenty miles."

"He moved away from us?"

"Yes, sir, we think so, but no data on that."

Admiral Kenner scowled. "What the hell is he trying to do?"

"Sir, put the fear of a Russian OSCAR into us. He could launch in a preemptive strike. By the time we tried to take evasive action it would be too late."

"I agree, Lieutenant. How old were you during the Cold War?"

"In my teens, sir."

"Do you remember living through the time of the feared intercontinental ballistic missile attacks? The Russians could target a hundred of America's largest cities, and the nukes would rain down before we could much more than launch a retaliatory strike. But by then, half our population and most of our culture would be in atomic ashes. A threat like the OSCAR is only that, a threat. We have the same threat against the Russian carrier with our missiles.

"That OSCAR is there to harass us, not to sink us. Report its actions from now on with an OPREP-3. Get the initial report in my hands within five minutes."

"Yes, sir, Admiral Kenner."

The flag officer went back by way of the Communications Center, and sent messages to the American ambassador, the CNO, and Don Stroh in the CIA. He told them all the same thing. The SEALs on board his ship now had a secret weapon they could use non-lethally, and should be able to attack the Japanese stronghold and capture it within four hours on a night operation. He suggested that the SEALs were ready to move anytime within the next thirty-six hours.

He telephoned Lieutenant Commander Murdock.

"I just sent messages to our ambassador to Japan, to the CNO, and to Stroh, explaining that you were ready to go and that you could take down the Japanese in a four-hour night operation."

"Good, Admiral. Stroh will yell at State, and they will scream at the CNO, and he'll talk to the President, and then they'll talk to the ambassador, and who knows, it all might work out."

"Did the weapons arrive?"

"Yes, but how do we test them? There should be no reaction to a board or chair or a wave if we fire them. Looks like our first test will be on a Japanese sentry when we hit the beach."

"How many weapons?"

"An even dozen. I'm surprised. We should be able to take down fifty men we expect are at or near the headquarters."

"Let your people get some rest. I've got a hunch the Japanese leaders are going to give you a go for tomorrow night."

"We hope so, sir. Yes, we'll get some rest. The instructions for these new rifles are first-grade simple. Take off safety, aim, fire, wait ten seconds to recharge. When the small red light comes on, you aim and fire again. Wish we had a hundred-and-fifty-pound Holstein heifer we could test the weapon on."

"Afraid we're fresh out of livestock on board, Commander."

"If Don Stroh says they work, we'll have to believe they work. If not, we have our backup weapons. We'll shoot to disable as much as we can if we have to use our usual weapons."

"Good enough for me. The Japanese can't expect to come out of this without breaking a few eggs."

"My way of thinking too, sir."

"I'll let you know of any developments."

"Thank you, sir."

They hung up, and Murdock went back to his men, who were staring in awe at the EARs. They looked a lot like the old M-l. About the same weight. The stock was made of plastic, and it contained some new kind of high-voltage battery. The barrel of the weapon was two feet long and had an inch-wide smooth bore. It was connected to a chamber between itself and the battery pack.

The chamber was sealed, and the SEALs could only wonder what went on inside. Murdock took one weapon on the flight deck and flipped off the safety. Ten seconds later a small red bulb glowed near the sights. He followed the instructions, aimed it off the side of the flight deck into the water fifty yards away, and pulled the trigger.

There was a snap, then a whooshing sound that he had long associated with rockets, but not so loud or so protracted. What seemed like only half a second later, the ocean boiled for a moment where he had aimed, then calmed.

Ten seconds later the red light came back on. Murdock pushed the safety on, and two seconds later the ready red light went out.

Ed DeWitt and Jaybird Sterling stood there shaking their heads.

"Looks like it fires, and in ten seconds is ready again," Jaybird said. "What happens if you have two targets in five seconds?"

"You let your partner take the shot," Murdock said. "We work in pairs—lead man takes the first shot, backup the second, and alternate at five seconds. We don't expect that many targets. Also, we'll have to set up a priority of firing if we're in a group. We don't want to waste three shots on the same target."

They went back down to their room six decks below the flight area, trying to work out any other problems they might have.

"Heavy bastard," Jaybird said.

They hadn't weighed it, but Murdock figured it weighed about eleven pounds. If it worked, it would be worth the extra weight. They wouldn't wear their wet suits or rebreathers. That would save six pounds on the suit and another five on the rebreather. The weight wouldn't matter, not if the EAR could do the job.

Back in their ready room, Murdock told them what the admiral had said.

"So, it's not a go, but a chance. We could be going in tomorrow at first dark. That's my suggestion. We'll see what the Japanese leaders think of the idea. Oh, if we go in, we'll take our new toys, plus lots of flashbangers and our regular weapons and a full load of ammo. Any questions?"

"How many bad guys we looking at, Skipper?" Horse Ronson asked.

"Two hundred on the island, about fifty at the central HQ and around it on sentry and guard duty. Just a guess. Not bad odds."

There was a buzz of talk, but no more questions. He told Jaybird to get the men out of there and back to their quarters. They were off duty the rest of the day.

At twenty thousand feet in the thin air over Kunashir Island, Sergei Viktor cruised in his assigned position, making a five-mile circle over the target below in his SU-33 Flanker, then doing a lazy eight, and coming back to circle his position the other way. He had been bored out of his mind all of this flight. His two wingmen were making similar moves at fifteen thousand and ten thousand feet. They had been on this station for over an hour.

Sergei bristled now just thinking about it. By rights, he shouldn't even be here. He had been born fifteen years too late. Before the dismantling of the Soviet Union, his family had been high up in the power structure of the Party. He would have gone to the Naval Institute in any case. But then he would have come out a lieutenant, and four years later would have been a captain, with his admiral's insignia another three years away.

It was the way the Party worked, rewarding those loyal to it. His family had earned those rewards. Now all of that special attention and those privileges were gone. He had attended the Institute, and come out only an ensign like everyone else. After six years, he was still a lowly lieutenant, even with his top ability as a fighter pilot. His name meant nothing. His family's heroics had been forgotten. He was just another pilot at the command of a trio of officers not fit to lick his boots.

Yes, half of his blood was Cossack. It flamed in his veins as he thought about how the fates had treated him. It was a damned conspiracy, and everyone in the whole fucking world was to blame.

Sergei remembered the good times in Moscow before the fall of the Union. There had been parties, grand waltzes, the ballet, and all the girls he could want even when he was fifteen. Glorious. His father had been promoted high in the Party, not yet in the Politburo, but on a fast track leading that way.

He had been accepted into the Naval Institute, and had been assured that he would do well, and graduate with honors. It was expected, it would happen. Rank and loyalty had its privileges.

Sergei remembered how it had all crashed down around them in two days. His father was arrested by the new government for crimes against the state. Their beautiful home and the dacha outside the city, both were confiscated. He and his mother and sister had to rush to her sister's house and hide.

Six months later, his father had been released, but he'd had nothing to come back to. No home, no land, no vocation, no money. He had killed himself after trying to get a job for six terrible months.

Sergei had changed his name, applied to the Naval Institute, and gained entrance on his abilities alone.

But now it had come to this. In a way he was following in his father's footsteps, being loyal to the regime in power. But how long could he put up with it?

Sergei felt his blood pressure rise, the way it did when he had to make two passes to land on a storm-tossed carrier deck. He didn't care. There came a time when he could stand it no longer.

His tactical plane-to-plane speaker came on.

"Sergei, don't you see them? This is Anatol, you having

radio problems? There's a flight of three American Tomcats at fifteen thousand feet making a slow crawl around our formation. Looks like they're on a joyride. Hey, Sergei, are you still with us?"

"Yes, yes, I'm here. Where? Where are they?" Sergei listened as his voice went louder, higher than he wanted it to go.

"To the north, climbing out to nearly twenty thousand," Anatol said. "You should be able to see them on their next pass."

Sergei craned his neck, and searched the sky to the north. He quit his circle, and flew north for a minute, then turned back. They wouldn't be expecting him from this quadrant. He had the highest Tomcat on his radar, but not where he wanted the plane to be. Sergei edged around more so he could come out of the sun at the Americans. Yes, just like in practice, and mock combat runs. He didn't care how long it took. He could wait for the exactly right moment so there would be no chance of failure. Yes, he had come to a decision. He was not doing himself any good here. This Navy life was not for him. Not anymore.

There had to be a change made, and it was about to happen. He nosed the SU-33 Flanker downward, and pushed on his radar fire controls. All he wanted to do was lock on. He had to lock on right now.

A mile and a half away, Lieutenant Jerry Vanhorst knew that they had three Soviet Flankers in the area. His RIO had kept him informed. He had seen one of them, but the other two were far below him as he climbed to his assigned station at 25,000 feet.

He had just reported on station, and carried full tanks of fuel. Vanhorst looked around in the pale blue of the thin sky.

"Hey, Mugger, you lose another one?" Vanhorst asked his RIO in the backseat. "Where the hell is that frisky Russian jet jockey we saw a minute or two ago?"

"Out there somewhere. He was circling at twenty thousand. Probably on the backside where we can't spot him."

"Vanhoast, old buddy," Lieutenant (j.g.) Phillips said from the Tomcat well below him. "You guys having trouble counting to three up there? I can come and help you find him if you need me."

"Not by your eyebrows, Phillips san," Vanhorst said. "Stick to your sampan ways. We've got this covered."

"Oh, shit!" Vanhorst's RIO bellowed. "Somebody's locked on to us. Get us the hell out of here, Jerry."

Lieutenant Jerry Vanhorst didn't have the slightest idea which direction to move. He hit the button releasing a load of metal chaff to try to detour any missile that could be coming, and at the same time kicked in the afterburner and made a screaming diving turn to the left that drained the blood from his brain. He had a feeling, a sick and cold premonition, that it wasn't going to be enough. How was he to know they'd be in a fucking shooting war up here?

Behind him, the Russian air-to-air heat-seeking missile from the bayonet-fighting distance for a Mach Two fighter of two miles tracked the targeted F-14, slamming through the thin air at Mach 1.4. Its heat-seeking sensitive nose ignored the chaff designed to distract other-type missiles, and zeroed in on the Vanhorst Tomcat's flaming afterburners.

The conditions couldn't have been better for the Russian missile. It streaked through the air following the jet's sudden left turn and dive, and in eight seconds rammed into the American Tomcat's tailpipe heat source and detonated.

18

Wednesday, 21 February

Kunashir Island
Kuril Chain, Russia

The Tomcat F-14 exploded in a horrendous roar as over six thousand pounds of fuel, four AIM-54-C Phoenix missiles, two AIM-9M Sidewinders, and two AMRAAM radar-guided missiles detonated in a blinding flash. A cloud of smoke and fire jetted upward, and pieces of the aircraft, and of the two human bodies, started their 25,000-foot drop into the Pacific Ocean.

Lieutenant Phillips had caught the frantic shout from the RIO in the highest F-14, that Vanhorst's plane had been locked on by targeting radar. The flash in the daytime sky was so brilliant that Phillips saw it from ten thousand feet below.

"Home Base, Home Base, missile hit on Red Tomboy Leader. I repeat, Red Tomboy Leader is splashed, no wreckage, no survivors. One big fireball. Request weapons free."

"Affirmative, Red Tomboy," the CAG said. "He vanished off our screens. Weapons free."

Even as he hit the tactical radio, Lieutenant Phillips had powered up, and slanted upward to where his RIO told him the offending Flanker circled the smoke.

The pilot of the third plane in the flight of Red Tomboy,

Lieutenant Pace Turlow, had monitored the radio exchange, and also gunned upward from his ten-thousand-foot beat.

He switched to plane-to-plane frequency and called.

"Phillips, there are three of them stacked. You taking the top one?"

"Right, Pace. I've got him gloating over his kill. We have weapons free. Get one of the bastards."

Then Phillips was breaking through 25,000 feet, and his RIO gave him a vector to the running Flanker. "He's heading down and toward the island. What the hell is he doing?" Lieutenant Patsy Fralic called into the ICS.

"He's still got three or four missiles left," Phillips said as he powered down toward the Flanker. "He might have orders to take out the Japs down there."

Phillips followed the Russian fighter down. It was faster than his Tomcat, not by much but a little, so he couldn't overtake him. He had no chance for a lock-on with his radar with the Flanker banking, turning, looping, doing maneuvers all over the sky.

"All we can do now is follow the bastard and watch him," Phillips said.

A minute later they saw the Russian jet level out and start a run at the small village of Golovnino on Kunashir island.

"Now's our chance to get a lock-on with him while he's on a bombing or strafing run. That's where the Japs' headquarters are," Phillips said.

"He just launched a missile," Patsy said from the backseat. "Is he trying to start World War Three down there?"

Phillips turned to tactical frequency, and called Home Base. But before he could transmit, another voice came on the speaker.

"American Tomcat. This is Russian Flanker. Not the one that shot down your plane. My English not good. Sorry about your friend. Sergei has gone crazy. My orders are to shoot him down before he launches more missiles. Can you help?"

"Be glad to," Phillips said. "Keep your two Flankers out of the area so we don't mistake you for him.

"Let's go get him," Phillips said in the ICS.

He slanted the F-14 to the left, picking up the Flanker as he started another missile run against the town.

"He knows we're here," Phillips said. "He's breaking off his run. Must have felt our radar. Here we go."

The Flanker pulled up in a steep climb, rolled over, and slanted away from them. Phillips matched his movements, but couldn't get into position to lock on with his radar. They swept around again, each fighting for an advantage.

Patsy had a Sidewinder AIM-9 infrared-homing air-to-air missile ready to fire when the lock-on was firm.

They were somewhere west of the island now, over the sea. The Flanker-33 had dropped down to wave-top altitude no more than thirty feet off the water. Phillips tried to lift up for a top shot, but the other plane pulled away and raced upwards in a vertical climb that left Phillips sweating to follow.

Then it was all but over. The Russian jet slowed, flying straight and level. They were at fifteen thousand feet, and Phillips raced in behind him, and he heard Patsy shout in the ICS.

"I have a lock. Fox three." She had fired the Sidewinder missile at the Flanker.

Phillips pulled the F-14 to the left to escape any blast particles, and followed the trail of the nine-and-a-half-foot-long missile as it homed in on the Russian Flanker. In its thousand-yard flight it never got up to its Mach Two speed as it smashed into the jet detonating, exploding the fighter's fuel system in a fireball that sent half of the plane slashing through the sky toward the water below.

"Splash one SU-33 Flanker," Phillips said on his tactical frequency.

"That's a Roger. Red Tomboy Flight, come home," Home Base said. It was CAG, and he sounded tired. "Contact Pri-Fly for instructions. We've got a hell of a lot of paperwork to do, and messages to send. Nice shooting, Phillips."

"Sorry, CAG, it wasn't. He slowed down and waited for me to shoot. It was like he gave up and committed suicide."

"Get back on deck, Phillips. We'll talk it through here."

"Aye, aye, sir."

There was silence on the ICS.

"Patsy, you still there? You all right?"

"I'm here. It's just that . . ."

"Yeah, Fralic, I know. Don't let it get to you. It's our job. What we trained for."

"I know. Still . . ."

"Yeah. I know too. Hasn't hit me yet. That was my first splash too. We suck it up, we tell the CAG exactly how it went, what that Russian Sergei did, what we did, the whole schmeer."

"That won't change a thing, Phillips. We killed a man."

"Yes, that's our job. He just killed Vanhorst and Mugger, remember that. It's still just one for our two."

"There is that."

The intercom went silent. Phillips contacted Pri-Fly for his rotation back. They didn't stack him up, bringing him right in.

"Hey, Fralic, are you still with me?"

"I'm here. I'm all right. I'll fly again this afternoon if we're on the sked. I'm not crying. There ain't no crying in baseball."

Phillips grinned. "Yeah, I saw that movie too."

On the way in, Phillips tried to figure out how he felt. He had been outraged when Vanhorst was shot down. He had done his best to outfly the Russian, and his Flanker, but never had. Then Sergei had pulled up and waited to be shot down. Why? The Russian pilot who spoke English said Sergei was crazy, and that *he* had been ordered to shoot down his wingman. Now what the hell?

Phillips tested his hand, holding it rigid in front of him. Dead solid, not the hint of a waver. He felt calm, in control. He had just killed a man. They had just killed a Russian pilot and destroyed a twenty-million-dollar aircraft.

True. Their job.

Phillips brought the Tomcat in on the approach precisely, took the landing signal, and dropped down on the three wire. He edged the plane into the assigned spot, and powered down.

"You still okay, Fralic?" he asked in the ICS.

"Yeah, I'm kicking ass if anyone asks. I just got my first kill. Now let's get the hell out of here and go see the CAG."

Five minutes later, CAG led them into a small debriefing room. He sat them down, gave them both cups of coffee, and took one himself. Irving Olson was a full captain, a former F-14 pilot himself, and had the respect of his pilots and RIOs.

"I'm sorry about the two good men we lost. Congratulations on the splash. We know how it happened, we're just not sure why. We've contacted Admiral Rostow on the Russian carrier with our questions.

"First a report to you. The missile Sergei fired at Golovnino wiped out three houses, two stores, and a small dock. We estimate no more than a dozen deaths resulted. He missed the military headquarters building by two hundred yards.

"We have monitored Russian air traffic to its planes. It's not coded just as ours isn't. We haven't translated the tapes yet to be sure, but it sounds like the remaining two MiGs were ordered to shoot down this Sergei."

The captain switched on a small tape recorder and put it on the table between them. "Phillips, will you go through what happened, step by step? No hurry. I know this is your first combat . . . kill. But I want a complete report."

Fifteen minutes later, they came out of the room and headed for their quarters. At a turn in a companionway, Lieutenant Patsy Fralic touched Phillips's shoulder.

"Hey, thanks for doing most of the work in there. I'm . . . I'm going to be all right, but it might take me a few hours. You never know how you'll react when it happens. I knew a cop back in Detroit. He said the same thing. When he saw his first dead body he threw up. A buddy of his got in a shoot-out with two punks, and when it was over the cop realized that he had shit his pants."

Phillips chuckled. "At least we avoided that."

"You better check, Phillips. I'm okay on that score. Right now I'm ·gonna have a shower."

Back in the debriefing room, Captain Olson stared at the recorder. No problem with his aircrew. Everything according to the book. Now he had to compose a supremely diplomatic yet stern communiqué to the Russian admiral. His message would be approved by, and go out under the name of, Admiral

Kenner. It had to be exactly right. They didn't want any more accidents, even if this one looked premeditated by the Russian pilot. The man had to have had a history of trouble in the Russian Navy.

In the small village of Golovnino, Japanese General Raiden Nishikawa set twenty of his troops to work putting out the fires and taking the injured to the small clinic. He brought a doctor from the prison compound to treat the wounded. Fifteen Russian civilians had died in the missile attack. One of his men had been wounded.

The missile must have been some kind of air-to-air type. It didn't seem to detonate at once, but skidded down a street, and then exploded near the dock.

He had been on the radio at once, speaking without any prepared statement, shouting at times at the Russians for their attack on his island.

"If there is another such attack, or an attack of any type on my island of Kunashir, I will summarily execute twenty Russian soldiers starting with the officers and working down. There can be no repeat of such an attack, or Russia will suffer many casualties.

"I know it was a Russian plane that launched the missile. Such actions are totally unacceptable. I expect a quick and total apology by the Russian admiral responsible for this pilot."

General Nishikawa put down the microphone. He had been speaking in Japanese, and he realized it would take some time for the Russians, and the Americans, to translate what he had said.

He had been outside before the attack, checking on his outposts, when he saw a brilliant flash in the air to the west. He hadn't been sure what it was, but shortly the Russian aircraft had attacked his island.

He shook with rage just thinking about it. This might slow down the Russians' plans to shell the island at the end of the seven days. He had no plans at all to leave the island. He had captured it, and he would keep it until he was driven off or dead in its defense.

The general left the military headquarters and toured the damaged area. The fires were mostly put out, and the wounded had been taken care of. Now the wails of the families who had lost loved ones could be heard. He wasn't used to such sounds of anguish.

They made him think of his father and mother each time he tried to worship at his ancestors' graves. There had been much wailing, and crying, and agony over the fate of their ancestors' final resting places.

Nishikawa went back to his office, knowing that he had done the right thing by coming here and capturing this island. He might not win in the military sense. Now he realized it was a heroic but rather stupid thing he had done here. Heroic because he had brought the plight of thousands of Japanese who had ancestors' graves here to the eyes and ears of the world through the medium of television.

Whether this had produced, or would produce, any long-lasting benefits was the question. If it did not, then indeed he would be branded as a fool, by his own family and by the countless other Japanese families out there who had suffered terrible losses at the hands of the Russians.

He slammed into his headquarters building, and found his second in command.

"Double the guards at the docks, around the bay, everywhere that someone could land a small boat. I think that it's time we understand that we will not win the diplomatic discussion. They will revert to an attack of some kind. I'm just not sure what it will be. All of our troops will be on alert now twenty-four hours a day.

"Those off duty will wear their uniforms, and weapons are to be in hand at all times. We will be facing a crisis soon. I'm just not sure what it will be, where it will come from, or what nation will be coming here to kill us."

19

Wednesday, 21 February

USS *Monroe*, CVN 81
Off Kunashir Island
Kuril Chain, Russia

The official statement came through an hour after Captain Olson's message had been delivered. He read it again to be sure he had it right.

"Admiral Kenner, Commanding, U.S. Task Force. Sir. We regret that one of our planes had an electrical and radar malfunction with the result that one of your aircraft was shot down. We offer condolences to the families of the two persons in the plane.

"We understand the immediate retaliation, and the destruction of the offending aircraft, even though the deadly accident had nothing to do with the pilot of the craft. We also have suffered a lost shipmate.

"We strongly urge that we both now maintain a separation between our aircraft. Since you were on the site first, we will relinquish the project of flying cover over the island to your aircraft. We will keep our flights offshore from the island, but in close proximity. This way there will be no reason why one force should be in the sights of the other, or that any lock-on by radar aiming should take place.

"We reserve the right to move onto the island when our seven-day grace period is over. It appears that General Nishikawa is making no preparations to leave.

"Our ships will continue to cover the area to the east of the island, and we will appreciate your recognizing this area and not interfering with our routine patrols.

"We hope that this entire situation can be cleared up with no more loss of life or equipment."

It was signed by "Admiral Vladimir Rostow, Russian Naval Forces Commander."

Captain Olson took the message at once to Admiral Kenner, who had approved the wording of the complaint to the Russians less than an hour ago.

"Accident my jockstrap," Captain Olson said when the admiral had finished reading the message. "Our pilots heard the Russian pilot of one of the other Flankers say that Sergei must have gone crazy and that the two other Flankers up there had been ordered to shoot down the one who splashed our Tomcat."

"We'll be lucky if that's the only deadly confrontation we have with the Russians," Kenner said. "This is a damn tense situation. I like the idea of keeping our forces apart this way. Tell the admiral that we accept his statement, and that we'll cooperate on keeping our forces separated."

"Good. I'll write it out and you can okay it."

Several decks below in the CDC, the watch commander looked over the shoulder of a chief manning a tactical display. This one was from their E-2C Hawkeye on station at thirty thousand feet over the fleet and monitoring anything that drove, flew, or sailed in a 250-to-350-mile radius.

"Look at that sucker go," the commander said.

"Estimate speed of seventy knots, Commander. Damn, that's eighty miles an hour over the water. Has to make it an air-cushion craft. The Russians have some. Last we knew, there were thirty-four of them in the Russian fleet. They could carry one in an amphibious ship if they have one in this fleet."

"Find the specs on them," the watch commander said. One man moved to a large book, and came back with the answers.

"Sir, they have three types, all about the same size from eighty feet to one-eighty-nine. The middle one can do seventy knots. It's called the Aist, type one-two-three-two-point-one. Has a crew of ten, and can carry two medium tanks and two hundred troops. Range is a hundred and twenty miles at fifty knots."

The commander reached for his phone.

"That's the picture, Admiral," the watch commander from the CDC said. "Figured you'd want to know. The craft has turned just south of Golovnino, and is circling about a half mile offshore."

"Thanks, Commander," said the admiral in his quarters. "Let me know what it does next. This is no violation of our agreement with the Russians, but it's a little pushy of them. They're telling the little general in there that they can move in with two tanks and two hundred men anytime they want to. The hovercraft is not exactly a quiet ship."

"Roger that, sir."

Kenner hung up and he told Captain Olson about the call. Then the admiral took off his shoes and stretched out on a couch in his cabin. "What worries me as much as anything is that damned OSCAR. What is a Russian submarine doing in our backyard? They have eleven of them, and the intel says five are based in the Pacific. What are they doing here?"

"We could ask Admiral Rostow," Captain Olson said.

They both laughed. "He won't even admit that he knows one is in the Pacific," Admiral Kenner said.

"You know what's missing in this whole damn scenario?" Captain Olson asked. "Where the hell is the Japanese Maritime Self Defense Force? Their damn Navy? I know they have over forty destroyers, sixteen submarines, and seventeen or eighteen frigates. They could put quite a screen around this damn island. Last time I checked they had almost forty-seven thousand men in their Navy. They have all kinds of smaller craft including LCIs and LCMs and patrol craft. All of their ships have the latest and best missiles and torpedoes. So why the fuck are they sitting in port, and we're out here on the damn firing line?"

"About time you thought of that, Irving. I had a signal on that the first day we took our orders. The Japanese Diet, their legislature, pressured the Prime Minister into ordering that none of the Self Defense Forces be used to solve this little problem. They said it wasn't self-defense, so technically the forces could not be used.

"What it came down to was that the Japanese didn't want their own forces shooting and killing each other. They said it could lead to a civil war."

"So the Japs, the Japanese, just don't want to be shooting their own people. It certainly wouldn't lead to a civil war, that's for sure. Damn, sounds like a thin excuse so we would have to come yank their fucking chestnuts out of the fire again."

A steward brought in coffee and each officer took a cup.

"Find out from TFCC what's happening to that hovercraft," Admiral Kenner said. "You might send one of your CAP planes down to take a closer look."

Captain Olson went to the phone, and in a few minutes came back with the information. "From what our F-14's say, the hovercraft probably isn't loaded. The loaded speed is about fifty knots. It's on a milk run, a display-only show of force."

"Let's hope it stays that way." The admiral sat up, put on his shoes, and tied them. "I've changed my mind 'bout that damn OSCAR. I better get down to the ASW module. I want to see what's happening with that Russian sub. If he's anywhere around, I want to know about it."

Five minutes later in the ASW module, the Admiral learned that they had no new data on the OSCAR.

"Seems she just fades away when she wants to, Admiral. She does keep us checking, and maybe that's the purpose."

The admiral nodded. "Get me on the horn with any new data on it."

Back in the CDC the Admiral watched the movement of the hovercraft. It circled a while, then drifted, moved back just off shore of the town, and circled again.

"Put a Seahawk out there and take a close look at him," Admiral Kenner said. It just might chase him away. If he's got no men or tanks, it's got to be a show. Let's give him a show and tell of our own."

"Just a fly over, Admiral?" The Watch Commander asked.

"Right, let them know we're here. Then have the chopper fly over and check out the damage of that Russian missile. Don't get too low and encourage any ground fire, but make a look-see."

"Aye, aye, Admiral."

The HH-60H Seahawk took off six minutes later and kept in contact with the carrier. At l47 knots it didn't take the Seahawk long to get over the hovercraft.

"Hawk One to Home Base."

"Go, Hawk One. What's happening?"

"Nothing. The eight or ten crewmen we see are waving at us, like they're on a picnic."

"Any sign of troops or arms?"

"Nothing. The boat is covered on top. Now something is going on. Yes, they're turning back north and heading up the coast. Their watch must be over. What now, Home Base?"

Admiral Kenner motioned to the man with the radio.

"Tell him to do a flyover of the town down there. Make an estimate of the damage that the Russian missile did. Keep him high enough so he doesn't antagonize the locals."

The message went out to the chopper, and they saw on the radar monitor that the Seahawk had swung toward shore.

"Home Base, Hawk One here."

"Go, Hawk One."

"Approaching the island at about three thousand feet. Doesn't seem to be many people on the streets. Not many streets. From the looks of it, the missile didn't explode right off. It must have slid down a street before it went off near a dock. Two buildings flattened. A couple more set on fire, but the locals have the fires mostly out. Don't see any bodies lying round. Figure they have been taken away by now. That's about it, Home Base."

"Roger that, Hawk One. Come on home before we get in any trouble."

"Yes, sir. On our way."

Admiral Kenner rubbed his face with one hand. "What the

hell is Admiral Rostow trying to do? Is he showing off his hardware for our benefit? Is he trying to scare this Jap general? Sure as hell would like to split a bottle of vodka with him and get this all worked out."

By 2000, Murdock had the SEALs back in their ready room. They all had seen the EAR weapons and knew how they worked.

"We betting our asses on these things, Cap?" Bill Bradford asked.

"Yes and no," Murdock said. "We're betting that they work. If the first two or three targets don't go down, we'll stash the EARs and go in with our usual firepower. Then we go with the idea of wounding and putting out of action the Self Defense soldiers, rather then simply wasting them. Which is going to be tougher. It'll be shooting for legs rather than heads or torsos."

"Lots of luck," Jaybird said. They laughed.

"So, I'm going to assign the new weapons. We've got twelve of them. Bradford, you've got enough to pack with the fifty and your rifle. The two machine gunners are also off the hook, and Jaybird. The rest of us will have the EARs. Any questions?"

"We have any word yet about going?" Washington asked.

"Not so you could write home about it," Murdock said. "My gut feeling is that we'll be going in with first dark tomorrow night."

"By IBS like we planned?" Ed DeWitt asked.

Murdock shook his head. "Who knows? That's what we laid out for the admiral. They should have some kind of amphibious craft out here that can get us into a mile offshore."

"Must be an amphib ship with a task force this size," DeWitt said.

"I'll ask the admiral," Murdock said. "Check over your gear again. Let's be ready to move in an hour in case we get the word tonight."

Murdock called the admiral. He wasn't in his quarters.

Murdock found him in the TFCC and asked him about transport in to the one-mile point.

"We'll use two River Patrol Boats from the *Nashville*. She's an Amphibious Transport Dock, an LPD-13. The river boats can get you in there with no trouble. Lash your IBMs on the bow and there's room for eight men. Be a short trip. We'll bring two over tomorrow morning from the *Nashville* and have them on hand."

"Thanks, Admiral. That's the last of it. We're ready to move as soon as we get clearance from the politicians."

"That's the way it usually works these days, Commander."

Murdock hung up, and told the SEALs about the PBRs they would ride in.

"Is that the fiberglass hull or the aluminum one?" Ken Ching asked. "Lots more room in the aluminum one."

Murdock shook his head. "We'll find out about that when we load on them. What I'm more concerned with right now is how are the walking wounded? Doc, you keeping tabs on them?"

"Right, Commander. Ching is the worst one. That leg wound is healing, but I'm not sure he can do wind sprints yet. You'll have to ask him."

"So, Ching?" Murdock asked.

"Yeah, it still hurts, but when I don't think about it, I do fine. I just won't think about it. I'm fit for fucking duty!"

Murdock grinned. "Sounds like it if all we had to do was yell at the general." He looked at Ron Holt.

Holt jumped up and began to shadowbox. He stopped and laughed. "Hell, Skipper. I'm five by five and ready to dive. Count me in. My arm is fine. For four or five hours over there I can walk on my shit-picking hands."

"What about the Shrapnel Kids?" Murdock asked.

Joe Douglas stood, then dropped and did twenty fast push-ups. "Now, Skipper, does that arm look all right to you or what?"

"Seems to be working. Adams, what about you?"

"Commander, you've still got more shrapnel in your ass than I have in my arm. You can do it, I can do it."

"We'll get a second opinion. Doc, I want you to run all four

of these gung-ho sailors past the duty doc down in sick bay.
Have him check them out, but don't let him put any of them
in a bed. The rest of you, get a good night's sleep. We'll be
busy tomorrow, and maybe when it gets dark we'll get into
action. Now get out of here."

When Murdock got back to his quarters, there was a
message for him to call Don Stroh at the office.

Murdock went to communications, where they put through
a voice call on the SATCOM. Stroh came on the line at once.

"Good buddy, how is the water over there?" Stroh asked.

"Hot and getting hotter. We lost a plane. When do we go in
and close this one out?"

"The old men are talking. From the President right on
down. I hear he's made a call to the Japanese Prime Minister.
Should know sometime soon. You're what, about fourteen
hours ahead of us. It's morning here. We could get the word
while you're in dreamland. The second we get a firm
go-ahead, you guys will be sent the word. How's the team
holding up?"

"Perfectly. We're SEALs, remember? The guys want you
to go on the next training session with us. The hike, the swim,
the explosive pit. You'll enjoy yourself."

Stroh laughed. "Yeah, like I do when I do the triathlon.
Closest thing I come to physical work is climbing in and out
of bed."

There was a pause.

"Anything you need, Murdock?"

"Just a go-go-go from your boss."

"You'll know one way or the other when you get up in the
morning. My promise."

"Holding you to it."

"You got it. My dime's worth is up. Take care, Murdock."

Murdock said he would, and hung up. So, tomorrow and
tomorrow and tomorrow. What was that from? He couldn't
remember. Tomorrow it was.

Admiral Kenner had just taken off his shoes, and was relaxing
in the big chair in his quarters, when the phone rang.

"Yes?"

"TFCC here, Admiral. Something is developing you may want to take a look at. We've had a separation of about twenty klicks between our screening ships and the Russians, but now one of their outer destroyers is moving toward the edge of our far screen."

"I'll be right down."

A few minutes later, the admiral looked at the display screen in the TFCC and scowled. "How far is that Russian destroyer from our ship?"

"About twelve miles, Admiral."

"What's our closest vessel?"

"That would be the guided-missile destroyer *Callahan*."

"Tell her to set General Quarters and notify her of the Russian ship."

"Aye, aye, Admiral."

"Then get me Admiral Rostow on the radio. We need to have a talk."

"The Russian still seems to be closing, sir. She's on a collision course at a little over seventeen thousand yards. She appears to be of the Sovremenny class, with eight Raduga SS-N-22 missiles each having a three-hundred-kilogram warhead in a sea-skimmer mode."

"That's point-blank range, for God's sakes," Admiral Kenner said. "Where is that Russian admiral? Can you raise him? Tell the captain of the *Callahan* to prepare counter-measures and watch for any radar targeting."

"Sir, the Russian vessel is closing at thirty-two knots."

"Get that damned Russian admiral now!" Admiral Kenner bellowed.

20

Wednesday, 21 February

Off Kunashir Island
Kuril Chain, Russia

Admiral Kenner listened to the radio operator calling for the Russian admiral. He felt as if he was stuck in mud up to his knees and trying to run. Everything slowed down—even the voices seemed to drag out each word to ridiculous lengths.

One of the techs looked at him.

"Admiral, I have a later report. The Russian destroyer has closed to sixteen thousand, five hundred yards, and is continuing on course at thirty-two knots."

The admiral closed his eyes and nodded. "Yes, I heard. There's just not a damn thing I can do about it right now."

The radio man handed him a mike. "We have the Russian admiral, sir."

"Admiral Rostow, why is your destroyer threatening our outer screen? Your ship is on a collision course with one of our destroyers. Do we have to fire at it to get your attention?"

"Admiral Kenner," the English translator said. "Our ship is in the open sea with the rights of passage. Have we in any way threatened your destroyer? We have not. Our ship is simply on a maneuver to test its crew. We have meant no threat to your fleet."

"Admiral Rostow, you have a strange way of showing it. Have your destroyer turn away or, at fifteen thousand yards range, we will open fire on it."

"Admiral Kenner, you are not on your most diplomatic behavior. It may take some time to contact the captain of the *Bespokoiny,* but we will attempt to contact her. You will hold your fire, yes?"

Admiral Kenner set his jaw and slammed his hand down on the worktable. He keyed the mike again. "Admiral Rostow. You undoubtedly are in voice contact with the *Bespokoiny* at this very moment. We will open fire if your destroyer comes within fifteen thousand yards of our destroyer."

There was no return comment.

"How close is the Russian ship?" Admiral Kenner asked.

"Sixteen thousand, sir. Same speed."

"Read off the distance every one hundred yards."

"Aye, aye, sir."

They waited. Everyone in the TFCC watched the display screen. The line kept moving toward the destroyer *Callahan.* Admiral Kenner closed his eyes and took two deep breaths.

"Fifteen thousand, five hundred, Admiral. Same speed. No change in course."

"Contact the *Callahan.* Authorize one star shell to be fired over the approaching Russian ship when it reaches the fourteen-thousand-nine-hundred-yard range."

The message was sent to the American destroyer.

CAG Olson slipped into the TFCC and watched the developments. He looked at Admiral Kenner, but didn't speak.

The chief looked up from his screen. "Fifteen thousand yards, sir."

Less than a minute later word came on the tac frequency.

"We have fired one star shell from the *Callahan* above the approaching Russian destroyer. It is red in color. The time is 2242."

Admiral Kenner touched a bead of moisture on his forehead. He looked at the screen.

"Range, fourteen thousand, seven hundred. The Russian ship is starting a starboard turn, Admiral."

Kenner could feel the tension break in the TFCC. Captain Olson looked at him, gave a short nod, then left the room.

"Well done, Chief. I'll expect an after-action report on this incident on my desk by zero-eight-hundred."

"Yes, sir. Looks like the Russian is doing a one-eighty, Admiral. She's probably going back to her screening position with the fleet."

Murdock didn't hear about the Russian destroyer probe until the next morning at breakfast. It reminded him of the way the Indian warriors used to harass their enemies in the Wild West when they had someone surrounded. A dozen warriors would ride hard and fast directly at the enemy, then just out of range they would whirl, screech, and yell, and then ride back the way they had come.

It was a chess game here as well, one side testing the other. The star shell was a great response. It showed ability and intent without killing anyone or damaging any hardware.

Murdock checked with communications, but they had no word for him from Washington, D.C.

"When a message comes in, we'll get it delivered to you at once, sir," the chief on duty said. "I'll bring it up myself."

Murdock opened the door to their assembly room at 0800 and found all of his crew on hand.

"Nothing yet, no orders. I want every man to break down his personal weapon, clean and oil it, and make sure all of his equipment is packed and ready to roll. We might get an hour's notice, it could be four hours, or maybe fifteen minutes. The more time we can save here means more dark time on the island."

"If we go," Colt Franklin cracked.

"We'll go," Murdock said. "Stroh guaranteed it."

"Oh, yeah, now there is a hidebound, genuine, fucked-up guarantee if I've ever heard one," Jaybird Sterling said. Half the men hooted their approval.

After the shouts died out, Jaybird grinned. "Okay, you sad-asses, let's get at it. Breakdown and cleaning. Go."

Murdock left, and checked the commo shack again. Nothing. He stopped by the TFCC, and watched the input from the dozens of radar scanners. One of the techs gave a yell.

"Commander, you better take a look at this," the chief said to the watch commander. "We've got a ship moving down the coast again, just like that hovercraft did yesterday. Not so fast—say, fifty knots—hugging the shore."

"What's his range?"

"About fifteen klicks. Nothing firm yet."

"Keep on it, I'll call the admiral."

Five minutes later Admiral Kenner and the CAG watched the progress of the line on the screen.

"Definitely slower," Admiral Kenner said. "Captain, have one of your cover guys take a look and see if it's manned this time."

The order went out, and Tom Two soon reported back from the sky over Kunashir Island.

"This is Tom Two, Home Base. That's a Roger. Dropping down now to take a snoop."

In the TFCC, they waited, watching the thin line representing the hovercraft move south along the coastline.

"They can't think they're fooling anyone," Captain Olson said. "They have their surveillance command-control planes up too. They know we can see the ship."

"Another bluff maybe?" the watch commander said.

"We'll see soon," Admiral Kenner said.

"Home Base, this is Tom Two."

"Go ahead, Tom Two."

"Just made a pass over the craft. She's a hovercraft, all right. The stern loading hatch is open and I see what looks like a tank in there. She's covered on top, so can't be sure if she has more tanks."

"Take another go-round, Tom Two. Look for troops topside."

They waited. CAG Olson scratched his head. "Admiral, if they are loaded, and if they do get to a spot where they could make a landing near the captured town, what should we do?"

"That's an easy one, CAG. If they turn and head for shore, your Tomcats are to splatter six rounds of twenty-millimeter across their bow."

"If that doesn't stop them?"

"Then you have another follow-on Tomcat put four rounds into the elevated wind propellers. Put her dead in the water, but with enough power to keep afloat and killing as few Russians as possible."

CAG nodded, and talked to the two Tomcats.

"Tom One and Tom Two. Any more intel on the hover-craft?"

"Home Base, the hatch is now closed so we can't see the tank. Spot no troops anywhere on the craft."

"Thanks, Tom One. I have a mission for you." The CAG gave them the orders. "The second he turns toward shore on a landing run, one of you has to be in position to do the bow firing. First one across gives them the warning shots. If they don't stop, the second one blasts those stern air propellers with four to six rounds of your best twenties."

Both pilots acknowledged the orders.

Murdock stood to one side watching it all. At last he spotted the marks on the screen that showed where the Tomcats were flying. Both moved closer to the small town on the Pacific side of the island.

Time crept by for Murdock. He watched the lines on the screen, the blips of the planes. Then he saw the hovercraft line turn toward shore.

"The hovercraft has turned toward shore. You have weapons free on the twenties, Tom One and Tom Two," the CAG said on the radio.

"That's a Roger. Tom Two making my warning run."

Lieutenant Jerome Wilcox lined up his Tomcat F-14 so he had a small lead on the hovercraft, then nosed down and put his finger on the trigger for the 20mm cannon rounds.

He pointed the nose of the F-14 just ahead of the Russian Hovercraft and hit the trigger for a ten-round burst. He saw some of the rounds explode on the water forty feet ahead of the small craft; then he was pulling up the Tomcat less than a hundred feet off the Pacific waves.

"Tom Two. I fired approximately ten rounds in front of the target."

"This is Tom One, Home Base. Looks like the craft is not changing course. It's about a quarter of a mile off shore."

"Tom One, you have weapons free on the twenty-mike-mike rounds. Hit those aboveboard air propellers if you can."

"Roger that, moving into position."

Lieutenant (j.g.) Ronson flexed his fingers and pulled the F-14 into a flanking attack on the hovercraft. He felt sweat bead on his forehead. He'd never fired at a Russian boat before. Hell, he'd never fired at anything that had human beings on it. He could very well kill several men in the next few moments.

He pushed that out of his mind, and flew the bird. He came up on the hovercraft, angled slightly to keep it in his sights, then nosed down and began his strafing run. He'd been the best at this in his squadron on target practice. This was just another target.

His hand gripped the trigger, and he decided to fire on this side of the stern and across it over the four huge air propellers, and then put some rounds beyond just to be sure.

Lieutenant Ronson wanted to wipe sweat out of his eyes. He didn't. Then it was time. He nosed down a little more, knowing he was dangerously close to the water. He hit his mark, and pressed the trigger. He saw the first few rounds hit the water on this side of the Russian hovercraft, then rake across the deck and explode on at least the first double set of pusher/puller propellers before he was past the target and pulling out of the dive slowly, yet staying above the spray of the waves below.

"Tom One, Home Base. Firing mission completed."

"The target is slowing, Home Base," Tom Two said. "Tom Two over her now. I can see that she took several hits. The big air props are winding down. One looks half blown away."

"Good shooting, Tom One. This is Home Base. The hovercraft is now dead in the water."

"Home Base, Tom One. She seems to be getting under way again, slowly but reversing course. I say again, the Russian hovercraft seems to be reversing course heading north."

"That's affirmative, Tom One. Our plot shows she's now

moving back toward her fleet. Observe but don't follow beyond ten klicks."

"That's a Roger, Home Base."

CAG Captain Olson looked at the admiral. "At least we didn't sink her. Could have. You'll probably be getting a message from your buddy Admiral Rostow."

Admiral Kenner shook his head. "Don't think so, CAG. He tried a bold move to get his attackers inside and it didn't work. He'll have to lick his wounds and try for a stealth move by night. No, I don't think that we'll hear a peep out of our Russian Naval officer friend."

The admiral turned to Murdock. "You hear anything from your man in Washington yet about a go for your team?"

"Not a word, Admiral. Today, I hope."

"Be best. You said you think the Russian commandos will be sent in tomorrow night."

"Yes, sir. We need to go in tonight to get there first."

On the Russian island of Kunashir, in the small village of Golovnino, Japanese General Raiden Nishikawa stared in delight as he saw the Russian hovercraft take the strafing by the American fighters. He cheered as it stopped amd then turned slowly and moved back toward the north at no more than ten knots.

His second in command had been with him on an inspection of the security outposts, and both had seen the warning rounds, then the attack on the boat.

"They were going to land?" Major Hitachi asked.

"Yes. I'm sure they wanted to. That class hovercraft can carry a tank, maybe two, and at least two hundred combat soldiers. We were lucky today that the United States drove them away." Nishikawa shook his head, and stared at the retreating hovercraft making less of a spray of water than when it had arrived at what he guessed had to be over thirty-five knots.

"But tonight, after dark. What is going to happen then? We still have three days on the seven day deadline. But the Russians were ready to violate their own limit by invading us today. What will they do tonight? We must be especially alert as soon as darkness falls."

Murdock returned to the compartment as soon as he talked with the admiral in the TFCC. The SEALs had finished with cleaning, checking, and oiling their weapons. Each man had his gear laid out for inspection, mostly so each one could check and double-check to be sure he had with him what he wanted on the mission.

Murdock went to his table, and laid out his gear again. Yes, it was all there. They would not take the big, heavy Mark 23 H&K O .45-caliber pistol. He wanted the men able to move quickly.

A sailor came in the door and looked around. When he saw Murdock, he went up to him and held out an envelope.

"Commander Murdock?"

"Right. I hope you bring good news."

The man grinned and hurried out of the room.

Murdock tore open the envelope and read the typed-out message.

The ready room's chatter tapered off as one after another of the SEALs saw the messenger and wondered what the message would say.

Murdock read it quickly, and looked up. "We have a go."

The room exploded with cheering and stomping, then quieted again.

"Stroh says we got past the Japanese Prime Minister with the EAR weapons. He hopes to hell that they work. He also said that he figures we'll have to take our regular weapons in, but he won't be telling the Prime Minister about that. Looks like DeWitt and I better go see the admiral."

By the time they tracked the admiral down in his quarters, it was a little after 1100.

The admiral already knew of the go.

"Your PBRs are already on board. You can load them with your IBSs and get them lashed down while they are in the hold. Then they'll go out a hatch near the waterline and you can board them. What's your time schedule?"

"Sir, dark here is about seventeen hundred. How far from shore and the town are we?"

"I checked. We're fifteen miles off shore and about five miles south of the town. The PBRs will do twenty-four knots. If you leave here an hour before dark, you should have plenty of time to get offshore a mile at dark and get into your IBSs."

"Good. We'll be ready at fifteen hundred to load the boats, then plan on casting off at sixteen hundred."

"Any last-minute special equipment or gear you need, Commander?"

"No, sir. We're ready. We'll have our SATCOM tuned to the carrier's tactical frequency for voice, and check it before we get onshore. I think we're all set, sir. Thank you for your help."

Admiral Kenner smiled. "No problem. Oh, you could put in a good word for me with the CNO next time you have lunch with him."

Murdock laughed. "Admiral, I hardly know the man. If I take him to lunch, I'll be sure to mention you."

Back at the ready room, Jaybird Sterling hurried up to Murdock when he came in.

"Skipper, I've got our guide here to take us back to the stern. That's evidently where our IBSs are and the patrol boats. He says we'll launch the PBR craft there and then board them."

"True, after we lash the IBSs on the bow of each of the PBRs."

Murdock looked around. "Jaybird, get these guys to chow, and then we'll do the last-minute packing up. We'll be pushing off from the carrier at sixteen hundred—that's a little over four hours. Now chew some tail and get these guys fed."

21

Thursday, 22 February

USS *Monroe*, CVN 81
Off Kunashir Island
Kuril Chain, Russia

By 1530, the SEALs had lashed one of the bulky, inflated IBS boats to each of the river patrol craft. Murdock didn't recognize the craft. The ones they had were the Mark II series, the older variety. They were thirty-two feet long, displaced 8.9 tons fully loaded, and had two GM V-6 diesels to produce 420 horsepower to run two Jacuzzi water jets. They had a top speed of twenty-four knots, and were set up to haul ten combat troops. They had four 12.7mm machine guns and two Mark 19 grenade launchers.

Murdock talked to the coxswain.

"We need to get from here to a mile off Golovnino, and arrive just at full dark. We want you to come into a mile off as quietly as possible. We don't care if you throttle down to five knots, just so nobody onshore knows we're out there."

"Understand," the coxswain said. "I'll be the lead boat. We've got enough speed to get up there and then move in the last mile or two on low power. Keep your guys inside the boat. We don't want to have to go back and pick anybody up."

"You ever worked with SEALs before, Chief?"

"No, sir."

"I didn't think so."

The Navy crew lowered the patrol boats into the water out the hatch that was three feet off the waves. Both the IBSs were lashed down securely.

At 1550, Murdock had Ed DeWitt load in his seven men. Five minutes later the Second Squad was on board the patrol boat, and Murdock put his squad in the other one.

It had been a while since Murdock had been on a thirty-five-foot boat in the open sea. They left the carrier slowly, then picked up speed. At twenty knots the spray coming over the bow soaked all of the SEALs, and the February weather was not balmy.

"Next time let's take a nice dry chopper," Jaybird said.

The rest of them were too cold to shout back at him.

At 1645, the coxswain tapped Murdock on the shoulder.

"We're offshore of the town and about five miles out. Not much of a glow, but you can see some lights."

Murdock saw them. It was almost dusk. "How long to move in to a mile off?" Murdock asked.

"We can do it in ten minutes, or twenty, or anywhere in between. Your choice."

"Let's make it twenty."

Fifteen minutes later the small patrol boats came to a stop, and two SEALs on each craft unlashed the IBSs and got them in the water. The SEALs loaded carefully. The engines had been tested just before they left.

They had their Motorolas on, and Murdock called for a net check. All fifteen men sounded off in his earpiece.

By that time it was fully dark. They tied the two boats together with a twenty-foot buddy line.

"Ed, take the lead," Murdock said in his mike. They watched the two river patrol boats back away and ease out to sea on low throttle.

"Let's do it," Murdock said. The IBSs' motors coughed softly, then purred, and the craft began their hushed approach to the lights the SEALs could now see plainly on shore.

DeWitt powered the small craft along at five miles an hour so the boats wouldn't produce a wake, and so the softly hushed motor could not be heard from the shore. He and Murdock had agreed that they would go in where there were no houses or buildings, maybe a half mile from the village itself.

The lead craft's motor coughed once and quit.

Joe Douglas, on the tiller, grabbed the starting rope and pulled twice on the starter; then it coughed once more and purred into a steady rhythm.

Ten minutes later the first boat scraped on the gently sloping sandy beach; then the second IBS came in right beside it, and the SEALs jumped out and ran into some small hardwood tree growth just beyond the beach. They took everything they brought with them. The IBSs were expendable.

The twelve men with the EAR weapons led the squads as they worked along the beach a hundred yards. Joe Lampedusa was the lead scout. He had tied his Colt carbine over his back, and carried the EAR in both hands. The glow of the ready light on the weapon showed, and all he had to do was pull the trigger. He went down to one knee, and tried to see through the darkness.

He flipped down his Night Vision Goggles and checked again. He could see no people. They were still a short ways from the village. Now he could see plainly which way to go.

They came to the edge of town, a street with a dozen houses on it. He saw few people and no military.

When he was about to move ahead, a uniformed soldier stepped out of the shadows of a house and walked across the street. Murdock had given Lam the freedom to shoot. He lifted the EAR, sighted in, and pulled the trigger.

The soft whooshing sound came, and a moment later the Japanese Ground Self Defense Force soldier slumped down, his rifle clattering on the hard-packed earth.

Murdock ran up beside Lam, who pointed to the EAR and to the man ahead in the street. "A sweetheart of a weapon," he said. Together, they ran forward, cinched plastic riot cuffs around the man's wrists and ankles, and carried him behind a house.

The rest of the SEALs moved up, and word whispered down the ranks that the EARs worked fine.

Half-a-dozen civilians hurried cautiously from one building to another. When they had left the street, Murdock moved his men forward into a vacant lot. Ahead they saw more buildings, some with lights on. Before they could decide which direction to go to find the military headquarters, a small Russian-style jeep growled around the corner. The headlights brushed over two SEALs who had just stood up.

There was no outcry from the jeep. Murdock and two men he designated fired at the jeep while it was half a block away. The three men in it slumped over, and the rig nosed into a building with a small crash and the motor died.

Three civilians ran out of the building and looked at the unconscious men. They chattered for a moment, then went back inside without offering to help the men.

Ching slid in beside Murdock. "I didn't get it all, but the Russian civilians said these stupid Japanese must be drunk again. Another one said all they wanted was the Russian vodka and their women."

Murdock sent Mahanani up to put riot cuffs on the three; then they moved on forward.

Another sentry walking a post came around a corner and saw them. He reached into his pocket for something. Before he could get it out, Washington had dropped him with a blast from his EAR. The sentry slumped to the ground without a sound. Washington ran to him, cuffed hands and ankles, and rolled him into the shadows.

Murdock studied the street ahead. It led down to the small bay. No good that way. He looked the other way on the street. There were more lights that direction. He thought he could see a two-or-three-story building, but he wasn't sure.

Lam came back from a quick scouting mission.

"Best way is to stay a block this side of that main drag. Lots of people out there moving around. Also, I saw another jeep patrol and looks like a sentry on every other block. We can work toward the center of town and hope the military headquarters is down this way."

Murdock nodded, and the two diamond formations moved

down the street, with Murdock's squad in front. Lam found another sentry and put him down with the EAR, but not before the man let out a shrill cry.

No one came to help him. The SEALs moved forward.

Murdock heard some music coming from one house they passed. He figured it was a balalaika. At the next intersection they spotted a half-ton truck with a heavy machine gun mounted in back and a gunner on it. He had aimed the weapon down the main street.

Ron Holt and Murdock took the shots. Murdock's went inside the cab. Ron Holt nailed the gunner. The man slumped down, fell off the seat, and into the body of the truck. Murdock heard nothing from inside the cab. He and Holt raced forward. Murdock found two men unconscious in the cab. He put plastic cuffs on them, and Holt said his man was secure. They moved on another block; then they could see a two-story concrete-block building to the left. It was half a block off the main street, and had a series of floodlights around it.

In front Murdock saw three jeep-like rigs, a six-by truck, and two smaller vehicles. This evidently was the motor pool as well. Murdock called DeWitt and Jaybird up for a conference. His men were against buildings, in moon shadows, off the street so the civilians wouldn't be alarmed.

"That it?" DeWitt asked, looking at the two-story building.

"My guess," Murdock said. "How we going to do it? I see one door on this side, small windows up high like a fortress. Lam, come up here," Murdock said on the radio.

Lam ran up and flattened out beside the others.

"Take a quick look around that building. Don't let anyone spot you. What we need is another door or some man-level windows we can use to shoot through. Take a check."

Lam nodded, and left sprinting across the street and past some buildings. Then he cut through the block and vanished.

"If we can find three openings to shoot through, we should get enough bounce around inside there to do in anybody who's home," Jaybird said.

"Agreed, but we need the openings," Murdock said.

"Are there drivers in those vehicles?" DeWitt asked.

"Can't tell from here," Jaybird said. "I'll go up and check."

"Wait until we get ready to do the headquarters," Murdock said. "Then we'll do them all at once."

Two soldiers left the one door they could see in the headquarters. Both had rifles. They talked, and laughed, and headed directly at the SEALs.

"I've got them," Murdock whispered into his lip mike. He pointed at Jaybird and DeWitt. Both sighted in on the soldiers and fired. The whooshing sound of the EARs came again like a heavy sigh, and the two Japanese Self Defense soldiers crumpled like rag dolls without uttering a sound.

"Leave them," Murdock said in his mike.

They looked for Lam. It was almost five minutes later when he came around the side of the house next to the one where they lay hidden. At the same time, three more soldiers came out of the headquarters. They saw the two men down in the street and ran to them. Murdock nodded and he, DeWitt, and Jaybird all fired. The three soldiers joined their unconscious comrades out cold on the ground.

Lam slid in beside Murdock.

"Don't look good, Skipper. Just one door on the other side. No back door, no windows worth shouting about."

"One squad on each side?" Murdock suggested.

"Yeah, but only one unit to enter the place; otherwise we might be blowing each other away—or knocking us out."

Murdock made up his mind quickly. "Ed, take your squad to the far door. Lam, you show them the safe way. Take out any guards or soldiers you find on the way, but don't touch any civilians. Go."

Murdock brought his squad up front. They were still forty yards away from the headquarters.

Commander Murdock surveyed the target again. He used his lip mike. "When we're ready, we move up to that house about thirty yards from the door. We wait for someone to go in or come out and open the door. Then we put five shots inside and let them rattle around.

If no one comes out, we check the trucks for drivers; then we'll storm the headquarters with our live-ammo weapons ready. DeWitt will be firing in the door on the other side but he won't go in. Questions?"

There were none. Murdock hit the lip mike. "Ed, how is it going? How long yet?"

"Just got into position thirty yards from the door. Can we fire through the door, or wait for it to open? One window we can use on the second floor. Three rounds in each one?"

"Roger that, Ed. We're waiting for an open door here. I'd say the sound won't go through the door. Has to be open. Yes, there it is for us. Everyone in First Squad fire except Jaybird, me, and Lam. Fire."

Two men had just come through the door. It swung open wide as the last one came out. The first shot hit both men, and they went down. One of them blocked the door so it stayed open.

The other four rounds went inside.

Murdock waited.

No one came boiling out of the building.

"Any action back there, Ed?" Murdock asked.

"Nothing. We got three rounds inside when somebody came out just after you hit the front. Nothing is moving."

"We wait two more minutes," Murdock said. "Then First Squad checks the trucks, then hits the door on this side. Inside, we can't use the EARs. Any ricochet would get us too. Have your regular weapons ready, and the EAR on your back. Put them there now."

Murdock strapped the long stun gun on his back, and brought around the MP-5 blaster.

He checked his watch again. "Twenty seconds, First Squad. Bradford, you're closest to the trucks. Check them for drivers. Then get to the door and hold it open wide and stay back. I'll be the first one inside, then formation order with Ching as rear guard. Now, let's do it."

The First Squad came out of the dark shadows on the run. Bradford checked the trucks, then got to the door and jerked it open. Murdock rushed inside.

Lights were on in the building. First he found a long anteroom, then the open door to an office with rooms off a long hallway to the left. Two officers sat in chairs behind a big desk. Both had slumped over the desk. The SEALs found six more soldiers inside, all unconscious. They quickly put on riot cuffs.

"Ronson and Ellsworth, cuff those five outside and drag them around to the side, then get back in here. Anybody see stairs to the second floor?"

"No second floor, Cap," Jaybird said. "Damn high ceiling, though, and some windows up there."

Murdock looked at the two Japanese officers. Neither of them had stars or shoulder boards. One was a lieutenant, the other a captain. Where were the big brass?

They found only one man not unconscious. He was in the bathroom. They cuffed him and left him there.

"Clear in here, Ed, come on in," Murdock radioed.

They collected in the big room with a lookout on each of the doors. They still had to find the general.

"Those outposts," Jaybird said. "Maybe the general went on an inspection tour."

"Company," the earpieces reported. Lam told them from the front door.

"How many?" DeWitt asked.

"Looks like six from a half-ton truck. All have rifles."

"Let them come in, then we surprise them. No shooting," Murdock said. "Out of sight, everybody."

They moved into offices. Murdock hid behind the two officers' big desk.

A few moments later, the six men came in chattering in Japanese. They moved toward the center of the big room. Then one of them noticed the two officers slumped over the desk.

One shouted.

"Now," Murdock said, and the SEALs rose up and ran into the room all with weapons pointing at the six.

"Surrender and you'll live," Ching barked at them in Japanese. "Try to fire your weapons and you all die quickly," he continued. One Japanese bent and put his rifle on the floor. The other five let their weapons fall and held up their hands.

"*Joto ichi ban,*" Ching said. SEALs rushed up, took the

weapons, and quickly tied all with plastic riot cuffs on both hands and feet.

One of the men was a captain.

"Ask the captain where General Nishikawa is," Murdock told Ching. Ching did so, squatting in front of the captain, who now sat on the floor.

An answer came at once. "The captain says the general could be at the grave site of his ancestors, or he might be inspecting the outposts. He drove away in a jeep about an hour ago."

Murdock frowned. "Ask him how many men work out of this building and where the rest of them are."

Ching asked the captain, but he shook his head, refusing to answer. Ching asked the other prisoners, but they shook their heads.

Murdock walked up to the group, picked out the smallest, and cut his ankle cuffs off. He grabbed him by the cuffed wrists and started to lead him toward one of the doors.

"Tell the captain if he doesn't tell us what we want to know, we will kill one of his men each time he refuses. Jaybird. Take this one into that room. Leave the door open. If the captain here refuses to answer again, shoot one round into something solid so it won't ricochet. But don't kill the guy."

Jaybird grabbed the Japanese man and pushed him toward the door.

"Tell him, Ching."

Ching told the captain what would happen if he refused to answer the questions. Ching asked him again how many men worked out of this building, and where the rest of them were.

The captain looked at the open door, took a long breath, then shook his head.

"Now," Murdock said into his lip mike.

The shot sounded like a cannon inside the concrete-block building. The captain collapsed on the floor.

Ching moved beside him, lifted his head, and asked the question again. This time the answer came quickly.

Twenty men worked out of this building. The rest were at the outposts. The general had just started a new outpost at the bay where he expected the invasion to come. Twenty men were out there.

The captain said he did not know where the general was. The next question was about how many men were in the invasion force. The captain said they had 180 men.

"Now, Ching, find out where the jail is where the Russian military is kept locked up."

Again the answer came quickly.

Murdock had the headquarters searched. They found Russian handheld radios like walkie-talkies.

"Bring one with us, we might be able to use it later," Murdock said. "Right now, let's get over to that jail and free the Russians. They can take over control of the headquarters here, and maybe lead us to some of the outposts."

Ed DeWitt and two of his men remained behind to keep control of the headquarters, and to capture any more returning men. Murdock moved out with the Japanese captain to show them the way to the jail.

They found it five minutes later. It was a large warehouse that had been used to hold crab meat. Murdock saw three guards patrolling outside. Ching asked how many guards were inside, and the captain said none. Murdock gave the word, and the three guards were shot with the EARs and collapsed.

Murdock and his men ran forward, found the locked doors, and opened them. Ching went to the door and talked with the ranking Russian officer, a major, and quickly the men in the jail were released. However, Ching told them they would soon be able to go back to the military headquarters building, but they could not use deadly weapons against the Japanese.

"Why not?" the major asked Ching. "They killed four of my men."

Ching translated for Murdock. Murdock spoke strongly, and the Russian heard the translation.

"We are here to free you, but restrict your activity until the last of the Japanese are gone. That's our job. Your job is to hold the central headquarters and capture any Japanese who report there. Do so bloodlessly. Understood?"

At last the Russian grinned. He looked at the unconscious

Japanese guards and asked how they'd done it. Ching explained it to him, and the Russian major was amazed.

"Now, that bay outpost," Murdock said. "Time we move down there and see if we can bag General Nishikawa."

As he said it they heard rifle shots, then some automatic weapons.

"Sounds like it's coming from the military headquarters building," Lam said.

"Let's move it," Murdock said. "Ed DeWitt and his men must be in trouble."

22

Thursday, 22 February

Kunashir Island
Kuril Chain, Russia

The SEALs ran flat out from the temporary Russian prison toward the military headquarters four blocks away. Lam outran the rest of them. The Russian military troops came along lagging to the rear.

Lam edged around the last building before he came to the headquarters, and spotted ten to twelve soldiers. They were behind the trucks and firing at the HQ front door and windows. Lam flipped down his NVG, and studied the dim greenish view.

"Twelve of them, Skipper," Lam said. "Behind those trucks."

"Use your EARs," Murdock said to his lip mike. "No time to ration our shots. Grab a target and fire."

Lam got off two shots before the last of the Japanese Ground Self Defense Force men crumpled to the ground unconscious.

"DeWitt, you guys okay in there?" Murdock asked on the Motorola.

"Have one wounded, but outside of that we're alive. A

patrol of some kind came back, and sensed something was wrong. They jabbered in Japanese, then opened fire."

"We've got company for you, about forty Russians. You come out and we'll let them go in."

Murdock found the Russian major panting up to the trucks where the SEALs were cuffing the Japanese troops.

He frowned at Murdock. "You shoot them but don't kill them. How do you do that?"

Ching translated.

"Major, it's our little secret," Murdock said. "We're giving you back your headquarters. The only stipulation is that you don't shoot any of the Japanese. These men are only unconscious. They'll wake up in three to six hours and be thirsty as hell. Take care of them. You can put them in your old jail if you want to. We're looking for the little general who started all this."

When Ching translated, the major offered to send along troops. Murdock accepted two men who knew the island, knew where the defense points were, and the outposts.

"The bay," Lam said. "When we gonna check it out? Bet that little Nishikawa guy is down there."

"The rifle fire up here will have alerted him that something is wrong," DeWitt said. "You think he's down there?"

"Best way is to go down and see," Murdock said. "Who got wounded?"

"Washington. Took a round in the ankle. Looks broken. Doc is tending to it."

Murdock went over to where Doc Ellsworth had splinted Washington's right ankle and leg.

"He's on the shelf for the rest of this one, Skip. Suggest he stay here with the Ruskies."

"Hey, no way, man," Washington protested.

Murdock punched him in the shoulder. "Your lucky day, Washington. You can find some pens and paper and work on that novel you tell me you're writing."

Washington brightened. "Yeah, I could. Good idea."

Some of the freed Russians ran into the headquarters building with shouts. Others grabbed the rifles of the unconscious Japanese.

Murdock turned to Lam. "Which way are those docks and the bay?"

Lam pointed, and the SEALs fell into their diamond formation and moved down the street. They found one walking sentry, and zapped him with an acoustic gun before he could get off a warning.

The bay was six blocks away, and Murdock and his men took it cautiously, working from cover to cover. They stopped when they had a good view of the small bay and the finger pier that extended out into deeper water.

The bay was only two hundred yards wide and about that long. A protective strip of land extended nearly to the mouth, giving the anchorage good protection. A dozen small fishing boats dotted the bay. Murdock figured they were for crab fishing.

One warehouse stood at the shore end of the pier. It was dark and evidently closed. Murdock used his NVGs and spotted a machine-gun emplacement complete with sandbags halfway down the one-hundred-foot pier.

A military jeep was parked fifty yards from the far side of the bay, and Murdock could see a dozen men there gathered around the vehicle.

"DeWitt and Adams," Murdock said on the Motorola. "Take out the gun emplacement on the pier. We're using the EARs. The rest of us, check out the jeep to the right. Let's see how many of them we can put down. We'll freelance on targets. Do it now."

The whooshing of the acoustic guns came again and again. Men around the jeep went down. Murdock heard the jeep engine gun, and a moment later the small rig blasted away from the scene, making sharp turns and twists, then darting behind a nearby house and down a street out of sight.

Four more men tried to run away from the scene, but they were zapped by the EAR guns and put down. Ed and Adams had worked the machine-gun emplacement and cut down the two men on the gun.

"Cuff all the Japanese and throw their rifles into the bay," Murdock said. "Then we have to find that damn little general.

Holt, fire up the SATCOM on the TAC frequency and let's talk to Home Base."

A minute later Holt handed Murdock the mike.

"Home Base, this is SEAL."

The reply came back quickly. "Go ahead, SEAL."

"We're on land, have control of the headquarters, and have released the Russian military. Have cautioned them not to shoot any Japanese, but that's problematical. Searching for the general who was not at the HQ. We have Tomcat cover?"

"That's affirmative, SEAL."

"Can they watch for any headlight movement? It's possible that the general learned of our move here and is cutting out for some fallback position."

"Will have the Tomcats watching your end of the island, SEAL. How are the new rifles working?"

"Home Base, they work better than expected. Perfectly. So far no other weapons have been used."

"That's a Roger, SEAL. Stay in touch."

Murdock tossed the handset to Holt. "Keep the TAC frequency open so we can receive. Now let's get back to the headquarters. Where's Douglas?"

The platoon's top mechanic and driver jogged up to Murdock.

"You bellowed, Skipper?"

"Those trucks back at the HQ. Let's go see if you can get that six-by running. It will make our moving around this rock a lot quicker."

It took them ten minutes to get back to the military headquarters building. The Russians were in total control. Murdock sent Ching in to talk to the Russian major. He came out grinning and pleased to be free.

"Of course you can use the truck," the major said through Ching's translation. "We're pleased that you came to our aid."

Murdock put Douglas in the cab, and had the SEALs jump in the back of the canvas-topped truck. It held all of them easily.

Ching asked the Russian guide the major had sent with them where the closest outpost was. Ching listened.

"Skipper, the man says the outpost is about nine clicks to the north on the Pacific Coast side."

"Ching, you and the Ruskie get in the cab and let's get up there. The general may be watching for us, but we'll have to take that chance. Do we still have that Russian walkie-talkie?"

Ching said he had it.

"Turn it on and see if you can get in contact with the general. Call him in Japanese."

The truck ground away from the HQ, and the men settled down to a few moments' relaxation.

"So far this has been a Sunday stroll through Central Park," Jaybird said.

"I like it this way," Horse Ronson said. "Let's hope this is as hard as it gets."

They were out of the tiny village then, on a dirt road leading close to the coast.

The SATCOM came to life.

"SEAL, this is Home Base."

"Go, Home Base," Holt said.

"Our night flyer reports one vehicle is on the road moving north out of the village."

"Roger that, Home Base. That's us SEALs in a six-by truck heading to an outpost. Any other traffic heading north?"

"Not exactly a freeway down there, SEAL. Night Fly reports you are the only one moving."

"Can we get on his frequency, Home Base?"

"Go to TAC Two, that should do it. Home Base out."

Holt switched the SATCOM set to TAC two.

"SEAL calling Night Fly."

"Hey, ground-bound SEALs. This is Night Fly. I have one rig moving north."

"That's us in a six-by. Any other lights heading that way?"

"Not a one. I'll keep watch."

"Thanks, we'll stay tuned."

General Nishikawa had received a radio call five minutes after the first jeep was hit by enemy fire. One of his sentries had seen the attack by the camouflaged invaders. The frightened soldier had wept. He'd said some new weapon had blasted his friends in the jeep, and they'd fallen to the ground apparently dead. There had been no sound of a rifle, no explosion, just a gentle hiss and then the men had gone down.

The general had been at the southernmost point of the island, around from the bay, and had reacted at once. He'd ordered his second in command to strengthen the force at the bay, set up a machine gun, and prepare for the invasion. He'd guessed that the commandos who had attacked had come to weaken his defenses before the main body invaded through the bay.

Again, the Russians had violated their own agreement to give him seven days. He figured the Russians would attack the HQ, so he didn't return there. Instead he turned the lights off on his jeep and proceeded slowly out of town and north up the coast road. Soon he passed the first outpost. He had taken a six-by-six truck with him, and twenty men fully armed. They would be his personal guard. Now it looked like good planning.

He made one call on the walkie-talkie radio for all outposts to report. Only the three north of the city checked in. The one on the bay evidently had been captured.

Quickly he assessed his resources. He had his twenty men, all armed. He had the two vehicles. Not much of an army. The outposts would surely fall soon. But by that time he would be in his backup position. Only yesterday he had completed stocking the supplies in the hideout.

It was not totally impregnable, but it would be hard to take with regular troops. That part he had planned well. So much for his lofty dreams. At least he had brought to the world stage and the world press the plight of the thousands of Japanese who could not worship their ancestors. The injustice of the giveaway of the Kuril Islands chain and the inhumanity of uprooting thousands of Japanese and rushing them away from their ancestral homes had now become known throughout the world.

Perhaps he had made one small footnote in history. Thousands of Japanese would thank him for his efforts. He would have a small legacy to leave to the Japanese people whether he succeeded or not. The matter had to be addressed sometime, someday. Why not now?

He wondered if he was far enough away from the village to turn on the trucks' headlights. They could go twice as fast with the lights on. He hesitated. Another few miles just to be safe.

In the captured six-by-six army truck on the coast road heading north, Ching turned up the volume on the walkie-talkie and listened again. It was the fucking Japanese general. If they could receive him, they could talk to him.

"Hey, Commander, listen to this." Ching gave the set to Murdock, who hit the listen button. He looked up.

"Who is it?"

"The bastard Japanese general. If we can hear him, we can talk to him. Should I try?"

Murdock laughed and nodded. "Fucking right. Tell him we have control of his headquarters, have captured twenty-five of his men, and released the Russian prisoners. See what he says."

Ching waited for the general to finish his transmission, then spoke in Japanese.

"General Nishikawa. This is the United States Navy force that has come to move you off this Russian island. We have captured your headquarters and released the Russian prisoners. Do you receive me, General?"

There was a pause. Ching shrugged and said it again. "Do you read me, General Nishikawa?"

Another short pause, then a tired voice answered. "Yes, I receive you. And I put a curse of a thousand years on you and your issue. You have disrupted the legitimate challenge of a whole people to be able to worship as they see fit, to sit at the graves of their ancestors and commune with them. Diplomats have taken this right away from us, and you and your kind are to blame as well for enforcing the diplomats' shame.

"Yes, I hear you, but will the world hear the wailing and gnashing of teeth, the screams of our ancestors' spirits as their sacred graves are desecrated, bulldozed away, razed and torn down so some Russian may raise a pod of peas?"

"General, it is time to come in, to submit to our control and end this whole military campaign," Ching said. "That will allow you to continue to wage your civilian campaign, your political effort to have some of the islands restored to Japan so your ancestors may be once again consecrated and protected."

There was another pause as the truck rolled along the dirt roadway.

"Could I ask if you are Japanese?" the general said.

"No, I am Chinese."

"Ah, so."

The air was dead for some time.

"General, are you still with me?"

"Yes, I am here."

"It is time for you to put down your arms, to order your men not to fire, and to come in to the village and surrender. There is no dishonor in ending a good fight with an honorable closure."

"I will never surrender."

"The lives of your men depend on your decision. Are you willing to see them slaughtered by overwhelming forces, just so you can have your last moment of glory?"

"Yes, more than willing. You may never find me."

"We will find you. We have many ways. For instance, right now our surveillance planes are tracking your radio signal."

"That is not true. I am not stupid. It would take triangulation by at least three receivers to locate my signal. You don't have that. But it was a good try."

In the dead air time, Ching turned to Murdock and summarized what they had said, and the position of the general that he would never surrender, even if it meant the deaths of all of his men.

"Afraid of that," Murdock said. "He's on the Japanese warrior crusade. We'll have to dig him out, wherever he lights. Try him again."

"General Nishikawa. My commander understands your position. He wants to meet with you, face to face, and negotiate."

There was no response, only dead air.

Ching tried to contact the general again, but he had no answer.

"He's probably turned his set off," Ching said.

Murdock looked ahead with his NVGs. "It was a good try. Do you have an evaluation of him?"

"I'd say he's a typical Japanese warrior. He'll go flat out for what he believes. I also got the impression that there's something of the samurai in him. No idea how that might play out in a showdown."

"That's what we'll have, it looks like. A showdown. The only trouble is, he's been here longer than we have. He probably researched the place before he came. He might know of some places to hide out and defend that we don't."

The big truck rumbled on at twenty miles an hour on the rutty, pothole-filled road near the Pacific Ocean.

Five minutes later, Murdock heard his SATCOM radio speak.

"SEALs, this is Night Fly. Did you get that transmission from Home Base on TAC One?"

"Negative, Night Fly," Ron Holt said.

"Home Base says they have radar showing a Russian hovercraft fast approaching the southern shore of your island somewhere north of the village. They assume it's a Russian landing of troops, Marines or commandos."

"We'll switch to TAC One, Night Fly, thanks."

Holt turned the knobs.

"Home Base, this is SEAL."

"Yes, SEAL. We have a possible landing by the Russians. We'll give you an approximate site in tenths of a mile north of the village of Golovnino. It looks like they will be landing to the north."

Murdock took the mike. "Understood, Home Base. This is Murdock. Can the admiral talk to Admiral Rostow? We have the situation under control. There is no need for Russian troops."

"Negative, Commander. We've tried twice to reach the admiral on the right frequency, but the Russians do not respond. We believe they're mad about that hovercraft we shot up."

"Roger that. Give us that landing spot as soon as possible. We're about five miles north of the village. We'll hold here for the landing location."

"SEALs. You might want to reverse course. The hovercraft is past that position already. Estimate they are three miles from the village."

"Will do, Home Base."

Murdock punched Douglas. "Turn it around and motor three miles back south and watch the surf for company."

They rode back the way they had come. At the three-mile mark, they stopped and waited.

"Turn off the motor," Murdock said. They listened.

Lam heard it first.

"Something out there is making noise, Commander. Could be the damn Ruskies slipping into shore."

"With a hovercraft you don't sneak in anywhere," Jaybird cracked.

Then they all heard it. The hovercraft was coming at the beach fast, and couldn't be more than a quarter of a mile away.

"Put up a white flare," Murdock said. "Then we'll see how in hell we can meet these guys without both of us getting our asses shot off."

23

Thursday, 22 February

Kunashir Island
Kuril Chain, Russia

Murdock watched the white flare burst fifty yards at sea. The road swung within seventy-five yards of the beach here. When the flare died, Murdock pulled down his NVGs and watched the water. At first he could see only the Pacific waves rolling into the sandy beach. "Everyone out, disperse along the road and in cover," Murdock said in the lip mike. The SEALs left the six-by and spread out along the road ten yards apart.

The sound of the hovercraft increased.

"Try them on TAC Two, Holt," Murdock said. "Tell them there are friendly U.S. forces in front of them. We fired the star shell."

Holt sent the message twice, but had no response.

"Don't think they heard you, SEALs," the radio reported. "This is Night Fly One. They're damned near the beach."

"Thanks, Night Fly One," Holt said. "We've got them."

"Fire another white flare," Murdock said. Jaybird fired one over the edge of the beach. It burst, and now in the glow, they could see the hovercraft heading straight at the beach fifty yards south of them.

"Ching, on me," Murdock snapped on the Motorola.

Ching ran up, and flattened out beside Murdock.

"You and me, Ching. We're getting as close to that landing area as possible. When the hovercraft motors stop and it goes quiet, I want you to yell at them in Russian that the United States SEALs are here and we're friendly. Ask them to hold their fire."

When they'd checked the Russian hovercraft in the book on the carrier, Murdock saw that this larger boat had four 30mm/65's with twin-mounting AK630's with six barrels per mounting. They could fire three thousand rounds a minute up to two kilometers. Murdock didn't want them to think they had to soften up their landing site with a few thousand rounds.

Murdock's request to hold fire was said so the rest of the men heard it on the radio. Then Murdock and Ching rose up and ran bent over toward where the Russian hovercraft would come out of the waves and power straight up on the beach over the sand. It would continue over the grass and land until the drivers wanted to stop it.

The pair was still twenty yards from the big craft when its fans blew dry sand into a cloud as they rammed the air-cushioned craft onto the beach and across it, and came to rest on the dry land covered by grass and weeds.

The big propellers pushing the craft forward slowed and died. The huge fans that had lifted the boat on a cushion of air off the water and the land wound down. A minute and a half after the craft came to a halt, the last motor sounds faded to silence.

Murdock tapped Ching on the shoulder.

Ching took a deep breath and yelled in Russian.

"Hey, Russian friends. Hold your fire. We are United States SEALs here putting down the Japanese invaders."

He stopped, and both men dug low against the ground in case of any Russian fire. Nothing happened. Ching yelled out his welcome again. Two minutes later, a thin voice came back. Ching translated.

"How do we know you are friendly? You disabled one of our hovercrafts and killed three men."

"If we had not been friendly your craft would have been sunk," Ching said in Russian. He whispered what he had said to Murdock, who nodded.

There was a long silence.

"Tell them about the prisoners and the HQ," Murdock said.

"We have captured the military headquarters building and twenty-five Japanese soldiers. We have released your local Russian garrison from the Japanese prison. They now control the HQ. Contact them on your radios for confirmation."

"We hear you," the Russian voice answered.

Again they waited.

Then the Russians answered with a new voice in English. "We have talked with our men in the headquarters. You speak the truth. Send out two of your officers for a conference. Come to the lighted area near our bow."

A moment later a light blossomed at the front of the dark hovercraft.

"Let's go talk," Murdock said. "You did good, Ching. Remind me to tell you that later."

They stood and walked toward the pool of light. Fifteen yards from the light they were aware of men lifting out of the darkness and following them.

"Always nice to be escorted," Ching said.

"Tell them we're coming in," Murdock said.

"We're coming in," Ching said in Russian. "We're about ten yards out with your troops behind us."

"Good," the voice said in English. "We would give you a typical Russian welcome, but you can understand our suspicions."

They saw a Russian then, standing in the light. He was dressed all in black, wore a floppy hat, and carried a submachine gun. When he saw them, he lowered the weapon and held out his hand.

"Hello, Americans, and welcome to Russian territory. I am Captain Radiwitch."

Murdock took another few steps and gripped the Russian's hand. "Hello yourself, Captain Radiwitch. I'm Commander Murdock of the U.S. Navy SEALs."

Murdock's EAR weapon was held in one hand and

pointing down. Ching had also lowered the muzzle of his EAR.

"What happens now, American?"

"Now we work together. The little general who started this is still at large. We're not sure where he is. We have two Russians with us who were in the garrison here. They can help us find the rest of the renegades."

"I will talk with our commander," the captain said. "Wait the moment one, please." He vanished out of the light, and two soldiers with weapons slung moved into his place.

"Send over the two Russians," Murdock said into his mike. "Ching, tell the two guards here that two Russians are coming from the darkness." Into the lip mike Murdock said: "The rest of you SEALs stay put. We don't want any accidents here. Wait until we get total agreement and clearance. It looks like a friendly situation, so far."

As he finished whispering into the mike, two men came into the light. One was the captain; the other had silver leaves on his epaulets. He was not dressed in black, but in the traditional Russian winter uniform. He stepped forward and held out his hand.

Murdock took it. "I'm pleased to meet you, Colonel. I'm Commander Murdock, Navy SEALs."

The Russian looked to the captain, who translated. Then the colonel smiled and shook his hand again.

"I am Lieutenant Colonel Hartzloff, in charge of this strike. How many men do you have?" Ching translated.

"I have fifteen SEALs, Colonel." The captain translated.

The colonel nodded. "I have a hundred, all seasoned veterans." He paused. "You have done all of this so far with only sixteen men?"

"We're specialists in this kind of work, Colonel. Have you talked to your men at the headquarters building?"

The colonel nodded. "We have. They tell me you have weapons that shoot men and put them to sleep, but don't kill them. How do you do this?"

"Sorry, we can't tell you that, Colonel. What we can do is work together on this problem, and bring the Japanese general to bay before it gets light."

The translation took longer this time.

The two Russians from the SEAL group walked into the edge of the light.

They said something in Russian, and the colonel smiled.

"So, they are helping you. Have they told you where this rebel general might be?"

"No, sir. We're taking out the defensive outposts as we come to them and working north."

Murdock's earphone spoke. He held up one finger and listened.

"Skipper, Holt. The Night Fly boys tell me they have a two-truck or two-car convoy out about twenty klicks and heading north along the Pacific side."

"They have a guess, Holt?"

"No, sir, but I do. Got to be the general and the rest of his men."

"Thanks, Holt. Stay in contact with the pilot. We've got to do some planning." Murdock took a step toward the colonel. "One of our aircraft reports a two-truck convoy about twenty kilometers to the north. We believe it is the general. I have a suggestion."

The colonel waited for his translator to do his work.

"So?"

"We divide your force. A third of it can move to the road and use the six-by-six truck there. They can continue to suppress the outpost north of here three or four kilometers. There may be no one there. Then these men can fan out and secure the rest of the island, and work back to the village."

The Russian nodded when he had the words translated.

"Then what?" the translator asked.

"Then our fifteen men join you on your hovercraft, and we go back up the coast twenty kilometers. We land, find the truck convoy, and engage the general and his forces. Either he surrenders or his entire force is killed."

The Russian colonel nodded as the translation went on.

"Yes, yes. I like," the colonel said in English. "I have very bit English." He beamed. "Yes, we do."

He turned and snapped orders to some men in the shadows. Murdock watched as thirty soldiers formed up just out of the

light and marched off toward the truck with one of the
Russians the SEALs had brought with them.

"Colonel, should I have my men come over?" Murdock
asked.

The colonel looked up and nodded. Murdock used the lip
mike and told them to get front and center.

Ten minutes later, the SEALs were on board the Russian
hovercraft. Before the big engines started, Murdock talked to
the planes overhead on TAC Two.

"Night Fly, this is the SEAL bunch. Any more action on
those truck lights?"

"SEALs, not much. Estimate they are about twenty-five
klicks from the town's lights along the Pacific coast. The
movement has stopped. Headlights are off. Best we can do
from up here."

"Thanks, Night Fly. Tell Home Base we've met the
Russian air-cushion craft. Have talked with the commander
and we're now on board ready for a fast run up the beach to
where you boys saw the headlights stop. We won't be able to
hear you when the engines start. Thirty Russian marines are
now combing the lower part of the island from where you saw
the air cushion rig come ashore. They'll work down to the
town.

"We're linked up with the other seventy Russian commandos for a surprise party for the general up north."

"That's a Roger, SEALs. Will relay the information to
Home Base. Good luck down there."

The air-cushion engines began, and Murdock handed the
mike back to Holt.

A minute later they edged down to the water, skimmed
over it, and turned north. At forty-five knots it would take
them less than thirty minutes to cover the twenty miles
northward.

Murdock looked around the vessel. It was 155 feet long,
he'd been told, and over fifty-eight feet wide. The troops and
gear were all stowed in a hold that was covered. He wondered
how the flyboys had decided that the first hovercraft the day
before had been empty. He would never know. He tried to

memorize as much about the craft as possible. It would come in handy for his after-action report.

The colonel sent the captain to take him to the bridge.

"We want you to see more of the ship," the Russian captain said. "The bridge is the best. Perhaps your radio will work from there, and your aircraft can give us some direction."

It did. The Night Fly team could follow the wake of the air-cushion craft. They had a previous fix on the headlights, and brought the ship into shore as close to the lights as they could determine.

"We can do seventy knots without a load," the Russian captain said. "That is much faster than your American air-cushioned boat, the LCAC, which has a top speed of forty knots."

Murdock laughed. "You win that one, Captain. This is a remarkable ship. You can carry four light tanks and how many combat troops?"

"No secret. It's in *Jane's Fighting Ships* book. We can carry four light tanks, or two medium tanks, and two hundred combat-ready soldiers."

By that time they were nearing their target. The Night Fly planes had agreed to do a flyover of the suspect area. They would come in off the sea and across the land so their flaming tailpipes could be seen by the hovercraft pilot. The plan worked remarkably well.

The craft headed for the beach, then diverted a quarter mile south.

"Too many sharp rocks and bad beach for landing," the Russian pilot explained.

The craft slashed through the Pacific Ocean's swells, rode the breakers, leveled out on the sand, and raced up the wet part to the dry sand. Then it slid easily over the weeds and small brush to a stop fifty feet from the shoreline.

When the motors cycled down, Murdock heard rifle fire and one machine gun.

"Looks like we're at the right spot," Murdock said. "Colonel, like we said on the way up, let my men go out first and try to get the general's rear guard in a cross fire with our weapons. If we can't dislodge them, we'll have your man call you in."

The colonel, who said he wasn't wild about getting his men killed, gave a curt nod, and the SEALs left by the rear of the big ship out the tank-access door. First Squad swung to the right and Second Squad moved left. They could hear the Japanese firing.

"Sounds like six or eight men," Murdock said into his mike. "Let's get a clear field, then fire at the muzzle flashes."

Three minutes later Ed DeWitt called on the Motorola that his men were ready. Murdock moved around another ten yards, and found an opening through which they could see the flashes.

"Open fire," Murdock told his lip mike. He sighted in on one muzzle flash and pulled the trigger. The soft whooshing sound came, and then he heard six more down the line.

At once the number of shots coming from the Japanese trailed off. Three more rounds hit the defenders; then the last guns in the rear guard went silent.

"Let's move in and mop up," Murdock ordered into his mike.

They ran forward, their EAR weapons off safety with ready lights glowing. In the pale Japanese moonlight they found the six defenders. All had two weapons each. All lay sleeping beside their still hot rifles and the one machine gun.

"Cuff them, and call up the troops," Murdock said. The Russian with Murdock used the Russian walkie-talkie, and soon the first elements of the Russians moved up. They stared in surprise at the six defenders all unconscious.

Colonel Hartzloff checked the pulse on two of the men, and shook his head. He came up to Murdock.

"Commander, must know about your weapon."

Murdock laughed. "Colonel, it's like your Akula-class submarines."

The colonel took a step backward. "You know about Akula?"

"About them. They are in *Jane's Fighting Ships*, right? But we don't know all the scientific and secret aspects of them.

Like this rifle. Now you know about it, but not how or why it works. We must leave it that way."

The colonel frowned, then shrugged. "We will leave it this way for now. But after we have captured the Japanese general, we will deal with it again." He paused. "You realize that we have five times as many weapons here as your fifteen men have?"

Murdock smiled in the moonlight. He stared at the Russian commando. "I'm aware of that, Colonel. But have you realized that our weapons are fifteen times as effective as yours are?"

24

Thursday, 22 February

Kunashir Islands
Kuril Chain, Russia

After a moment of staring, the two officers looked away from each other.

"I wish we had one of them conscious so we could find out where the general went," Murdock said. He motioned to Lam.

"Make a couple of swings out there and see what you can find. Even in the dark you should be able to see where twenty men went on a hike."

Lam grinned, and ran into the darkness toward the looming upthrust of a hill in front of them.

The Russian guide who had come with them from the prison came up and talked with Ching. The interpreter hurried over to Murdock.

"Skip, we might have something here. This guy says he's been in this area many times. There is a series of old caves high on the cliffs back there. He says it would make a perfect hideout and fortress for somebody trying to hold off a superior force."

"How far from here?"

Ching asked the Russian, then turned. "He says it's into the mountain where the jeeps can't drive. Maybe four or five miles, maybe more. None of his group ever went all the way back there."

Murdock moved over to talk to the Russian officer.

"Colonel Hartzloff, we may have a direction to go." He told the officer what the Russian guide had told Ching. The colonel motioned to the guide, who was a corporal, and talked with him.

Then the colonel turned to Murdock. "Yes, sounds good. My trackers and my scouts will lead. Your men in the middle and my commandos as rear guard. We will go now."

Murdock shrugged. Getting there wasn't the problem. What to do once they found the general would be the tough part. He could wait.

They found Lam coming back to meet them. He lifted his brows when he saw the SEALs in the middle of the line of march.

"What the fuck, sir?"

Murdock shook his head. "Not the time to worry now." He told the scout what the Russian from the prison had said.

"Good, they went up this way for fucking certain," Lam said.

They hiked along silently for two miles. Then ahead, a machine gun chattered. Murdock and his men hit the dirt. The Russians went down as well. Murdock and Holt began working forward past the prone Russians. They didn't look like blooded veterans right then to Murdock.

The machine gun fired again; then they heard the lower-pitched rounds from the Japanese rifles. The Russians at the front of the column returned fire. Murdock heard the flat crack of the AK-47, now called the AKM, and the stuttering fire of a Russian machine gun. He and Holt went faster, pushing past the Russians until they came to the front of the column.

Murdock bellied down behind a fallen pine tree. There were a lot of good-sized pines here higher on the slope.

"Captain, how many up there?" Murdock called to the Russian officer. Radiwitch rolled toward him.

"We don't know. Four, maybe five. I've got a wounded

man. They are in a good defensive position among a jumble
of rocks. Hard to get a good shot."

"Let *us* try," Murdock said. He motioned to Holt, who had
an EAR now as well. They waited for another volley of fire
from the rocks a hundred yards ahead, then took turns firing
at five-second intervals. After three shots each from the
EARs, they waited. The firing from the rocks had stopped.

"I figured the sound would bounce around those rocks like
it did in a room," Murdock whispered to Holt.

Captain Radiwitch rolled over to Murdock again, and
stared at the EAR from two feet away.

"I must have one of those. No more firing from the
Japanese rear guard. How did you do that?"

"With these rifles. Captain, do you want to send two men
up there and check," Murdock said.

"I will go," the captain said. He rose and sprinted forward.
There were no shots fired by the Japanese. Radiwitch ran the
hundred yards in fifteen seconds. Another five seconds and he
called out loudly in Russian and his men advanced slowly.
Murdock and Holt went with them.

The four Japanese rear-guard defenders lay unconscious
beside their weapons. Murdock and Holt bound them with
plastic cuffs, and Murdock pointed ahead. The Russians
talked excitedly for a minute until Captain Radiwitch silenced
them.

The Russian commando sent out two point men; then the
rest of the Russians and SEALs moved out following them.

They were still on the right trail.

A mile higher on the slopes, they found another rear-guard
position. Murdock and Holt had drifted back with the other
SEALs and told them about the action.

"That's why we should be the fuck up front," Lampedusa
said. Murdock agreed with him, but he didn't want to
antagonize the Russians. They might be needed later on.

The new rear guard was in a patch of foot-thick pine trees
with an open field of small rocks and gravel in front of it. The
area looked as though an old landslide had wiped out
vegetation there sometime within the past year or two. There

was no cover going the last five hundred yards to the position where the Japanese kept up a steady but spaced fire.

Murdock and his squads were still out of the range of the guns ahead. He waited. He felt more than heard a squad of the commandos move through the woods to the right of the open space. Captain Radiwitch was trying to outflank the defenders and get around them. The sound of two grenades exploding in rapid succession came a minute into the Russians' move. Trip wires and hand grenades, Murdock guessed. He and Holt worked to the front of the safe zone.

Captain Radiwitch came back carrying a dead commando over his shoulders. He dropped him to the ground and sat down hard. A medic ran up and treated the captain's shrapnel wounds in his leg and both arms.

"Lucky, he said. "One dead, two wounded bad." He turned and said something to a sergeant, who gave another order. At once a squad of seven men took rifle grenades from their packs and rested the butts of their AKMs, the newest model of the AK-47 standby, on the ground. Each had grenade-launching attachments. The commandos fired at will, each man putting six grenades into the general area of the machine gun and the rear guard ahead.

The machine gun stopped firing. Only an occasional round came from the Japanese rebels above. After another five minutes, Captain Radiwitch led a squad of six commandos through the woods again. They kept to the fringes, sometimes in sight of the spot where the rear guard had been.

Murdock could see them assault the position with full automatic fire. If anyone had been alive before they made the assault, it was certain none were alive now.

The walkie-talkie rumbled, and the Russian commandos got to their feet and moved up the hill. Murdock and his SEALs went along.

At the rear-guard position, Murdock checked the bodies. There were only three men there, with two machine guns and six rifles. All were dead. No chance to question a Japanese prisoner again.

Captain Radiwitch found Murdock.

"Lead out with your men, if you wish," Radiwitch said. "Your weapons may be more effective in this situation."

Murdock said they would take the point. He realized that he hadn't seen the colonel. Evidently he was a commander who directed his men from the safety of the hovercraft.

The trail now wound higher in the hills. The timber was mostly pine now, and thick in places. Other areas were bare rock where nothing could grow. Lampedusa led the SEALs with the Russian scout they brought from the prison. He and Lampedusa communicated with signs. They wound up a valley, over a small hill, and the Russian pointed ahead. They could just make out a peak with a jagged, rugged-looking cliff just down from the summit.

Lam scowled. In the dark, the place looked to be another two thousand feet above them. He figured there was only one more ridge between them and the last slant of the mountain. Would they be in an open field of fire all the way up that last slope?

Lam pointed at the place and tapped the Russian on the shoulder. "General, Japo?" He pointed at the cliff. The Russian nodded and chattered in Russian, which didn't help at all.

"If you say so, buddy. We got ourselves some heavy climbing to do."

Lam had seen evidence of passage recently. He'd found a canteen back a ways. On a bramble, he saw where a uniform had ripped and left a swatch of dark cloth. Now the work was harder. They were not at a timberline, but the rocky terrain prevented any but the hardiest of small shrubs from growing there. That meant there was practically no cover or conceal-ment.

They worked up to the ridgeline and down the other side. Lam had been right. Now it was one long climb up a slant of rock to what must be the general's hideout above. Lam estimated it was a half mile up the slope. If they were caught out there in daylight, the Japanese could pick them off like targets in a carnival shooting gallery.

Lam looked at his watch. Just after 2200. They had a lot of dark yet. He waited for the troops to catch up. Time they had a conference on just how they were going to get up all this rock without attracting attention.

A few minutes later, Murdock and the platoon came up to where Lam waited.

"Need to talk, Skipper."

Murdock looked at the landscape ahead, and up to the top of the slope. "Up there?"

"That's what our local guide thinks. I've found enough shit to know they came this way."

Murdock checked his watch. It was 2215. "We should be able to move across this open space in the dark. They might know we're down here, but they won't shoot and give away their positions. Ching."

The lanky SEAL dropped down beside Murdock.

"Tell the captain and his men that we must have absolute silence as we move up from here on. No talking, coughing, no sounds."

Ching nodded, and headed for the Russian troops just behind them.

"Route?" Murdock asked.

Jaybird had been looking at the shadows in the moonlight. "Looks like there's a ravine over there a few hundred yards we could use like a staircase."

"For a ways," Lam said. "Looks like there's a rockfall at the far side near the top. That might be how the rebels go up the last few yards to the cliff top."

"Is it a cliff or a cave up there?" Mudock asked.

"Supposed to be a shelf-like place with a cave behind it," Lam said.

"So from a low angle, our EAR shots would bounce off the rocks and slant out into space hurting nobody," Murdock said.

"Let's hope it looks different by the time we get up there," Ed DeWitt said from the other side.

"So let's do it," Murdock said. "Silent movement, keep our interval. Lam, lead out."

They worked across the slope to the ravine, and walked up that for two hundred yards; then it ended. It was hard going. The slant of the hill increased, and at times they had to reach down to the ground to help themselves to take the next step. Murdock could hear the sound of the Russian commandos behind them. That was not good. If the general had any sentries out at all, they had to be able to hear the seventy-five men moving toward them.

An hour later they were still a long way from the top of the mountain. Murdock called a halt. DeWitt and Jaybird came up for a talk. Now their voices were whispers.

"How far to the top?" DeWitt asked.

The estimates were from six hundred yards to twelve hundred.

"Where is the closest cover for our eighty-five bodies?" Jaybird asked. They all stared into the softly moonlit night.

"There isn't any," Lam said.

"Got to be some somewhere," Jaybird countered.

They were near the middle of the slope of rocks and dirt that led up to the peak.

"Off to the left more," Murdock said. "Another wash. Looks big enough for half of us. The rest can stay back farther and be out of the line of fire."

"Might work," DeWitt said. "But that gully still puts us six or eight hundred yards from the target."

Murdock used his lip mike. "Ching, ask Captain Radiwitch to come up for a conference."

A few minutes later the Russian commando sat down beside the others. Murdock showed him the situation, letting him use the NVGs to check out the top and the new gully.

"What we suggest is that half of our force move into the gully," Murdock said. "Then I'll take one squad of SEALs and work up silently as close as we can get to the top. We think that rock field to the left is the access route to the top. Once there, the squad will have cover from any fire from above."

"Your sleep guns. Can you use them?"

Murdock shook his head at the Russian. "The angle is wrong. We can't hit the Japanese and we can't get any bounce effect up there the way we did the last time. We'll have to move in closer and probably use our regular weapons."

"How many men up there?" the captain asked.

"We've captured or killed nine or ten. That should leave him with maybe ten or fifteen."

"It's a good defensive position," the Russian captain said.

"We'll try grenades," Murdock said. "But the overhang on that cliff is going to deflect all but a few chance rounds that get inside."

The Russian stared at the slope. "You take squad of ten?"

"No, we use eight men."

"Then I take squad of eight men, we go together."

Murdock had expected it. Russian pride. "Agreed. Bring your men up. Automatic weapons, lots of grenades, hand and rifle."

The captain nodded and slipped away.

"First Squad, get up here," Murdock said into his lip mike. "We're going for a walk in the park."

Ten minutes later, the sixteen men crouched in the ravine. The rest of the SEALs and twenty handpicked Russian commandos filled the area behind. The rest of the Russians were farther back.

Murdock had been checking the slope above with his NVG. He had monitored the lip of the cliff looming over them, but could detect no bodies and no movement.

He spotted what looked like a trace of a trail that wound through sedan-sized boulders fifty yards ahead of them. Lam checked it and nodded.

"Sure as hell looks like a trail, Skipper. Let's give it a try."

Murdock and his men moved out first, slipping quietly up the rocky slope toward the rocks. Lam reached them first, and vanished behind a huge boulder. Murdock and the rest slid in between the giant's marbles. The Russians were close behind.

Murdock looked around his big rock at the cliff above. It was still fifty yards away. He grinned. Now he saw the path. Someone had cleared away most of the smaller rocks and pushed aside larger ones. The path wound around some of the large boulders slanting upward to the end of the shelf. They provided what could be enough cover for an assault on the cliff. The cave must be just behind it.

Murdock waved at Ching, and he edged up beside him.

"Stay undercover and call out to the Japanese general. Tell

him we come for his surrender. Enough men have died. He should send his men down without arms."

Ching moved closer, then called the message over a protective rock. When he finished, there was a long pause. Then a short reply came back.

Ching looked back at Murdock. "He said never, just the one word."

Captain Radiwitch came up and heard the exchange.

"Time for Russian power," he said to Murdock. "My men will blow them out of there with grenades."

"Captain, it's only fifty yards. The shelf over the cave extends well out. It's a hard shot to get a rifle grenade in there. Coming up here, I thought it might work. Now I'm not so sure."

"We can do it. Do not worry. Russians good with rifle grenades."

Murdock shrugged. "Go ahead. I hope that none of the misses start a landslide and cover this place up with rocks."

"Russians never miss," Captain Radiwitch said. He turned and spoke quickly in Russian. Six men with grenade launchers on their AKMs came forward and found firing positions.

Murdock touched his lip mike. "Our friends are going to try to use rifle grenades to soften them up. Let's watch it. Some of those little bombs could set off a landslide in this unstable part."

The Russians began firing. Murdock watched the flight of two rifle grenades. They sailed high, came down short on the bare rocks outside the ledge, and exploded. A few rocks loosened and tumbled down the slope. None came toward the SEALs. Half a dozen more grenades exploded. Murdock saw two shatter inside the parapet around the cliff. Then three more went off on the face of the cliff below the cave.

It began slowly. Then more and more rocks loosened. A moment later it was a full-sized landslide rumbling down the mountain straight at the SEALs and Russians.

"Watch out," Murdock shouted. "Incoming from those damn Russian grenades."

25

Thursday, 22 February

Mt. Kunashir
Kunashir Island
Kuril Chain, Russia

The dirt and rocks in the landslide cascaded down the slope. The larger rocks rolled faster, bounced, landed, and bounced again. The first few hit the huge boulders. Some shattered, others bounced once more and went past the men.

Tons of rocks and dirt pounded down. The group of huge boulders the men crouched behind acted as a divider for much of the landslide. The first roll of rocks and dirt hit the boulders and split to each side; then more of the Plymouth-sized rocks nudged the flow of dirt and rocks farther to the side.

The sixteen men in the forward position huddled behind their boulders and waited. The roaring, grinding sound of the landslide enveloped them, then passed by and was gone. The men were covered with a foot of dirt and small rocks, but none of them was injured.

Murdock did a net check, and all seven of his SEALs reported in. "Just hold in place while we figure this," he told them on the Motorola.

Captain Radiwitch came up brushing the dust and dirt off

his uniform. Lam moved over as well and motioned to Murdock.

"Commander, might have a suggestion. Look at the layout of the rocks up the hill, the big ones. With a little covering fire, we can leapfrog up there to the end of the rock field. The boulders are plenty big enough for cover up to thirty feet from the ledge where the cave is."

The Russian listened. Murdock took another look at the rock field and nodded. He turned to the commando. "Looks possible, Captain. What do you think?"

Captain Radiwitch stared up at the rocks, then the path the men would take. At last, he nodded. "Eight men fire, eight men move. We go first, you give cover fire."

"Sounds good." Murdock brought his SEALs up in a rough line with fields of fire on the top of the ledge, and told them the plan.

Radiwitch got his men in position and pointed at Murdock.

"Let's do it," Murdock said to his men. "Sustained fire, real ammo, but don't run short on rounds. Fire."

The eight weapons spoke, and then again, and again. The eight Russians darted from rock to rock, working up the hill thirty yards. They slid behind boulders, and Murdock called a cease-fire.

A moment later the Russians set up a fire pattern on the top of the mountain, and Murdock led his men in a charge toward the spot the Russians had claimed.

They made it, and Murdock tried to remember if there had been any return fire from the top. He couldn't remember hearing any.

"Hand grenades," the Russian officer said. His men threw six grenades into the mountaintop fortress. All went off with a thunderous roar. Just after they exploded, the Russians charged up the last twenty yards to the shelf of land. They went in with assault fire, the AKMs and the AK-47's blasting on automatic. Then the firing stopped.

Captain Radiwitch stood on the top of the ledge and waved.

"Nobody here," he called.

Two minutes later, Murdock and his men were in the

temporary fortress. All they found were three dead Japanese and several weapons that had been ruined by exploding grenades.

Lam explored the cave, then the sides of the mountain. He came back a minute later.

"Small cave to one side of the large one. It has a back door, and a good trail down the mountain on the back side. We've been snookered."

Murdock and the SEALs rushed out the opening and looked downhill. Five hundred yards down the mountain, they saw two forms slide behind some cover in a gully. Murdock checked the route they had to follow. There was a large rock slide well down the mountain the Japanese would have to cross.

"Machine guns and Bradford. Set up here and zero in on that rock field. You're going to have some targets down there soon. Bradford, what's the range?"

"Eight hundred yards."

Joe Douglas shook his head as he spread the bi-pod on his H&K 21E chattergun. "Got to be closer to a thousand."

"Work it out. The three of you cover that slide area. The minute you see any men on it, start firing. It won't be us. The rest of you SEALs on me. We're going hunting."

Captain Radiwitch listened. He had no machine gunners in his team. When the SEALs left moving quickly down the trail, he put his men in line behind them.

It was almost ten minutes later when the three gunners spotted figures in their NVGs as they worked into the slide area. The gunners charged their weapons and opened fire. Bradford was short, even firing downhill. Douglas and Horse Ronson blasted the rock slide with five-round bursts. They saw at least two of the Japanese who did not continue the trip. The rest hurried, and some slid down the slope, creating a new, small landslide.

After three minutes of sporadic firing, the gunners checked with the NVGs again. There were no more Japanese moving across the slide.

"Let's pack up and haul ass," Bradford said. He had slammed fifteen of the big .50-caliber rounds into the area.

He wasn't sure if he'd hit any targets, but he must have scared hell out of them.

The three big men trotted down the trail, making as good time as they could.

When Murdock and the SEALs came to the rock slide, the guns firing above had silenced. They found three bodies there, and evidence that the rest of the general's army had kept to the very edge of the slide in some small growth to mask their movements. The SEALs followed.

The moon seemed brighter now. Murdock noticed that it was three-quarters full, and thanked the heavens for their help. The SEALs hurried forward, then stopped to listen. Each time they could hear the Japanese rushing through the brush and more trees below.

The SEALs took a quick break in an open area. Murdock called the captain up. "What's the maximum range on your rifle grenades?"

"Four hundred meters."

Murdock grinned in the darkness. "What would you think of sending six rounds out at max range where we think the Japanese general is?"

Captain Radiwitch smiled. "Yes, I like." He turned and spoke to his men, who quickly readied their rifles and fired six rifle grenades forward where their captain pointed.

They waited for the six distinct cracking explosions of the grenades. They heard no shouts of surprise or wails of pain.

"Worth a try," Murdock said, and got the men moving again.

An hour later, the sixteen men were in heavy pine timber working down another small hill. Lam said they were still on the right trail. "They leave a highway of signs," Lam said. "Some of the troops must be discarding equipment to make their load lighter. I've found a pistol, a shirt, and three loaded magazines. They are still ahead of us and we're gaining on them."

Murdock looked at his watch. The soft light glow showed him that it was 0505. An hour, maybe two, to daylight. He talked to Lampedusa on the point as they walked through the brush.

"Any logic to his route?"

Lam shrugged. "Not that I can see. Downhill is his trademark right now. I'd guess we're heading toward the coast. We're on a small stream that must come out at the beach sooner or later."

"Any way to cut him off at the pass?"

"Not so you could notice, Skipper."

"Afraid of that."

Ten minutes later, the small stream had grown to a roaring river. Lam figured that the Japanese couldn't cross over now if they wanted to. The brush thinned out in the pine woods, but there was still plenty of protection. Lam didn't consider an ambush by the Japanese. They were running, not looking for a fight.

"Figure there are no more than eight of them, Skip," Lam said. "My guess is we're about a half mile behind."

"Double time?" Murdock asked.

"Yeah, no brush, ground is stable. Let's do it."

Murdock told the Russian captain the plan. He shrugged. "SEALs do it, Russians do it."

Murdock set up a ground-eating trot that he figured was seven miles an hour. That would be about an eight-minute mile. They should be able to sustain that for an hour.

Lam stayed out in front by thirty yards, and Holt made a connecting file to him. They jogged down the bank of the river, across small feeder streams and up a slight rise, then down to the bank again.

A half hour later, Lam stopped and held the rest. They all listened. Ahead they could hear talk.

"Japanese words, but I can't understand them," Ching said. They moved ahead again slower, but on full combat alert. Lam spotted them first. The Japanese had taken a break. None was on sentry duty watching the rear. Two were drinking at the stream.

They were forty yards ahead.

"Don't kill them," Murdock said into his mike. He caught the Russian captain. "We capture them. We don't kill them." The captain nodded and whispered to his men. Murdock sent Lam and three SEALs into the brush to get even with the

Japanese. Lam clicked his mike when he was set. Murdock had moved up the other four SEALs and set up a field of fire.

"Shoot over their heads, three rounds each. Then, Ching, sing out and talk the general into surrendering."

Murdock began the firing with a three-round burst from his MP-5. For a moment the woods rang with the gunfire. Then, just as suddenly as it began, it stopped.

Ching bellowed at the Japanese, who had frozen in place. None of them even reached for a weapon.

"General Nishikawa, you are surrounded. You must surrender or your men will be slaughtered like pigs and you will have to watch them die."

The general stood and turned toward the voice.

"We surrender. My men will lay face-down. No more need to die. They have been loyal and true. You must urge world opinion to consider the plight of twenty thousand Japanese who can't worship at their ancestors' graves. You may approach now."

The general moved away from his men and sat down on the ground with his back to the others. Murdock and the SEALs moved forward cautiously. They kept their weapons ready, but none of the Japanese made a move to protest. They were cuffed by the wrists as the SEALs came to them.

Murdock walked over to where the general sat. He took Ching with him.

"Tell the general we respect his military moves, but it's time now to surrender."

Ching said it, but there was no comment from the general.

Murdock told Ching to speak to the general again. Ching said the same words, but the general did not turn.

Murdock rushed ahead just as the general toppled over to the side. When they got there it was too late. General Raiden Nishikawa lay on his side with a ceremonial samurai short sword in his stomach. He had thrust it in, turned it sideways, and sliced through his bowels.

He had died in the few minutes it took the SEALs to approach his position.

Murdock crouched on the ground in front of the general. The man had had a mission and had been willing to die for his cause. At least now he would be with his ancestors. The world would have a martyr for the cause of giving the Kuril chain back to Japan.

Murdock had an idea that he let ferment and grow and expand as he thought about it. Why not? What would be better for this small Japanese man than to be left here on Kunashir with his ancestors?

How? They had no entrenching tools, no shovels, nothing to use to dig a grave. Murdock called Jaybird over and put the problem to him.

"Easy, Skipper. We do like the Indians used to. We find a low place in the land, scoop it out with sticks, lay him in it, then cover him with rocks out of the stream. Then we pile brush on top of that so no animals can get to him. Makes a fine grave."

Captain Radiwitch came up frowning. "Why didn't you use your sleep guns on the Japanese?"

Murdock smiled. "Hey, if we had, then we would have had to carry them out to the coast. This way, they walk." The Russian laughed and went to talk with his men.

"We get him and his Ruskies out of here, then we bury the general," Murdock said. "We'll make up a story that the general killed himself and fell into the river and we couldn't find his body."

Ten minutes later, Murdock had convinced Captain Radiwitch that he should lead the way downstream to the coast, then contact the Russian hovercraft to come get them. He still had his walkie-talkie, but he couldn't use it here in the mountains. He also took the Japanese prisoners, who were now willing captives.

When they were gone, the SEALs made a grave for General Raiden Nishikawa, much as Jaybird had suggested. They finished it with a stack of dead limbs and brush that no animal could get through.

Then they marched off downstream toward the coast.

Holt fired up the SATCOM on TAC Two. The planes did not respond. He tried TAC One, but reception was not possible through the mountains.

"We get to the coast we'll try it again," Holt said. "It should work out there."

Murdock had grilled the seven SEALs on the death of the general. They had to have the same story. The general had committed hara-kiri with his samurai sword, then toppled into the surging river, and they hadn't been able to find him.

It took them another two hours to hike down the stream to the coast. Then the Tac One channel worked and Murdock talked to the admiral.

He explained their chase and the final capture and what had happened to General Nishikawa. The admiral said he would report it to the embassy and to Washington.

"Well done, Commander. You need transport?"

"First we have to find the other half of our platoon and about thirty Russians."

"That would be Lieutenant DeWitt and the Second Squad. When you assaulted the mountain, he pulled back his squad with the Russians and worked back to the coast. One of our choppers picked him up about an hour ago. The Russians commandos with DeWitt are on their air-cushion craft. They radioed to us to come and get the SEALs."

"Wondered about that. You might tell the Russian floater to move about four klicks north to find their captain and his eight men."

"Will do, Commander. We'll see you soon."

Murdock sat down with his back against a tree ten yards from the beach and watched the waves roll in. The seven SEALs were close by.

"I'd kill for an MRE," Ronson said.

"Hey, didn't you bring one?" Jaybird asked. "Thought everyone did. Hell, no, I'm not sharing."

The six SEALs rushed him, rolled him on the ground, and made certain he didn't have an MRE in his pack.

"Doc, how about a casualty report," Murdock said.

"Nothing I know about. Some nicks and scrapes, and Jaybird is getting strangled. That's about all. We left Washington back at the village with that broken ankle."

"Yeah, we still have all of our EARs? Count them, Jaybird."

A minute later he reported. "All present, Commander."

"Good. Stroh would skin, roast, and feed us to alligators if we lost one of them. We should have a bird here soon. Sack out if anybody wants to." Murdock grinned. Even before he said it he heard two of the SEALs snoring. Yeah, great idea. His chin dropped to his chest and he slept.

26

Friday, 23 February

Mid-Coast
Kunashir Island
Kuril Chain, Russia

Murdock awoke to feel snowflakes hitting him in the face. It was a light fall of cold, dry flakes. He licked off a couple, then checked his watch. Almost 0830. Somewhere in the background he heard the Russians on a radio.

He dozed again, then came alert.

Chopper.

No doubt about it, the sound came again, the *whup, whup, whup* of the big rotors. He looked over where the Russians had been. They were gone. Captain Radiwitch had talked with Murdock and knew a chopper was coming. The Russian hovercraft must have come well before the helicopter. Murdock had shaken hands and said good-bye to the Russian captain. The Russians had brought out their one dead and four wounded.

Murdock checked seaward. The chopper sound persisted. He looked in his combat vest and found a red flare.

Two minutes later he could see an outline of the chopper through the light snow. He popped the flare and threw it down on the beach sand. At once the chopper changed directions, did a low flyover, then circled around and came in for a landing just inside the dry sand.

The chopper hatch slid open and a crewman jumped out.

"Up and at them," Murdock barked. "Your limousine is here."

Jaybird made sure everyone was awake; then they moved through the light snow flurries toward the twin-rotored Sea Knight, and climbed in the forward hatch.

"Glad you guys showed up," Murdock told the crewman. He went to the cockpit and tapped one of the pilots on the shoulder. The aviator turned and nodded.

"Hey, can you contact Home Base and ask them if Lieutenant DeWitt picked up Washington, or if he's still down there with the Russians in Golovnino."

The pilot asked him to repeat the message, then got on his radio. A minute later the pilot looked over at Murdock.

"Home Base reports that your man Washington was brought out by DeWitt when the rest of his squad was evacuated. They are all on board the carrier now."

Murdock thanked him and went back with the other SEALs. Five of his men had sat down and promptly gone back to sleep.

"Been a long day," Jaybird said. "When did we get any sleep last?"

"A week ago Thursday," Ken Ching said. He dropped his combat vest and slumped against it. "Don't wake me up until Christmas," he said.

Murdock walked among the bodies counting. They still had their six EAR weapons. Good. It would take them about twenty minutes to fly back to the carrier, get in the flight pattern, and come in to land, a crewman told Murdock.

Murdock waved. "Hey, take your time. I'm in no hurry. Not now."

As soon as they hit the carrier deck, Murdock told Jaybird to get the men below and into the ready room. He'd be along shortly. He found a white shirt and followed him off the deck, and then a seaman took him to sick bay.

Washington was under the knife. DeWitt waited for the surgery to be over. Murdock found him.

"How's Washington?"

"Looks like a clean break, but they wanted to be sure. The X-ray was a little dicey. The bone may need a pin, but no reason he can't come back to full-duty status."

"Good. We finally nailed the little general."

DeWitt nodded.

"See you in our assembly room."

Murdock had little to say to the SEALs. All were there except Washington and DeWitt.

"Good work. Get out of here and hang some sack time or chow call, whichever you want first. We'll get together here again about fifteen hundred."

Murdock found his way to the Communications Center and asked them to make a call to Don Stroh's number in Virginia. The encrypted call went from one satellite to another, then into the Washington, D.C., antennas.

Don came on a moment later.

"Yeah, SEAL kind of guy, hear you scored a touchdown."

"Might have been a safety. At least we won. How is Japan taking the whole thing?"

"State says they are pleased. They pleaded for non-lethal, but they had to know it couldn't hold up for the whole affair. From what I gather, the Russians were fascinated by your new sound toys."

"I figured they would steal one before they left, but we still have twelve. I counted."

"Good work, again, Murdock. You'll probably want a long leave again so you can come to Washington."

"Don't know, Stroh. First I'm going to sleep for a week, then eat four meals a day. After that we'll talk."

"When does the fishing improve out in California? I'm still looking for some yellowtail and maybe a big-eye tuna."

"You're talking at least April or May. We'll keep your toys safe. I do want to get two of them on permanent loan. They might come in handy again for a stealth approach."

"I'll have to talk to the boss about that."

"Stroh, what else is cooking? We have a couple of months

to get patched up? I've still got some guys with bumps and bruises, and one new broken leg."

"Depends on what pops first. That Korean thing is still hot, but it's cooled off a little. We plan to hold you guys on the carrier there for a few weeks, so don't plan any reunion. Looks now like the Korea situation will taper off and might not blow up this time, but I have a feeling it's coming sooner or later.

"Then we have a problem in the Middle East again. I mean a real bad one that could go ballistic on us. Hey, you guys have the easy part. You just sit there and wait for us to decide where you go."

"Yeah, sure, Stroh. I can't fight with you when I'm this tired. It's sack time for me. You take care, and don't call us. When we're ready for something really big, we'll call you."

Stroh laughed and they said good-bye.

Murdock got a guide to help him find his quarters. Tomorrow he'd call Washington again, only this time he'd talk to Ardith Manchester. Yeah, let her know he was safe and sound. He frowned. Did that mean he was getting serious about this woman?

Murdock gave up even trying to think about that, and hit the sack. First sleep, then food.

SEAL TALK

Military Glossary

2IC: Second in command.
40mm Grenades: Fired from launcher on Colt M-4A1, others.
Aalvin: Small U.S. two-man submarine.
Admin: Short for administration.
Aegis: Advanced Naval air defense radar system.
AH-1W Super Cobra: Has M179 undernose turret with 20mm Gattling gun.
AK-47: 7.63-round Russian Kalashnikov automatic rifle. Most widely used assault rifle in the world.
AKM- or AK74: 5.45mm round.
AN/PRC-ll7D: Radio, also called SATCOM. Works with Milstar satellite in 22,300-mile equatorial orbit for instant worldwide radio, voice, or video communications. Size: 15 inches high, 3 inches wide, 3 inches deep. Weighs 15 pounds. Microphone and voice output. Has encrypter, capable of burst transmissions of less than a second.
AN/PUS-7: Night Vision Goggles. Weigh 1.5 pounds.
ANVIS-6: Night Vision Goggles on air crewmen's helmets.
APC: Armored Personnel Carrier
ASROC: Nuclear-tipped antisubmarine rocket torpedoes launched by Navy ships.
Assault Vest: Combat vest with full loadouts of ammo, gear.

ASW: AntiSubmarine Warfare.

Attack Board: Molded plastic with two handgrips with bubble compass on it. Also depth gauge and cyalume chemical lights with twist knob to regulate amount of light. Used for underwater guidance on long swim.

Aurora: Air Force recon plane. Can circle at 90,000 feet. Can't be seen or heard from ground. Used for thermal imaging.

AWACS: Airborne Warning And Control System. Radar units in high-flying aircraft to scan for planes at any altitude out 200 miles. Controls air-to-air engagements with enemy forces. Planes have a mass of communication and electronic equipment.

Balaclavas: Headgear worn by some SEALs.

Bent Spear: Less serious nuclear violation of safety.

BKA: Bundeskriminant: Germany's federal investigation unit.

Black Talon: Lethal hollowpoint ammunition made by Winchester. Outlawed some places.

Blivet: A collapsible fuel container. SEALs sometimes use it.

BLU-43B: Antipersonnel mine used by SEALs.

BLU-96: A fuel-air explosive bomb. It disperses a fuel oil into the air, then explodes the cloud. Many times more powerful than conventional bombs because it doesn't carry its own chemical oxidizers.

BMP-1: Soviet armored fighting vehicle (AFV), low, boxy, crew of 3 and 8 combat troops. Has tracks and a 73mm cannon. Also has an AT-3 Sagger antitank missile and coaxial machine gun.

Body Armor: Far too heavy for SEAL use in the water.

Bogey: Pilots' word for an unidentified aircraft.

Boghammer Boat: Long, narrow, low dagger boat, high-speed patrol craft. Swedish make. Iran had 40 of them in 1993.

Boomer: A nuclear-powered missile submarine.

Bought It: A man has been killed. Also "bought the farm."

Bow Cat: The bow catapult on a carrier to launch jets.

Broken Arrow: Any accident with nuclear weapons or nuclear material lost, shot down, crashed, stolen, hijacked.

Browning 9mm High Power: A Belgium 9mm pistol, 13 rounds in magazine. First made 1935.

Buddy Line: 6 feet long, ties 2 SEALs together in the water for control or help if needed.

BUDS/S: Coronado, California, nickname for SEAL training facility for 6-months course.

BUPERS: BUreau of PERSonnel.

C-130 Hercules: Air Force transporter for long haul. 4 engines.

C-2A Greyhound: 2-engine turboprop cargo plane that lands on carriers. Also called COD, Carrier Onboard Delivery. Takes people, supplies, mail to and from CVN carriers at sea.

C-4: Plastic explosive. A claylike explosive that can be molded and shaped. It will burn. Fairly stable.

C-6 Plastique: Plastic explosive. Developed from C-4 and C-5. Is often used in bombs with radio detonator or digital timer.

C-9 Nightingale: Douglas DC-9 fitted as a medical evacuation transport plane.

C-141 Starlifter: Airlift transport for cargo, paratroops, evac for long distances. Top speed 566 mph. Range with payload 2,935 miles. Ceiling 41,600 feet.

Caltrops: Small four-pointed spikes used to flatten tires. Used in the Crusades to disable horses.

CamelBack: Used with drinking tube for 70 ounces of water attached to vest.

Cammies: Working camouflaged wear for SEALs. Two different patterns and colors: jungle and desert.

Cannon Fodder: Old term for soldiers in line of fire destined to die in the grand scheme of warfare.

Capped: Killed, shot, or otherwise snuffed.

CAR-15: The Colt M-4A1. Sliding-stock carbine with grenade launcher under barrel. Knight sound-suppressor. Can have AN/PAQ-4 laser aiming light under the carrying handle. .223 round. 20- or 30-round magazine. Rate of fire 700 to 1,000 rds/min.

Cascade Radiation: U-235 triggers secondary radiation in other dense materials.

Cast Off: Leave a dock, port, land. Get lost. Navy: long, then short signal of horn, whistle, or light.

Castle Keep: The main tower in any castle.

Caving Ladder: Roll-up ladder that can be let down to climb.

CH-46E: Sea Knight chopper. Twin rotors, transport. Can carry 22 combat troops. Has a crew of 4.

CH-53D Sea Stallion: Big Chopper. Not used much anymore.

Chaff: A small cloud of thin pieces of metal, such as tinsel, that can be picked up by enemy radar and that can attract a radar-guided missile away from the plane.

Charlie-Mike: Code words for continue the mission.

Chief to Chief: Bad conduct by EM handled by chiefs so no record shows or is passed up the chain of command.

Chocolate Mountains: Land training center for SEALs near these mountains in the California desert.

Christians In Action: SEAL talk for not-always-friendly CIA.

CIA: Central Intelligence Agency.

CIC: Combat Information Center. The place on a ship where communications and control areas are situated to open and control combat fire.

CINC: Commander IN Chief.

CINCLANT: Navy Commander IN Chief, atLANTtic.

CINCPAC: Commander-IN-Chief, PACific.

Class of 1978: Not a single man finished BUD/S training in this class. All-time record.

Claymore: An antipersonnel mine carried by SEALs on many of their missions.

Cluster Bombs: A canister bomb that explodes and spreads small bomblets over a great area. Used against parked aircraft, massed troops, and un-armored vehicles.

CNO: Chief of Naval Operations.

CO-2 Poisoning: Occurs during deep dives. Abort dive at once and surface.

COD: Carrier On board Delivery plane.

Cold Pack Rations: Food carried by SEALs to use if needed.

Combat Harness: American Body Armor nylon mesh special operations vest. Has 6 pouches, 2 magazines each, for drum-fed belts, other pouches for other weapons, waterproof pouch for Motorola.

CONUS: CONtinental United States.

Corfams: Dress shoes for SEALs.

Covert Action Staff: A CIA group that handles all covert action by the SEALs.

CQB: Close Quarters Battle house. Training facility near Niland in the desert training area. Also called the Kill House.

CQB: Close Quarters Battle. A fight that's up-close, hand-to-hand, whites of his eyes, blood all over you.

CRRC Bundle: Roll it off plane, sub, boat. The assault boat for 8 seals, all ready to go into combat.

CRRC: Combat Rubber Raiding Craft. Also the IBS or Inflatable Boat Small.

Cutting Charge: Lead-sheathed explosive. Triangular strip of high-velocity explosive sheathed in metal. Point of the triangle focuses a shaped-charge effect. Cuts a pencil-line-wide hole to slice a steel girder in half.

CVN: U.S. Carrier with nuclear power.

CYA: Cover Your Ass, protect yourself from friendlies or officers above you and JAG people.

Damfino: Damned if I know. SEAL talk.

DDS: Dry Dock Shelter. A clamshell unit on subs to deliver SEALs and SDVs to a mission.

DEFCON: DEFense CONdition. How serious is the threat?

Delta Forces: Army special forces, much like SEALs.

Desert Cammies: Three-color desert tan and pale green with streaks of pink. For use on land.

DIA: Defense Intelligence Agency.

Dilos class patrol boat: Greek, 29 feet long, 75 tons displacement.

Dirty Shirt Mess: Officers can eat there in flying suits on board a carrier.

DNS: Doppler Navigation System.

Drager LAR V: Rebreather that SEALs use. No bubbles.

DREC: Digitally Reconnoiterable Electronic Component. Top-secret computer chip from NSA that lets it decipher any U.S. military electronic code.

E & E: SEAL talk for escape and evasion.

E-2C Hawkeye: Navy carrier-based Airborne Early Warning craft for long-range early warning, threat assessment, and fighter direction. Has a 24-foot saucerlike rotodome over the wing. Crew 5, max speed 326 knots, ceiling 30,800 feet, radius 175 nm with 4 hours on station.

E-3A Skywarrior: Old electronic intelligence craft. Replaced by the newer ES-3A.

E-4B NEACP (called Kneecap): National Emergency Airborne Command Post. A greatly modified Boeing 747 used as a communications base for the President of the United States and other high-ranking officials in an emergency and in wartime.

EA-6B Prowler: Navy plane with electronic countermeasures. Crew of 4, max speed 566 knots, ceiling 41,200 feet, range with max load 955 nautical miles.

Easy: The only easy day was yesterday. SEAL talk.

ELINT: ELectronic INTelligence. Often from satellite in orbit, picture-taker, or other electronic communications.

EOD: Explosive Ordnance Disposal. Navy experts in nuclear material and radioactivity.

Equatorial Satellite Pointing Guide: Used to aim antenna for radio to pick up satellite signals.

ES-3A: Electronic Intelligence (ELINT) intercept craft. The platform for the battle group Passive Horizon Extension System. Stays up for long patrol periods, has comprehensive set of sensors, lands and takes off from a carrier. Has 63 antennas.

ETA: Estimated Time of Arrival.

Executive Order 12333: By President Reagan authorizing Special Warfare units such as the SEALs.

Exfil: Exfiltrate, to get out of an area.

F/A-18 Hornet: Carrier-based interceptor that can change from air-to-air to air-to-ground attack mode while in flight.

Fitrep: Fitness Report.

Flashbang Grenade: Non-lethal grenade that gives off a

series of piercing explosive sounds and a series of brilliant strobe-type lights to disable an enemy.

Flotation Bag: To hold equipment, ammo, gear on a wet operation.

Fort Fumble: SEALs' name for the Pentagon.

Forty-mm Rifle Grenade: The M576 multipurpose round, contains 20 large lead balls.

Four-Striper: A Navy Captain.

Fox Three: In air warfare, a code showing that the aircraft's machine gun or cannon is being fired.

FUBAR: SEAL talk: Fucked Up Beyond All Repair.

Full Helmet Masks: For high-altitude jumps. Oxygen in mask.

G-3: German-made assault rifle.

Gloves: SEALs wear sage-green, fire-resistant Nomex flight gloves.

GMT: Greenwich Mean Time. Where it's all measured from.

GPS: Global Positioning System. A program with satellites around Earth to pinpoint precisely aircraft, ships, vehicles, and ground troops. Position information is to a plus or minus four feet. Also can give speed of a plane or ship to one quarter of a mile per hour.

GPSL: A radio antenna with floating wire that pops to the surface. Antenna picks up positioning from the closest 4 global positioning satellites and gives an exact position within 10 feet.

Green Tape: Green sticky ordinance tape that has a hundred uses for a SEAL.

GSG-9: Flashbang grenade developed by Germans: a cardboard tube filled with 5 separate charges timed to burst in rapid succession, blinding and giving concussion to enemy, leaving targets stunned, easy to kill or capture. Usually non-lethal.

GSG9: Grenzschutzgruppe Nine. Germany's best special warfare unit and counterterrorist group.

H&K 21A1: Machine gun with 7.62 NATO round. Replaces the older, more fragile M-60 E3. Fires 900 rounds per minute. Range 1,100 meters. All types of NATO rounds: ball, incendiary, tracer.

H&K G-11: Automatic rifle, new type. 4.7mm caseless ammunition. 50-round magazine. The bullet is in a sleeve of solid propellant with a special thin plastic coating around it. Fires 600 rounds per minute. Single-shot, three-round burst, or fully automatic.

H&K MP-5SD: 9mm submachine gun with integral silenced barrel, single-shot, three-shot, or fully automatic. Rate 800 rds/min.

H&K P9S: Heckler & Koch's 9mm Parabellum double-action semiauto pistol with 9-round magazine.

H&K PSG1: 7.62 NATO round. High-precision, bolt-action sniping rifle. 5-to-20-round magazine. Roller lock delayed blowback breech system. Fully adjustable stock. 6 x 42 telescopic sights. Sound suppressor.

HAHO: High Altitude jump, High Opening. From 30,000 feet, open chute for glide up to l5 miles to ground. Up to 75 minutes in glide. To enter enemy territory or enemy position unheard.

HALO: High Altitude jump, Low Opening. From 30,000 feet. Free fall in 2 minutes to 2,000 feet and open chute. Little forward movement. Get to ground quickly, silently.

Hamburgers: Often called sliders on a Navy carrier.

HELO: SEAL talk for helicopter.

Herky Bird: C-l30 Hercules transport. Most-flown military transport in the world. For cargo or passengers, paratroops, aerial refueling, search and rescue, communications, and use as a gunship. Has flown from a Navy carrier deck without use of catapult. Four turboprop engines, max speed 325 knots, range at max payload 2,356 miles.

Hezbollah: Lebanese Shiite Muslim militia. Party of God.

HMMWU: The Humvee, U.S. light utility truck, replaced the honored Jeep. Multipurpose wheeled vehicle, 4 x 4, automatic transmission, power steering. Engine: Detroit Diesel 150 hp diesel V-8 air-cooled. Top speed 65 mph. Range 300 miles.

Hotels: SEAL talk for hostages.

Humint: Human intelligence. Acquired on the ground, from a human as opposed to satellite or photo recon.

Hydra-Shock: Lethal hollowpoint ammunition made by Federal Cartridge Company. Outlawed in some areas.

Hypothermia: Danger to SEALs. A drop in body temperature that can be fatal.

IBS: Inflatable Boat Small. 12 x 6 feet. Carries 8 men and 1,000 pounds of weapons and gear. Hard to sink. Quiet motor. Used for silent beach, bay, lake landings.

IR Beacon: Infrared Beacon. For silent nighttime signaling.

IR Goggles: "Sees" heat instead of light.

Islamic Jihad: Arab holy war.

IV Pack: Intravenous fluid that you can drink if out of water.

JAG: Judge Advocate General. Navy legal investigating arm.

JNA: Yugoslav National Army.

JP-4: Normal military jet fuel.

JSOC: Joint Special Operations Command.

JSOCCOMCENT: Joint Special Operations COMmand CENTer in the Pentagon.

K-bar: SEALs' combat knife.

KATN: Kick Ass and Take Names. SEAL talk, get the mission in gear.

KH-11: Spy satellite, takes pictures of ground, IR photos, etc.

KIA: Killed In Action.

KISS: Keep It Simple, Stupid. SEAL talk for streamlined operations.

Klick: A kilometer of distance. Often used as a mile. From Vietnam era, but still widely used in military.

Krytrons: Complicated, intricate timers used in making nuclear explosive detonators.

KV-57: Encoder for messages, scrambles.

L-T: Short for lieutenant in SEAL talk.

Laser Pistol: The SIW pinpoint of ruby light on a weapon emitted for aiming. Usually silenced weapon.

Left Behind: In 30 years SEALs have seldom left behind a dead comrade, never a wounded one. No SEAL has ever been taken prisoner.

Let's Get the Hell out of Dodge: SEAL talk for leaving a place, bugging out, hauling ass.

Light Sticks: Chemical units that make light after twisting to release chemicals that phosphoresce.

Loot and Shoot: SEAL talk for getting into action on a mission.

LZ: Landing Zone.

M-16: Automatic U.S. rifle. 5.56 round. Magazine 20 or 30 rounds, rate of fire 700 to 950 rds/min. Can attach M203 40mm grenade launcher under barrel.

M-18 Claymore: Antipersonnel mine. A slab of C-4 with 200 small ball bearings. Set off electrically or by trip wire. Can be positioned and aimed. Sprays out a cloud of balls. Kill zone 50 meters.

M-203: A 40mm grenade launcher fitted under an M-16 or the M-4A1. Can fire a variety of grenade types up to 1,200 feet.

M-3 Submachine Gun: WWII grease gun, .45-caliber. Cheap. Introduced in 1942.

M-60E3: Lightweight handheld machine gun. Not used now by the SEALs.

M-86: Pursuit Deterrent Munitions. Various types of mines, grenades, trip-wire explosives, and other devices in anti-personnel use.

M1-8: Russian Chopper.

M1A1 M-14: Match rifle upgraded for SEAL snipers.

M60 Machine Gun: Can use 100-round ammo box snapped onto the gun's receiver. Not used much now by SEALs.

M61(j): Machine pistol, Yugoslav make.

M61A1: The usual 20mm cannon used on many American fighter planes.

M662: A red flare for signaling.

MagSafe: Lethal ammunition that fragments in human body and does not exit. Favored by some police units to cut down on second kill from regular ammunition exiting a body.

Make a Peek: A quick look, usually out of the water, to check your position or tactical situation.

Mark 23 Mod O: Special operations offensive handgun system. Double action, 12-round magazine. Ambidextrous safety and mag-release catches. Knight screw-on suppressor. Snap-on laser for sighting. .45-caliber. Weighs 4 pounds loaded. 9.5 inches long, with silencer 16.5 inches long.

Mark II Knife: Navy-issue combat knife.

Mark VIII SDV: Swimmer Delivery Vehicle. A bus, SEAL talk. 21 feet long, beam and draft 4 feet, 6 knots for 6 hours.

MAVRIC Lance: A nuclear alert for stolen nukes or radioactive goods.

MC-130 Combat Talon: A specially equipped Hercules for covert missions in enemy or unfriendly territory.

McMillan M-87R: Bolt-action sniper rifle .50-caliber. 53 inches long. Bipod, fixed 5- or 10-round magazine. Bulbous muzzle brake on end of barrel. Deadly up to a mile. All types of .50-caliber ammo.

MGS: Modified Grooming Standards. So SEALs don't all look like military and can do undercover work in mufti.

MH-53J: Chopper, updated CH053 from Nam days. 200 mph, called the Pave Low III.

MH-60K BlackHawk: Navy chopper. Forward infrared system for low-level night flight. Radar for terra follow avoidance. Crew of 3, takes 12 troops. Top speed 225 mph. Ceiling 4,000 feet. Range radius 230 miles. Arms 2 12.7mm machine guns.

MIDEASTFOR: MIDdle EAST FORce.

MiG: Russian-built fighter, many versions, used in many nations around the world.

Mike Boat: Liberty boat off a large ship.

Mike-Mike: Short for mm, millimeter, as 9-mike-mike.

Milstar: Communications satellite for pickup and bouncing from SATCOM and other radio transmitters. Used by SEALs.

Minigun: In choppers. Can fire 2,000 rounds per minute. Gatling gun-type.

Mitrajez M80: Machine gun from Yugoslavia.

MI5: British domestic intelligence agency.

Mocha: Food energy bar SEALs carry in vest pockets.

Mossburg: Pump-action shotgun, pistol grip, 5-round magazine. SEALs use it for close-in work.

Motorola Radio: Personal radio, short range, lip mike, earpiece, belt pack.

MRE: Meals, Ready to Eat. Field rations used by most of U.S. Armed Forces, and the SEALs as well. Long-lasting.

MSPF: Maritime Special Purpose Force.

Mugger: MUGR, miniature underwater locator device. Sends up antenna for pickup on positioning satellites. Works underwater or above. Gives location within 10 feet.

Mujahideen: A soldier of Allah in Muslim nations.

NAVAIR: NAVy AIR command.

NAVSPECWAR: NAVal SPECial WARfare section. SEALs are in this command.

NAVSPECWARGRUP-TWO: NAVal SPECial WARfare section GRoUP TWO, based at Norfolk.

NCIS: Naval Criminal Investigative Service. A civilian operation not reporting to any Navy authority to make it more responsible and responsive. Replaces the old NIS, Naval Investigation Service, that did report to the closest admiral.

NEST: Nuclear Energy Search Team. Non-military unit that reports at once to any spill, problem, or Broken Arrow to determine the extent of the radiation problem.

Newbie: A new man, officer, or commander in an established military unit.

NKSF: North Korean Special Forces.

NLA: Iranian National Liberation Army. About 4,500 men in South Iraq, helped by Iraq for possible use against Iran.

Nomex: The type of material used for flight suits and hoods.

NPIC: National Photographic Interpretation Center in D.C.

NRO: National Reconnaissance Office, runs and coordinates satellite development and operations for the intelligence community.

NSA: National Security Agency.

NSC: National Security Council. Meets in Situation Room, support facility in the Executive Office Building in D.C. Main security group in the nation.

Nsvhurawn: Iranian Marines.

NUCFLASH: An alert for any nuclear problem.

NVG One Eye: Litton single-eyepiece Night Vision Goggles.

Prevents NVG blindness in both eyes if a flare goes off. Scope shows green-tinted field at night.

NVGs: Night Vision Goggles. One eye or two. Give good night vision in the dark with a greenish view.

OAS: Obstacle Avoidance Sonar. Used on many low-flying attack aircraft.

OIC: Officer In Charge.

Oil Tanker: Regular-sized tanker: 885 feet long, 140 feet beam, 121,000 tons, 13 cargo tanks that hold 35.8 million gallons of fuel, oil, or gas. Crew of 24. Not a super tanker.

OOD: Officer Of the Deck.

Orion P-3: Navy's long-range patrol and antisub aircraft. Some adapted to ELINT roles. Crew of 10. Max speed loaded 473 mph. Ceiling 28,300 feet. Arms: internal weapons bay and 10 external weapons stations for a mix of torpedoes, mines, rockets, and bombs.

Passive Sonar: Listening for engine noise of a ship or sub. It doesn't give away the hunter's presence as an active sonar would.

Pave Low III: A Navy chopper.

PC-170: Patrol Coastal-class 170-foot SEAL delivery vehicle. Powered by four 3,350-hp diesel engines, beam of 25 feet and draft of 7.8 feet. Top speed 35 knots, range 2,000 nautical miles. Fixed swimmer platform on stern. Crew 4 officers, 24 EM, and 8 SEALs.

Plank Owners: Original men in the start-up of a new military unit.

Polycarbonate material: Bullet-proof glass.

PRF: People's Revolutionary Front. Fictional group in *Nucflash* SEAL book.

Prowl and Growl: SEAL talk for moving into a combat mission.

Quitting Bell: In BUD/S training. Ring it and you quit the SEAL unit. Helmets of men who quit the class are lined up below the bell in Coronado. (Now the bell is no longer rung. Just place your helmet and go.)

RAF: Red Army Faction. A once-powerful German terrorist group not so active now.

Remington 200: Sniper rifle. Not used by SEALs now.

Remington 700: Sniper rifle with Starlight Scope. Can extend night vision to 400 meters.

Ring Knocker: An Annapolis graduate with the ring.

RIO: Radar Intercept Officer. The officer who sits in the backseat of an F-l4 Tomcat off a carrier. RIO's job: find enemy targets in the air and on the sea.

Roger That: A yes, an affirmative, a go answer to a command or statement.

RPG: Rocket Propelled Grenade. Quick and easy, shoulder-fired. Favorite weapon of terrorists, insurgents.

S&W Mark 23 MOD: .45-caliber Special. 12-round magazine. Large handgun. Has suppressor.

SAS: British Special Air Service. Commandos. Special warfare men. Best that Britain has. Works with SEALs.

SATCOM: Satellite-based communications system for instant contact with anyone anywhere in the world. SEALs rely on it.

SAW: Squad Automatic Weapon. Usually a machine gun or automatic rifle.

SBS: Special Boat Squadron. On-site Navy unit that transports SEALS to many of their missions. Located across the street from the SEALs' Coronado, California, headquarters.

SD3: Sound-suppression system on the H&K MP-5 weapon.

SDV: Swimmer Delivery Vehicle. SEALs use a variety of them.

Seahawk SH-60: Navy chopper for ASW and SAR. Top speed 180 knots, ceiling 13,800 feet, range 503 miles. Arms: 2 Mark 46 torpedoes.

SEAL Headgear: Boonie hat, wool Balaclava, green scarf, watch cap, bandanna roll.

SERE: Survival, Evasion, Resistance, and Escape training.

Shipped for Six: Enlisted for six more years in the Navy.

Shit City: Coronado SEALs' name for Norfolk.

Show Colors: In combat, to put U.S. flag or other identification on back for easy identification by friendly air or ground units.

Sierra Charlie: SEAL talk for everything on schedule.

Simunition: Canadian product for training that uses paint balls instead of lead for bullets.

Sixteen-Man Platoon: Basic SEAL combat force. Up from 14 men a few years ago.

Space Blanket: Green foil blanket to keep troops warm. Vacuum-packed and folded to a cigarette-sized package.

Sprayers and Prayers: Not the SEAL way. These men spray bullets all over the place hoping for hits. SEALs do more aimed firing for sure kills.

SS-19: Russian ICBM missile.

STABO: Using harness and lines under chopper to get down to the ground.

STAR: Surface To Air Recovery operation.

Starflash Round: Shotgun round that shoots out sparkling fireballs that ricochet wildly around a room, confusing and terrifying the occupants.

Stasi: Old-time East German secret police.

Stick: British 2 4-man SAS teams. 8 men.

Stokes: A kind of Navy stretcher. Open-coffin shape of wire mesh and white canvas for emergency patient transport.

STOL: Short TakeOff and Landing. Aircraft with high-lift wings and vectored-thrust engines to produce extremely short take-offs and landings.

Subgun: Submachine gun, often the suppressed H&K MP-5.

Suits: Civilians, usually government officials wearing suits.

Sweat: The more SEALs sweat in peacetime, the less they bleed in war.

Sykes-Fairbairn: A commando fighting knife.

Syrette: Small syringe for field administration, often filled with morphine. Can be self-administered.

Tango: SEAL talk for a terrorist.

TDY: Temporary DutY assigned outside of normal job designation.

Terr: Another term for terrorist. Shorthand SEAL talk.

Tetrahedral reflectors: Show up on multimode radar like tiny suns.

Thermal Tape: ID for Night Vision Goggles user to see. Used on friendlies.

TNAZ: Trinittroaze Tidine. Explosive to replace C-4. 15% stronger than C-4 and 20% lighter.

TO&E: Table showing organization and equipment of a military unit.

Top SEAL Tribute: "You sweet motherfucker, don't you never die!"

Train: Men directly behind each other. For contact in smoke, no light, fog, etc. Right hand on weapon, left hand on shoulder of man ahead. Squeeze shoulder to signal.

Trident: SEALs' emblem. An eagle, with talons clutching a Revolutionary War pistol, and Neptune's trident superimposed on the Navy's traditional anchor.

TRW: A camera's digital record that is sent by SATCOM.

TT33: Tokarev, a Russian Pistol.

UAZ: A Soviet 1-ton truck.

UBA Mark XV: Underwater life support with computer to regulate the rebreather's gas mixture.

UGS: Unmanned Ground Sensors. Can be used to explode booby traps and Claymore mines.

UNODIR: Unless otherwise directed. The unit will start the operation unless they are told not to.

VBSS: Orders to "visit, board, search & seize."

Wadi: A gully or ravine usually in a desert.

White Shirt: Man responsible for safety on carrier deck as he leads around civilians and personnel unfamiliar with the flight deck.

WIA: Wounded In Action.

Zodiac: Also called an IBS, Inflatable Boat Small. Fifteen by six feet, weighs 265 pounds. The "rubber duck" can carry 8 fully equipped SEALs. Can do 18 knots with a range or 65 nautical miles.

ZULU: Means Greenwich Mean Time, GMT. Used in all formal military communications.